ChangelingPress.com

Second Chance Omegas

Will Okati

Second Chance Omegas
Will Okati

ISBN: 978-1-60521-862-5

Publisher:
Changeling Press LLC
315 N. Centre St.
Martinsburg, WV 25404
ChangelingPress.com

Printed in the U.S.A.

Editor: Crystal Esau
Cover Artist: Bryan Keller

The individual stories in this anthology have been previously released in E-Book format.

Table of Contents

Second Chance Omegas Series Notes

Welcome to the world of Second Chance! Located roughly halfway between Chicago and Albany, the Alphas and Omegas who call it home are unique in some ways but are all in need of another shot to make things right with the loves of their lives -- the ones who got away.

The Alphas and Omegas in this world are descended from various animal bloodlines and clans. Some can shapeshift to a degree, and everyone has at least one aspect about them that hints at where they come from. A man with a wolf in his ancestry might have eyes that change from brown to green and teeth that get sharper when he's upset, or a man descended from dragons might have a faint pattern of scales on his forearms and calves.

Alphas and Omegas both have a unique scent that gets stronger when emotions run high, and -- with Omegas -- changes when they conceive. Omega pregnancies last approximately nine weeks. If an Omega is aroused, they are fertile. *Very* fertile. Family planning is one thing, but you can't fight fate forever -- especially in Second Chance.

Some Omegas -- not all -- can become physically ill when separated from the Alpha their body has chosen as its mate. Alphas do not have a corresponding reaction. Which is unfair, but Omegas also have the biological bonus of an internal cousin-to-a-clitoris as well as a prostate. They can reach dry orgasm multiple times before their grand finale.

All books in the Second Chance series share a world and the occasional character might pop in and out for a cameo, but each of the stories is written to stand alone and can be read in any order. All stories also focus heavily on Omega/Mpreg themes and contain childbirth scenes.

Only You (Second Chance Omegas 1)
Willa Okati

Second Chance -- a small town where anything can happen -- and does.

Once upon a time, a teenaged Alpha named Alex fell in love with a pretty Omega boy from the wrong side of the tracks. Zachary was everything he'd ever wanted -- sweet, sassy, and sexy as hell. Alex would have married that boy and raised baby after baby with him -- if Zachary hadn't run away when Alex popped the question.

Alex doesn't give up easily. When a train derails on its way to Alex's hometown, he's finally got another shot at the one who got away, and he's not going to waste it. Now he's got Zachary in his sights, and he's never letting go again.

It killed Zachary to let Alex go the first time. He loved that man as much as Alex loved him, and he's never fallen out of love, but he left to give Alex his best chance at living his best life. Zachary can't -- won't -- be sorry for that, no matter what it cost him.

Stranded in Second Chance with nowhere else to go and no way to get there, Zachary's got no choice but to accept the help and shelter Alex offers. The chemistry's still there. The desire. The connection. The yearning. But when the secrets they've both been keeping come to light, will they shatter their bond for keeps, or bring them together in a forever kind of love?

Prologue

Alex

Three months. Three months since they'd started doing this. Since Alex had been allowed to have it. To have *him*. Zachary. To have him like *this*, both of them naked and hard, Zachary kneeling on top of Alex and looking down at him like he was the only thing in the world he'd ever wanted. Alex knew he was looking up at Zachary the same way. Maybe even more so, because of the way Zachary shook his head fondly and stroked his cheek, teasing the edges of his smile with one thumb. And -- why not? It was true. The basement of the empty house they usually snuck away to might be freezing and dusty, and they might have to keep their voices down so no one would hear them, but Alex wouldn't have traded it for anything. Not even the world.

What did the world have that could compare to *this*?

Nothing he could think of, for damn sure.

"The way you smile could melt snow, sweetheart." Slow, smooth and easy, Zachary pressed his palms flat against Alex's bare chest, pushing him down until he came to rest with his back against the floor. The old linoleum was enough to make Alex shiver, but he didn't care, and he didn't stop grinning. Zachary stroked one fingertip against Alex's cheek. "God, look at you, you beautiful baby, you wild dog. You're gorgeous."

Alex laughed. To tell the truth? He loved the pet names, and he did mostly have forest-hunting canines, wolves and mastiffs, in his animal heritage, but the other one -- come *on*. He couldn't let that slide without at least a little snapback. "Baby? Really?"

"Mmm-hmm." The way Zachary grinned at him, brazen and predatory as the wildcat bloodlines *he* came from, told Alex he'd been angling for exactly that reaction. Not many men could make a full shift, but bits and pieces came out in everyone, like the way Zachary's eyes went cat gold with oval-slit pupils when he was on the hunt. "What, you don't like it?"

"I didn't say *that*." Alex reached up to take Zachary's smooth, bare hips in the cups of his palms; he was a big guy, built sturdy and tall like most Alphas, and Zachary was small like Omegas usually were, all slim bones and delicate joints with a pointed chin and a shoulder-length tumble of silky dark hair. Alex could hold those hips with room for his fingertips to curve around and knead at Zachary's ass cheeks, making both men hiss at the contact.

But there was never an ante Zachary wouldn't up and no challenge he wouldn't rise to. He'd been stubborn and feisty as hell like that for as long as Alex had known him, and he'd known Zachary since, God, they were snot-nosed kids growing up in the same neighborhood. They'd played soccer on the same team at the same high school and worked summer jobs at the same community pool. Genderless kids could do that until they presented as either Alpha or Omega and were separated until their hormones settled down or they paired up. They paired up more than they were supposed to and got together as often as they could.

Really, really together.

Like this. Even if it had to be in secret because they were still young, not twenty yet, and the second an Alpha started sniffing after an Omega the whole damn world wanted to get involved. It was *their* business and no one else's, Zachary insisted; he'd been with a handful of other boys before any of them presented as one gender or the other and he'd already dealt with more than he wanted of the whole "neighborhood bike" bullshit.

So Alex hadn't argued too hard and anyway, Zachary had been right. They'd needed time to figure this whole thing out between them, and it was easier this way.

Private. Protected. Nothing but the two of them together in the shadows.

And it was -- good, *so* good. Perched on top of him Zachary was warm, light enough his weight barely registered but so solid and there, his cock dark and hard where it rested against Alex's belly. He rolled his hips in a tease, moving slowly against and with Alex's hands. "There you go, that's good, like that," he murmured, his slow roll asking Alex to join the fun.

Alex couldn't resist the temptation. His hands shook as he reached up to stroke whatever parts of Zachary he could reach, sliding from here to there every time he saw another part he needed to touch -- and there were so many he had to sit back up, balancing Zachary in his lap, to reach them all and to taste them too. He moved his mouth over everything he could reach on Zachary -- his slim hands, for starters, especially where they were marred with a few scars from the carving he liked to do sometimes. His nipples, flat brown discs with the centers raised up hard as little pebbles. The dip of his navel and the shudder and flex of his stomach muscles underneath. Between his collarbones, where he tasted sweet; at the softness of the skin on his throat, and the tendons that stood out hard when he arched his head back. Zachary hummed when he mouthed at them, and made small, desperate noises when he bit them.

The whole time, he kept his gentle rhythm going. Maybe he couldn't help it, maybe he liked it, but God, he was good at it. He smelled as sweet as he tasted, the scent Alex had come to recognize as a gentle release of Omega hormones. Hormones, and the slick wetness his Omega body produced, making them both slippery and sticky where their hips fit together. More so when Alex reached down to guide his cock into the space between Zachary's legs and slide there in the tight heat between the muscles. He could feel the Omega channel between balls and ass, open and dripping, wetting him when he nudged his cockhead there.

"*Oh.*" Zachary arched above him. He wasn't even inside the guy, but Alex had made him shudder and made his cock jerk up with what he was doing. Made him feel like he was more than human, like he was a god or something, or like -- like -- he didn't know the right words. Yet.

Or maybe he did, and it wasn't the right time to say them.

Or was it?

Alex put his face to Zachary's chest, wanting his mouth on Zachary's nipples again. No. Not yet. There was time. They had all the time they wanted.

How'd he gotten so lucky? Alex had gone over and over it and he didn't have a clue. Seemed like it'd happened all of a sudden one day, when he was looking at Zachary, hungry but not willing to say so when Zachary never seemed to look back the same way, but then suddenly Zachary *was* looking back, crossing whatever room they'd been in, driving straight into Alex's arms and demanding to be kissed.

Alex had. He could still feel the first shock of Zachary's mouth on his. He never wanted to forget it.

And ever since then: this.

Zachary shuddered again as he caught his breath. He threaded his fingers through Alex's hair to push his head back. "You're thinking so hard I can almost hear you," he teased. "Where'd you go?"

"Nowhere. Right here."

"Good answer." Zachary let go of Alex's hair to slide back a little and took hold of his cock, shiny-wet, and give it a couple of lazy pulls. "Because right here is exactly where I want you."

Alex wasn't going to argue with him, especially when the change pressed their bellies together with both their cocks trapped between them. The friction made him grind his teeth and press his forehead hard against Zachary's shoulder. They were both shiny with sweat, hot and red, and if it weren't for the difference between their scents, his Alpha musk and Zachary's Omega sweetness, he wouldn't have been able to tell the difference between them.

So maybe he might argue a little. This was -- amazing, this was like getting drunk off nothing more than touch, but -- Alex wanted more. Something he'd gotten once or twice and craved like a junkie going after a fix. Zachary was an addiction, and he wanted to feed on it.

It made him brave. Bold.

"You want me right here?" Alex asked, sliding his hand between Zachary's thighs. He found his way to Zachary's entrance and slipped two fingers inside. So *tight*, so wet, muscles clutching at him as he curled his fingers to stroke up the way Zachary had taught him. "Or here, instead?"

"Oh. *Oh*, Alex. Oh God." Zachary leaned forward to capture his mouth in a kiss, rougher than he'd been since the very first time they'd kissed. He only stopped kissing Alex when he ran out of air and it left him panting. "Oh God, you're going to make me come."

Alex laughed into the softness of Zachary's open mouth and slipped out of him, making him whine in protest. "Uh-uh. You think I'm done yet? I'm not. Baby."

Zachary laughed with him, breathless but light and sweet and pure. "You're a menace. Come back. I want more."

"No." Alex bit at Zachary's chin. "I'll come, and I don't want to. Not yet."

"But soon." Zachary's hips moved faster. He'd gotten harder, leaking trails over Alex's groin. Alex could tell he was leaking too, slow clear strings drooling from the head of his dick. He murmured against Alex's mouth the way Alex had with him, quick sharp breaths fed between his lips. "Soon. I know you. Soon."

Or maybe now. Like he'd said before, Zachary made him feel bold.

Alex moved his hips too, sliding Zachary back where he needed them both, his cock nestled again between Zachary's cheeks. This time he didn't glide through. He found the right angle and nudged his cockhead harder, with intent, against Zachary's opening.

Zachary's back went stiff, and the rest of him went still as he stared down at Alex.

"Or this," Alex said. He sounded older to himself. Deeper. Stronger. Rougher. "We could do this. I want to know what you feel like inside. Really feel it."

Zachary caught his lip between his teeth, biting down so hard the skin went white there. Alex didn't want him hurting himself; he reached up to gently thumb his sweet boy's lip free.

Slowly, but as if he couldn't help it, Zachary wound his arms around Alex and clutched at his back. "You want to fuck me?"

"So much." Alex shifted up, nudging harder at Zachary's opening. It almost didn't seem like he'd fit, but he already knew better. It opened wide enough to let his fingers in, and one day it'd let a baby out. The thought made his pulse thump hard everywhere, from chest to cock, with the idea of Zachary all rounded out with his child. Heavier, moving slower, but still so sweet in his arms, so hungry for him. He touched Zachary's cheek. "I've never wanted anything like I want you."

"Oh God." Zachary let his breath out in a rush and shivered. His cock throbbed against Alex's, but he was getting himself back together now. Alex could tell, and he liked it. Liked being taught, when Zachary wanted to teach him. He'd been with others himself, but never a presented Omega, and God, there was so much left to learn, and he wanted to know it all.

He caught Alex's face in his hands, bent his head, and kissed him *hard*, his teeth leaving imprints in Alex's lips instead of his own. "There's a condom in my back pocket. Use it."

Then he'd wanted to go all the way too. Enough to think about it and get some protection ready in case they needed any. Alex had to thrust up one more time, he couldn't help it, and almost slid inside. He stopped himself, barely, and tilted Zachary's chin up, far enough back so Alex could look at him.

"Don't worry about it," he said, grinning. "I brought one of my own."

Zachary laughed, breathless again but fully present, wicked the way he could be when he was on top of his game. "Then put it on and show me what you've got." He curled his fingers and raked his nails lightly up and down Alex's spine. "If you've got it in *you* to get it in *me*."

Alex grinned at him, feeling fierce and just as wicked as Zach. "Watch me."

"Oh, I do. All the time, I do."

Alex had to kiss him again, one more for the road before he had to lean back and crane at the awkwardest angle, one that made Zachary laugh until he almost toppled off, to reach his jeans. Alex didn't mind, because he knew he looked ridiculous, and he knew he stopped looking dumb when he found the foil packet and held it up for Zachary to see. "Told you."

"And I told you." Zachary took the condom from him, snapped it right out of his hand, and pushed Alex back down, flat on the floor. He rocked on top of him, letting him nudge a fraction deeper before lifting away. "Now, you watch me. You let me do the work."

Alex wasn't going to argue with *that*. He arched

back, gritted his teeth and counted backward from a hundred to keep himself from coming at the soft/hard touch of Zachary's hands on his cock, rolling the condom down him like they'd already done this a dozen times, maybe more. He lifted himself up and lowered himself slowly, moaning as he took Alex deep, deep, deep inside, not stopping until they were pressed skin to skin.

Oh. God. It was heaven. It was torture, and it was the best kind.

And it made Alex -- different.

He surged up, holding Zachary tight as he could, and ground them together before raising him and letting him slide back. Zachary was light as a feather, and holding him so easily made Alex feel like a king, like someone who knew the world and how it worked, and how to make things happen. He fucked Zachary the way he'd burned to since they started this. Fucked him until his moans bled into each other, a steady keening he didn't bother stifling. Alex kissed him everywhere, and bit him too, leaving marks that'd make bruises and leave red spots behind. He took Zachary's left nipple between his teeth and used the edges of them to make it sting and make Zachary hiccup with a caught breath.

Someone was babbling, mumbling words that didn't really make sense, and it took Alex a second to realize it was him. They mostly got muffled against Zachary's skin as he thrust inside the Omega, drunk on it and addicted all over again. Perfect. This was perfect, it was all he wanted, and --

And it could get better. An idea came to him, not a new one, and it made him dizzy. Made him go harder still, until he thought he was rattling all their bones.

"Listen to you," Zachary said, slack-mouthed and red as a rose. "Noisy. I like it."

He bit the curve of Alex's neck. "I like *you.*"

Alex couldn't help it; he jerked up and came buried

as deep as he could go. Zachary must have felt it. His nails dug hard into Alex's back before he reached out blindly to take his own cock in hand and pump it.

Uh-uh. Alex wasn't having any such nonsense. He swatted Zachary's hand away and replaced it with his own, stroking almost too hard and rough, the way Zachary liked it best. Worked him until Zachary arched his back into a beautiful bow and came, hot and sticky and so, so much, gripping Alex's cock so hard he would have come a second time if he could.

He panted to keep himself under control, and caressed Zachary lighter, lighter, until the Omega winced from being too sensitive and lifted himself up until Alex slid out of him. Zachary let himself fall on top of Alex then, lying chest to chest and with mouth against mouth. Alex licked Zachary's lips, one last tease, and sighed contentedly when Zachary laid his head over Alex's slowing heartbeat and snuggled against him.

The condom came off easy when Alex reached down to remove it. He held it for a moment, looking over Zachary's shoulder. He didn't think he'd ever come so hard, or so much, and he didn't know if it was an Alpha-with-an-Omega thing, or a Zachary thing. Maybe both.

He ran the tip of his nose over Zachary's chest and neck. An Alpha could almost always tell from their scent if an Omega's body was *really* satisfied, and the only thing that truly did the job was when his womb caught a seed that would start to grow. They glowed when that happened, went luminous-pale and loose-boned, taking the change deep, deep, deep inside.

Zachary's scent was the same as before, and he was still red with exertion.

So. Not this time.

But Alex *wanted*.

And he didn't want to wait to say what was on his mind.

Zachary raised himself up and rested one elbow on Alex's chest. *Ow. Pointy.* Whatever, though. Alex couldn't give less of a damn with his body still humming.

But Zachary was still Zachary, and after only a minute or so of lolling bonelessly he bounced back from his exertions like a rubber ball. He glanced over his shoulder and wrinkled his nose. "Okay, a used condom isn't something people usually like to keep in their line of sight unless they have a thing for cooling come and let me tell you, that's not my kink. Where's your head at?"

The teasing made Alex snort. There weren't any trash cans down here and he didn't feel like getting up anyway, so he went for the shortcut of picking up a stray sock that'd landed within arm's reach and stuffed the condom in it without looking. "Fine, it's out of sight. Better?"

"Ugh, no. That was mine, you dick." Zachary poked him. "Next time, use your own."

"Next time." Alex squeezed Zachary's hips, nudging him to sit up.

Zachary sighed impatiently, but he went with it and looped his arms loosely around Alex's neck once they were more or less upright. "What? I was comfortable there."

At this angle, Zachary sat a little higher than Alex, and Alex could enjoy looking up at him all tousled and pink and contented. Could smell both of them more deeply than before, all the scents on them -- sex, hormones, sweat -- trapped between their bodies. He took a deep breath in, the better to taste it all. He felt the light brush of Zachary's thumb on his cheek and heard his quiet hum of amusement before he said, "You look like a cat asleep in the sunshine." He didn't mean to keep talking, but the words kept coming like someone had pulled a cork from a bottle and let everything in there spill free.

"I love you," Alex blurted. "I do, Zachary. I love you."

* * *

Silence answered him.

Absolute, total silence, except for the slight catch in Zachary's lungs. His hands trembled almost imperceptibly where they rested on Alex's back.

"I'm scared too." Alex kneaded at Zachary's sides to soothe himself as much as Zachary. "But -- I've been wanting to say it for, I don't know, it feels like weeks now."

"We've only been together for a few months," Zachary said. He sounded -- odd. Neutral.

Probably the surprise, Alex figured. Alphas usually didn't go in first with the big love confessions. He opened his eyes and laid his head to rest on Zachary's shoulder, because if he was going to buck stereotypes then he'd buck 'em all the way, and if he was going to do this, he'd go big or go back home. "I don't think time matters when it feels the way this feels between us," he said. "That's why I was looking at the condom."

He couldn't see Zachary's owl-eyed blink in response, but he could sure imagine it. "Come a -- I beg your pardon?"

Alex laughed and nuzzled Zachary's shoulder. "You almost said 'come again,' you dork, didn't you? But... yeah." He pulled Zachary a little closer. Swear to God, he could almost feel himself buzzing, totally high on it all. So damn *happy* to be getting this out. "Not next time. Not even the time after, but before a lot longer, I want to do this without the protection."

Zachary didn't move an inch. "You mean you want to knock me up."

"Don't say it like that, like jocks dragging their balls out in the locker room. I mean I want to have babies with you, that's what I mean. We could be a family."

"We're not even twenty."

"So? My grandparents got married when they were teenagers."

"Married?"

"Well -- yeah. We could find a place like this, you know? Maybe small to start with, but I could get a job instead of going to college. Or we could find a place where you decide to go to school, and I can find a job and take care of things. I can take care of you, and if we have babies then I can help take care of them too. I want a family with you in it, Zachary. I want it so much."

Now he'd started talking, Alex couldn't seem to stop and the words kept coming faster and faster, rattling out of him.

"I've wanted you ever since I saw you, you know? I think maybe I wanted you before I even knew what wanting like this really was. And then I got to have you. And I want to have this, always. I want us to be our own family. We can do it. I know it. You make me feel like I can do anything. I *love* you." He pressed his lips to Zachary's neck, feeling the almost too-fast thrum of his pulse underneath the skin. He could taste the Omega of him there, even stronger now, the scent that said his body was responding to all the words coming out. "And I know you love me too."

Silence.

Then, Zachary took a deep breath. He shook himself all over, then brushed the backs of his knuckles along Alex's cheekbones. "Oh, honey. Alex. Honey. Look up at me right now. Please."

Alex did, his smile so broad it almost hurt his cheeks, and looked at Zachary's face. Happily.

At first.

Only at first.

Because what he saw looking back at him wasn't... It wasn't happiness, and it sure as hell wasn't love. It was

-- confusion? No. No, not that. It was dismay. Almost horror, only held back by the thinnest layer of wariness. At what he'd said.

Alex's smile faded away as his heart lurched sickeningly sideways. "Zachary?"

Zachary held Alex's face so gently between his hands it still *felt* like love, and that almost made it worse. "Honey. I'm sorry. No. I --" His ribs moved with the sharpness of his breath. "That isn't what I feel, and it isn't what I want."

Alex's ears rang, but no. No way. He took hold of Zachary's shoulder, hard, and pressed his nose to the spot where arm stopped and pit started. "You're lying."

"I'm not, and don't you dare yank me around like that again." Zachary pulled away from him and sat back, realized he was still perched on Alex, and made an impatient noise. He would have climbed off if Alex hadn't seen his intention half a second before he would have moved and held him in place. "Let me go."

Alex set his jaw. "No. You're lying to me. I can smell it."

"You're a horny Alpha, Alex! Of course you smell 'it.' You smell exactly what anyone would smell after they'd fucked their first Omega, you idiot." Zachary punched him in the pec. "We're not even legal adults yet, and you're talking about marriage? Babies? We've never even left this town. We've never even had a chance to see what else is out there. We haven't started our real *lives*, for fuck's sake."

"I don't care about any of that." Alex reached up to comb roughly through Zachary's hair. He held him there instead, fingers tangled in the soft locks. "All I care about is you."

"Then I'm sorry, but the answer is still no." Zachary held his gaze without flinching. "What did you want me to say, Alex? Did you want me to lie to you?

How would that be fair to you at all, to string you along and give you false hope? To take away all your chances at a real life before you even got to see what they were? How would that be fair to *me*, when I --"

He stopped there, clamping his lips tight like a book clapping shut.

Didn't matter. Alex finished for him, numb all the way down to his core. "When you don't even love me a little, you mean."

Zachary didn't even blink. "I think I should go."

"Yeah, I think you should." Alex shoved the Omega off his lap. He was still sticky with sex and sweat, but it'd turned sour and all he wanted was to wash it off, and -- to hurt like he'd been hurt. "You knew how I felt about all this before, didn't you? You did. But you figured I'd never say anything, so you kept on doing what made you feel good anyway."

Something unreadable passed over Zachary's face. "And if I did?"

"You bastard." Alex dropped back down to the floor, covering his face with the crook of his arm to hide his humiliation, the pounding anger at being played like this, the hurt that went right down to his bones. "Get out. Just -- get out."

He stayed there, listening to the almost-silent sounds of Zachary getting dressed, then the quiet patter of sneakered footsteps walking to the door, the latch turning, the door itself opening and closing.

When Alex looked up, Zachary was gone, and he knew -- somehow -- he wouldn't see the Omega again for a long time.

Maybe not even ever.

And the worst part of it? The very, very worst? Alex still loved the son of a bitch.

He didn't know if he could ever stop.

* * *

Zachary let the door click shut behind him, as softly as he could manage with his hands shaking as hard as they were. It wasn't a particularly thick door; both sets of neighbors, if they were home, had to know absolutely everything he and Alex had been up to for the past few hours.

Would they realize his leaving meant he'd cut the cord? Walked away from the man he loved with all his heart, no matter what he'd just said?

Probably not.

None of them would know this had been Zachary's first time letting a man inside his body. No one in town would have believed *that* -- they all thought he was the town bike, ready and willing for anyone to take a ride -- but it was still true. He'd gotten wet for others because he liked to feel good and there was nothing wrong with enjoying sex, but Alex was the only one he'd opened his legs for. Not that he'd have let Alex know. Zachary had always had too much pride for his own good, and he'd wanted this to *be* good.

It'd been selfish of him, but he'd done it anyway. He'd known the end would come sooner or later, if not this soon, and he'd wanted one taste to take with him. A memory he could hold tight to his chest. He'd brought everything he knew and could guess at to the table, some of it instinct, a lot of it imagination, and put it to use.

Maybe too much so. He'd been half a second away from letting instinct take over, stripping that condom right off Alex and letting the man come inside him.

At least he hadn't been *that* selfish.

Getting pregnant would have doomed Alex to a life stuck on the wrong side of the tracks, tied forever to a bad seed with no chance of getting out there and living his best life. Alex deserved better than that, and Zachary would be damned if he'd let himself stand in the way.

Even if it broke both their hearts. Which it had.

Zachary could hear Alex weeping clear through the thin door. He knew those kinds of tears; they were born out of confusion at having your heart crushed under someone else's foot. He'd shed them before for one reason or another, but somehow he'd never expected to hear that noise when he was with Alex. It made him press the balls of his hands against his cheeks to try and stop from crying too, but it didn't work.

Stupid. So stupid that he'd let himself fall in love when he knew better. Wanting everything Alex wanted -- lovemaking without a barrier between them, a stupid white wedding because fuck the rules, babies who had his eyes and Alex's chin. A home of their own. Family. Love. So much love that it made his ribs ache, and it was only partly because he was crying now too.

"I love you. And I know you love me too."

"I'm sorry. No. That's not what I want."

He'd lied to Alex. But he'd had to.

So stop this. Zachary gave himself a sharp, impatient shake. It didn't matter what he felt or what he wanted when he knew it was better this way. He'd learned how to live with pain before. He'd learn how to live with this too, and he'd let Alex live the best life he could. Sooner or later, Alex would get over him.

First love never lasted. Wasn't that what people said?

But God, he couldn't stand any more of that heartbroken weeping now. That depth of pain couldn't last. It'd shift to anger, then humiliation, and then turn south toward bitter hate. The tears were bad enough, but feeling that love turn to hate would break him.

Zachary needed distance. As much of it as he could get.

He swiped at his face one last time, squared his

shoulders, and walked away without looking back.

And that might have been the end of it all, right there.

But sometimes -- sometimes -- fate had other plans.

Chapter One

Seven Years Later

"This is your conductor speaking. Sorry for the delay, folks --"

Zach jolted out of the light doze he'd fallen into, momentarily disoriented by the movement and the too-bright lights in the train car. He blinked dazedly and looked around, searching for who'd woken him and why, so he could *break their necks*. The first sleep he'd gotten in days, and --

The PA system gave a burst of jarring static.

"...running a little behind schedule due to some technical issues and maintenance being done on the tracks ahead," the conductor droned on. "They should be almost done, so hold tight and we'll have you reaching your stops only a few minutes late."

Well, that was... absolutely swell.

Zach -- he hadn't gone by Zachary in years -- rubbed his face hard, trying to stimulate enough blood flow to help him wake up. No use trying to go back to sleep. He doubted he'd be able to drop off again for hours, if not another couple of days. Insomnia, the single Omega's unfriendly best friend. That and constant, gnawing hunger. Never being able to get warm. Bond sickness didn't happen to every Omega, but a handful of them couldn't cope with any kind of distance from the Alpha their body had laid claim to.

Like Zach. His body wanted Alex and wanted him now. Had wanted him for seven years without ceasing.

Everyone and their cousin had a theory about the phenomenon: that it was all psychological, that it was hormonal, that they didn't have enough of one chemical or another in their brains, or some bizarre instinct figured the less they slept the more they'd be inclined to fuck their way to a solution.

Zach clicked his tongue, frustrated as ever with the

entire mess. He hadn't known, when he was young and stupidly in love, that when he gave his body to Alex he'd forged a link like that. That he'd sentenced himself to fade away into a ghost of his former self, his body demanding what he refused to give it, until one day he would disappear completely.

Once upon a time he'd asked himself: if he had the chance to do it all over again, would he?

Zach would have liked to say *no*, that he'd have better sense, but -- he would. *Yes*. God help him, he would. He had the memory of that one night before it all went sour, and that was worth holding on to. He could be confident Alex wasn't afflicted -- Alphas were lucky that way. If the odd Alpha ever did get a touch of bonding flu, he'd address it by hunting his man down. To the ends of the earth if need be.

As for himself, he'd live off strong coffee and willpower for as long as he could. Travel when he had the chance, looking for warm places and willing Alphas who could satisfy him for a night even if they didn't fool his body chemistry for long.

Could always be worse, and he could comfort himself with knowing he'd done the right thing even if he was paying for it.

Zach waved a *no thank* you to a train attendant who walked past, asking if anyone wanted a warm towel to help with the dry air in the carriage, and leaned back in his seat. Surprisingly comfortable, soft on his aching bones, and the headrest was well cushioned, but they didn't have the central heating cranked nearly high enough for his comfort. He rubbed his hands together to try and warm them when shivering and wrapping his arms around himself didn't help.

Probably should have taken that hot towel after all.

He glanced out the window. If it hadn't been dark, he'd have liked to watch the countryside fly past. Almost no one took trains anymore, not when planes and cars were so much more convenient, but Zach did. He liked them. Liked the romance of them, the way the countryside rolled past and gave you time to read or to simply be quiet and think. If you were alone, it wasn't the worst thing in the world. It was how he'd lived his life from eighteen to twenty-five and that was *fine*, that was the way he liked things. Getting involved equaled getting in trouble. Romance was a complication best avoided, a lesson he'd learned the hard way.

He glanced back as the attendant started back up the aisle, this time pushing a rattling cart with one squeaky wheel and enough coffee on board to give a horse heartburn.

Oh God. Yes. Zach waved him down.

"Coffee, sir?"

"As much of it as you can fit in a cup. No cream but double the sugar. Please."

The train attendant shook his head, but with a smile and a finger briefly pressed to his lips as he passed over not one but two Styrofoam cups filled to the brim. He was an Omega too, in his mid-thirties by the look of him, but he wore an obsidian widower's ring instead of a wedding band.

Zach took a grateful gulp, not caring that the coffee was hot enough to scald his throat, and asked, "How far behind schedule are we?" Stretching his legs at the next station would do him good; they ached when he stayed still for too long.

"About half an hour, at this point." The attendant nodded at him with a sympathetic grimace before pushing his cart forward.

Half an hour. I can do half an hour.

Wishing wouldn't make the wheels turn faster, but with nothing to look at outside in the dark, Zach adjusted his position so he could get a better view of the passengers in his car. Like most Omegas he wasn't very tall. Some new folks had gotten on and others disembarked while he'd dozed, and he liked wondering what their stories were.

Two young Alphas who acted like frat bros; interesting, they weren't the usual size for Alphas, but small and compact and they weren't at each other's throats but laughed and joked like best friends. A couple that had to be recently married from the way they could barely resist climbing all over each other; an Omega with a contented smile, probably on his way back home, and --

Oh.

Oh, God. Zach's heart jumped into his throat and wedged there. Three rows ahead, a profile almost as familiar as his own turned to smile at the attendant as he refused the offer of coffee. It couldn't be, it *couldn't* be, he hadn't seen that profile in real life since he was eighteen, but --

Alex.

He'd changed -- no, he'd grown up, the way everyone did, the bones of his face maturing from soft boyish cuteness to strong, masculine definition. His hair had gone from somewhere between red and blond to full-blown ginger, with a slightly darker red beard that he'd trimmed and shaped to his strong, stubborn jaw. He wore the kind of casual suit that would have cost the equivalent of a month's rent in a big city, but it wasn't as lovely as his hands. Zach remembered them all too well. Elegant hands with sturdy knuckles and deft fingers. If Zach had closed his eyes, he could have *felt* those hands on the bare skin of his memory.

He did and didn't look a thing like the boy Zach remembered but it *was* him.

Alex.

You never forgot your first.

"I love you. And I know you love me too."

"I'm sorry. No. That's not what I want."

Zach had to stop staring. Alex would sense it any second now and look around.

Stop.

He tried looking at his tablet to calm down. Someone passed by, walking down the aisle and back again, but Zach barely noticed. He focused so hard it made his head ache, but even with the coffee humming through his veins the words swam on the backlit page, and he couldn't help it. His gaze drifted back up, drawn like a moth to a flame.

Zach's body twitched with the first pangs of arousal, wanting what he'd had once upon a time. He remembered it all, and he remembered it perfectly. He dreamed about it, when he slept. The taste of Alex's skin, the softness and hardness of his mouth and how his eagerness had nearly rubbed the insides of Zach's thighs raw. The fullness, almost too much and too tight, when he slid inside Zach.

"I love you. And I know you love me too."

"I'm sorry. No. That's not what I want."

Anger slowly took alarm and unhappiness's place -- anger, and frustration with himself. Zach should have sensed this train was to be avoided. Dodged. Something! And Alex, sitting there as if he didn't have a care in the world -- it was everything Zach had wanted for him, the entire reason he'd left Alex in the first place, but seeing it in the flesh opened all those old wounds back up and made them bleed afresh. The pain from that moment of saying no to what Alex had offered with all his big, warm heart cut sharper than any knife -- but he'd had to. You didn't do that to your first boyfriend. You didn't take him up on a marriage proposal and tie him down to a shitty life based on a few promises made in the afterglow.

Alex...

No.

They must have been traveling farther and faster than Zach had realized, or he was more out of it than he'd known. Between one blink and the next the train's PA system crackled to far-too-loud life again, announcing they'd reach their next station at Second Chance in ten minutes.

Second Chance? What kind of name was that for a town?

Alex looked up at the speaker, nodded in an absent sort of way, and stood to open the overhead compartment. He took out a bulging messenger bag, slung it over his shoulder and stuffed a pair of thick gloves and a warm knit hat in the pockets of his coat. Second Chance must have been his stop.

Zach caught his lip between his teeth, torn between his body's demand that he go to Alex and the common sense of staying right where he was. His heart might be breaking all over again and he *hated* doing it. It made him so angry his temples pounded, and his hands curled into tight fists, but fury was better than grief. He'd rather rage against the dying of the light than cry over a candle.

Or what if -- maybe if he kept it to a simple hello --

Stop. Zach dug his fingernails into his knees. He knew better, for God's sake, and he hadn't kept his distance this long to crumble like a pillar of salt just from catching sight of Alex again. *Let it go.* Let it be nothing more than a missed connection on a connecting train.

Let him go as many times as you have to, until it takes.

And Zach would have. Really he would.

But as Alex walked past him -- always so eager to do things, that one; he *would* start heading for the exits before the train had even come to a halt -- he only made it two steps past Zach's seat before he stopped. As Zach's heart sank down past the pit of his stomach he sensed Alex pause, then turn to look back.

He stopped, almost exactly the way Zach had,

blank with surprise. "Do I know you?"

Zach held his breath. Could he lie? Yes, but this new, matured Alex would have the life experience not to believe him, and he hadn't changed nearly as much as Alex had. He opened his mouth, but nothing came out.

"I do know you. I know your face," Alex said. His voice had matured with the rest of him as he aged, going from sweet to firm with a rasp on the edges. "Zachary?"

"I go by Zach now." That wasn't what Zach had meant to say at all, and the annoyance helped alleviate the fluttering in his stomach. "And I know your face too, Alex."

Alex grinned at him, as boyish as he used to look when seen from this angle. "I go by Alexander now. That's funny, isn't it? We did the same thing in reverse. I went longer, you went shorter."

Without being invited, he dropped into an empty aisle seat across from Zach and turned at the waist so he could keep on looking. No, not looking, that wasn't a strong enough word. Studying him, intense in a way he'd only started to be when he was young and it made Zach want to fidget, but he'd be damned if he showed his soft underbelly now. "I would say I can't believe it's you, but if I see a thing, I believe it."

"An interesting philosophy," Zach managed.

God, how awkward. He sounded like the primmest queen who'd ever quirked his pinky finger drinking tea, but he would swear he could feel Alexander's body heat radiating gently away from him and all he wanted to do was lean in and finally warm up. He couldn't. He daredn't, which probably wasn't a real word but ought to be.

He cleared his throat and tried again. "This is your stop?"

"I wasn't planning on taking a flying leap off with my luggage like Superman." The corner of Alexander's mouth lifted in a sideways quirk. He leaned a little farther forward, closer to Zach. "Yes, this is my stop. Not yours?"

"No, I'm headed -- north," Zach said, then pretended he hadn't nearly slipped up. God, Alexander smelled *so* good, like some warm, spicy custom cologne that cost a king's ransom per ounce. Every Alpha had their own unique fragrance, which got stronger as they aged. Omegas were the same, only their scent changed when they were were and weren't with child. Or when they wanted to become that way. Alexander's scent had been faint but addictive when they were young. It nearly intoxicated Zach now.

All the more reason to keep a cool head, he warned himself. And it was, by far, better not to let Alexander know exactly where he was headed. He made a vague gesture upward. "The New York area."

"You would have to be, seeing as the train's pointed that direction."

Flip, flip, flip, wasn't he? And so damn witty. Zach wasn't at all sure he liked it. It made him want to tap his foot and scowl. But the train hadn't come to a stop yet, so -- one more try. "You look well."

Alexander snorted quietly. "Do I? You look tired. And cold."

"A few days of not sleeping well. Nothing to worry about."

"Mmm," Alexander vocalized, a noncommittal noise. Suddenly -- so quickly and smoothly Zach didn't see it coming in time to relax -- Alexander had reached out to brush the backs of his knuckles along Zach's jawline. He'd come closer still while he was at it, so near that if he'd wanted to Zach could have counted his eyelashes. He wasn't smiling now. "It's been the better part of a decade. I never thought I'd see you again."

Was he waiting for an answer? "Neither did I."

"On purpose?"

The question hit hard and fast like a jab under the ribs, and Zach's mouth dropped open for a startled second before his temper kindled. "I didn't choose this train knowing you'd be on it."

"Hmm. The whims of fate."

"I don't believe in fate," Zach lied flatly. "There's chaos, and there's random chance, and sometimes things collide. Nothing else. What are you doing?"

He reached up to catch Alexander's wrist, but too late.

Alexander had moved his knuckles to Zach's cheek, his touch so light but so very *there*, so *present*, it nearly burned the skin. "Your face," he said, turning Zach slightly toward the light. "I remember those cheekbones. They were softer then." He traced the sharp line. "You grew into your bones. More beautiful than I'd imagined, and… I've imagined, Zach."

An electric spark, not visible or tangible, yet still somehow very real, jumped between him and Zach, who couldn't seem to catch his breath. He wanted to snap back something witty, something sassy, but --

Alexander wanted him. Maybe willingly, maybe not. Zach couldn't tell. No Omega could miss those signals, and if they cared in any way, they couldn't help but respond. Alexander would be able to smell it -- already had; he'd broken out that sideways quirk of his mouth again. Oh, he knew. But what did he expect to happen? This was his stop, not Zach's. Ten more minutes and Zach would be gone again and besides, he couldn't jump the bones of a man he'd broken up with years and years ago even if he wouldn't mind!

Damn him for being himself.

Zach pulled away from Alexander's touch and put his hand up between them to stop him trying again. "Don't. Just -- don't."

Alexander opened his mouth, no doubt ready with

another quicksilver retort, but he never got it out. With no
warning, with a sudden and sickening lurch and the
screaming of metal against metal, the train car jerked
sideways and sent them flying one against the other, and
both bodies against the window, hard. The lights buzzed,
sparked, and went out.

Darkness.

Silence.

Alexander lay on top of him, chest to chest, breath
to breath, in the abrupt and utter quiet of the night.

Chapter Two

Zach might have -- not screamed, exactly, though the noise was close enough to make no difference -- at the shock of impact and the vanishing light. It was too short a sound, cut off by the abrupt impact of Alexander's weight on top of him, nearly full-length, his face pressed to the man's shoulder. Blind in the dark, he reached up to scrabble for anything he could find to hold onto, and twisted his fingers into the thick, warm fabric of Alexander's coat. Only enough to stop himself shaking quite so thoroughly. He'd dare anyone to blame him for it, though! After something like that?

"Shh," Alexander said, his breath warmer still where it fanned against Zach's cheek. "Shh. Don't move yet. I've got you."

He did. More than, Zach realized. The momentum might have started them off, but Alexander -- he'd thrown his body across Zach's, hadn't he? Shielded him from whatever was coming with his whole self.

Oh God.

"I love you. And I know you love me too."

"I'm sorry. No. That's not what I want."

A trickle of something warm and wet ran down Zach's cheek. Blood? No. Salt. Tears. He squeezed his eyes shut, ordering himself to *not* be so weak again, but he should have known he couldn't fool this new Alexander. He pressed his forehead to Zach's, murmuring quiet things, not really words, more like simple, soothing sounds. "It's all right, sweetheart, I think it's over. Don't be scared. I've got you; I'm not letting go."

Oh. *God.*

Zach didn't do it on purpose, but he didn't stop himself. With his hands knotted in Alexander's jacket, he raised himself a few inches and it was easy, so easy, to tilt his head and press his mouth to Alexander's. Alexander stilled for half a beat, made a brief breathless sound, and then -- melted -- into Zach, warmer and heavier, his hand cupping, cradling Zach's cheek. He pressed his thumb to the soft spot beneath Zach's ear, by his jaw, firm and gentle, as he deepened the kiss.

Alexander tasted like Zach remembered. Exactly the same. Even if he didn't kiss anything like the boy he'd been, back when --

Zach jolted away from Alexander, shocked at himself. "I --" He stopped there, lost for words, but unkinked his fists and pressed his palms flat against Alexander's chest until Alexander moved back far enough he could take a full breath. "I shouldn't have -- I don't know why I did that."

He felt, rather than saw, Alexander's sigh, and felt the brush of Alexander's thumb over his lower lip too. "People do things, sometimes. Don't they?"

Zach didn't know what to say in reply. He shivered, colder still now the train's heating had cut off, wishing he could see something besides darkness. There should have been emergency lights and there weren't, and it frightened him. "What happened? Some kind of explosion?"

"No." Despite the quickness of his answer, Zach couldn't help noticing Alexander was still shielding Zach's body with his own. He sounded thoughtful. "No flash, and the vibrations felt like they came from somewhere deep. Maybe something happened at the quarry."

"There's a quarry?"

Alexander wasn't paying attention to him any longer. Probably listening for other things like the train creaking, maybe tipping -- *no, don't even think about the possibility, it's over, he said so.* "Second Chance has a quarry, yeah. And a mine. The old families built the town around them. They use dynamite and blasting caps to open up new seams. Something might have gone off when it shouldn't, or it could have been a tree falling across the tracks. I don't know. Are you sure you're not hurt?"

"I'm fine. You?"

"You couldn't tell?" Alexander's short beard scratched Zach's cheek when he shook his head, and if his chuckle was a little unsteady Zach decided he could be kind enough not to call him on it. "Whatever this was, it didn't hurt me."

"Good. That's good." The emergency lights finally flickered on, pale blue and weak, but anything was an improvement. Zach could tell now they'd landed at a forty-five-degree angle, leaning sharply to one side. Sounds started to filter through the shock now he could see: screams, sobs, and the rumble-thump-scramble of panicked people. "The others in the car. The steward! He was so kind. Can you see if anyone's hurt?"

Alexander went still again, though God only knew why because Zach certainly didn't. "I don't know, but if we're all right I'm going to find out."

Zach shot out a hand to grab him by the wrist before he could move. "Not by yourself, you're not."

"I'm not leaving you here alone, don't worry." A flash of white, a sharp smile, quick as lightning, darted across Alexander's face. "You think I would, now? Hold still. I'm going to get up now, help you up too, and we'll do what needs doing. See if we can find out what happened."

* * *

It wasn't as bad as it could have been. *Thank God.* Once they were on their feet and steady enough to walk up the car's new slope, everyone Zach and Alexander checked was shaken, but no one had taken any damage worse than a bump here and a bruise or a scrape there. The steward had broken or twisted his ankle and either bitten his tongue or split his lip. He made Zach think of a

B-movie vampire with blood trickling from the corners of his mouth, but he was lucid. He'd found a lump of ice to tuck in his cheek and waved Zach off with a garbled directive of some sort.

"I'm sorry, what?" Zach asked, baffled.

Alexander must have been more fluent in *muffled* than Zach, because he nodded. "I'll check with the engineer and come back, or have someone else come back to fill you in. All right?"

The steward gave Alexander a thumbs up, but the second his back was turned he gave Zach an impressed look and brought the second thumb up too.

Oh lord. But there wasn't time to hang around and explain; Alexander had taken hold of Zach's hand, not leaving him behind, and started forward. His legs were so long that Zach's only choice was to keep up or get dragged, and he wasn't quite badly off enough to let an Alpha go full caveman on him, thank you very much.

Ah. There was his backbone. Zach had missed it when it'd gone AWOL. He took as deep a breath as he could, and felt the steadiness come back to his legs too. He gripped Alexander's hand tighter, and when Alexander looked back over his shoulder with one eyebrow cocked in a question, he nodded to the Alpha. *I can do this. Let's go.*

Alexander grinned at him, approving, squeezed his hand back, and took off at top speed.

Together they hurried through cars that went from plush and passenger-oriented to greasy and industrial. Alexander stopped at the first man wearing what looked like an engineer's name tag and got his attention with a hand to the shoulder. He held both hands up when the man all but snarled at him. "Whoa! Stand down. I won't keep you, but the passengers need to know if you have any idea what happened."

The engineer ran a frustrated hand through his

hair, already standing up in spikes. "Look, I don't know for sure. The original delay was for a warning about a car on the tracks, but --"

"A what?" Alexander shouldered a few inches in front of Zach. "Whose car?"

"No telling yet. No one inside, no clue why they left it. Maybe it got stuck and they ditched? Shitty of them not to let us know somehow but could be there wasn't time. Fuck me if I know."

"Are engineers supposed to use that kind of language?" Zach asked, fascinated and, to his embarrassment, so inappropriately. He didn't need Alexander's reproving glance to prompt him to grimace an apology.

"So no one in the car was hurt. At least there's that." Alexander grimaced at Zach, which was an improvement from a nonverbal scolding. "I know most of the people around here. Don't want to think of any of them in that kind of trouble."

He still had a kind heart. It made Zach feel somehow better to see it -- and it made him want to take Alexander's hand and hold it. He diverted quickly into curiosity, inappropriate or not. "A car on the tracks, at *first*? What came second?"

"Whatever the hell the *boom* was. Maybe the quarry, but there's some nasty weather moving in, a big storm that was supposed to go up the coast but took a hard left and pointed itself this way. Might have gone through up ahead and done some damage."

"Not likely. It's barely started raining, and a fallen tree wouldn't make that much earth shake," Alexander said. He looked grim. "Is there anything we can do to help over there? In here?"

The engineer's expression softened briefly before he shook his head. "Someone who doesn't know what they're doing, real specific-like, they'd just be in the way.

Best clear out and give the professionals room to work."

There was a definite hint to get out of the way in his last comment. Zach tugged at Alexander's cuff, intending to nudge him aside in case he'd missed the point. Or rather, he tried to nudge Alexander out of the way. It would have been easier to move a fallen tree with a feather. How much stronger had Alexander *gotten* since they were kids? Either he benched more than Zach weighed or he'd acquired the ability, like a cat in front of a keyboard, to gain as much mass as he needed to stay firmly put when he didn't want to be moved.

Oh God, Zach needed some sleep.

He rubbed at his eyes. *That* Alexander noticed, and *that* took him back two steps and redirected his attention to Zach. "Are you sure you're all right?"

Zach swatted him aside. "I'm fine." He risked his luck one more time with the engineer, who he frankly wouldn't have blamed for chucking them bodily off the train by then. "Are there any cars stable enough for passengers to wait in until the train's fixed?"

"Too risky. All the stewards steady enough to walk are getting folks out as quick and safe as they can."

"Going where?" Zach blurted. He crossed his arms, trying to tug his jacket tighter, and shivered. "The station?"

"Unless they're local, like your boy here." *He's not my boy*, Zach started to say, but neither the engineer nor Alexander was listening.

"Does the station have heat?" Alexander asked.

The engineer made a face. "Looks like their power is out. It's pretty drafty, but there's probably blankets somewhere around and benches folks can nap on."

A drafty, empty station, a thin blanket, metal screeching within arm's reach. Zach blanched. He didn't shy away from -- much -- but he wasn't certain he could cope with that. His head would split open or he'd shiver himself sick.

Alexander gave him an odd look, but the engineer was still talking. "It'll be five hours at least, maybe more, before we're moving again. Depends on how fast we can get equipment and workers down here to get us back on track and that's *if* something else doesn't happen. Fuck knows, it might. It's that kind of night. Clear out while the clearing's good, that's my advice, and if you guys would let me get back to work now before someone kicks my ass for lying down on the job?"

"If anyone tries, send them to me," Alexander said. He had a way about him, even now, that made the engineer's tight shoulders relax. "I'll let them know you had a reason. Thank you for taking the time."

The engineer waved him off. "Take the employee exit, if you want. Probably less crowded, but mind you're careful of the drop-off."

"Good idea, and I will. Thank you again." Before Zach knew what he meant to do, Alexander had taken his hand to tug him away. "Come on. Let's get out of here."

"I wasn't the one holding us up," Zach protested, but he didn't object enough to being hauled around to stay in the engineer car. Much. The thought of having to hole up in that station -- but good Lord, Alexander had long legs, and even in spaces as tight as these he could move fast. "Alexander, slow down! You're going to pull my arm out of its socket."

"No I won't, and I'm going this fast so we can get where we want before you have a chance to change your mind. Or I change *my* mind."

"What's that supposed to mean?"

"You'll see." Alexander stopped in front of an exit door, far more industrial than inviting in its design, to the tilted left of the train. He glanced back at Zach. "Hold on tight to my hand, okay? Don't look down, and don't let go."

Well, that didn't sound ominous at all, did it? But what choice did he have?

Zach gripped Alexander's hand tighter. "Fine, but I just survived a literal train wreck. If you get me killed now, I'm going to come back and haunt you."

Alexander snorted lightly. "It wasn't a wreck. More of an accident. Still, fair enough." He shoved the door open, and no matter how strong he might be, he really had to put his shoulder into it. "Step where I step."

"You're really selling this," Zach said, and let Alexander guide him off the train. Whistling in the dark, graveyard humor, call it what you liked. "You should go pro."

Alexander gave him a warning look. "I'm not joking. Step where I step, don't slow down, and don't look down. Got it?"

"I don't understand."

"You will."

He wasn't wrong. The second Zach set foot on the ground, he understood completely. There was solid ground for them to walk on, sure, but maybe -- *maybe*, when measured with a generous eye -- eighteen inches between them and a narrow, rickety bridge rail the only safeguard against a fifty-foot drop into a flooded gully.

Zach froze, unable to take another step. Surprisingly strong winds made it nearly deafening out there, but he'd have been very surprised if Alexander couldn't still hear the rattle-bang-slam of his heart in its panic. He gritted his teeth out of sheer frustration at his own weakness, his fear of heights, then buried his face against Alexander's back in paradoxical need for comfort. Alexander's body hitched in a rueful *I told you you wouldn't like this* sort of movement, but he pried and pulled and nudged until he'd guided Zach in front in front of him, sheltered by his body and arms.

He put his lips to Zach's ear. "It'll be okay. I'll

guide you. I promise I won't let you fall. Trust me."

As if he had a choice? Again? Zach would have to do as he was told and put his trust in Alexander to take care of him.

Wasn't that just the kind of irony fate loved best?

Zach closed his eyes and took a step forward. One. And then, another, and one more.

* * *

He held his breath until they'd circled around the front of the train and were on solid ground, at least ten feet between them and the bridge, before letting go of Alexander's sleeve -- promptly balling up his fist and socking Alexander in the ribs.

"Hey! What was that for?"

"As if I could hurt you," Zach retorted. He shook out his fist. "That was -- I don't know. It felt right."

Alexander rolled his eyes. "God, I love gratitude," he muttered. "I told you to trust me. I got you out of there safely, didn't I?"

"I didn't say otherwise." Damn, his knuckles stung. It'd felt more like punching a brick wall than a man, but it'd been worth it. Zach gaped at the drop-off. "Why is that even there? Aren't they just asking for someone to take a great big dramatic nosedive right over the edge?"

"It's there because it's been there since the tracks were laid down, and the straightest path was right next to the original quarry," Alexander said tiredly. "I've lobbied for years to get an actual barrier there, which makes me the latest of a few generations to try. Town council won't bite."

"They all have historic authenticity boners?"

"You could say so. I'd call it stupidity, myself."

Zach chanced a look over his shoulder, and caught a glimpse, quickly hidden, of a fear matching his own. He stopped. *Oh.* Alexander been scared too, even if he hadn't let it stop him.

There was a certain irony in there as well, which Zach chose to tuck away and not examine -- yet. Instead, he took Alexander's hand and gave it a quick squeeze: *thank you.*

Alexander squeezed back, just as quickly. *You're welcome.*

Though it was hard to let go, Zach managed. He turned to face the station where he'd have no choice but to bunk down, first curiously and then with his fingers pressed to his lips in growing dismay. "Oh my God."

Drafty? Understatement. The brick building looked like it'd been slapped together by drunken builders a hundred-odd years ago, and at least three of the topmost windows were broken, probably by kids throwing rocks. He shivered -- no, shuddered -- at the imagined chill and how it would go straight down to his bones. It'd be days before he got warm again.

You could warm up a lot faster if you wanted, a sneaky part of his mind suggested.

Zach would have scolded himself for the stray thought if his brain hadn't been startled into silence by the sudden, heavy, body-heated weight of Alexander's coat being draped over his shoulders. It smelled of both Alpha and some rich, spicy cologne, and Zach couldn't help but cuddle into its folds in immediate relief. It made him want to melt to the ground, and to dig in his heels at the same time.

He started to peel the fabric away. "Stop it, Alexander, this is yours and you need it."

"Somehow, I knew you were going to do that." Alexander settled the coat back into place and gave Zach a warning look. "Don't. I can see how cold you are."

"I'm fine."

"Sure you are," Alexander said dryly. He studied Zach again. "No. It's too cold out here and it's going to be worse in the station. You're coming home with me."

Zach stared at him. "What?"

"You're coming with me," Alexander said again. "No arguments."

"No," Zach said without hesitating. "Not going to happen, Alex." Damn it; he'd slipped. It was harder to get used to the grown man's preferred name than he'd thought it would be. "*Alexander*. Sorry. But the answer's still no."

He could see Alexander's frustration building. "Would you put your pride away this once? I can't go home and leave you all by yourself in the cold."

"It's not about pride!" Mostly. Partially. "It's about going with you being a bad idea, and me knowing you know as much." Zach's teeth chattered, and he had to clamp his jaw shut to stop it until the fit of shivers passed. He laid his hand on Alexander's forearm. "You're kind to offer, but I can't. Don't you see?"

"I see if you don't cooperate, I'm going to toss you over my shoulder and carry you back to my place," Alexander said frankly. "Your choice."

Zach gaped at him. "You're serious."

"My hand to God, I am. I swear, you're worse than any cat in your bloodlines ever was."

"And you're worse than a hunting dog!"

Alexander crossed his arms. "Do you think I'm taking you back there to seduce you?"

Zach's face warmed.

Alexander sighed and settled his coat a little more snugly around Zach's shoulders. "It's going to start raining again any second, you know. You need a place to warm up and stay dry while they're fixing the tracks. I have a couch and a gas fire if the power goes out. That's all. It's nothing but an offer of hospitality, no funny business involved."

Frustrated with himself, Zach bit at his lower lip, thinking furiously while Alexander waited. He meant to say no. He did.

He didn't. The *cold*.

What choice did he have? "All right," Zach said, putting his hands up in surrender, and sighed. "You win. And. Thank you."

"There. Was that so hard?" Alexander's ire passed as quickly as a stray breeze. "It's a couple of blocks down the road."

He offered Zach his arm like a proper gentleman, and when Zach didn't take it he shrugged and tossed it over Zach's shoulders instead.

Zach shook his head. "I can't stop you, can I?"

"You're not the only one who can be stubborn." Alexander led him away from the train, whistling a few casual notes that made Zach's spine prickle in warning; no one acted so very innocent unless they had some devious plan up their sleeve. "You really didn't know I was there? It's funny."

"What is?" Zach asked warily.

"I've learned to know what it's like when someone's watching me. Some of the places I've been it matters more than you'd think to pick up on it, though I guess you'd know about that too. But for miles now, I'd felt someone staring holes through the back of my head."

"What are you saying?"

"Me? Nothing, really. Just saying." Alexander tugged him left, giving him no choice. "Mine's this way."

Truer words, Zach muttered to himself, but he followed Alexander anyway.

* * *

"You live here?" Zach whistled, staring up at the terrace house Alexander had led them to. Wall to wall with its neighbors, old, built from a darkly veined stone carved to look elegant as well as inviting. Someone took good care of the entire block. There wasn't a cigarette butt or an empty beer can to be seen in the gutters, and all the paint on the windowsills and doors looked fresh, new. The stones themselves almost gleamed, they were so clean, and the flecks of quartz mica in them must have glittered in the daylight. "Swanky."

"I know what I like, and I like nice things." Alexander guided Zach up the steps. He didn't need to; Zach's knees were steady -- enough -- now and the coat had warmed him up until he could breathe freely.

Still, it would be the better part of valor to pick his fights carefully if they were going to be sequestered together for a few hours. Zach had zero doubt there would be plenty to choose from.

"Not to your usual taste?" Alexander arched an eyebrow at Zach as he dug into his hip pocket. "What don't you like?"

"I didn't say I didn't like it, I..." Zach didn't mind *huge* as a general rule; no Omega did; every one of them had at least a crumb or so of "size queen" in their stockpile of jerk-off fantasies. But this house... Alexander was a big man, but even he would rattle around in there like one dried pea in a tin can, all alone. "Do you have roommates?"

"Not as such." Alexander frowned as he started patting the pockets he hadn't searched yet. "What kind of place do you have?"

"An uptown studio. Smallish. Almost enough room for a bed *and* a bath, and there's a good view of the skyline." Zach loved his studio's view. It made the otherwise cramped conditions worth his while. He'd wedged a small chair between bed and window solely so he could curl up in the seat with a cup of coffee and watch the sun rise or set. "It suits me."

"Sounds like it." The way Alexander looked at him, even sideways, made Zach catch his breath. As unexpected -- or maybe more so, because he hadn't seen it coming -- and as intimate as a kiss, as knowing, as personal as a hand sliding up smooth, slick skin in the middle of the night. "Sounds like you."

"I…" Zach hesitated, lost for what to say. He swallowed hard. "I wouldn't have chosen it if it wasn't what I wanted."

"Hmm. You should see the views here when they don't involve industrial accidents." Alexander looked away, finally, letting Zach breathe again -- but he hadn't found what he wanted in the pockets he wore, and with a shrug started digging through the pockets in the coat he'd loaned Zach instead. "Hold on, let me…"

Zach swatted him away in alarm. Wandering hands made it far too hard -- difficult! -- to think and if all the blood in his body divided itself equally between cheeks and dick, he wouldn't be able to think at all. "If you're going to do that, would you please take your coat back?"

"No, I've almost got it. I know I put my keys in one of these." He barely glanced at Zach as he added, "Keep it on, so you don't get chilled again. Or keep it, period, if you want. It's a good winter coat and you're so thin I can almost see through you. You need the warmth."

"Flattering." Zach twitched from side to side, trying to dodge Alexander's touch coming too near any danger zones. "I swear, you never could find what you're looking for, even if you'd laid both hands on it less than a minute ago and that was when you *had* someone to remind you of things."

He hadn't meant to say that out loud. Damn.

Alexander snorted quietly. "So imagine how bad I am when I don't have someone to keep me on the straight and narrow. Aha. Found them." He jingled a key ring at Zach. "Now I can actually let you in. Welcome to my humble home."

"You were never humble a day in your life. And by the way, you didn't distract me. Your coat. Take it."

Alexander made a disgruntled noise but took the coat back and draped it over his arm as he unlocked the door. "You really are as bad as a cat."

"Independent," Zach corrected. "You're saying independence is a bad thing?"

"See? That's what I mean, right there." Alexander glanced back and grinned, teasing. "No, you always reminded me of a cat. Sleek and slimlined and prickly and slinky, and..."

Zach's cheeks went cherry red and hot all over again. He swept his hair over his cheek and smoothed it down, his hands dancing nervously as they moved. "Yes, well. You've heard the old saying about herding cats, I'm sure."

"A few times. Just a few. And speaking of which... uh-uh-uh, hey!" Alexander put out one foot as the door swung open, blocking a huge black and white cat's escape attempt, and crouched to nudge a tiny Siamese mix back before it made a break for freedom too. It hissed at him.

Zach's mouth dropped open. "I thought you said you didn't have roommates."

"Cats count as roommates?" Alexander wrinkled his nose fondly at the contrary Siamese mix and scratched lightly behind its ears, dodging the swipe it aimed at him in return. "Little thing, you and your buddy know the rules. Back inside."

The huge cat glowered, then flipped its tail straight up and marched away as if a dignified retreat had been its idea in the first place. The little one licked its forepaw twice before following, absolutely careless of being commanded. Zach had to fight the urge to smile. Alexander could grumble all he wanted, but it was perfectly plain to see those cats had Alexander firmly wrapped around their forepaws -- two cranky, cantankerous, crosswise cats that enchanted Zach right away.

Maybe Alexander was right, and he *was* a lot like the ancient cats in his bloodline. Maybe he'd just met some long-lost family.

He offered the two domestic pets a metaphorical fist bump. *Represent.*

Alexander winked at Zach as he stood. "The way I remember it, herding cats is supposed to be impossible. But I've learned a few things over the years. Come inside."

Chapter Three

Inside, the brownstone was -- *huh*. And *hmm*, as well.

Zach frowned at it, turning in a slow circle and trying to figure out why the polished wood and off-white walls rubbed him the wrong way. They were too much like the outside, weren't they? Polished until they gleamed, picture perfect, and possessing absolutely nothing resembling individual charm. He'd stayed in cozier motel rooms during his early years away. "You really do live here?"

Alexander glanced around at the four walls as if they were almost as unfamiliar to him as they were to Zach. "When I'm in town, yes. Once every couple of weeks or so, maybe for a day or two. Sometimes less often."

Ah. Now it makes sense. Zach nodded. The missing personality would have gone hand in hand with the kind of clutter that accumulated whenever you hung your hat in a particular place for a while. The chair next to the window in his apartment, for example, or the collection of coffee cups he kept on wall hooks.

As Alexander kicked off his shoes and gestured for Zach to do the same -- sensible, shoes of any kind and floors so highly polished did not mix -- Zach couldn't help but wonder why. Though it didn't come easily to him he was a stranger in a strange land here, not at all on his own territory, and he tried a little beating around the bush. "What made you pick this town? What with the death-defying drop-offs and exploding quarries and all?"

Still frowning at the walls, Alexander shrugged almost disinterestedly. "It's got its own charm. Friendly people, sort of 'everybody knows your name,' but not too Hallmark. It's a little like a northern New Orleans, old history and new charm. Things happen here --"

"Including train wrecks," Zach couldn't help

murmuring.

"-- and I like being where things happen," Alexander went on. He put his bag down and flicked a lamp on that looked small but illuminated a surprising lot of the room with a soothing amber glow. "Keeps life interesting. Besides, like I said, I don't *live here*, live here. It's a place to hang my hat when I'm in town."

"And when you're not?" Zach drifted toward the edges of the room to poke curiously at the very few bits of bric-a-brac on end tables and the mantel of a gas fireplace. Mostly cat paraphernalia and a stack of unopened mail. It seemed so wrong, still, that there was almost nothing personal scattered around. Nothing to point to the enthusiastic force of nature the house's owner could be.

Zach couldn't shake a feeling of *wrongness* about it all.

"Where do you go? What do you do?" he asked. Underneath the stack of mail, he found a sheaf of travel magazines both new and old, and held one up. Comprehension dawned. "You write for them, don't you?"

"Blogs, columns. Mostly food related."

Alexander always had loved food, and though he hadn't been much for writing way-back-when people did change. All the stretching his legs around the globe and dining daily on the good stuff would explain how he'd grown up so big and strong. And -- the things he must have seen, the things he must have done. He'd accomplished all of it, everything Zach had left him for.

"I sit on the town council in absentia as well, so I can fight to fix the drop-off," Alexander went on. "And I'm a resident coordinator at the college during summer sessions. I like to stay busy."

He'd made a life. A good one.

"So." Zach dropped the magazines and tossed a

little sass into the mix to hide how much this new understanding touched him. "Your job is eating your way around the world. Nice work if you can get it. How are you not as round as you are tall?"

Alexander's laugh never got old, even when it had been familiar; more so now, when it was new again. Zach had forgotten what it really sounded like, the timbre of it, the warm depths. It'd aged well, gotten richer like a good brandy, but it was the same way the eager boy he'd once been had laughed when staggering home arm in arm with Zachary-as-he'd-been, both drunk as lords off cheap beer and bravado. "Trade secret."

"Hmm." Sass seemed to go over well, and Zach wasn't above using what worked to his advantage. "So do you only do columns and the part-time town gigs?" He held out his arms to display the luxe of Alexander's coat, then waved at his shoes and messenger bag. "Travel journalism and odd jobs don't pay *that* well."

"Nope. But the investments I've made over the years -- those do. Dating sites, mostly." Alexander gave him the wickedest possible wink. "You've heard of Grindr? And a few others."

Zach's mouth dropped open. "Wait. Really?"

"Houses like this don't pay for themselves. As to why I bought it? Call it another of my investments." Alexander threw himself carelessly down on a cream-colored chaise lounge, putting one leg up on the cushion and bracing his other foot on the floor. "Are you hungry? You look hungry. I've got a freezer full of almost everything. Name your poison."

"I had a sandwich on the train," Zach lied.

"Uh-huh." Nope, Alexander wasn't buying it. "Even if you had, the best they offer is two slabs of cardboard with some kindergarten paste smeared on one side and a couple pieces of anemic lettuce. You're hungry." He paused, studying Zach too closely. Zach fought the urge to fidget. Alexander was a grown Alpha. He knew what it meant when an Omega looked as thin and weak as Zach did. At least he was kind enough not to say it out loud. "Do you still like Indian food? Or Thai?"

"Hmm," Zach vocalized absently, watching the cats stalk past to make sure both humans knew they were good and annoyed.

Wait.

Zach pivoted, too startled and indignant to tread lightly. "You go off and leave the cats alone all the time? Are you crazy? No wonder they don't like you."

Alexander gave Zach a look flatter than a sheet of marble. "You think I neglect them?"

Outside, the promised rain kicked from light patter to steady drumming against the windowpanes. Nicely dramatic, as if he had charmed the weather into being on his side, the bastard. It even sounded freezing, and it made Zach furious for some reason he didn't care to dwell on long enough to identify. He'd rather get good and pissed than cower in a corner. If he had to start a fight, well, he knew how to fight. Fair or dirty, either worked for him.

"I wasn't saying before, but you know what?" Zach put his hands on his hips. "I am saying now."

Alexander's eyes narrowed to slits, a danger sign for an Alpha. "Not that it's your business, but the furballs and I get along fine. I like how they don't smother me with love. I wouldn't know what to do with slobbering and fawning. They're themselves, and I like them the way they are. And when I'm gone, I have a pet sitter who comes in every day. He plays with them, feeds them, spoils them rotten with treats."

There was so much to unpack in there Zach didn't know where to start and he still didn't want to. "Don't explode all over me, bitch. No one gave you permission to play lord and master, ever."

"Seems like I remember differently, unless you were begging someone else to fuck you like a good little bitch in that empty house." Alexander bent to collect his shoes and Zach's, dropped them in the same bin, and in the same fluid movement slid forward into Zach's personal space, close enough to feel the heat of his breath and the fire of his temper. "No matter what you think, I wouldn't leave them alone. *I'm* not the one who runs off, Zach."

His words were a knife cutting straight to the heart, and left Zach open-mouthed with sharp-stinging hurt. Alexander wasn't as over it as he obviously wanted to appear, was he? Even so, Zach wasn't going to take a slap like that lying down. He bristled up, temper flaring. "Refresh my memory, Alexander. Who was it telling who to get out?"

"And who couldn't wait to run like his ass was on fire?"

"Don't." Zach pointed at him in warning. "I mean it, Alexander, don't you fucking dare. You have no idea what --"

Alexander caught his pointer finger at the knuckle and knocked his hand aside. "This is my fucking house, Zach. I'll do what I goddamn please. And what don't I have any idea about? I have a fucking good idea about more than you think."

"Fuck you!" Zach's fist followed the second Alexander let go of his finger, and this wasn't any semi-friendly punch in the ribs, this was aimed at the Alpha's jaw and almost connected. "If you say one more word, one more --"

"One more, and what?" Alexander crowded closer to him, chest to chest, trying to dominate him, the testosterone-laden... *fucking* Alpha. It made Zach want to bite him. "What'll you do if I do dare, hmm? Run again? Where are you going to go this time? Out in the cold to freeze to death?"

Zach pushed back, head forward and ready to crack skulls if need be, showing Alexander the sharp edges of his teeth. "Maybe I will. Maybe I'd rather."

"You're not going anywhere."

"Stop me, then!" Zach shoved at Alexander, and -- meant to turn. Was halfway there before Alexander's broad hands had cuffed his wrists and wrenched him bodily back around to face him, and then -- and then --

Then Alexander's mouth was on Zach's, and there was nothing, *nothing* gentle or careful about this kiss. He shoved Zach backward until Zach's shoulders hit the wall, and he was strong enough to do it, angry enough not to care how rough he was. The scent normally kept muted under his clothes burst out in waves of bittersweet myrrh and burning woodsmoke and pheromones, so purely Alpha that no matter what Zach wanted, his Omega side rose in a rush to meet it with a cloud of burnt-caramel coffee and saline.

Alexander bit as much as he kissed, fierce in his attack on Zach's mouth, and he didn't hold back *his* teeth as he moved from mouth to jaw to nape, pulling Zach's shirt open at the collar. Cold poured through the opening but Zach hardly noticed. He'd started kissing Alexander somewhere in there, who knew when or where, but giving as good as he got and leaving marks from his nails and his teeth behind. Clawing at his hair, his back, the hard muscles at his hips and ass. Alexander tasted so *good* his mouth watered and he had to swallow it down or make a mess.

More of a mess. His legs shook like aspens until he wrapped them around Alexander's waist and made the man groan from somewhere so deep down it drowned out the beginnings of thunder outside. He could smell himself, his thighs Omega-wet, jeans soaked, and he could feel his insides hurrying to open too, eager to be --

To be bred.

Oh God.

Alexander must have caught the scent at the same time. He jerked back, mouth swollen and eyes wide open, startled. For a second he looked exactly like the boy Zach remembered, stunned stupid with sex and crazy dreams. Zach lay still with his mouth open, knowing he looked ravished and ripe and ready, and if Alexander tried to press his point right now he wasn't sure he'd be *able* to say no --

"Shit!" Alexander dropped Zach and pivoted as fast as he'd turned in the first place, putting his back to Zach and dragging his hands through his hair. Zach could hear his teeth grinding. His jaw would break if he wasn't careful. It sounded like it hurt. If Zach hadn't been struggling to rein himself in too, panting for breath, he might have gone to the man and caution be damned.

He didn't. He didn't dare.

"Shit," Alexander said again, quieter, after a minute. He scrubbed hard at his face and gave Zach a bewildered look over his shoulder before turning very carefully and slowly. "Zach, I'm sorry. I don't know why I did that."

"You're not the only one," Zach retorted, even if he knew why *he'd* done it. Omega bodies didn't listen to reason, damn them. Or -- other things. Especially when emotions ran hot and high. "I warned you."

"Yeah." Alexander touched a bite mark Zach had left as if he couldn't believe what he felt there was real. Zach had broken the skin enough to draw a pinprick's worth of blood. "And I didn't listen. I get -- tense -- when I think about that day."

Zach crossed his arms, more tired than angry now. "You're still not the only one. And if you didn't know as much before, you do now."

"Yeah." Alexander let out a long, frustrated breath

and then shook himself. "Food. We lost the thread there. I have Thai in the freezer, made by a couple of first-generation grandparents who don't cut corners. It's good stuff. I can heat it up for us."

Zach bit savagely at his lip, angry at the rush of heat that went through him when he tasted Alexander there. He was still too angry to feel the slightest bit hungry, but... oh hell, he didn't have the energy to fight until he'd gotten something with calories inside him. "Thai is fine."

"Good." Alexander didn't look at him as he stalked past and didn't even give him a backwards glance -- but under his stubble, his face was pink. He touched his bite mark again, almost caressing it, so absently Zach didn't think he knew what he was doing. "I'll be right back. Wait for me here, and we can start over."

* * *

Start over. Could they, though?

Zach should have left, of course. He had the best opportunity right there, with Alexander safely out of the room, to shove his feet back into his shoes and slip silently out the front door. Go back to normal, to what he was at least used to.

He didn't, and he still hadn't figured out why by the time Alexander came back.

"Here, while we're waiting. This'll warm you up." He wrapped a thick cable-knit blanket around Zach and made sure it was secure before he doubled back and returned with a glass. "This'll help too." He held it out in offer, a cut-glass tumbler with two fingers of something peat-colored, a whiskey stone clinking gently at the bottom.

"What is it?"

"Unique." Alexander let Zach take the glass, but as he handed it over, he held on long enough to brush his fingertips against the back of Zach's hand. "I really am sorry. The last thing I want to do is fight. Do you believe me?"

Zach searched his face narrowly. He'd heard that before, and he knew better than to believe a word of that kind of speech -- usually -- but that old tie was still there, and he could *tell* Alexander wasn't lying. He meant every word.

Always making this harder than it had to be.

"I believe you," he said quietly. "This time. Do it again, and I might feel differently. Understood?"

Alexander let go of the glass in visible relief. "Understood."

Zach didn't believe him for a second. Maybe *Alexander* couldn't smell a lie on himself, even one so deftly danced around, but there was no way Alexander was letting anything go. Zach thought about calling him on it, but he still didn't have the reserves for a good head of steam. He sniffed at the glass instead, curious, and thought he could pick out mingled hints of clove, wild berries, tobacco, and the smoke from a fire on a cold night. "You didn't answer me, and before I try this I want to know what it is."

"I did answer. It's unique," Alexander said, crinkling his nose in amusement. "Not exactly whiskey or ale or wine but kind of a little of each. It's probably easiest to call it mead. You'll like it, but if I'm wrong and you don't then I have some tequila somewhere."

"I want to get warm, not hammered. Maybe. This sounds terrible." Zach tried a sip, and if there was anything closer to heaven, he'd never tasted it. "Oh my *God*."

Alexander laughed, freer, easier. He sat on the edge of the chaise he'd dropped into earlier; must have been his favorite. "Told you so."

"Shush." Zach cradled the glass reverently. "If you have any more of this, say goodbye to it because I'm taking it with me when I go."

"You can finish the bottle tonight if you want. Or two."

Zach gave him a quick sharp look. *Trying to get me drunk?*

Maybe not. Alexander just looked loose-limbed with pleasure at being right, not like a schemer. He grinned at Zach. "One of the local breweries has a guy who likes to play mad scientist, and sometimes he comes up with a stroke of genius. They bottle a limited batch every December, and I always have them save me a case because it's my favorite no matter what time of year. I've barely touched the last shipment, so you can have as much as you want."

"Twist my arm." Zach took another reverent sip. Tasted like being in Scotland, huddling by a fire on the moors -- and it must have been stronger than strong, if it had him indulging in flights of fancy after barely a shot's worth. "I really will steal this from you, you know. Try and stop me."

"Nah. There are better things to do." Alexander stretched out both legs to loll properly on the chaise. He watched Zach idly, only taking the occasional sip from his glass. "So tell me."

"Tell you what?"

"Everything, I guess. What you've been doing -- since. With your life. I can glean a bit here and a piece there, but I don't have the full picture." Alexander ran the pad of his thumb around the glass he held; his hands were big enough to manage it without dropping or spilling. "I'd like to know."

Zach shifted his weight. How much to share? "There's hardly anything to tell," he tried to evade. "I've had a mostly normal life. Quiet. I've done whatever I could find work doing, mostly slinging coffee, and I've gotten by."

"Ah," Alexander murmured quietly. "Do you still carve?"

"You remember that?"

"I remember you liked to work with wood, and sometimes stone. You made beautiful things, even if you do still have the scars from slipping with your knife. I remember those too."

Zach glanced down at his hands, turning them from back to front. The marks there were so familiar he never even noticed them anymore, but Alexander had.

"The marble from the quarry here is good for carving," Alexander remarked. "Or so I hear."

"Yes. Well." Zach buried his face in his glass.

"Go a little slower there," Alexander cautioned. "It's stronger than it tastes. Nearly knocked me down the first time I tried it, and I must weigh twice what you do. Do you eat at all? You look like a strong breeze would blow you away."

"Not all of us can be musclebound globetrotters. Mind your own."

Alexander held his hands up, palms out. "My apologies. God, you're touchy."

"You say it as if it's a new thing," Zach muttered. "I don't like being this way, but I can't help it."

"I know." Alexander regarded him a little longer, quiet and thoughtful. "You're as tightfisted as you always were with details. You give long answers, but they don't have any real content."

Zach raised his shoulders. "I am what I am, and even if I could help it --"

"Twenty questions," Alexander said abruptly. He swung his legs over the edge of the chaise and sat upright. "And we can even make it interesting."

"I'm sorry, what?" Zach raised an eyebrow. "You want to play twenty questions? That's a kid's game."

"Not the way I play it."

Zach didn't doubt it. Yet Alexander had piqued his curiosity. Zach leaned forward to mirror Alexander's pose. "Make it interesting, how?"

"Truth for truth, answer for answer, turn for turn. And… no lies allowed. No evasions."

Oh. Zach swallowed.

"Or can you not bend that far, even now?" Alexander asked, far too quietly. "Even now, Zach?"

"That isn't fair, and it's almost cruel," Zach replied, equally quietly, then lifted his chin. "I want five 'I reserve the right not to answer' options."

"One."

"Three," Zach countered, even though he already knew what Alexander's answer would be. "All right. One. You win."

"For once." Alexander lifted his glass. "I tell you what, if you go first we'll cut it down to ten instead of twenty -- unless you lose. Deal?"

God, he'd turned devious, but two could play the same game. "That's one for you, but -- all right. One for me: can I have a refill?"

"You've still got at least a shot's worth in your glass."

"Only temporarily." Zach tilted his glass back and drained it, then held it out. "And not anymore."

Alexander shook his head, but he took the glass from Zach and filled it deftly. Zach bit his lip as he watched; there was, somehow, something of a turn-on about the easy way Alexander poured a level shot. "You keep surprising me. With things like this. I meant."

Alexander cocked his head. "Oh? What did you think I'd keep in my liquor cabinet?"

"That's two -- no, three -- of your ten. And frankly, I'd have bet on either top shelf Scotch or the cheapest, shittiest beer you can buy at a corner store."

Alexander chuckled as he swirled the alcohol

around his glass. "The kind of beer that tastes like skunk spray smells?"

"Four," Zach murmured. "And you asked out of turn. I'm winning."

"Whatever. God, I remember drinking those with you. Thinking we were so grown up when we could barely get through a can each without gagging."

Zach wrinkled his nose at the memory. "Thanks for reminding me. I'd almost managed to block out the taste."

"Sorry."

"You're really, really not, are you?"

Alexander made a fond-sounding sort of noise as he sat back down and tucked an arm behind his head for an impromptu pillow. "Four for me, two for you. You know, I've missed this. The way you zing it right back, everything anyone dishes out to you. The human slingshot." He glanced at the window as a bolt of lightning was followed, alarmingly quickly, with a roll of thunder that made the building rattle. "They weren't kidding about the weather rolling in. Listen to it, would you?"

"Five questions from you. You're terrible at this, did you know?" He held up a hand to stave off Alexander's fist pump of triumph. "I know that's three for me. And of course I hear it. I can't help listening." Zach shivered again and wished he still had Alexander's coat on, or a second blanket to wrap around himself. "I hope it doesn't get worse, or any second now the power's going to --"

Obligingly, because nature was a bastard and had a sadistic sense of humor, a crack of thunder made them both jump half out of their seats a split second before the room went dark.

Zach pressed a hand to his face in the pitch blackness. "I had to say it, didn't I? I had to say it."

"And we're at four questions for you. Also, quick, threaten me with winning a million dollars. The way you're going tonight, it might happen."

"Don't make me come over there." Zach tapped his watch for the few seconds of light it would provide, even if it was sterile and cold. "It's not even eleven yet. Fuck me, this is going to be a long night."

"Twist *my* arm," Alexander said dryly. Zach could hear him stirring, standing up in a businesslike manner, so he probably hadn't meant it seriously. Probably. "Could be worse. The stove's gas, so we'll still have hot food. The drink's strong enough to stand up to a little chill, I have plenty of coats and blankets, and -- here."

Abruptly, the room filled with a much better, warmer light than that from Zach's watch, and with it a gentle, rolling wave of warmth. Alexander stood by the fireplace, arm propped on the mantle, and gestured at the flames. "If you stand about where I am, you can warm up and..." He cleared his throat. "Dry off. I'd offer you some clean clothes, but anything I have would swallow you like a tent, and I don't think you want to hang around naked."

Embarrassment nearly bowed Zach in half. He'd forgotten, but now he was paying attention again he could smell himself, and he *reeked* of Omega. Alexander wasn't as badly off, but he definitely carried a strong whiff of Alpha.

"It might be the lesser of two evils," he said, which was the alcohol talking for sure. He chanced a glance up to find Alexander watching him, so intent, and yes, serious this time.

He'd opened his mouth to say so when Alexander murmured, "Maybe. But I wouldn't say no, if you said yes."

Zach's insides did a slow, lazy flip, hinting at what they'd been headed for and wanted to get back to again.

No. He refused, and he made sure that showed when he said, "You said you didn't want to fight, Alexander."

"I know," Alexander said, still watching him. "I was there."

He wasn't talking about the immediate past now, but a moment seven years back. Zach could tell.

"Don't. Please don't."

Alexander shook his head slowly and didn't answer or ask a question. Just waited. And waited.

One moment before Zach would have howled in frustration, the man stood up and stretched. "Food smells ready."

"Say again?"

"The food. Thai, the stuff I said I'd heat for us. I'll plate it up, and you go sit by the fire. I can't stand seeing you half frozen in my own house. Come on already."

Zach nibbled on a rogue cuticle as he eyed the hearth. Contrariness argued against doing as he'd been told; yearning got him on his feet and moving. He elbowed Alexander aside and stretched his cold hands out to the flames, sighing as they started to thaw.

He'd almost forgotten Alexander was there when the Alpha rested his hand on Zach's shoulder, then tipped his chin up so they were looking at each other. "Even if you don't want to, one way or another we *are* going to talk about it tonight. All of it. I've waited too long for this chance to let it slip away."

The warmth of his touch almost burned. Zach couldn't look away, try as he might. "You're doing this to keep me off balance, aren't you?"

"Maybe a little," Alexander replied. He brushed along the line of Zach's cheekbone, almost -- almost -- cradling his face. "Just a little. It's my turn, after all."

Zach could have argued, but... he didn't want to fight any more than he wanted to be fought with. He was so tired of fighting, even if he couldn't give in gracefully no matter what. He bent his head in stiff agreement, stepping back as he did so he wouldn't press into Alexander's touch and give him the wrong idea. It was one of the hardest things he'd done in a while.

Alexander squeezed Zach's shoulder once, rubbed the muscle with his thumb, and then he was gone.

Zach watched after him for a moment, too much going on in his head to process any of it. In the end, he shook his head and turned back to the fire. No matter the weather outside, this pause was the calm before the storm and they both knew it, didn't they?

Might as well take what he could get while the taking was good. Though that was a thought that didn't bear any more thinking...

* * *

Alexander didn't take long with the plating. He really did know his way around a kitchen, if not the actual cooking involved. He came back a scant handful of minutes later with two plates, one bearing a normal portion and one heaped so high he'd rounded it off to stop it spilling over its edges.

Somehow Zach wasn't surprised when he got handed the second one, and good lord, it was even heavier than it looked. He had to balance it with both hands. "How much do you think I can eat?"

"I don't know, but I want you to get as much of what's on your plate down as you can." Alexander shook his head firmly when Zach started to protest. His eyebrows drew together in a frown. "I've seen your kind of skinny before. I don't know who you bonded with or why they aren't with you now, but it doesn't take a genius to figure out why you got so thin."

Zach bit his lip, blushing hot as a coal even though the rest of him was still shivering-cold.

Alexander watched until Zach bent his head over the plate in submission, then shrugged and smiled with a mercurial shift of mood. "By the way, that made five questions for you. Or was that number six?"

"I've lost count."

"Me too, so go ahead and eat while I tally them back up. I promise you, it really is good." He leaned against the wall, his balance easy, and shoveled a forkful of something savory-looking in his mouth. "Mm-mmf."

Trying to set an example, Zach supposed. He wasn't sure he *could* eat now, his stomach making warning noises at him, but the smell was too much to resist. He tried one small bite, and then another. The warning noises took a sharp left into rumbles of hunger and demands for more. He had to make himself eat slowly, taking small, deliberate bites because Alexander was right, and it *was* good, too good to risk his stomach rejecting it if he ate too fast.

Even if he could feel Alexander watching him keenly the whole time. "Would you stop staring at me?" Zach said when it became too much. He pointed his fork at Alexander. "You're going to put me off my whatever-this-is."

"Nah. You like it."

And of course he didn't specify *what* he thought Zach liked. It could have been the food, but most likely not. Zach stabbed his fork into a heap of something mysterious but delicious, left it there, and put his plate aside. "I'm done."

"Uh-uh, no lies. Those were the rules."

"You didn't ask a question."

"No, but I can." Alexander was watching him like a hunting lion now, and it made Zach's skin tingle. "You're still hungry enough to keep eating, aren't you?"

"Yes, but that doesn't mean I will. Are you going to make me? Try to take care of me like an Alpha should?"

"Six. Seven. And I am an Alpha. Shouldn't I?"

Not with someone who wasn't his Omega, and he

damn well knew it. God, there they went again. "I'm. Done. Eating. Stop babying me, *please*. I can take care of myself."

"I know," Alexander said, his jaw working as he looked down and away. "You taught me that a long time ago when you left and never came back."

If Zach hadn't put his plate down, he would have dropped it. They were only words, but they felt like a slap.

Alexander pushed himself abruptly away from the wall. "My grandparents used to say some people were so sharp they'd cut themselves. I never really knew what that meant before." He headed across the room toward something Zach couldn't identify at that distance. Not until Alexander turned a knob and it crackled to life with a burst of static. "Battery operated. There's a local station that usually plays oldies."

But it wasn't, at least not at the moment. An announcer's voice rolled through, stressed and taut. "-- an explosion at the quarry has been confirmed. As previously reported, the explosion damaged the railway passing through town. Additional rescue workers are en route and employees on site are working to assist those who were in the quarry and mine when --"

"Change it." Zach was too raw to listen to more. "Unless there's anything we can do to help."

"No. I wish there were, but we'd only be in the way." Alexander twisted the dial. The flow of something soft and smooth, a little bit of jazz, a little bit of rock and roll, replaced the announcer's voice on another station. He nodded slowly. "I mentioned my grandparents. This was theirs, back in the day. Built to last."

"They usually were. Back in the day."

"Hmm." Alexander tapped his foot lightly against the floor, moving ever so slightly to the beat of a song far older than either of them was. "Do you remember we were going to go to prom together? How excited you were, when you always worked so hard never to act excited about anything? Like we were going to be fairytale princes for the evening." He paused. "And then we never made it there."

No, they hadn't. Zach wondered what'd happened to their tuxedos. Were they tucked up safe in a closet somewhere, wingtips stuffed with tissue paper arranged neatly beneath them, or had they gotten tossed in a dumpster long ago? It'd been the stupidest fantasy, the notion of spinning around and around the floor in Alexander's arms, but he'd *wanted* it, and --

"I remember." He'd been sleeping in an alley the night after leaving, hiding in a corner where he'd cried until his eyes burned. Even now, the memory made him swipe at them. "Damn you for bringing that up, and that's nine. You only have one more."

Alexander tucked his hands in his pockets for a long moment, then nodded as if making up his mind and turned his head toward Zach. Half a smile crooked up the corner of his mouth as he held out a hand in invitation. "Then I'll make it count. May I have this dance?"

Chapter Four

Zach's jaw dropped.

Alexander simply waited, holding out his arm as if he could stand there all day. "I'm serious. Come and dance with me."

"You… what?" Zach stood too quickly, his knees wobbling and his head spinning, but he clenched his jaw and stayed put until the dizziness passed. "You're angry with me. I get that. I deserve it. But don't be cruel."

"I'm not. You weren't the only one who wanted the whole fairytale dream ending," Alexander said quietly. He curled his fingers, beckoning. "One dance, Zach. Let's listen to the music, and the storm, and just be together, for a few minutes. Let that old scar heal. If you won't do it for yourself, then do it for me. Please."

Let it heal. Please.

There was no way to say no to that, even if Zach had wanted to. God help him, he didn't. And he didn't care if it was right or smart or sensible or for the best; he couldn't think clearly enough for that.

So he acted. He let his body lead. He went to Alexander, and he let the man wrap him up in his arms.

Taking it while the taking's good, if only for one last dance.

* * *

"Good. Just like that. That's good." Alexander let Zach nestle against him and was still so gentle when those strong arms came around to support his slighter weight. "You always were strong, even when you thought you weren't."

"I'm not. I'm really not."

"That's what you think." Zach felt something brush the top of his head, the lightest pressure that might or might not have been a kiss but with no sound to give it away for sure.

He curled a little tighter against Alexander. "What

is this song?"

"I don't know, but I like it. No, wait, I do know the name. My parents played it at their vow renewal. *Unforgettable.*"

"Nat King Cole," Zach said, remembering too. It'd been on every station for a while. "The remix with his youngest Omega child. It was made years and years after he died."

"And yet they found a way to come back together."

Zach pushed a breath through his nose. "Don't take that as an omen. The universe isn't tuned in that well to what anyone wants."

"Isn't it?"

Zach didn't have an answer for that. He wasn't sure Alexander had it wrong. The way things kept happening tonight...

Alexander moved slowly, still, not really dancing but doing more than swaying with him. Simple steps, executed slowly, that turned them in lazy circles around a five-odd-square patch of floor by the window. He bent his head, letting Zach feel it for sure this time, and breathed in. "You smell better."

"You must have a cold. I haven't showered yet."

He felt Alexander's chuckle and shivered when Alexander held him a little closer. "That's not what I meant, smart-ass. 'Better' means... you smell warm. You're not shivering, and you're not wound so tightly you're a flinch away from pulling your joints apart."

Zach winced at the mental image but -- he knew that feeling, and he'd been afraid of it sometimes himself. "You run hot. You always have. I can't help but warm up, this close."

"I warm you, but the gas fire on full blast didn't?"

"Smart-ass, yourself," Zach muttered. He butted his head against the sturdy muscle below Alexander's collarbone. "Don't get cocky."

"To thine own self be true."

"Except when it makes you a pain in the ass."

That made Alexander laugh, too loudly at first until he brought it down. "I really did miss the way you can whip everything right back. No one's ever called me on the carpet like you can."

"No one dared take a whip to the big bad Alpha mastiff?"

"Something like that. I spent a while looking for someone who would, you know."

Zach stiffened slightly as Alexander turned them in another circle. "Did you ever find anyone?"

"A few. Some that tried." Alexander paused. "Does that make you jealous?"

Another punch to the solar plexus, another flare of frustrated anger, a slower ebb. Zach ground his teeth together -- he knew when someone was trying to yank his chains. Alexander didn't play fair, and he really had gotten a little mean as he got older, but who could blame him? Not Zach. He'd taught that lesson himself and it was time he owned up to it.

"Yes," Zach said. "It does. Does that make you happy?"

"Not really."

Now that took Zach by surprise. "Why not?"

"You don't need me to answer that." Alexander raised one shoulder. "But I will. They weren't you, and it wasn't the same, and after a while I wasn't interested in pale imitations. So I looked for something as different as possible, and I found that. Lots of that."

The first attack had made Zach angry. This one hurt.

But he was who he was, and he said, "Good. That's what you should have done. I hope you *were* happy with that."

"Sometimes. Not for long enough. Some of them

stuck it out for a while, but they mostly called it quits before too long."

"Why?"

"I called your name in my sleep one too many times."

The hits kept coming, and any second now they'd crack Zach open. He knotted one fist and punched Alexander in the ribs again, even though he bruised his knuckles doing it. *Ow.*

"Neither of us ever learns," Alexander said. If he'd even felt the hit, he didn't show it. He tucked his chin against Zach's shoulder, resting it there. Which put him in the ideal position to whisper to Zach, lips tickling his ear. "I've already asked way more than ten questions, but I'm not in the mood to play by arbitrary rules tonight. Do you ever wonder what would have happened, when I asked what I asked that day, if you'd said yes?"

Zach drew in a shivering breath. *Yes. So many times, yes.* He shut his eyes tight and pressed his head tighter still to Alexander as he lied, because he couldn't help it, "No."

Alexander shook his head slowly, the rasp of his stubble harsh on Zach's neck, but let that go too -- diverted, if not forgotten. But he wasn't one to give up either. The roughness of that beard scruff should have irritated both Zach's skin and temper, but somehow it made him want to moan and lean closer instead. "I can smell the difference between truth and lies out of you again. And I have wondered," he said. "Sometimes during the day. Mostly at night."

His hand drifted down Zach's back, as slow as the tide and equally unstoppable. Equally unforgettable.

He would *not* tell Alexander what those words did to him, the hot clench inside, the empty yearning it woke in his belly and pelvis. Aching. Burning. "You dreamed about me? Really? Sap."

Alexander's chest vibrated with amusement. "You say that like you only now figured it out."

Zach made a *pfft* noise. "What did you dream about? Hearts, flowers, big church weddings?"

"Sometimes. Those were mostly during the day. But at night..." He touched his lips to Zach's neck, lips parted. Hot breath, a flicker of tongue, then a sweep, tasting him. "At night, it was different."

Zach's eyes slid shut. He reached up to pull Alexander away, but somehow his fingers ended up tangled in Alexander's hair, holding him there. "Stop it."

"Make me."

Zach didn't. His fingers flexed once, and that gave away the kind of picture that a thousand words couldn't.

"You dream about it too." It wasn't a question, but a sure and certain statement. Alexander's arm fitted more snugly around him now and his hand dipped lower still, brushing the small of his back. Where did he learn that? That a hint, a whisper, did more than a shout and a fistful of ass? "I think you dream about the same things I do. Where we'd be if you'd let yourself say yes."

How had this turned so fast, so sharply?

"I can't help your dreams."

"Can't you?" Alexander took Zach's earlobe between his teeth. "I dream about you saying yes. Fucking you again and again that night, not giving a damn about anything else, until you were pregnant and there was no going back, not ever, and you *wanting* every goddamn bit of it." His words were warm, straight into Zach's ear, and they made him quake under his skin. "The way you do now."

Zach's body rippled, his muscles flexing and bunching, going wet where he shouldn't. "No."

"Liar." Alexander's mouth moved again, resting over where Zach's pulse was hammering so hard that he must have felt it. Bastard. He teased his fingertips ever so slightly lower. "Liar."

"And what if I am?" Zach shoved him, for all the good it did, a weakened Omega and an Alpha at the peak of his strength. "You want the truth? This is the truth. I. Did. The. Right. Thing. We were too young to even think about mating, getting married, *children* for God's sake, no matter what I --"

He stopped himself before he could finish that and turned, fast -- and realized, right away, what a mistake that'd been.

Alexander's arms tightened, holding him steady around the ribs and hips, back to chest. Pressed this close, he could feel how hard Alexander was, and when his breath went shaky he knew Alexander guessed the state of him too. He slid the hand at Zach's hips around, down, where he could tease a few fingertips along Zach's belt buckle, hook the tip of one underneath and tug.

"Don't lie to me anymore tonight."

He ground against Zach's ass, rougher now, insistently hard, so hard he must have ached. Zach's body moved back against his, pressing into it. The sound they made was obscene, wet and sticky, and so goddamn sweet it made both moan, both groan, made Zach reach back for whatever he could grab onto and hold.

"You like that," Alexander murmured. He turned Zach around again and fitted them together. Thrust his thigh between Zach's, the friction so good that he almost sobbed as he hitched forward. He had his hands knotted in Alexander's hair again, pulling as hard as he wanted. "I like this. I like you the way you've always been, wanting me to want you. I remember your body like it was yesterday. I hear it. It's shouting at me, telling me how much you want to fuck. I can almost feel you coming open. You need a cock. You want mine."

"My body doesn't know what's good for it," Zach whispered. He couldn't let go. "I don't have to listen to it.

We were -- dancing. Just dancing."

"We still are." Alexander pulled Zach tight against him, hips to hips. He was *so* hard. They both were, yet the abruptness shocked Zach. Too much sensation. Too fast.

He tried to push Alexander far enough away to let himself breathe. "I didn't mean for this to happen."

"I know," Alexander said. "But I did."

Zach stiffened, then pulled away in a rush, retreating. "That's not fair."

"Should it be?" Alexander advanced on him, taking back every inch Zach had gained, and he didn't look cruel the way Zach had accused him of being, but like a man who had reached the very end of his tether, and there was no telling what would happen now. "I have everything -- everything -- on the line here, Zach, and I know this is the last chance I'll ever have so no, I'm not being fair. Nothing about this is. I want to fuck you, and you want to fuck me. Say it. Say it, out loud."

Zach gritted his teeth, but he couldn't stop himself. "*Damn* you, Alexander. *Yes.* Are you happy now?"

Generals on the battlefield must have given commands and barked responses with the same kind of fire in their bellies: forward, forward! And to hell with the consequences. "*Yes,*" Alexander hissed.

Now he was the one who was lying.

No. Zach could tell Alexander wasn't happy. He was angry, frantic, desperate, and starving as badly as Zach was. But Zach, God help him, had reached the end of his tether too, and there was nothing left to do but let it snap, and *fall.*

He crashed into Alexander before Alexander could crash into him. His mouth on Alexander's, eating at him open-mouthed and messy, his legs around Alexander's waist, his weight held up as if it were nothing and yet Alexander dropped them both to the floor so fluidly they barely jarred. They landed with Zach on top, Alexander taking the brunt. Between one kiss and the next he'd rolled them both over to put Zach under him, and the things he said made Zach burn.

"I want you, oh God, I want you, I want you so much, I never stopped wanting you, I --"

He pressed his mouth to the gap where Zach's shirt had come open. A sharp jerk and the fabric gave way, parting as he pulled, giving him room to bite a string of burning marks all the way down. Zach's hips jerked up as his insides melted, flowing and shifting as if he were made of water, not flesh and bone, and he went hard, so hard, so fast. Alexander felt it, or saw it, didn't matter which. He put his mouth over it without bothering to shred his jeans off and pressed his tongue --

Zach's arms were around Alexander's shoulders, without knowing he would do that.

Zach's knees were locked around Alexander's waist, without meaning to put them there.

Zach's back arched till his neck ached, desperate, willing to --

To do --

Anything --

And get the ending right, this time.

"Zach." Alexander kissed his way down Zach's hip before he let go of him, breathing hard and swallowing dry, cheek pressed to the inside of Zach's inner thigh. "God, Zach, I need you."

Want. Need. Was there a difference? Yes. No.

He drew one deep breath, and then another, and reached down to brush his fingertips through Alexander's hair. His hand shook too much for more. "Yes. Alexander. Yes."

Alexander's eyes flew open, and he stared at Zach with such pure shock that it would have made him laugh at any other time. Not now.

"Now." Zach found his grip, and pulled at him; he

wasn't anywhere near strong enough to haul a big Alpha up, but he'd be damned if he wouldn't try and once he got the idea there was no stopping Alexander anyway; he came in a rush, a surge, dropping with all his weight on top of Zach and kissing him as if he'd die if he stopped.

Zach's hands weren't shaking now.

Somehow, somewhere in all the sensation, every other piece of clothing vanished, peeled away where they were tacky-sticky or slipped off, tossed to the side. Hot skin warmed Zach all the way through, right down to his bones. He couldn't follow where Alexander put his mouth, he moved so fast and with such hunger, but he felt every one of those kisses and he ran after them, collecting each one to keep safe in his head for later. Kisses on his hips, his navel, the very last bit of skin above his cock.

"Don't --" Zach found the breath to warn. "Don't. Too much. I'll come."

Alexander nosed at him, but only once, and backed away. "Not yet you don't. Not till I'm in you."

"Fuck!" Zach bit at the back of his hand, but barely stopped himself from coming even so. He couldn't catch his breath; he was burning alive. He raked his nails down Alexander's back so he'd feel some of the flame too. "*Fuck*. Oh, fuck. If you want that, Alex -- no, Alexander -- hurry. I can't wait. *Alexander*."

"Call me whatever you want," Alexander breathed, sliding on top of him, high enough for their bodies to fit. He lifted Zach's thighs, kissing beneath them as he guided himself where they both wanted him, and then -- in --

Tight, hot, easy as a tongue sliding through molten honey. Hard, so hard inside him, as good as he remembered; no, better, he knew what he was doing now; they both knew, and Zach still couldn't get him deep enough or hold him tightly enough. He panted hot and open-mouthed against the salt-slickness of Alexander's shoulder. Biting him.

"Oh God." Alexander seized his head and pulled it back to crush, to bruise him with the kind of kiss that said *I want to eat you alive, I want to have all of you*. His cock throbbed inside Zach as he groaned and curved his back, pressing deeper still. He couldn't go deeper, but he worked his hips as if trying to, grinding their bodies together. "God, so good, so good for me, you feel so good inside."

He did, oh fuck, he did. Zach rolled up, but that wasn't enough. He had to *feel*. He reached between them, gliding slickly on the sweat and his own lubrication, flowing so smooth, making everything easy, easy. Alexander arched up with a sharp moan at the feel of Zach wrapping a hand around the base of his cock, barely able to fit but pressing himself down to make room. Zach stroked him once, then -- could he get in there? He didn't know, but he had to try -- slid two fingers inside himself alongside Alexander's cock, and --

Oh. Oh God. An ice-cold shock shot down Zach's spine. "Stop."

Alexander wouldn't ignore him, but he wasn't hearing him. Too gone. He rolled his hips and bit at the hollow under Zach's chin, slid his own hand between them and kneaded over the concavity of Zach's stomach. "Thin. Too thin, but the way you'll look when you have my baby in you... Wanted you, wanted this for so long -- "

Zach understood, with a sickening drop from his throat to his guts, what Alexander had *thought* he meant, why he'd done it this way even if all of it hadn't been a conscious choice.

His head spun with thoughts coming too quickly to process. If they made a baby together right now the way their bodies wanted, the way Zach wanted *so* much --

wouldn't that be as bad as tying Alexander down by doing it years ago? Alexander had gone out and seen the world, but not all of it. There was so much left and Zach couldn't steal that from him, he *couldn't*.

"Alexander." Zach gasped at a thrust so deep it made him pulse inside, and -- no! He pushed hard at Alexander's chest -- clutched at him instead -- *no, no, focus, focus* --"Stop. Alexander. Stop." Taking hold of Alexander's hair, he pulled up hard. "Stop!"

Alexander looked up, confused. His hands flexed on Zach's hips. "What's wrong?"

"Stop," Zach said again, gentler this time. Didn't he know what it felt like, even if he'd only done it to himself sometimes, to be so deep and wanting nothing more than to go *deeper*. It wasn't easy to come back from, but he had to, he had to. "Stop." He slipped his fingers out of himself, up, and showed Alexander the streaks of white trailing down the backs of his knuckles. Not come, not yet, but so damn close it made his heart pound at the risk of it all. "You're not wearing a condom. Stop."

The ragged sound of their breathing filled the silence. Zach couldn't feel anything but body heat and the shaking of their muscles, both of them shuddering with the effort it took.

"Oh. Oh, I -- I get it. I think. You don't want that part yet?" Alexander asked, plainly trying to work through it, to make himself believe anything but what he was trying to deny. "No, you're right. You need to be healthy first. Then we can try."

Zach moaned. He shouldn't touch Alexander when he was like this, when they were both so *weak*. Yet he couldn't stop touching either, no matter how unfair it was. He arched his hips, unable to help it even if it *was* cruel. His body would gulp down any seed it could catch hold of. Swallow it like dust swallowed rain.

Alexander moved his mouth over Zach's throat.

The tip of his tongue traced a pattern through the light sheen of sweat on his skin. "Please, Zach, please. I love you. I could pull out. At the end. I'm strong enough. I don't want to, but I --"

"I don't want you to either!" Zach tried to punch Alexander in the pectorals, but his wrists wouldn't work and his fingers wouldn't make a fist. "Don't you get it?"

"No. I don't. I can feel it in you. I can smell it on you. You do want me. You care about me. You're holding me so close that I --" Alexander thrust deep, and Zach could almost feel Alexander swelling inside him when he hit that spot that made Zach bite back a cry. It escaped when Alexander whispered to him, full of confused desperation, "You said yes. I heard you say yes. Don't take it back now."

Zach smoothed Alexander's hair back, but he couldn't speak. The only words he could think of was that old refrain, and he couldn't. He just couldn't.

"I --" Zach swallowed, so hard. "I never said I didn't want this."

Then, the fierceness faded and left the lost boy in its place. "Then why? I don't understand. Why?"

"Because I want it so much I might give it to you, and I can't. I can't!" Zach shoved Alexander, angry and rough now. "Pull out now. Do it! If you care about me at all, Alexander, then let. Me. Go."

Alexander shuddered again, a motion that made Zach think of earthquakes that tore the earth apart. But he did it. He had to use his hand, and it almost didn't work. Once an Alpha was inside an Omega, and the Omega needed it this much, muscles clamped down and wouldn't easily let go. Slick dripped down his legs as their bodies separated. Soaked and soaking, his body leaking in slow pulses that made him quake inside and out. The scent had to be overwhelming. Alexander's cock gleamed with the stuff, shiny over the dark, stiff rod that still strained toward Zach's body.

"You won't ever, will you?" Alexander asked after too long and raw a pause. "You won't love me. You won't let me love you. Not now. Not ever. You didn't mean anything but 'fuck me' when you said 'yes.' I meant forever. All you meant was 'tonight.' Again."

So pieces of a shattered heart could break into even more fragile shards. Zach felt them crack. His and Alexander's.

He slid himself backward, naked and dripping but away, his body protesting at the emptiness inside and cold, so cold, all over again. "I..."

That wasn't what I meant at all, he would have said, but he didn't get the chance. Alexander shoved himself bodily up and away, turning his back and burying his head in his hands.

Zach couldn't sit there and wait for him to say it. Not again. He staggered to his feet, unsteady as a colt, wet to his ankles and up to his navel, reeking of sex and frustrated lust. "I told you," he said before Alexander could open his mouth. "I told you, Alexander, and now look where we are. Right back at the beginning, and I can't --"

No. He couldn't do *this* anymore. That was what he couldn't do.

He could damn himself for a coward, and he could hate himself for it later, but right now all Zach could do was pick up enough clothing to cover himself with and run.

Chapter Five

He had to -- he didn't know. Get out of there. Before he did something he'd regret, regret even more, whatever that might be. A pile of clothes in his hands, throwing on whatever he could manage on the move, Zach ran for the front door on bare feet because he'd forgotten his shoes.

When he wrenched the heavy door open, he jerked back. Rain with temper and teeth lashed through at him, drops as sharp as needles on his oversensitive skin. He couldn't even see the sidewalk through all of that, and he had to slam the door shut before it drove him to his knees.

He leaned against it for a second, panting, cold and wet but hot and hard as well. Wrapping his arms around himself, he rocked on his heels and stifled a moan against the rain-swollen wood. His body still wanted what it'd almost gotten, and it wasn't happy with him. Muscles clenched and cramped in his legs, his arms, all through his insides. He was still leaking, humiliating himself, but he smelled bitter now, so bitter he almost gagged.

Zach made himself get to his feet. If he couldn't run he could hide. God knew this house was big enough. There had to be somewhere.

Something furry bumped against his bare ankle and made him jump away with a yelp. "What the hell?"

When Zach looked down, the giant black and white cat glowered up at him. "What do you want? Go find Alexander. He's the one who owns you."

The big cat's tiny, sandy-furred friend popped out from behind its buddy and hissed.

Zach shook his head. "Don't think I don't get the irony. Either of you."

The giant cat sneered at him, turned with an imperious flick of the tail, and strode away. When Zach didn't follow, it turned its head and yowled. The little one bit his big toe -- for emphasis, he supposed. They either wanted him to follow them, or feed them, and... why the hell not? Stranger things had happened.

The cats walked well ahead of him, measured now that they knew they had Zach's attention, and they didn't go far. Down a short flight of steps, across old-old-old flagstones, and to what he guessed must have been a butler's pantry once upon a time. When Zach peeked inside, he saw two empty pet food bowls sitting against the far wall.

Big Cat yowled again, lashing its tail. Feed them it was.

Zach snorted quietly, a little wetly, but there was no reason not to make *something* glad he was there before his body got over the surprise of being herded *by* cats and turned on him again. He had to get control over himself somehow.

If he could. Maybe he couldn't.

His legs were shaking again, and he had just enough strength left to fill the bowls before he stumbled to the far wall and used it to slide down so he didn't fall. The second wave was worse than the first; he did gag this time, acid flooding his throat. Nothing else came up. His body had already sent those few bites of Thai on their way down his guts, too hungry to let them go to a second's waste. He wished it hadn't. The acid made his nose run and his mouth burn, and when he swallowed it back down without thinking, it lit a sour flame in his belly that made him gag all over again. He was on his hands and knees before he'd finished and his stomach still hadn't stopped cramping in long, sick waves.

Zach pressed his hot face against the wall and let the tears go. He wept for everything he could have had, and all the things he never could have had, either.

He wasn't sure how long it lasted before he heard footsteps, Alpha-heavy, treading a slow path down the steps. *Figured.*

"I might have known," Zach said, tired. "Alphas always follow their trails to the bitter end."

"Did you really expect anything different?" Alexander asked. Shuffling noises sounded like him sitting down outside, but not opening the door any farther.

"Expect, no. Hope -- maybe, yes. But I never knew anyone so bent on banging his head against a brick wall as you."

"Haven't met yourself, then, have you?"

Zach aimed a narrow look at the crack in the door. "More often than I've liked. Look, I have to stay until it stops raining, but then I'll get out of your hair, Alexander. You don't have to worry about me."

"Don't have to --" Alexander stopped. "Zach, you -- " He made a noise more like a roar than a groan, sheer frustration let out of its bottle like a furious djinn. "How do you not get it, not even now? I want to -- I --"

He stopped mid-sentence. Small sounds followed, the quiet noises of a man struggling to get himself under control and mostly failing at it.

"God, I could tear you limb from limb sometimes," he said, starting off so abruptly that Zach flinched. "You keep saying I don't get it, but you know what? There are things *you* don't get. Like how I never knew what anger really was, before you. I never, never understood how you could walk away like you did."

Zach pressed the heels of his hands -- cold -- to his sore eyes -- hot from tears. "It hurt me as much as it hurt you, Alexander. Don't you ever think differently."

He heard Alexander exhale and drop back with a dull thud against the corridor wall. "I always wondered."

"Now you know. So please -- go away, until I can go away too."

Silence. Zach angled a bit to the right and realized

he could see a few inches outside the cracked door, enough of a patch of wall for Alexander's shadow to fall against. He could identify his movements now and there was no one to see him drinking them in. The way Alexander rubbed at his face, and how he turned his head when he spoke. "Do you want to know something true?"

Zach flinched back again. "No."

The stubborn man heard him, Zach knew he did, but he kept on talking. "If I'd known what you just told me, I'd have gone after you."

"I know. That's why I made sure you didn't." Zach's chest ached so that he rubbed over his breastbone to try and ease it. "If I'd let you, if I'd let me... It would have happened exactly the way you wanted. We'd have fucked until night fell and the sun rose and we'd have walked out of there with me pregnant, both of us on our way to the courthouse. And you'd have smiled like the sun every step of the way, not knowing any better. We were so young, Alexander."

"I know." Alexander sounded thoughtful. Zach could picture him so easily, lost in the images his mind conjured up for him as they spoke. "If we'd stayed together, do you think we'd have more than one kid by now?"

It wasn't funny, but Zach still almost laughed. It was laugh or howl, and his hormones were doing the picking and choosing. "Probably? We never stopped going at it back then, and we've barely stopped tonight. Every chance we get, we're on each other."

"In each other," Alexander murmured. "I'd have liked to see what it felt like if you fucked me, for once." He laughed when Zach hissed, half shocked and half jolted by a new wave of lust. "Thought you'd like that idea. But the way it was when I fucked you -- no, we wouldn't have stopped. We'd have a litter by now. A whole ball team's worth of babies."

Zach's breath hitched. He pressed his thighs together to stop the surge of yearning that provoked. A sharp tongue was the only defense he had left, but somehow it came out sounding rueful instead. "If you were an Omega and had to go through a pregnancy *and* give birth, I don't think you'd sound so thrilled about the idea."

"This is thrilled?" Alexander asked.

"You know it isn't." Zach looked up at the blank wall across him. Even the cats had run away. Smart cats. "Stop. Please? All this is doing is hurting us. Please stop."

He heard the soft scrape-scrape-scrape of Alexander's palm rubbing over the stubble on his cheeks and chin. "Yeah. About that. I'm not sure I'll ever be able to hear you say 'stop' again without flinching. I didn't do it on purpose. I wasn't thinking."

"Yes, you were. With the wrong head, but that's neither here nor there." Zach let out a long sigh and dropped his hands between his knees. The shudders were easing, finally, ebbing down to the occasional shock and quake, but he'd leaked -- was still leaking -- so much that it puddled beneath him, and his face went hot with shame. "So was I. Or so wasn't I. I don't know which is right. I let my hormones call the shots. Too many of them."

Alexander's shadow tilted its head a little more to the left. "Can I ask you a question?"

Zach raised one shoulder. "You can ask. I can't promise I'll answer."

"Is it scary to think about? The general concept of it, I mean. I never got to ask an Omega before."

"What, pregnancy, birth?" Zach's hand drifted down to rest over the concave dip of his belly. "No. I want children. Babies. I always did." He ached for them, and not only because he was an Omega. He yearned for someone he could love without reservation, who'd love him without bias. Who the world hadn't ruined and he could keep safe, teach how to be tough but -- he hoped -- how not to wall himself away. Someone who was half him, and half... "I don't know if I'm past that now, though. I might be."

"You're not even thirty. That's not old."

"I'm not talking about chronological age." Zach's fingers flexed. He could feel the gnawing emptiness inside that happened whenever he let his mind go to places like these, and that hurt too. "I've been fighting what my body wants, needs, for so long that I could have done myself some damage. You don't hear a lot about it, but it *does* happen. The spirit is willing and eager but am I even capable anymore? You leave anything too long and it withers. Seeds don't grow in scorched earth. *Fuck.*" He rubbed his face against his knee. "Please stop listening to me and go away."

"Oh, Zach," Alexander said. Only that, but with all his heart in his voice for once instead of on his sleeve. "Zach. No."

"Don't pity me," Zach snapped. "Don't you dare do that. It's done, and what's done is just -- done."

He saw Alexander's shadow's shoulders go tense. "You know, I hate it when people say that."

"Why? Because it's true?"

"No. Because it's bullshit."

Zach lifted his head and blinked at the door. "What?"

"I told you there were things you didn't get, but I didn't say them all," Alexander said, speaking slowly, thinking each word through as it came out. "When you left me that day --"

"Alexander, no." Zach pushed himself away from the comfortingly cool plastered wall, his heart pounding too hard and too fast again. "I don't want to hear it."

"That's too bad, because you're going to. When you

left me, I hated you. I hated you so much that it almost choked me. You're a cat, and you turned me into this -- this junkyard dog with more teeth than tail, taking bites out of everyone."

Bad enough to have imagined it every day, since. Worst of all to hear it out loud, even now. Zach wrapped his arms around his knees and pressed his face against them. "Alexander. Please."

Alexander's shadow shook its head. "I don't remember when I stopped hating you. A year, maybe. Two. A few boyfriends who didn't want strings, and one who was ready to tie me down with all the strings he could get his hands on."

He stopped there.

Zach couldn't constrain his curiosity. "What happened?"

"I thought about saying yes. I almost did say it. He was right for me in every way. Wanted a home, a huge family, a big noisy gorgeous life, and he had a smile that could stop traffic. I still couldn't."

"Why not?"

"Because he wasn't you." The door opened, and the small amount of light from a candle Alexander carried cast up long shadows as he dropped to a kneel in front of Zach, gazing steadily at him. "Here's something else true: I knew who you were the second I set foot on the train."

Zach pressed the back of his hand to his mouth. "No."

"Yes. Long before you realized I was there. I had almost an hour to look over my shoulder and think about what I was going to do. When I could. When I wasn't caught up in watching you, feeling like I was drowning, feeling *all* of that come rushing back while I was trying to keep my head above water. What you look like -- you look like the only happiness I'll ever know, and you look like you're one missed meal away from being six feet under -- and that junkyard dog inside me lay down and went to sleep. It curled up next to you so it could keep you safe, and I wanted that too. I wanted it. I wanted you like I'd never stopped."

Zach ground his hand against the edges of his teeth. He wanted to bite down to distract himself from how much pain he could sense coming from Alexander. How had he been so blind to it before? Selfishness? But now that his senses were open he could feel the deep-down thrumming of loneliness radiating from Alexander.

"I couldn't let you go. I had to at least try. I thought you wanted that too, but -- I still don't get it, Zach. Help me understand why I'm --" He stopped, then visibly made himself go on. "Rip the bandage off. Tell me why I'm not good enough for you."

What?

Zach's lips parted. "That's what you think?"

"What else should I think?" Alexander spread his hands in frustrated hurt. "You couldn't make it any plainer if you tried. You don't want me, and you don't want me so much that you spent years running as fast as you could. So just -- tell me why you don't love me, even if you still want my cock enough to make me crazy. Let me put that to rest, at least."

"But that's not it. That's not it at all."

He'd finally caught Alexander off guard. "What?"

"Idiot, yourself. God!" Zach lifted himself, balancing unsteadily but on his own two feet. He caught Alexander's wrist as he stumbled and went back down to his knees; the shock of hitting the stones hurt but he didn't care. He needed Alexander to listen and hear. "I *always* loved you."

"But --"

"How did you not know? I loved you so much it broke me to leave you. There wasn't a night I didn't wish it could be different."

"Then why?"

"It was the only way you'd ever have something better for you than me!"

He'd stunned Alexander into silence with that. It wasn't anywhere near satisfying. Zach gestured broadly, frustrated into nearly babbling to get it all out. "You deserved so much more. The world. Everything in it. And you *got* it, don't you see? You got out there and you took it all by the balls and you got what you wanted, and I am so *fucking* proud of you for that I'm almost not mad at you for whole seconds at a time."

Zach bent his head; his neck ached so, as if his skull were nearly too heavy for it to support.

"And there's the other side of the coin," he said after a minute, when Alexander didn't say anything at all. He couldn't stop. "My God, Alexander. We never stopped fucking, but we never stopped butting heads, either. And here, now? Look what's happened in one night. An explosion, a train wreck, a storm -- what's it going to take to convince you fate doesn't want us together? A lightning strike right down the middle of your head?"

Alexander regarded him for a long, unreadable moment. "Maybe," he said at last. "Stranger things have happened. And you know what? I don't care. All those things you say you wanted for me, Zach. Did you think I couldn't have done them *with* you?"

Zach's mouth opened and closed, stunned silent.

"Think about it," Alexander said quietly. He stood. "What we could have done -- both of us -- if we'd had each other's backs instead of always stopping to look over our own shoulders. Maybe making a choice that big, when we were that young, would have slowed us down. But it wouldn't have stopped us."

"How can you be so sure?"

"Because you changed everything with nothing but

a few words."

Zach closed his eyes.

"I love you. And I know you love me too."

"I'm sorry. No. That's not what I want."

Alexander nodded as if he'd heard those words running through Zach's mind. "Two little sentences, and you ended the world for me. That world. So do you really think you couldn't have kept us going with a few others, different ones? No. I know you. You'd have kept us moving, if you'd chosen that. If you'd trusted me."

"I loved you too much to trust myself to do that."

"Ahh."

"Ahh, what?"

"Now I understand," Alexander said. So simply. So surely. "Now, I know what to do."

He stood, taking Zach by the hands as he did so that he could bring Zach up with him, and supported his weight as he looked down at him. "You're so cold." He chafed Zach's hands gently, frowning when they didn't warm to his touch. "Is it always like this for Omegas, when they...?"

"Sometimes. Mostly, for me." Zach struggled against the urge to snatch his hands back ashamed of how thin and chilly they were. Who'd want to hold those? "Yes."

"Does it have to be that way?"

"Don't ask me that. God." Zach dashed a tear away from his eye, impatience making him hit a little too hard. "You know it doesn't."

"I do." Alexander guided Zach's hand away from his face and held it a bit tighter, clearly to keep him from doing that again -- and Zach let him. He looked down at how Alexander's hand swallowed his, so much bigger and warmer, and all he could do was swallow, himself, around a knot that wouldn't go down his throat. "And here's what I think, Zach. Neither of us can change the past. No one can. But we *can* change the future."

"Can we, though?"

"You know we can." That stubborn, never-dying hope of Alexander's shone through him. "If you try, with me. If you just try. You've been running for too long. It's time to come home. Let me be yours. Let yourself be mine."

Zach moved toward him, drawn like a magnet -- then flinched back. "I don't know how."

"I can show you." Alexander touched a fingertip to the soft skin beneath Zach's left eye, prompting him to open them again, and caught him like a deer in the headlights with how close he was. He could see the hazel starburst around his pupils that made Alexander's eyes look more green than blue, and was mesmerized. "I want another chance to try."

Zach shivered once, his lips parting even as he shook his head. "Alexander…"

"No, I mean it. You've been so cold for so long, and I want you to come home to me. Let me take care of you and let me love you." Alexander brushed his mouth against Zach's.

"Don't." Zach cringed. "I taste like vomit."

Alexander cupped his cheek without a flinch. "Ask me if I care about that right now. Let it be easy, Zach. It could be. This one time, let it be easy. Stay."

"Why me, though? You're crazy, Alexander. What have I ever given you except a hard time and a fistful of drama?"

Alexander laughed. "Where do I start? What do you give me? The idea of babies with your sass and my hair, for one. I still want them. Don't you?"

Zach's lips parted as he caught his breath.

"And the way we fight? Didn't it ever occur to you that if I didn't like it, I never would have been with you in the first place? I know you, Zach." Alexander reached into his pocket and came out with a chip of peppermint candy that he unwrapped and slipped through Zach's lips, nestling it on his tongue. "You've got so much fire in you, Zach. So much life, so much energy. So much more than you think, and if you chose to share it then you could."

"You could have that with anyone," Zach said. One last line of defense. "Any other Omega."

"All I want is you. Stay with me. Love me, or try to. That's all I ever wanted. That... and to hear you say it too. The way we couldn't when we were young, because we didn't know how -- but we aren't young now. We can say the right words this time. But it's your choice. It's always been your choice. Say yes, Zach. Or say no. Either way, what you say, that's how it'll be."

He held Zach at half-arm's length and simply watched him then, waiting. The boy he'd once been in the way he drank Zach in, and the man he'd become in the strength of his arms.

Zach turned his wrists so that he could stroke the muscles corded in those arms. Up and down, watching gooseflesh pop up where his fingers brushed. He really didn't know how, but...

He swallowed and swallowed again. He'd spent so long... but maybe Alexander was right. Maybe the past didn't have to be a life sentence. And if he could dare to believe that, then...

Then.

Zach took a deep breath and made up his mind. He clawed inside himself until he found the courage he kept buried under the bravado, and he dragged it, kicking and screaming the way he'd lived his life, all the way to the surface.

"I'm staying this time," he said. "Do you hear me? I'm not running anymore."

He was terrified, he'd never been so scared, but he

lifted himself on his toes, caught Alexander's face in his hands, and kissed him back. He fell for the last time, and Alexander caught him.

Chapter Six

It was different, this time. Not like the first, back in that basement. Not like the almost-second, with that kiss. Not like the third, split down the middle. This was its own beast, and it didn't roar. It purred.

Soft kisses, flowing smoothly, peppermint-sweet. Zach tasted Alexander's skin for the first time in so long. Salty sweat, the last traces of soap from a morning shower, cologne that smelled of red oak and wild earth. He must have looked ridiculous and he didn't even care a little, his hair tousled in every direction, his mouth wet and red, his clothes askew and half ripped away.

And -- what about Alexander? Big tough Alpha like that, brought to his knees like this by a little bitty Omega? There was a power in that he'd always liked, and it would -- could -- be so very interesting to see what happened if he rose to the moment and bent it to his will.

He could, he thought. He knew how.

And he wanted to. And he could, this time.

Zach laid his palm flat against Alexander's chest to pause him before he could go too deeply and backed a few steps away. "You have a bed upstairs?"

"I do. It's big enough for two," Alexander said, not looking away. As if Zach fascinated him still. "Tell me what you want."

It still took an effort, but Zach found he had the courage now that he knew where to reach for it. He bent to touch his forehead to Alexander's and murmured, "For you to take me there. Now."

* * *

Odds were, Alexander had a nice bedroom. Something elegant and tasteful and as untouched by personality as the rest of his house -- well, before *now* -- but Zach didn't bother looking around. Alexander had taken *take me there* as a literal command, carrying him up the stairs like a silver screen Omega queen and twirling him around to finish that dance before setting him on his feet. "All these years of wanting you, and you're letting me have you again. I almost don't know where to start."

"I think you'll figure it out," Zach said. He cocked a hip and made a beckoning gesture. He'd forgotten how much *fun* it could be to play and tease with a lover, it'd been so long. How remarkable that in one night, he could be this way with Alexander again. "Start with being nakeder than this. Go on. Let me see."

Alexander's eyes crinkled at the corners with amusement at being bossed around like that, but he didn't hesitate to do what he'd been told. When he was naked, fully bare, he turned in a slow circle, finishing with a *like what you see?* tilt of his head.

"I do. Very much. But now it's my turn." Zach let the too-big shirt he'd never buttoned fall off his shoulders. It pooled around his bare feet, leaving him in nothing but a pair of shorts with the inseam halfway torn apart.

Alexander's pupils dilated, watching him. He let out his breath in a great puff and dropped heavily to the edge of the bed, never looking away.

So he liked that, did he? Zach cupped his cock through his shorts and stroked once, slow and lingering, watching Alexander watch him. The man wanted to eat him alive, didn't he? It could go to an Omega's head, if it hadn't already.

He wanted more.

Zach plucked at the torn seam of his shorts, fraying it away as he shimmied his hips, ever so slowly freeing himself, then stepping out of them. With nothing left to hide behind, and not ashamed -- how could he be, with that kind of hunger in an Alpha's eye? -- he held his arms out at his sides and let himself be seen. All of him. Stiff cock jutting proudly up, feet planted flat and apart, his thighs gleaming.

Alexander shook himself out of his trance and reached for Zach, but there was one more thing. Zach took a half step back and warned, "Don't let me run, no matter what."

"I won't."

"Hold me to this, all of it."

Alexander had arms long enough to reach across that half step and collect Zach, reeling him slowly in. "I will."

"And keep holding me, even when neither of us deserves it." Zach came to a stop between Alexander's knees. "Keep me warm."

"I'll do that too," Alexander said, and kissed him.

There was, Zach discovered, another world's worth of difference in this kiss. One well worth exploring.

He hummed as their mouths parted. "Once, twice, and three times lucky. Let's try that again, my way."

Alexander shook his head, slow and wondering and appreciative. "If you tell me what you want."

"This." Zach took hold of Alexander's cock; it hadn't softened at all, and it was still slippery enough from his own body to stroke hard and fast. "And whatever put that look on your face I saw right before you were in me the last time. I want *that*."

Alexander bit the stiff peak of Zach's left nipple. One tiny nibble, but sharp, sharp enough to make Zach's belly clench. "Oh, Zach, be careful what you wish for." He bit the right, making them a matching, aching pair. "You sure you're ready for that?"

"You think this isn't ready?" Zach lowered himself to straddle Alexander's lap. He rolled his hips, making a glorious sticky mess between them, and hummed when Alexander hunched forward with a shudder of appreciation. "I want you *so* far inside me. I want you to fuck me until you come and I come and I want you to stay inside me until you're hard again."

"Oh, you don't play fair."

"No," Zach said. He tilted his weight forward without warning Alexander, all for the fun of tipping him onto his back and putting himself in a very satisfying position astride. "I don't think anyone's ever said that I did."

"Then isn't it lucky for both of us I like it that way?" Alexander raised himself on one elbow and studied Zach. Finally, he shook his head, but before Zach's heart could plummet he flipped them to lie side by side and leaned crossways over the tumbled sheets to tug open his bedside table's top drawer.

Zach watched, not surprised but touched as Alexander rummaged until he found what he wanted, a silver-wrapped packet, and dropped it between them. "I didn't buy them for anyone in particular. They might be a little old."

Zach blew a fine layer of dust off the crinkling wrapper and teased, "You think?"

"Wiseass." Alexander rubbed the tip of his nose against Zach's, chuckling when Zach swatted at him. "A guy gets into the habit, that's all. No one's ever shared *this* bed with me."

"Mmm. Good. No one else will ever get to."

"There's the Zach I remember," Alexander said, so admiring that Zach damn near preened. He'd forgotten how much he used to enjoy having *fun* in bed, teasing and laughing and tweaking each other's chains.

With a little luck, he'd relearn all his old tricks. He thought he'd like that.

Alexander started to tear the packet open, but Zach reached up, without thinking, to stop him. They blinked at each other, equal in their surprise.

Courage. Zach bit at his lip, then blurted, "You don't have to."

Alexander considered it, resting all his weight on

one arm, then shook his head. He took the packet back from Zach. "No." He made a wry, amused sound as he unrolled the rubber and slid it on. "One life changer at a time. I have you again. I can wait for the rest."

That man. Zach reached up to caress his face, making a purring sound when Alexander pressed his cheek into the touch. Who was acting like they had cat bloodlines now, rubbing up against him like that? "I love you," he blurted. "I do. I love you."

Alexander's smile came out like the sun rising after a long and rainy night. "Would you look at that," he said. "Two life-changers after all."

Zach ducked his head, but not for long. Alexander wasn't done.

"One more thing," he said. "Do you have any idea how brave you are?"

No, that couldn't be right. "What?"

"Brave. Courageous," Alexander said, stroking his face -- and no, he wasn't lying or trying to butter him up. "You're right. We were so young. You did what you thought was the right thing, and I know now what it did to you, to make that choice. I don't think I would have been brave enough."

Zach stared at him, disbelieving.

"I mean it," Alexander said. "Every time I think you're done amazing me..." He skimmed one hand between them and wrapped his fingers around Zach's cock. Not stroking, seeming simply to enjoy the feel of him and appreciate how even so light a touch made Zach roll his hips and groan. "I think I understand what you're saying, and why. But I'm not forcing anything anymore. We'll see what we'll see, go as we go, and we'll handle it together."

Zach had to reach for his hand and take it. "There. There's the third life-changer."

"Good." Alexander lowered himself, *finally*, to kiss

Zach, so deep, so sweet and so good.

Zach wrapped his arms around Alexander's neck and raised himself to meet the man halfway. Even better.

"What do you want?" Alexander asked between kisses. "Anything you want. Name it."

"Mmm." Zach leaned back, letting Alexander hold him up. He let his head tilt as he breathed deeply. His body *hummed*, and the urge, the driving need was still there, but it'd been tamed and purred like an engine. Idling, but ready to leap when it was told. Only he got to choose that too, now.

So many choices. He licked his lips lazily, letting the ideas tumble through his mind, chuckling when for all his romantic words Alexander started to shift impatiently.

What he really wanted was... well, why not?

"I want this." Zach raised himself on his knees, slid forward, and took Alexander in hand to show him what he meant, and where he wanted the Alpha. He arched both head and spine, posing a little, but no one there minded.

Not Alexander, who took hold of Zach's hips to help him out. "Oh God," he breathed. "Yes. This."

Though his eyes were still closed, Zach let his mouth curve into the wide smile he felt from the inside out. "That. And maybe this."

He let his other arm drift down to touch himself too, and stroked light, deft, as Alexander guided him down, bringing him home.

Zach bit his lip as the emptiness inside him was filled, and more than. No matter what else had happened that night, Alexander was more than most could handle, and for a moment his head didn't know whether it was coming or going or going to come in less than a minute. Maybe all of the above. If he did, he wouldn't be alone. But an Alpha's strength of will...

"Need a minute?" Alexander held himself stiller than any man would want to and kneaded at his hip, gazing up at him in a way that Zach could feel without having to see it.

He breathed out -- and -- he knew how to do this, when he let himself -- let his body open, let himself ease the way. "No."

"Do you want a minute?"

Zach laughed. "No."

"Good."

He rode the roll when Alexander sat up to balance Zach in his lap, still joined, and wrapped him up to hold him close, and that was the last of the -- gentleness -- but not the intimacy of this time. Alexander's mouth was on his, all the hunger he'd held in check unleashed. Ready to eat him alive and lick the bones left behind clean. Zach gave back as good as he got, the way Alexander liked it, biting when Alexander bit, meeting him thrust for thrust. They melted together, liquid where they weren't hard, and hard where they needed to be. His big, broad hand jostled Zach's out of place and encircled him on the right side of too hard, the way *Zach* liked it.

"*Ohh*," Zach moaned as he leaned into Alexander's presses and pushes, his hips moving into the touch and taking Alexander deeper at the same time. He knew what it would feel like, muscles flexing and squeezing around Alexander, and when Alexander sped up he did too. Tempo and rhythm, they had both, and even when one missed a beat the other caught them and pulled them back.

Zach only stopped once, panting, though he didn't stop Alexander. His throat worked, swallowing hard, but not in fear.

He made the choice to be brave, as brave as Alexander believed him to be. Took Alexander's face in his hands to kiss him as deeply as he wanted to -- had wanted to for so, so long.

"Oh fuck. Oh, fuck." Alexander buried his face in Zach's shoulder as he swelled inside, locking their bodies together. Nothing would separate them now, not until the end. "Fuck, Zach, oh fuck," he repeated, slurring it together as he said it over and over, a rush of noise like music in the background. "Zach, Zach --"

Zach took in a sharp, shocked breath as it all become too much, almost too fast, and he couldn't have stopped if he'd wanted to, he couldn't have helped coming with a full-throated keen that made his throat and chest burn. Alexander's mouth fastened on his neck, because he couldn't have not followed an Omega's lead there, coming the way Zach knew in his heart he wouldn't have in years. Seven years.

They took forever at it, and not long enough, but when they fell against each other, shaking in every muscle and lax with satisfaction, the last kiss -- this time -- was ripe with satiation, and *that* went on and on until they weren't kissing but only moving their mouths together, each tasting the other's scent and breath. Their bodies parted on their own, though Zach didn't budge from Alexander's lap before he eased them both down to lie on the bed in the glorious mess they'd made together.

Zach couldn't wipe the smile off his face, and it only widened when Alexander flipped onto his stomach to nuzzle under his chin.

"Say it one more time?" he asked, hand over Zach's heart with the fingers spread open.

Zach covered Alexander's hand. "I love you."

"Not that." Alexander laced their fingers together and shivered one more time, shifting closer. "The other."

Ah. "I'm staying," Zach said. His smile turned into a laugh as he gave their joined hands a jostle. "Try and get rid of me."

"I won't."

Zach looked up at Alexander and said, "I know."

Alexander let out a sigh, believing him, and let himself relax. He pressed his mouth to Zach's arm, then raised himself up on his elbow. His grin bent sideways. "We might be genuinely stuck together if we don't wash some of this off. Join me in the shower. It's big enough for two as well."

Probably true, but Zach wasn't ready to move yet. "You go on," he said, lazily stroking Alexander's chest. "Get the water warm for me. I'll be there. I promise."

"I believe you." One more kiss, and Alexander rolled out of bed. He stretched, arms over his head and raising himself on his toes until his fingertips brushed the ceiling -- grinned over his shoulder at Zach, who had to laugh at him a little -- and moved away with the rolling grace of an Alpha who'd given and taken until he was replete.

For now. There was a promise of more in his walk, and Zach didn't mind. He let his eyes drift shut again as he heard a glass door slide open, and then the patter of water on tile. Warm. So warm, inside and out, and hungry, but for food. Real food, as much as he could hold, and that he knew Alexander would provide.

He might need it more than usual. Zach glided his hand across the sheets and let it rest on his belly. It could only be his imagination, it probably *was* even with how he'd responded to Alexander claiming him so good and hard, but he seemed even warmer there, his body no longer shifting inside but throbbing with a slow pulse he'd never felt before. His scent seemed to be changing, ebbing from bitter to something sweeter.

It might be true. It might not.

But no birth control was effective one hundred percent of the time, especially if an Alpha didn't have it in place the moment he got hard. Zach was almost sure a little piece of Alexander had taken root inside him. That

what was happening now would become the baby he'd --
they'd -- wanted seven years ago.

He made a low, pleased noise, and slid out of the
bed. His hips rolled as he went to join Alexander in the
shower, maybe a little looser already. Yes, almost sure.
But they'd see what they'd see, and one thing he
especially wanted to see was the look on Alexander's face
when steam made his scent bloom around them and the
penny dropped.

Now, and later, and always.

And soon.

Epilogue
Nine and a Half Weeks Later

Alexander eased sideways on the window seat, giving Zach a little more room to stretch out. Alphas were mostly taller and wider than Omegas, but his legs were long enough that he could let one fall to the floor and rest his foot there. "Better?"

"Hmm," Zach sighed, easing his legs into the empty space. "Mmm. Yes."

Alexander pressed a kiss to the back of Zach's head. Whatever it took, he'd do it to keep Zach snuggled in the cradle of his body and Alpha pride be damned. He liked this, both of them covered in the warmest blanket he owned and not a stitch on underneath. Zach's back and head rested against Alexander's chest, his hands lay draped over Alexander's knees, and the rest of him was kept safe between Alexander's thigh on one side and the picture window at the other.

There with him, here and now after so long spent apart. Alexander wouldn't trade it for anything.

He drew Zach closer and glanced up at the glass. They'd been there for hours, letting the night pass as they held each other close. "Sun's rising."

Zach made an absent but pleased noise, his eyes half-open like a sleepy cat as he turned to look too. He touched his fingertips to the glass, but he didn't say anything else. He'd been quiet for a while, not like his usual self, but there wasn't much of the "usual" this night. Alexander preferred hearing Zach put all his thoughts into words. Once Zach got going there wasn't much he couldn't go on -- at length -- about.

Alexander jostled him as gently as he could. "Are you comfortable?"

"As I can be," Zach said, still watching out the window, tracing a pattern in the faint mist forming on the glass. He hummed a snatch of song to himself, quiet and dreamy. "It's not that old chair in my old place that I loved, but it'll do."

"Glad to oblige."

Alexander would have gone on, maybe teased him a little -- winding Zach up was almost as good as setting him off -- but Zach fidgeted abruptly, hands dropping back to Alexander's knees and gripping them tight. He stiffened and pressed his face to the crook of Alexander's arm, and the abrupt movement made the blanket slip away from both of them.

And there they were, both of them. Naked, one holding, and one laboring.

Alexander put his hand over the heavy curve of Zach's stomach, so weighty that it amazed him Zach had been able to walk around like that. When he'd mentioned it, Zach had given him a look that could have melted the glass, then laughed at him and minced away. Never had lost his grace, but the only place he'd put on weight despite Alexander's efforts to feed him up was around the middle.

That he'd done that, was willing to do this, and for *him* --

Zach was stubborn about not making noise, but as he reached the worst of it he keened quietly into Alexander's elbow. Alexander didn't shush him but started counting the seconds out loud. He knew how long it lasted, and it took a full sixty seconds to ease. Zach slumped against him, panting short breaths through his nose.

"Sun's almost up," Alexander said, drawing him back from that odd dreamlike state he fell into so easily because he needed Zach to be present for the moment. "If I didn't know better, I'd think you planned it this way."

Zach laughed breathlessly. "No. It's luck." He licked his lips, dry and sore-looking from being bitten. "Maybe fate."

He might be right. Alexander kept up his slow stroking; Zach had said it helped. Even so, he shook his head doubtfully. "Are you sure you don't want to go somewhere? Get a doctor?"

"We've had this conversation before. I choose what I choose. I want to do this the old way."

"We're *going* to call a doctor if you need one."

"I won't. I can do this. It's entirely possible that I'm -- oh -- going to kill you before this is over, but..." Zach had to pause there and breathe a moment before he could speak again. "There's nowhere else I'd rather be." He rolled his forehead against Alexander's arm. "All I want is the two of us, here, at home."

Alexander stroked lower as another contraction started. They weren't far apart at all now, and he could feel Zach's body opening wider with each rippling spasm. He shook his head in alarm and awe. "There's no 'used to be' for your first time giving birth, and you're scaring the shit out of me. How do Omegas do this?"

"Same as they have since the world started spinning. I need it this way." Zach finally relaxed fully, limp with fatigue. When Alexander made to pull the blanket back up, he made a face and pushed it away. "Too hot."

"And if someone looks in, now that the sun's on its way up?"

Zach scoffed. "Let them look. That's the way things used to be as well."

The way things used to be, indeed. Alexander hooked his chin over Zach's shoulder and stroked his massive belly, big enough to make him worry ever since he'd popped. There *was* only one in there, but... Even for an Alpha, Alexander was a large-scale man, and Zach was as small and fine-boned as a reed. Omega hormones produced a few natural painkillers and having their Alpha this close supposedly made it all go easier, but even so...

"You are never, ever doing this again," he said into Zach's sweat-damp hair. "Not if I have to wrap it up in three layers every single time you look sideways at me."

Zach's laugh bubbled up, exhausted but still bright and gorgeous. "You say that *now*."

"And you'd better believe I mean it."

That got him a dismissive noise. "Please. You're an Alpha to the bone, you --" Zach stopped and went stiff.

After a moment, Alexander started to worry. Zach was too still, not fidgeting or moving through it. He jostled Zach gently. "Hey. Talk to me."

Zach shook his head. He gripped Alexander's knees tightly enough to make them creak. He winced, but Zach had already left bruises there and Alexander honestly didn't give a damn about that.

"Wuss." Zach laughed breathlessly, let go of Alexander's knee and took his hand, guiding it down between his legs. "Kiss me," he ordered, panting. "Now. Please. And touch me, help me."

Alexander did. Both. God, Zach was so wet and open, so open, but different too. As another spasm took him in its grip, he felt a pressure against his palm, one that slid forward and then back, then forward again until Zach had to stop for breath.

And then, again. Again.

Alexander lost track of time after that. The only thing that mattered was holding Zach and being held. It seemed to take forever, both of them caught like that, soothing him when his moans got so loud they echoed against the window. Helping him catch hold of his ankles, then putting his hand back between Zach's legs.

It took forever, and no time at all, and then it ended with their son's head cradled fully in his hand.

"Oh my *God*," he said, as horrified as he was thrilled, his heart beating as hard as Zach's, gorgeous

Zach's. "You're doing this. You're doing so well."

"Says -- you." Zach shook his head. "Don't let go. Don't ever let go."

Alexander had meant to look, but he couldn't. Zach shuddered like a willow tree caught in the wind, and this time it wasn't passing but only rising and falling. One more tremendous effort, two more, three times, and then with a gasp that wrenched him nearly in two, it was over. He fell back, going limp, while Alexander only barely caught the slippery creature that'd slid free of his Omega's -- his Zach's -- body.

"Help me." Zach tried to reach down. "Alexander, help me."

Alexander had been too caught up to move before, but he did now even if he *was* shaking like a willow tree. He almost dropped their son -- poor kid! -- before he could lay him in Zach's open arms, laughing at how he was already shrieking about how *very* unhappy he was with the past few hours and this new indignity.

Zach cradled the baby, hands shaking. "Alexander… look. Look."

As if he could turn away, or would ever want to. Alexander cupped their son's head again, awed down to his core as the infant shrieked at a volume fit to make the glass rattle in its frame, and made them both wince and laugh.

"Oh, we're going to have to buy some earplugs, aren't we?" Zach looked back at him, so delighted that Alexander had to kiss him.

"I kind of like the noise. He takes after you." Alexander brushed his thumb over Zach's temple. "He's beautiful, he's so beautiful, Zach. Love him. Love you, always. Thank you for this. For loving me enough for this."

"Finally," Zach breathed against his mouth, and came back for another kiss. Alexander tasted salt on

Zach's lips, and knew Zach could taste it on his, but that was all right. Neither let it stop them, because they weren't letting anything do that now. No shame, no blame. No going back. Only the two of them holding their son, bathed in the light of the rising sun of Second Chance.

Yes, You Are (Second Chance Omegas 2)
Willa Okati

Everyone always assumed small, pretty Darian would be an Omega. He ticked all the boxes -- except for the temper and the tendency to cuss a blue streak. But whatever, right? And everyone always assumed big, athletic Coby would be an Alpha. Just stood to reason -- as long as you paid no mind to his tender heart. When they met in passing as teenagers, both boys had no reason to doubt that was who they'd be. Everyone said it, after all. But everyone was wrong.

When Darian and Coby meet again in grad school, Darian's still small and pretty but he's one hell of a ferocious Alpha -- and tall, muscular Coby still struggles with having turned out to be an Omega. The college is short on space due to storm damage, and they've got no choice but to share living quarters and come to terms with themselves and their past -- and when Coby gets pregnant, their soon-to-be future.

Opposites attract like lightning and steel rods when they meet again in Second Chance, but do they have what it takes to overcome the unexpected for the long haul?

Prologue

Darian hit the asphalt track ass first, jolting backward on his bony butt, and oh *hell* no, he was not about to let that one slide.

He lashed out with his left foot and caught one of the guys who'd knocked him down in the ankle. Good and solid too, not breaking any bones but making him yelp like Darian had gotten him in the nuts instead and hop-stumble off balance like a fool until he caught himself. Cleats were better for more than a little traction.

Darian glared up at the group. He didn't know which of them had shoved him, and frankly he didn't give a damn. They were big guys, all of them, chunky around the middle and spattered with about as many zits as strands of wayward facial hair. He'd only caught one guy's nickname -- Snickers, because my God, that bastard loved his candy, and he'd already gone through two king sized bars in one morning at this Goddamned field and track camp he'd been dragged to.

What the fuck even, seriously.

"If you're going to spend your life picking fights you'd better know how to run when you get in over your head," his dad said, exasperated, right before he booted Darian out of the car. "Now either go have fun or at least try not to kill anyone, okay?"

"No promises." Darian bared his teeth.

After that, his dad had muttered something under his breath and driven away.

Anyway. Looked like Snickers and his clown crew buddies had finished razzing each other over getting nailed near the crotch and were back to hooting like they'd pulled the cleverest prank in the world by pushing Darian over.

"Little bitch went down easy, didn't he?" Snickers jeered.

"Yeah, you know boys like him do." One of the

others grabbed his crotch, and *ugh*, unless he was a grower and not a shower, that bastard was in for a whole lifetime's worth of disappointment. "You want to go down on me, pretty boy?"

Darian wiped a smear of wetness away from his upper lip and scowled when it came away red. Damn it, they'd given him a bloody nose. "Not even with someone else's mouth on someone else's dick."

While they were gaping at that, trying to figure out what he'd said and what it meant, Darian shoved himself to his feet. "If you unpresented wannabe Alphahole dickheads think you can toss me around like a chew toy" -- because he was small and skinny and probably going to be an Omega --"I will be *so* happy to teach you better. You want to go? Let's go."

"You got some kind of mouth on you," one of them sputtered. "You want to use that mouth for --"

"Hey!"

Darian jerked his head around to look because that voice right there? That was the kind of voice that made everyone sit up and pay attention. It wasn't the coach getting involved. *He'd* spent at least an hour bitching about Omegas being allowed on the same teams as Alphas, never mind that none of them were old enough to draw that line yet. Right now *he* was too busy pretending he saw no, heard no, and spoke no evil to do anything, and his assistant was setting up hurdles on the opposite side of the track.

Nope, it was the biggest of the guys on the field that day, and Darian meant *big*. A full head taller than any of the clown squad, wider at the shoulders, with hands that could probably palm a basketball and a jaw set like a battering ram.

Also? Super pissed off.

Darian could not tell a lie: that was pretty hot.

Big Guy thrust himself between Darian and the

others. "Knock it off and leave him alone."

Darian shoved back. Big Guy wasn't easy to move, so he shouldered up side by side with the dude instead and jabbed an elbow into his side. "Fuck off. I can defend myself."

"No you can't, little pretty boy. Who's going to stop us?" one of them jeered.

"You think I can't?" Big Guy doubled up his fists. "Let's go."

"There's one of you and three of us."

Darian rolled his eyes. Some people never learned unless it was the hard way. "Three of you, and two of us," he corrected. "And I don't know about him, but me? I don't fight fair."

He dropped his shoulder and charged into the middle of the group at top speed, and before they knew what'd hit them he leapfrogged forward and pinned Mr. Candy Monster down. Drew back his fist and smashed the guy a good one right in his potato face. *Pop* went some cartilage, and scarlet flew everywhere.

"Now *that's* how you give someone a bloody nose," Darian said with a sharp grin.

Big Guy gaped wide-eyed at Darian. Wide and abruptly gold-eyed, like a hawk. Must have been his animal nature coming through, and Darian wouldn't lie, that was pretty hot too. "Holy shit, dude."

Darian smirked at him, letting his animal nature show with a bared canine too sharp to be a human's, then let them *all* go good and pointy as he waggled his fingers at the two jackasses left standing. "Anyone else want to see what a pretty little thing like me can do to you?"

And of course, *that* was when Coach decided to get involved. He blew his whistle at top volume. "Separate!"

"I'm sorry, did you not see him knock me down first?" Darian demanded, climbing off the blubbering former bully, who now had red snot bubbles dribbling down his chin. "You don't see the blood on my face?"

The assistant coach must have noticed what was going on. He jogged over to put his two cents in. Big like all Alphas were, but not that much older than Darian and probably Big Guy either. "They did start it." He pointed at the three aggressors. "I saw the whole thing. These two were defending themselves."

"Separate!" Coach's fists were shaking and white-knuckled with all the things he couldn't legally say to an Omega these days. Fucking genderist bastard. "You three, go see the nurse. You two, far end of the field where I can keep an eye on you."

"Wait, what?" Big Guy jostled forward. "Are you serious? That's not fair."

"Corner! Another word out of you and you're out of here, understand?"

Coach stormed off without giving either of them a chance to explain, muttering those things about Omegas -- and weakass bleeding heart Alphas too -- out loud now but being super solicitous of the bastard with the bloody nose. The assistant shook his head and set out after them, shooting back arguments that Coach wasn't listening to.

"That's not *fair*." Big Guy started to go after them, but Darian caught him by the edge of his loose-sleeved tank and yanked backward.

When Big Guy aimed a surprised scowl over his shoulder, Darian gave the dude his best unimpressed look. "That's not going to make a difference. Pick your battles."

"Like you do?"

"We're talking about you, not me, and I *do* pick my battles," Darian retorted. "I just pick all of them."

"It's still not right. They did start it, and they can't get away with it scot-free."

"Oh, they're not." Darian dug in the loose pocket of his gym shorts and came out with the last of Snickers' three candy bars, waving it at Big Guy. "He'll go for the comfort food pretty soon and when he figures out he lost this somewhere, his head'll explode."

Big Guy started to grin. "How'd you do that?"

"I have my skills. Come on, you. Coach said 'go to the edge of the field,' I say we go to the bleachers. I've gotten too familiar with the turf already and if he doesn't like it, he can bite me."

At that, Big Guy snorted. "He can try. I already know you bite back."

"Which makes you smarter than him, so you're already ahead of the game." Darian waved Big Guy ahead of him, surprised when he didn't drop onto one of the lowest bleachers but climbed a few up before picking a seat. He shrugged and followed him. "What are you, a hunting hawk bloodline or something? And what's your name, anyway?"

"Mostly falcons. Some deer. Don't ask. And my name's Coby. It's not short for anything. Just Coby. Would have been Kobe but my dad misspelled it on my birth certificate. He was a fan." Coby bit at his thumbnail, looking torn between righteous wrath and some kind of inner conflict.

Normally Darian wouldn't have considered that his problem, but for some reason he elbowed Coby in a rough kind of sympathy. "Sucks to be you, doesn't it?"

"Tell me about it." Coby cocked his head. "Wolf bloodlines?"

"Fox." Darian broke the Snickers bar in half and passed over an equal share of it, wondering if he'd heard or imagined Coby muttering *I'll say* before deciding that was one step too far into *what the fuck* for the moment. "Here. And I'm Darian. Not Darry, not Dare. Darian."

"Darian. I'll remember." Coby's stomach let out a basso rumble, but he had some manners on him and he hesitated before reaching for the candy. "Are you sure?"

"We're getting rid of the evidence. Eat up."

Coby thought about that for a second, but he was already grabbing for his half of the candy bar, and once he had it in his hand he shoved the whole damn thing in his mouth.

Darian's eyebrows flew up. "Okay, hungry much? You're going to choke yourself."

"Mmf." Coby chewed and swallowed maybe half his mouthful, going pink-faced. Strike what Darian had thought before about manners, but for some reason it didn't annoy him as much coming from Coby. Maybe he was in the mood to let it ride, and after he'd swallowed the other half of his mouthful mostly whole Coby did give Darian a sheepish shrug. "Couldn't help it. I'm always hungry. I grew six inches this year already."

"Big strong Alpha in the making, huh?"

"Well, I mean." Coby gestured up and down himself, and -- Darian sighed -- he wasn't going to be wrong, even if neither of them had presented as a real gender yet. "And..." Coby waved his hand awkwardly at Darian, sturdy but still short as hell with a heart-shaped face. "And. You know."

Yeah, Darian knew. He still crossed his arms defiantly. "I didn't need your help, you know."

"No shit," Coby shot back. "But even if you can take care of yourself, that doesn't mean I have to sit by and watch. I don't like how Omegas get shit on for being Omegas. I see enough of that at home. All that bullshit about them being good for nothing but fucking and babies." He grimaced an awkward apology. "Which is stupid, you know? I mean, look at you. There's a waiting list for this track and field camp and you don't get in because you're pretty."

He went beet red, juicy ripe tomato red, when he realized what he'd said. Darian couldn't stop laughing. He even tipped over sideways.

"Fuck it, whatever." Coby hauled him up only to give him a light shove back down and laughed when Darian shoved right back because that was the okay kind of shove, give and take and give again. "You are pretty." He went a deeper shade of red still while his eyes went hawk gold again, which actually kind of struck Darian as both weird and freaking cool. Still, he'd seen weird shit before. It didn't shock him or anything like that.

What *did* shock him was Coby leaning over, fast and awkward at the same time, and pressing his lips quickly to Darian's before zipping back like he was attached to a rubber band.

Darian stared at him, realizing half a beat too late he'd put his hand to his mouth in surprise like an Omega in a movie, for fuck's sake. "What the hell?"

Coby looked resolutely away, going from red to purple before he took a few deep breaths and the color started to recede. *He* touched his mouth too. "Like I said. You're pretty. And I wanted to. You're brave. I like brave, And the point I was trying to make before, smartass, is that if you weren't good at sports, if you hadn't earned your place the way everyone *says* Omegas can't, you wouldn't be here, so." He shrugged. "Do you want to kick my ass now for kissing you? I'll give you a free shot."

Normally Darian would do exactly that, but... Well, hell. He'd never been kissed before, and now he had. Kind of left him reaching for something to say, which was a rarity in his world. "Gender's not a hundred percent guaranteed," he finally came up with, and jumped on it in relief. "You do know that? But you're not the usual kind of probably-Alpha, are you?"

"I don't want to be. You're not the usual kind of probably-Omega, yourself."

Darian admired the bruises on his knuckles. Worth it, every one of them. "Nope. I don't want to be. I'm going to be a terrible Omega. The worst kind. Because I'm not going to let it stop me. I'm kicking every ass I come across that tries to take me for less than what I am on the inside. Bet."

"Yeah? Me too. Watch and see. Not that you can, I don't even know where you're from, but still. Respect." Coby surprised him one more time by holding out his fist for a bump.

Eh, why not? Courage should always be rewarded when it was the real thing. Darian tapped knuckles with Coby. "Respect," he agreed, settling back to rest his arms on the bleacher behind him. "Oh hey, you see? Dude just figured out his candy went missing. Told you he'd go apeshit. This ought to be good."

Coby laughed and copied him, though he had to stretch those long legs of his out across two sets of lower bleachers.

Darian watched him for a minute, shaking his head, baffled but pleased at the same time. Watch and see? If they'd lived anywhere close to each other, he'd have liked to do that. Besides, Darian was going to make a bad Omega, but Coby was -- *mmm* -- fine, fine, fine, and only going to get finer when the guy Alpha-fied. Darian would have liked to see that too. Maybe jump him in a totally different kind of way. Try that kissing business some more. A lot more. See what happened after that.

Well, hell. It really was too bad they'd never meet again. They'd have made a killer team all on their own.

Chapter One

Darian still thought about that day sometimes, because while he had no idea about Coby, hadn't seen him since then, the funny thing was they'd both been mostly right. Darian wouldn't have been a good Omega, no matter what anyone thought.

But as it turned out... he'd made a kickass Alpha.

He said as much to his friend Oscar, who shrugged and took a drag off his cigarette before passing it to Darian. "A weird, short one with a filthy mouth, but sure."

Darian took it, rolling the paper cylinder between his fingers, deftly avoiding the ember at its end. "Join the club. Why do you think we're friends, and why do you think I agreed to room with your bony tail?"

"'Cause you love me, jackass."

"Debatable," Darian scoffed, and knocked shoulders with his favorite fellow weird-as-fuck Alpha. They'd been buddies for years, ever since they'd presented and neither one of them fit the usual mold. Oscar was taller and broader than Darian but not *tall* and not beefy either. He made up for it with a trimmed beard and dressing butch enough he didn't get half the questions Darian did, but that was him doing him and Darian had no problem with it. *He* did himself, and he liked the Omega shit. Loose clothes, longer hair, a ring in one ear. Anyone who didn't like it could keep it to themselves or piss off.

Still, Oscar did have one good point: with the language and the willingness to dive fist-first into every fight he could find, Darian really should have known way sooner how he'd turn out. Showed him for making assumptions about the gender binary, didn't it?

Darian drew deeply on the cigarette and passed it back. "Would you look at us? We are such bad examples, smoking on school grounds." College grounds, but whatever. He and Oscar both had their bachelor's degrees in education, but neither of them wanted to stop there. All the way to the top with a Dr. in front of their names, or nothing at all, and specialized summer intensive courses like the one they'd come here for were a place to start. "We should be ashamed."

"Educators of impressionable youths that we're going to be and all that bullshit," Oscar agreed.

"*If* these assholes get their dicks untied any time before the summer session starts." Darian lifted his chin at the group of busily bickering housing officials clustered in a knot not far away around a registration table, heads bent worriedly together while discussing the usual: what to do with a problem like himself. "So there was a storm last week that flooded the graduate housing, and no one thought to tell any of us. Awesome."

The more things changed…

"Even so, I don't get what the deal is," Oscar mused. "I mean, I don't give a fuck about sharing if the only room left is a single, and I know you don't. They always put Alphas together anyhow. Don't see why they're all hot and bothered about it."

"Probably fire codes. Weight capacity. Plus all those crazy orgies you know boys like us throw."

"Because that happens so often."

"Pfft. I wish." Darian shook his head. "Nah. Five more minutes, and I'm going to put a word in, and you know how I feel about that."

Oscar shrugged as if to say *it's your funeral.*

Or theirs, maybe. Darian'd worked hard on reining in his lightning trigger after presenting a gender, partly because of Coby. He'd never expected to *be* an Alpha, but be damned if he wouldn't be the best one he could manage either. "Five more minutes." He stubbed the cigarette out to underscore his point. "Start your watches."

Oscar didn't have a watch, but he did have half a pack of cigarettes left, a brutal nicotine habit, and a willingness to share. He pulled out a second smoke and lit up before exhaling a thoughtful cloud. "Second Chance, huh?" Which was where they were, after a stupidly hair-raising trip on a train that should have been in a museum decades ago which finished up two inches away from a drop into the pits of infinity. "Think whoever named it had a thing for optimism?"

"Or irony. Don't know, don't really care. They have one of best secondary educator's courses on the East Coast."

"Say that five times fast."

"How about I don't?" Darian shifted forward, frowning at the clustered clusterfuck going on at the tables. "Something about that seem odd to you?"

"Like how?"

"They're looking at me, but they're looking down the way too." Darian couldn't see what they were gesturing at, or who, but at least half of them were trying to subtly jab their pointers to the left. One of them, a tall bastard with a jaw like a nutcracker, finally sliced his hands sharply sideways through the air, caught Darian's eye, and flicked a couple of fingers at him to gesture him back to the group. He stood, dusting off his ass with a few brisk swats, and stole one more drag off Oscar's cigarette. "Here we go."

"Me too?"

"Odds are. Besides, no matter what's going on you live for licking up spilled tea."

"I do love that," Oscar agreed. He didn't bother to dust himself off when he stood, comfortable ambling around with grass clippings stuck to his ass. "Let's roll."

And roll they did, deliberately taking their time about it even if they didn't have far to go. Hands in their pockets, moving with a comfortable slouch, showing the world: this is what we are, even if we don't look like it. No apologies.

Darian didn't see what the problem was until they got nearly close enough to reach out and touch it, and once he did he couldn't figure how he'd missed it in the first place. A couple yards past the knot of arguing administrators, on a low brick wall, hunched a fucking giant of a man. He'd curled in on himself so tightly, head down, that anyone who wasn't built like a Viking would have looked small. This guy had no chance of that, seriously ever.

Huh. Darian frowned at the man. Couldn't see his face, but there was something familiar about...

Then, the guy raised his head to sneak a glance at them, and the second Darian saw the flash of those hawk-gold eyes, he knew. He fucking knew.

"Jesus Christ. Coby?"

Coby -- because it was him -- gaped at Darian, his mouth dropping open in surprise.

One of the administrators facepalmed. "They know each other? I told you this wouldn't work."

"So? They have a history that doesn't involve --" Nutcracker Jaw stopped himself. "All the more reason it will work."

Okay, that was enough of that. "Would someone like to tell me what the hell is going on?" Darian demanded, louder than he needed to be to get their full and undivided attention.

Worked too. Oscar winced away from him, hands over his ears -- *sorry, Oscar* -- but the full contingent of admins stopped to blink at him in surprise and Coby's hawk eyes went wide as saucers.

Good. Darian put his hands on his hips. "We're here to be educated. Educate me."

The admins exchanged glances of varying disapproval and insistence, but Nutcracker Jaw -- who seemed to be in charge or at least willing to step up -- took the lead, and boy, was he everything an Alpha should be even if he didn't look the least little bit fazed by Darian's temper. Points to him. "We have a situation."

"No, really?" Darian took another look past him at Coby, who'd slumped down again and hugged himself around the middle. "Involving him, or what?"

"Yes. It's policy to put Alphas and Alphas and Omegas and Omegas together, like that ever stopped anyone from hooking up whenever they wanted to --"

Okay, Darian did like this guy.

"But." Nutcracker Jaw hooked his thumb back at Coby. "He's the only Omega left without a roommate."

Darian's jaw dropped. He'd kick his own ass for that later, but for now --"Say again? He's a what?"

Coby hunched deeper and fisted his hands in his hair, then shook his head and sat up straight. Darian could see the effort it cost him, *and* the angry defiance in his hawk eyes. He'd seen that look in the mirror most of his life. "I'm an Omega. *Me.* And you're not."

Behind him, Oscar whistled. "Holy fuck."

Nutcracker Jaw cleared his throat. "There's a single left, and a double. We could put him in the single, but he presented late, a year or so ago, and he's too much of a temptation without an Alpha around to watch his back." To his credit, Nutcracker Jaw looked like he didn't think it was fair either. "We want to put one of you two in with him. You can choose who, but I say it should be you. You've got enough scars on your knuckles that I can tell you'd do a good job of defending his honor *if* someone tries to take advantage of him not having a buddy, and whether he likes it or not, he needs it."

Coby kept his head high, but he was angry as hell now and red streaks of embarrassment marred his cheeks.

Shit. Darian couldn't blame Coby for that. And he

couldn't help admiring him, either. Any other Omega would have turned inside out with shame by now, but Coby had what it took to fight back. Mostly. He stared straight at Darian, daring him to kick up a real donnybrook.

Darian made up his mind in that second. "I'm in. Give me the keys, and let's go."

* * *

Keys in hand, Darian was five steps ahead before he realized Coby hadn't budged. He looked over his shoulder. "Well? Are you coming?"

Reluctantly, taking one more glance at the admins probably to make sure this was really happening, Coby unfolded himself. He was still half a foot taller than Darian, maybe more, and he'd filled out those lanky bones into wide shoulders and legs long enough to make a man want to try and climb him like a tree. *I mean -- damn.*

But Coby didn't walk like he used to, full of confidence. He sloped along with a slouching kind of gait that suggested bashful uncertainty, and the way he kept his head down indicated shyness, but the look on his face was nothing but pure, frustrated rage.

Darian couldn't blame him. Hell, this was fucking with *his* head. He could only imagine how tangled up Coby had to feel about it. Coby, an Omega? Seriously? He made an even weirder specimen that way than Darian did in his, so what the fuck *even*.

Behind them, Oscar gave them a wry salute before turning to head for his single digs.

"Bastard," Darian muttered before turning to give Coby a dose of straight eye contact. "This isn't how I planned for things to turn out either, but since they did, we can either bitch about it or make the best of it," he said bluntly. "So come on. Or don't, but if that's your call then I'm going to leave you behind. It's not even noon and I am fucking tired. So?"

Coby looked like he was going to argue, then shook his head and fell into step. He tried to stay behind, act like they weren't together, but his legs were too long not to catch up. When he did, Darian had the weirdest urge to take his arm. Just an urge, of course. An Alpha thing, a real throwback to the days when a gentleman would take a submissive's arm to guide him. If he tried that now, fuck knew if this new angry Coby would try and break his elbow.

Darian didn't do playing it safe, but unusual times called for unusual circumstances. He kept his hands in his pocket and his walk to an amble, and -- again, not his usual thing -- took a stab at small talk. Anything to calm Coby down before his head imploded. "You're a teacher too, huh? No kidding. Makes sense, now I think of it. I don't make sense, but I'd started the pre-classes before things turned out like they did, and I'd put in too much work to go back."

No answer.

Annoyed, Darian tried again. He hooked a thumb backward. "That was Oscar, a friend from back home. He can be a real douche sometimes, but deep down he's pretty decent. A good guy to count on, in case you were wondering."

Which Darian could tell Coby wasn't. Too lost in his own head and his flinching awareness of every single person who paused to give them either odd or shocked looks when they put two and two together. Darian would have ignored those -- he'd gotten used to them years ago -- but being with Coby made him glower at everyone, daring them to make a deal out of it, and he could only do that so much before he gave himself a fucking migraine.

One more shot. "What are you teaching?" Darian asked. "I'm math. Calculus, trig, and basic algebra as I need to."

Coby shook his head and kept his trap firmly shut, his head so far down that his chin almost touched his chest and yep, there went the temper Darian really did try to keep locked down. Didn't help that looking at Coby made his mouth water and that pissed him right off because for fucks' sake, his libido needed to mind its own business right now. The rest of him didn't like the way the Coby he remembered had changed, and his being Omega wasn't part of that.

He stopped in front of the big man, blocking his path, and lifted his chin. "Would you mind looking at me? And while we're at it, what the fuck besides the obvious is your problem? It's not like this is easy for me either."

Coby glowered at Darian and shouldered past him, strong enough to jostle him aside.

Okay. That was *really* it.

Darian put on a burst of speed and shouldered past Coby in turn, minus the passive-aggressive shove, and walked in front of him all the way to the housing they'd been assigned. Not much to look at, just your basic small dorm. Still, his key worked on the front door and, down the hall, the quarters he and Coby would be sharing. God help them.

Which were not bad, actually. Darian's eyebrows went up as he took it in. Roomy enough for two grown men to move around in without knocking elbows, decent closets, a closed door that was likely a private toilet. Even a mini-kitchenette with a sink, a cabinet, and space above a micro-fridge for a coffee pot and an illegal hot plate.

And of course, twin beds shoved in opposite corners.

Darian wrinkled his nose at them. "You're not going to be able to fit in one of those. You'll dangle off from the shins down."

Coby shut the door behind them, and holy shit, Darian had not expected what happened then, nor had he noticed the near-total lack of airflow in there with the windows closed. His own Alpha scent wafted out in waves that completely failed to mask Coby's Omega scent. Gunpowder and pennyroyal. They shouldn't have gone together at all, but somehow they did and they gave Darian an immediate half hard-on that he was glad as all hell his loose shirt covered.

The Omega -- *no, don't call him that, he's more than his gender* -- Coby -- was looking at him now, boy howdy, his hawk eyes gone so wide that the whites showed around his irises. "You really are an Alpha. How?"

"You really want me to explain biology to you?"

Coby ignored that. "You don't look like an Alpha." He started to reach for Coby with one hand, then pulled back at the last second. Even so, Darian had the strangest sensation that he'd followed through. He could feel the warmth on his cheek. "You're still little, and still pretty, and -- look at *me*."

Darian resisted the urge to rub his cheek. "I don't look like an Alpha, and you don't look like an Omega, so aren't we an equal pair?"

"Equal," Coby scoffed. He wrapped his arms around himself again squeezing tight. "Do you know the kind of shit I went through when I didn't present, and when I did --"

"About the same kind of shit I did, I'd guess," Darian retorted. "And if you're going to have an attitude about it all summer --"

"Like you're one to talk!"

Darian sailed past that. Mostly because he was right. "*If* that's how you want to be, then I'm setting some ground rules." He ticked them off on his fingers. "If we can't get along, we keep our mouths shut when we're in the same room. No bringing anyone back here to fuck, and that includes me with Oscar -- yes, we do fuck sometimes, because neither of us is all that sold on the standard rules. Find somewhere else or it'll confuse everyone's nose."

Coby looked at him, shaking his head. "I didn't ask for this. Any of it. I didn't ask to be an Omega."

"Who the fuck does? I didn't."

"You didn't get it, either," Coby fired back. "And you know what? I don't need your help. I can take care of myself. I didn't ask to share with you."

"No, the resident director or whoever-the-fuck he is did, so if you have a problem you can take it up with him, mkay?" It wasn't that Darian didn't feel any sympathy or empathy for the guy. Turning out not to be what you'd always thought was hard, right? Which meant something else needed saying. He held up a finger. "One last rule. No bullshit embarrassment. We are what we are, and we can't change that. In here, neither of us has room to hide."

"And you'd be damned if you even wanted to try," Coby scoffed. He dropped his bags in a messy heap, a deliberate insult from an Omega. "So it's really easy for you to say, isn't it? I'm out of here. There's got to be somewhere else."

He stormed out, slamming the door with a bang behind him.

"Shit," Darian said aloud. He rubbed at his forehead. Well, *this* was going to be a fun summer, wasn't it?

And that right there was probably the understatement of the year.

* * *

Darian couldn't sleep.

Coby might have slammed out, but he'd sure as hell left his scent behind and it permeated everything -- by which Darian meant *everything*. His skin. His clothes. His hair. His fucking *boots*, for God's sake.

He took a shower.

He opened both windows and then the door to let a cross-breeze through.

He took another shower, then tossed everything he'd been wearing except the boots in the washing machines he found in the dorm's basement. Which, by the way, belonged in a horror movie set. Just saying. Spiderwebs everywhere and probably some kind of Gollum-like creatures cringing in the darker corners that he hadn't stuck around long enough to poke into.

No luck. The second Darian got back to his -- their -- room, the sweet smell still saturated every molecule of air. What was it made of, Velcro? Jesus.

So Darian shoved every last one of Coby's bags into the back of the closet, shut its door, and stuffed a towel against the bottom jamb.

He thought about taking a third shower, but he didn't have a lot of skin left that wasn't scrubbed almost raw except for one specific area. Because, come on. Darian wasn't a complete bastard. He might have stayed hard after Coby left and sure, he was an Alpha, but that didn't give him the right to beat his chest, howl like Tarzan, and whack off to whoever, whenever.

But… it wouldn't have been the first time he gave himself a hand to thoughts of Coby, either, though the shoe had usually been on the other foot. So to speak. The dick in the other ass, if you wanted to get specific.

Which Darian was trying *very hard not to do*, okay?

When he opened the dryer to find his laundry smelling like dryer sheets *and Omega*, he took a third shower that mostly consisted of standing under the spray, so mad at himself that he was steaming more than the hot water. He glowered down at his dick, which gave him a one-eyed glare right back as it refused to take the hint.

Darian made his bed, stuffed wads of Kleenex up his nose, and fell into it the first time he caught himself yawning. Sleep. Sleep was the frustrated Alpha's friend.

Which meant, of course, that he didn't get a wink.

When midnight passed and Coby still hadn't come back, Darian stopped tossing and turning, scrubbed a hand through his hair, and decided if working this out of his system would let him get some sleep, then fine. Fine!

"You win," he told his cock as he took it in hand. Under the covers. Just in case. "I hope you're happy."

His cock was, in fact, very happy with this development. Well, it was usually one of his favorite parts about being an Alpha: growing all the way up. He might be short in stature, but he had enough inches to inspire envy where it counted. Resigned if not philosophical about the situation, Darian cranked up his mental Wayback Machine until it hit on a few old favorites. Idly stroking himself, he flicked through the assortment until he found the one he wanted.

Not the one where he rode Coby like a cowboy on that old town road, no... Definitely not the first simple, almost sweet daydreams he'd had about them figuring out how all this worked together, though that tempted... And not the one where Coby plowed him from behind until he made Darian scream. That didn't fit his mood.

Ah. The one where they woke up together and didn't have to say a word. They knew where they were, who they were, and what they wanted. That'd work.

Darian settled down to business. He liked the slow, lazy strokes; maybe that was why he'd picked that particular fantasy. That and the way they were both confident in this scenario: when he rolled onto his back Coby followed, sliding on top of him. He bit kisses into the side of Darian's neck, and made noises of deep appreciation when Darian wrapped both legs around his waist -- but it didn't stop there. A few dips and teasing nudges, and then they were switching, tumbling around and over until Darian was on top instead. He had Coby's cock in his hand then, not his own, and he knew so well what he was doing that Coby arched and groaned beneath him at the first touch.

"You like that, don't you?" his dream self asked, rocking his hips light and easy. "Which do you want more? This cock or this ass?"

Dream-Coby pressed his hands to his face. "Fuck you, like I can choose?" He laughed breathlessly. "Oh fuck. I don't care, but whatever you do, don't stop."

Should he -- oh yes. Dream-Darian flexed his thigh muscles, knowing he was wet and ready, and used his grip to turn them over one more time. Dream beds were always big enough for any acrobatics, and when they landed he lifted up, guided Coby down, and took every Goddamn inch of him so deep inside they both lost their breath.

Dream-Coby couldn't choose, but he could sure act, and his cock was proportional to his size. Not Alpha-big -- huh -- but enough to satisfy anyone looking to get pounded. He took it slow, though, pinning Darian's hands over his head and giving it to him in slow, languid rolls that made Darian grip at his back and keen in sharp, steady gasps. Most Alphas didn't like getting penetrated, but Darian had a taste for it even now.

Why shouldn't he?

In his dream, Coby reached down to slide two fingers in beside his cock, stretching Darian even wider. He knew how to crook those fingers *just* right and how to curl them good and hard, how to turn Darian into a thrashing mess of a man who could only clutch at him, call his name as he tried to keep up, and -- burst --

In the real world, Darian arched up into his hand and came hard.

His breath had gone ragged after and stayed that way even after the sweat cooled and the fucking glorious mess he'd made was going sticky. He still shuddered with the occasional aftershock too, but no complaints there. He'd lost the Kleenex nose plugs somewhere along the way, but when he breathed in all he could smell and taste was raw Alpha. God. So much better. Now he could sleep, he could --

The door opened.

He could dig a hole to the center of the fucking earth, dive in, and pull the firmament closed above him, was what he could do.

"Darian?" Coby asked, quiet, as he stepped inside. "I -- oh." He came to an abrupt stop. "Oh."

Oh, and *oh fuck* too. Darian slammed his eyes shut and did his very best at pretending to be asleep. He muttered something under his breath that hopefully sounded sleep-addled and suitably pissed at being woken.

Now, it wasn't that he minded getting caught jerking off but as previously stated, well, it was personal this time, and for once in his life, he'd have to call what he felt *guilty*.

God, he hoped Coby fell for the *I was asleep* thing. Then he could tell himself what he smelled was from Darian having a wet dream or whatever. That was the kind of thing a guy could write off as just biology being biology all by itself, and if Coby did assume that he wouldn't tie himself into knots over what it meant.

Darian hoped, anyway. Coby still hadn't said anything, and he didn't dare look.

He shoved his head under his pillow and muttered again, then went still and slack as if he'd dozed off.

Good God, the *smell* in there now.

Though Darian couldn't see anything, he heard Coby stand still for a minute longer, then heard his quiet exhalation as loudly as if it'd been a tree falling in the forest. Heard the soft sounds of him toeing off his sneakers, then the softer *pad-pad-pad* of footfalls coming toward -- him. He held as still as he could when Coby hesitated once more beside his bed.

The brush of contact made him think at first that Coby had touched his hair, but no. A crinkling wrapper and the smell of chocolate, caramel, and peanuts suddenly on the pillow beside his head made him go red with -- some kind of feeling -- and pray it was too dark in there for Coby to see. He didn't have to look to know what that was.

A Snickers bar. Coby had gone and left him the present of a fucking Snickers bar, and Darian would be damned if he knew how to feel about that.

And not even that candy could blunt the *scent*.

Darian held still while Coby retreated, shuffled around until he found where Darian had stowed his gear, and shook out what sounded like a blanket and gave a pillow a few thumps. Soft noises would be him wrapping the blanket around himself, and creaking springs were him climbing into bed without bothering to get undressed.

He sighed again, and Darian dared to take a peek over his shoulder. Coby had lain down with his back turned to Darian, curled up loosely on his side. "I wish…" He swallowed. "I wish you hadn't done that."

So much for wishful thinking and shitty acting. Darian made a fist and thumped the bed beneath his own pillow. *Damn*!

Chapter Two

Oscar took a long drag off the vape pen he'd switched to -- something about fire codes. Darian didn't know, he hadn't been paying attention. *He* had a cigarette and if anyone wanted to get in his face about it, let them.

In case Darian hadn't been paying attention, Oscar blew the smoke in his direction. "So," he mused out loud. "You're sharing living space with an Omega about as fragile as a broken jar, quicker on the trigger than a cheapshit pistol, and jumpier than a rabbit on the freeway."

"Judas fuck, you want to throw some more metaphors in there?"

Oscar ignored him. "All of that, and your response is to go full chest-pounding Alphahole and beat your meat until the whole place stinks of jizz and ownership?"

"When you say it like that..." Darian rubbed his forehead with his unoccupied hand. All he needed right now was to set his hair on fire.

"Then it makes you sound like a jackass?"

"More or less," Darian muttered under his breath. "And he brought me a Snickers bar, for fuck's sake."

"What?"

"Long story. Makes no sense out of context."

"I'm going to be a literature teacher, dude. I dig analysis on the macro and micro levels. But whatever." Oscar shrugged and shifted back to facing forward, mirroring Darian, both of them contemplating the campus quad. He twirled his vape pen thoughtfully between two fingers. "He brought you a candy bar, tucked himself into bed like a lost puppy digging under some newspapers to stay warm, and delivered a line that would break the Grinch's heart."

Darian jabbed his cigarette in Oscar's direction. "One more metaphor or simile and I'm kicking your ass."

"You could try."

"But..." Darian shook his head. "Yeah. When I woke up I could smell the anger, it was so strong. And he was so out of there, again, he damn near left a vacuum trail behind him."

"Least something would have been doing some sucking."

"Be cruder. I invite you."

"You're one to talk." Oscar cocked his head sideways. "You want to blow off some steam? Make love, not war. By which I mean 'go get laid.' The sooner the better. I'll volunteer as tribute if I have to. Wouldn't be the worst way to spend a few hours."

Darian looked sharply sideways, but as far as he could tell Oscar wasn't joking. *Huh.* Like he'd said before it wouldn't be the first time they'd gone there, and if he couldn't get in a fight, fucking a fellow Alpha came almost close enough to do the same job. "No risk I'd get you pregnant," he mused.

"You think I'd let you top me? Please, bitch."

"I think I could make you want me to," Darian said absently. He thought he saw a familiar face at the far end of the quad, coming out of the library and down the overdramatic stairs leading up to its doors.

Not hard to discern, since the owner of that face stood a good six to eight inches taller than most everyone else, Alpha or otherwise. And --

"Whoa," Darian muttered, sitting up straighter to get a better look. That was a different side of Coby, right there. He held his head high. His shoulders were squared like a stack of bricks, his stride long, and his face forward. Darian would bet those hawk eyes of his were hard and cold. All different from how he'd been before and -- Darian couldn't deny it -- just about as hot as hell.

"Huh," Oscar muttered under his breath.

Darian ignored him, too busy watching Coby. He flinched every time he passed someone who caught his scent and stopped to give him a shocked and/or baffled face, but now Darian could see his hands were knotted into fists and he didn't slow down once.

"Moody bastard, isn't he?" Oscar asked. "Look at that. He's copying you."

"What?" Darian frowned at his friend. "He is not."

"Yes he is. That's the way you walk, like you're stomping on the necks of your enemies. Or grapes."

"You're so full of shit." Darian shook his head, but he couldn't stop watching. Oscar was right. Coby hadn't been one to stalk or bring his boots down that hard before, but he looked like a damn dire wolf hunting for the first throat he could rip open.

Coby caught his eye -- maybe he felt Darian staring -- and his fists curled into tighter knots. He looked away and stalked past without breaking his gait. Tough, moody bastard.

Darian kind of liked it. Even turned to watch him a little longer.

On the turn back, he frowned in confusion when what he saw was Oscar busily patting the grass. "What are you doing?"

"Making sure nothing caught on fire with all the flame in that gaze, 'cause I see how it is now. You want him." Oscar did Darian's pride the kindness of not turning his way as he delivered that punctuated, underlined, and italicized declaration. "You want to fuck him till you break the bed. I know you."

Darian growled under his breath, then mumbled, "Shut the fuck up."

"Guess us having a quickie is off the table." Oscar twirled his pen again. "Any idea what you're going to do about the whole thing?"

"That won't fuck it up worse than it already is? I don't know. And to be honest, I'm pretty sure we're not talking now. He's different than he used to be."

"Lots of things used to be different for both of you." Oscar shrugged. "What matters is what you do about them now."

Well, there was a thought. What *was* he going to do?

To be determined, Darian decided as he stubbed his cigarette out on his heel. But he would be giving it some thought. Bet.

Because Coby might have gotten a nose full of him last night, but he hadn't been the only one.

Darian had scented how much Coby wanted him too.

* * *

Or at least thinking had been the idea. Darian hadn't gotten through nearly enough by the time dinner hour rolled around, and he hadn't had a chance to pick up any food for the room. If he wanted to eat -- and Alphas had all kinds of appetites -- he'd have to take his chances on what the skeleton staff cafeteria crew had cobbled together.

Darian wrinkled his nose. Fifteen feet away and all he smelled was meatloaf with a vegan option, plus green beans boiled until they were gray. Possibly grilled cheese sandwiches somewhere under there, and Alphas automatically got double servings of everything -- which was some kind of bullshit prejudice against Omegas now Darian came to think about it. He might pick that battle as one to fight.

The wrapper on the now-melted Snickers bar Coby had given him crinkled in his pocket with every step he took. He patted it, just once, as he walked in.

He sniffed the air. *Huh.* Maybe it was from having too much Coby on his mind, or the smell of melted chocolate so close, but he'd called the menu partly wrong: not meatloaf, but spaghetti with or without meatballs. Definitely grilled cheese. Darian made a disgruntled face as he weighed up his options, but what the hell. Food was fuel. He'd live for one night. Besides, might be a good idea to carb up before he ran into Coby again.

Darian took his place in a straggling line leading up to the hot food counter, then raised an eyebrow. Speak of the devil and he would appear, because be damned if Coby wasn't there again, right at the front of the line. Head and shoulders above the rest and still pissed at the world.

Caught his interest, for sure.

What'd happened to change him so much? Aside from the obvious. Or... Darian cocked his head. Maybe that was all he'd needed. He remembered a few things Coby had had to say about the way his family viewed Omegas. Pretty likely he'd caught some serious hell ever since he presented a gender, especially if he'd done it later than most. Lots of pressure beforehand to Alpha up already, and then -- boom.

Yeah. Got Darian under the collar imagining what that must have been like, and Coby'd lived through it. *Then* add on top the fact that he *looked* like an Alpha, top to toe, but he had to deal with getting wet and opening up every time his cock thought about going hard. That'd fuck with anyone's head.

Huh. Darian patted his hand over the Snickers bar, mind whirring away. Not paying that much attention to Coby himself, which as it turned out was what could be called a mistake. He jerked back to the present when he heard Coby raise his voice at the guy dishing out tonight's processed proteins, and that was just out and out weird. Coby'd even been soft-spoken when he was angry with Darian. Yelling out of him sounded like he'd had to force it out, and it was so unnatural it made his throat raw.

"I've got an exemption." Coby waved a yellow pass in the air. "I need that many calories in a day to function, all right? And that's the minimum."

"Can't do it. Rules." The cafeteria worker -- maybe sixteen, seventeen, pimple-faced and probably zit-assed, a brand new Alpha and so damn full of himself that it was almost coming out his ears -- shrugged with a smirk. "Next."

Coby's face went bright red, but he didn't quit. "Surgeon General calorie guidelines for Omegas don't apply to me. They can't. I'm too big."

"Not yet. Unless you want to fix that." Zits looked Coby up and down with a leer that said exactly how he'd like to do the job. All he thought of Omegas, right there: good for nothing but fucking and babies, like Coby's family insisted.

Darian made some fists of his own. *How fucking dare* --

Okay. No. That wouldn't be allowed to stand. Lucky for him, Darian was an educator and he *liked* teaching lessons.

He put both hands in his pockets and swaggered forward to the front of the line. Cut in front of a dozen others, but nobody noticed given the high drama and tea spilling everywhere. Well, they could notice this, and he'd cross his hidden fingers Coby didn't sock him in the face for it.

Casual, easy as anything, Darian slung his arm around Coby's waist and stood, embarrassingly on tiptoe but whatever, to kiss his cheek. "Hey, babe. Thanks for saving me a place."

To underline the point, Darian sent a wave of Alpha pheromones billowing out that nobody with a nose could miss.

Coby stiffened, but so did Cafeteria Boy. *You smelled it right. I'm an Alpha, so chew on that.*

Darian cuddled Coby a little closer -- which should have felt weird, foreign, but didn't -- and ignored the little bitch behind the counter. "Anything worth eating tonight?"

Coby shivered at Darian's touch, and Darian could feel how much he struggled between jerking away and otherwise, but he took a deep breath and stayed put. "If they'd play by the rules, maybe."

"They're not fucking with your exemption thing again, are they? They all know they could get fired for that shit." Darian met the cafeteria worker's eye and held it. "Don't they?"

Swear to God, he'd never seen anyone dish up two portions of everything available quite so quickly. In to-go boxes, but while Darian wouldn't have minded keeping up that steady stare at the sexist asshole with every bite Coby would probably be better off out of the limelight. He let Coby take the heavy boxes and kept his arm around the man's waist. Pretty comfortable, actually. Long torso and low-slung hips on that man.

Some people, though, they didn't have the sense to know when to quit. Once he'd shoved the boxes into Coby's arms, the worker looked back and forth between them, sputtering verbal question marks. "But you're... he's..."

"He's an Omega. I'm an Alpha. Welcome to us, the freaks of the known universe, and just so you know you could get fired for questioning anyone's orientation whether or not it matches your idea of how the world should work too," Darian remarked, more amiably than he'd spoken since he was a toddler with a whole cookie to himself. If the stories were to be believed, not even then. "Broke your brain, did we? Tsk-tsk. However will I live with myself? I don't know, though, something tells me I'll manage. Just. Fine." He gave Coby's waist a squeeze, half warning and half -- who knew. Time to blow this popsicle stand in any case. "Let's get out of here."

He half expected Coby not to follow him. But Coby

did.

Then, he mostly expected Coby to shake off his arm once they were outside. Coby didn't.

He fully expected Coby to explode all over him. Coby didn't.

Coby kept his mouth shut, though his expression was so haunted it hurt to look at, and somehow Darian couldn't find the right words to ask him what was wrong. He did say, in case Coby needed to hear it, "I won't hurt you. You know that."

Coby nodded once, only once, but Darian would take what he could get.

"Okay then." He tugged Coby again, guiding him left, letting the big man set the pace, however fast or slow he wanted. "Let's go home. We've got some things that need talking out, you and me."

* * *

They made it almost two-thirds of the way back to their dorm in that uncertain state of truce and with Darian's arm settled around Coby's waist before Coby fidgeted for the first time and gave him a quick, sideways glance. "I…"

"You?" Darian asked, not looking back. It was kinder. He didn't need the pressure of being looked at when he was trying that hard.

Coby shook his head and took a few more steps in silence. Darian noticed for the first time how Coby had slowed his steps to match Darian's so that Darian didn't have to skip-run to keep up with those stork legs of his.

Huh. Way to prove his point.

"I… I think that's the first time since we've met you've gone five minutes without swearing. Or talking. It's kind of unsettling." Coby's throat worked as he swallowed around whatever he was feeling. "I don't… Look, you're not a freak."

Of all the things Darian had been expecting him to

say, that wasn't one. "I know I'm not."

"But you said --"

"To Zit Face? Yeah, I did, because that's the language he understood. I could've balls-out lectured him on gender bullshit for days, but it would've gone in one ear, through the gaping hole where his brain ought to be, and out the other side." Darian scrubbed at the back of his neck with his free hand. "There, I cussed. Happy?"

"I think I am. You're not you without a hair trigger and a filthy mouth."

Darian snorted quietly. "I am what I am. And that's not a freak. Neither are you, by the way. We're different. So the fuck what? Who gets to say what normal is anyhow? Anyone who tries can come have a word with me."

"I don't know who'd dare." Coby freed himself, ever so carefully -- or was it gently? -- from Darian's arm, but he didn't go far. He clutched the food boxes tight to his body and carried on walking side by side with him, though he kept looking forward instead of at Darian. "I was trying to be like you."

Son of a bitch. Oscar had called that one. "Why?"

"Why do you think?" Coby gave him a mildly dirty sideways look that transitioned to an eyeroll before he let out a long exhale. "I wanted to fight too. Not with you. I mean, mostly not with you. I -- my family, when they figured it out -- I tried to hide it, but you really can't --"

Darian held up one hand to stop him. "You don't need to tell me any of this."

"But I want to." Coby's jaw went hard, and he took the next few steps at a stomping stalk before swinging around to face Darian. "You know what it's like. You're the only one I ever knew who did, and that was before. Now? I'm not sure if I hate you for being what I can't, or if I want to be like you used to, or if I --" He stopped himself. "Either way, I don't know what to do, or even how. When I try to act like you, I'm not me, even if I don't understand me anymore. It's all so different, and I never thought I'd need to know so I didn't learn. What do I even do with this me that I am, now?"

Darian rocked on his heels, frowning at Coby. "All you should be is you. Fuck the rest. Let everyone else figure out how to deal with it; it's their problem, not yours."

"You're missing the point." Coby came closer, bending at the waist to get their faces closer together. "I can't do what you're telling me to, I -- I've been alone in all this. I'm still alone, and I don't know *how*."

Ahhh. Now things started to make sense. Darian touched his thumb to his lip, thinking fast.

Before he could speak, Coby had one more surprise for him. He stood up soldier-stiff and said, equally stiffly, "So I'm sorry. All right?"

"I beg your pardon, but what the fuck?" Darian blurted in surprise, and it hadn't been on purpose but there was this little flash of warmth inside when that made Coby almost-laugh. "No. Back up. Why are you apologizing to me?"

"For being a -- what did you call it back then -- an Alphahole?"

Sweet pitchforking hell. That *he'd* think he needed to apologize... Well, might as well take him off balance too. Keep 'em even. "And I'm sorry too." Darian could be the bigger man. So to speak. "For last night, and you know exactly what for, last night. You want to talk Alphahole behavior? There's your ground zero."

Coby almost laughed again, and even that made him light up from the inside. Made Darian's heart twinge in empathy, so much so that he sighed out loud. God, this Omega needed help, and Darian wasn't usually the one in this position, but he wasn't a monster. Usually. Except to people who deserved it, and Coby didn't.

He held out his hand, folded in a loose fist. Took Coby a second to get it, but when he did, he grinned and tapped an equally non-combat-ready fist against Darian's.

Felt good. Made the air seem clearer. Cleaner. Easier to breathe.

Darian took a deep draft of it and nodded at the takeout containers Coby had somehow managed to hang onto. Grease had leaked out, staining their sides, and if it'd smelled like the wrong kind of ass in there, age hadn't improved it. He gestured at it, wrinkling his nose. "Do you really want to eat that?"

"Oh God no."

"Good. Get rid of it, would you?" They'd reached the front door of their housing, propped open with the trash can that should have been sitting to one side. Darian watched Coby drop the boxes inside and grimaced at the *splat* they made. "Well, that's good riddance to bad rubbish."

"I guess. What do we do for dinner, though?" Coby's stomach rumbled right on cue, and he rubbed it.

Darian looked away, fast, because the spark of heat *that* inspired came from a place that wasn't anywhere his brain needed to go. No thank you, and also fuck you, sir. Or not, as the case might be, because they'd just finished tidying away all the Alphahole bullshit and --

"You like pizza?" he asked abruptly, leading the way inside. "I'm going to order pizza. It's supposed to be shitty and greasy and if we're going to share a dorm room on a fucking college campus we might as well embrace the cliché. All the meats, all the veggies, and extra sauce and cheese. The kind of pizza you need a shovel and a stack of napkins to take the first bite out of. Sound good?"

If Coby's stomach had rumbled before, now it roared. "Sounds amazing," he said fervently. He rummaged in his pocket for his keys and had their room open in a flash. With the windows left open all day, the only thing the place smelled of now was the things that got ingrained from years of being lived in: dust, old sweat, dirty sneakers. Coby loped across the small space, easier in his movements than Darian had seen him so far as an adult and opened the closet Darian had chucked all his things in the night before.

Darian grimaced. "About that."

"I'm the one who left his shit tossed everywhere." Coby looked at him in a way that was as different as his walk. A lot less angry, a little more shy, a fraction hopeful, and a bushel more genuine. And warmer, even if it was a candle's flame and not the sunshine somebody like him should fucking well have radiated. "It's okay. I'm not mad."

Talking to each other like human beings and not a weird Alpha and a don't-wannabe-an-Omega kept getting easier. So weird. "What are you looking for?" Darian asked instead of saying *thanks*.

And because Coby understood how to speak his language, if not his own native tongue yet, he grinned back as he unearthed a bottle of -- oh, hot damn. Tequila, the good stuff, with a worm floating in the bottom and everything. "I like a good cliché too. Got anything to drink it out of?"

"The bottle itself works for me." Darian took it when Coby passed it over and deftly unscrewed the cap. He took one gulp, then wiped his mouth on the back of his hand and the bottle's mouth on his sleeve. Passing it back over, he said, "You're not alone now, and you're not going to be again if I can help it. Deal?"

There went that smile again as Coby took the tequila back and gulped a mouthful for himself. "Deal."

He passed the bottle back.

He wasn't the only one who shivered, entirely without meaning to, when their fingers brushed.

Chapter Three

"Are you done?" Coby asked.

Darian glanced over, if not up, at Coby. They'd given up sitting on the edges of their beds pretty soon after the pizza arrived, mostly since they didn't want their sheets to look like a murder in a marinara factory. So they'd shifted from the bed to the floor, cross-legged in front of Coby's laptop loaded with every Call of Duty and a few weird-ass alien shoot 'em up games, beating the electronic shit out of each other between bites. Then, one bite past one too many, they'd slid to the floor and sprawled out like starfish who'd completely failed an attempt to sixty-nine.

Probably looked like idiots, but what the hell. Darian's pride could take the hit this once. Coby's cheeks were pink, the tension he carried in his shoulders had mostly melted away, and with all the calories a body like his needed to run packed in there doing their thing, he was damn near content enough to purr.

Looked good on him.

Fuck. Darian looked away, pretending to be fascinated with the pizza box resting on his chest. "Done with this? I'm wearing more than I've eaten at this point, so I'd better be." He flipped the lid closed. He made a disgusted face at the mess on his hands -- when he'd told the shop they wanted a train wreck of everything bad and good and delicious and filling on a crust, they'd taken him seriously. "Take this away before either of us hurts ourselves."

He tossed the box frisbee-style at Coby, who groaned but laughed as he caught it and sent it skidding bumpily across the floor toward the kitchen. "There. Away."

"Out of sight, but not mind."

"I know how to fix that." Coby flailed an arm around until he found the bottle of tequila, carefully capped when the pizza came and set aside for later and waved it at Darian. "Think you can fit some of this in there?"

"You think you want to watch me do a technicolor yawn?"

"A what, now?" Coby laughed harder, then rolled on his side and groaned through the laughter. "Oh God, don't, you're going to make *me* hurl now."

"Then lie down like a sane person and digest already, dipshit." Darian crooked his fingers. "And pass that bottle over here. I'll fucking well make room."

Coby shook his head, but his arms were long enough to stretch across the distance between them and shove the tequila at him. He dropped bonelessly to the floor afterward, stretching luxuriously and contentedly. "Don't say you didn't warn yourself."

"Yeah, I'll keep that in mind." Darian crossed his arms behind his head and kept his gaze tilted Coby's direction, sizing him up while the Omega was distracted. And that was fucked up right there. Coby wasn't just a gender, Goddamn it. Darian scowled at himself and that Alpha hindbrain of his that kept on beating its chest regardless.

But Coby *did* look better now. Less ragged, less raw, more like -- hell, like someone was looking out for him, taking care of him. Wasn't as hard as Darian had thought, on the very few occasions he'd idled the *maybe someday I might want to with someone* idea around. A little pizza, a little shooting the shit, a little booze.

Kind of fun. No, actually fun.

Weird as hell.

He liked it.

Darian eyed the tequila bottle thoughtfully. On a night like this with anyone else -- Oscar, say -- he'd have figured the hell with it and poured a shot. Or two. Or three. But that had been excellent pizza, messy or not, and he didn't want to bring it up for a second look, and who knew if Coby was a sympathetic puker? Then he'd have to start from scratch with getting some calories into the guy, and one carb banquet had already stretched his credit card to its breaking point.

But there were other options.

Putting the bottle aside, Darian patted his pockets until he found the vape pen he'd lifted from Oscar earlier, clicked it on, and took an analytical drag that he let out with a satisfied sound. Yup. So that was why Oscar was wearing his wiser-than-thou philosopher's hat earlier: boy had been baked like a cookie. What he had in there was so not tobacco based.

He could hear Coby sniffing. "Is that what I think it is?"

"Probably. Try it and find out." Darian figured out a way to eel himself around where he and Coby were mostly at the same head level, about one of his arm's lengths apart, and offered him the pen. "You ever had some of the good stuff before?"

"No. Is that what this is?" Coby took the pen between two fingers, looking dubious and wrinkling his nose. "It kind of smells like... it smells bad. Almost like boiling broccoli or skunk spray."

Darian snorted. "You haven't smoked much, have you? That's not skunky weed. That's the good shit, or at least it's the best a guy can find on short notice. Or steal."

"Huh." Coby had to figure out how the pen worked, but once he had it down he took a thoughtful drag and only coughed a couple of times. His eyes went wide and dazed. "Holy shit."

"Hell yeah." Darian stretched out his legs, pointing his toes. They'd lost their boots and sneakers, and while the floor was cold it felt good on his bare feet. "Smoke 'em if you've got 'em, boys. Good life tip."

"Preach."

"And pass it back."

Coby made a *sure, if you want* gesture and handed the pen over. Once again, his fingers brushed Darian's. Darian was ready for it this time and held himself still, but he couldn't miss what that little bit of contact did for Coby: he shivered, curled briefly in on himself, and his muscles quaked on the exhale.

Goddamn, that poor guy. How long had it been since anyone had touched him without him having to get all tense about what they wanted? Darian doubted his family would've gone near him after he presented Omega -- probably thought it was catching or some such stupid shit -- and anyone else would have been on the prowl, looking to get their dicks deep and wet.

Someone in the room was growling under their breath -- wait. Damn. It was him, and Coby had heard it too and was giving him the oddest look.

Way to prove he wasn't like other boys. Darian shrugged it off with an irritated jerk. *C'mon, be better than this.* "Why teaching?" he asked, grabbing a topic partly purely out of the blue and partly because he'd been curious. "I know why I wanted to be a teacher. I like showing people they don't know as much as they think, and how things actually are. But you?"

"You mean, since teachers are mostly Omegas, why did I want to go into this when I thought I was going to be an Alpha?" Coby asked frankly.

Darian raised one shoulder. *Since you put it that way...*

He watched Coby take the question seriously, lifting himself to rest his elbow on the floor and his chin in one hand, thinking. A comma of dark blond hair flipped down over his forehead, making Darian's fingertips itch to nudge it back into place.

He didn't. Last thing Coby needed was another horndog Alpha fixated as fuck on his ass even though --

fuck it, fine, Darian wasn't into lying to himself and he wanted his cock as deep in Coby as he could go, but that wasn't what Coby needed. He needed a *friend*, damn it, so all that gotta-fuck-gotta-fuck-gotta-fuck could go ahead and piss off, mkay?

Not that it'd be *easy*.

"I want to be a teacher *now* because I know, in my head, I'm not the only one like me," Coby said slowly. "Even if I feel that way most of the time. Not this minute, but..." He glanced almost shyly at Darian, quick-and-gone. "I *wanted* to teach Alphas they don't have to be animals and say 'oh, we were born this way, can't help it.'"

"You can do that either way. Walk into a room, and you're your own best example."

"Yeah. That's the hard part." Coby looked down, mouth twisted. "I still can't wrap my brain around most of it, and I've tried, Darian, I swear to you I've tried. It's nothing like... what was it like for you?" He cocked his head. "When you, uh..."

"Grew a few extra inches of dick overnight and my voice dropped about as many octaves?"

Coby chuckled. "I always liked the way you put things. No sugarcoating." His fingertips strayed slowly toward Darian until they touched the edge of his sleeve and stayed there, idly playing with the fabric. From there he drifted downward, tracing a pattern on the back of Darian's hand. "Tell me?"

Darian wasn't entirely sure he knew he was doing it. Problem was, whether he knew it or not, having him so close, his scent pooling in the shared air between them, was going to make the issue hard to avoid pretty soon.

Hard. Ha. Like that wasn't an issue already. Whatever happened to whiskey dick when you needed it? Did tequila not do the same thing?

"I think..." He looked up at the ceiling, gathering

his words. "I think it wasn't much like what you went through. I woke up, took a deep breath, and thought *oh. Okay, now it makes sense.* Then I went apeshit for a while, had the sense to find a friend who was willing to fuck me blind and stupid and back into my right mind, got my shit together, and then I was still the same old me again. Only now I knew why I'd always been like that."

Silence fell, broken only by the soft shushing noise of Coby's fingers moving lightly across his. Without his permission, Darian's hand flexed, and somehow Coby took that as permission to link them lightly together. He still looked so faraway, though. Darian couldn't *tell* and Coby's scent wasn't giving away much in the way of hints.

"Did you learn to control that?" Darian asked. "Most Omegas can't."

"Mm. Seemed safer. You're right. It wasn't like that for me. I woke up that first day..." Coby's eyelids fluttered shut and he swallowed hard. "I woke up wet. You know? I thought it was the dream I'd been having... it wasn't. I'd... opened. I reached down looking for those inches and I found this tight pocket between my balls and my ass instead, all puffy and swollen and --"

He shuddered to a stop, lip caught hard between his teeth -- and would you look at that, he didn't have perfect control over his scent. Memories of what that must have felt like damn near wafted out of his pores.

"I fucked myself on my own fingers," Coby said in a rush, eyes shut tight and cheeks red. "I came, and I fucked myself some more, and I came, and I came. I made the biggest mess, and I made the whole house stink like we were renting rooms by the hour."

Darian scowled. Yeah, he bet he knew who'd phrased it like that, and if he ever crossed paths with any member of Coby's family they were going to have some words nobody but him would enjoy. And by words, he meant punches being thrown, but whatever. Coby wasn't done yet.

God, Coby had started panting. Darian watched him, a little awed. What *did* that feel like, for an Omega? An Alpha wanted to give, give, give, but an Omega -- did they walk around with that kind of hunger gnawing at them all the time? Alphas could take the edge off with willing partners, but did Omegas dream, every night, of being fucked until they were satisfied? When they did fuck, was it enough?

He licked his lips. "And then?"

Coby dropped his head onto his forearm. He shifted his hips, trying to be subtle about it, but a man that big couldn't hide it when he'd gone hard. "Checked into a strip motel and fucked myself until I was coming dry. I put on a hoodie big enough to hide my face and went into a shop and bought some things, and they still weren't enough." His hips shifted, and the smell of Omega arousal grew stronger. "Nothing ever was."

It was already a hot night, but Darian's skin went warm and damp with sweat. He rested his hand on Coby's forearm to ground him. "Okay. That sucked."

Coby snorted. "Tell me about it."

"But it was different the first time you had an Alpha," Darian said. "That helped some, didn't it?"

Coby went very, very still, and very, very quiet.

Darian didn't get it at first. Every now and then he could be slow, and pizza/tequila/pot/being horny as hell didn't do his brain many favors. When he did, he jerked back before he could stop himself, because damn it, he could feel the sharp spike of embarrassment coming from Coby right away at that.

He wasn't. He couldn't be. A man who looked like *that*, Omega or not --

Not possible.

Darian opened his mouth to ask anyway and

caught himself barely a breath away from blurting it out like an asshole. He tapped one fingertip on Coby's forearm to get his attention, to let him know he might have been surprised, but for shit's sake, not judging. Who the fuck was he to judge?

But he did need to know this, because everything else that hadn't made sense before would now, if he was right.

"You've never been with anyone, have you?" Darian lifted himself on his elbow because he needed to look down at Coby and study him when he answered. "Open your eyes. Look at me. You've never had sex, have you? Real sex."

Coby shook his head. "Who'd want me?"

"Anybody with half a working brain," Darian snapped back. "I told you before. You're not a freak." He slid upward a few more inches to take Coby's chin in his hand, wanting that attention fixed good and firm on him. With the height difference between them that meant his leg came up too and slipped between Coby's, but he didn't pay it any real mind. "You. Are not. A freak. Maybe you don't believe yourself when you say that, but you'd better believe me. Get that?"

Coby's mouth had fallen open as Darian spoke, and Darian thought at first it was the speech. And maybe it was. In part.

But a small part.

Slowly, uncertainly -- and Darian had plenty of time to move out of the way, dumbass, he didn't know why he didn't -- Coby let his legs slide apart, easing Darian down into the cradle between them. His hand shook as he reached up to slide his fingers through Darian's hair, and the way he looked at Darian made Darian wish he'd been a better person.

He absolutely hadn't. He caught Coby's wrist and though he wasn't strong enough to move his arm out of the way, he could keep him from moving forward. "Don't."

Hurt flashed over Coby's face, but he came back quick. He was learning. "Why not?" He twisted his wrist free, not that Darian had been holding it all that hard and slid his fingers through Darian's hair. "I want --"

"Your hormones want. Big difference."

"Not from here." Coby licked his lips. For someone who hadn't managed to make eye contact less than a day before, he sure had a handle on it now. "I want you." He lifted one knee, bringing it between them and barely against Darian's crotch. Still shy, but not nearly as shy as would be smart, he flexed his thigh muscles just enough to hint at a ride. "You want me too."

"No shit I do. Doesn't mean it's a good idea."

"Why not? I told you, I don't know anything. But I want to *learn*." Coby rubbed his thumb behind Darian's ear, looking at him like he was special or some kind of shit. "I want you to teach me."

Darian leaned back out of Coby's touch and raked at his own hair, but too riveted to look away from him. Judas fuck, he was an Alpha's wet dream. Hot-blooded and hard and from the smell of him, easing open. Pink and willing and on the edge of begging for it. "You don't want me to teach you this."

"I do."

For fuck's sake. Darian grabbed both of Coby's wrists, squeezing hard this time. "Okay, why? Why me?"

"Because you know how to be true to yourself."

"Yeah. An Alpha."

"I know." Coby was winding him in, slowly, inch by inch, with those long arms; somehow, he'd ended up lying on his back again, but he'd brought Darian with him until Darian had to brace his forearms on the floor and they were nearly nose to nose. "You can't teach me how to be an Omega. But I can find out what it's like to be an Omega from someone who gives a damn. And..."

He lost his words then, shaking his head instead, pleading with Darian to understand.

The bitch of it was that Darian did. He closed his eyes, letting everything going on here play through his head. Coby wanted someone who could teach him how to be true to himself, and glad to be that way no matter what anyone else thought -- rough like him, or sweet like Coby was on the inside.

"Don't make me beg," Coby said, moving so that Darian settled between the cradle of his legs. "But if I have to, I will."

He would too. Darian couldn't answer that out loud, and did the only thing he could instead, the thing he'd wanted to since the day they'd fucking met if he was honest with himself: he brought their heads together, put his mouth to Coby's, and kissed him with everything he had. Kissed the hell out of him and didn't stop.

No turning back now for either of them.

* * *

Coby arched up, kissing back -- and fuck, he really was a virgin. Darian hadn't been kissed like that since before he'd met the guy, all uncertain slides and tentative tongue and zigging left when he should zig right. Clumsy as hell, and he knew it. He broke away, his face cherry red. "I told you I don't know what I'm doing."

"That's all right," Darian said. "I do."

Because he wanted to -- and now he was letting himself want, he *really* wanted to -- he kissed Coby again, teaching him like he'd promised this time. How to tilt his head, how to give way, when to push back. The way tongues should slide and stroke instead of blindly jab, the way teeth didn't have to crack against each other. How to go deep, and wet, and to copy what it felt like to fuck and be fucked.

God -- damn it. Darian'd had a purpose in mind

when he started this. He distinctly remembered that but
following through took more than he'd thought it would.
He waited for Coby to be good and out of breath before
he took hold of the man's wrists and held both hard,
jolting him out of the moment on purpose. "One of the
things I know is when to set some ground rules. That
happens first. Understand?"

Coby was strong enough to fight back, but there
were instincts there too, and he didn't. He let Darian pin
him and stared up with his eyes wide enough to see the
whites around those gold irises. "You didn't strike me as
the type."

Fuck, a man could drown in eyes like…

Darian shook it off. *Focus, damn it.*

"I'm whatever type I want to be when I want it.
There's things you need to know, and I need to know you
know." He made sure Coby was tracking before he went
on. "You and me, this isn't the usual. We've got history
and chemistry and matching hard-ons, but I'm not
looking to fall in love with anyone. What you're feeling
right now? That's hormones. Don't go thinking you're in
love with me. All right?"

Had to be said. Good sex, if you wanted it to be
good, had to come with hard truths sometimes.

Hurt flashed across his face, but Coby had enough
sense and sanity in left amidst all the endorphins that it
passed fast, and he moved his head to say okay, he got it,
they were on the same page. "And?"

Darian put a finger to Coby's lips. "And let me
finish. I'm only going to say this once, because my *God*."
He rolled his hips down to check and make sure he'd
assessed the situation correctly and had he ever. "Let me
tell you from someone who knows, you've got a monster
cock for an Omega and I'm seriously about to either drill
you through the damn floor or flip over and ask to get
drilled, so we've got a limited window here."

Coby groaned and matched his grind down with a roll up before he got control of himself. Except for hands that shook, he did his best statue impersonation -- if statues could go pulsing, soaking wet between their legs, anyway. "Don't say things like that."

"Not into that?"

"Fuck you, I didn't say that. I just don't want this to be over before it starts."

Hmm. That'd do nice things for any man's ego, but fair point. Darian had never really liked going to town on someone who'd already blown their load. Felt too much like making use of a sex doll to him.

Not that he had to worry too much about it with Coby, not when Coby was the type to grin at him, full of mischief, and who knew how to play. The quick bastard caught the finger Darian had put to his lips, drew it into his mouth to suckle on it, then bit.

Fuck, and while he was at it, *hot damn.*

Darian rolled his hips down again against Coby's groin -- seriously, any Omega or Alpha would have been proud of *that* kind of dick -- and yeah, they were setting a rhythm but it was good and slow, promising instead of delivering, and it kept them both hot without boiling over. Still, he tugged his finger loose and rapped Coby sharply on the nose. "Bad dog. Rule one: condoms. Both of us. Not negotiable. I'm not getting you pregnant."

Another flash of hurt -- instincts again -- was followed by a flicker of horror, and then wryness. "Oh God. Can you imagine?"

All too damn well, and that was the problem because what the *hell*, Darian was so not into the daddy thing unless he was on his knees for someone with a hairy chest and a leather crop.

Moving on. "Rule two: no strings. You want to learn, and I'll teach. We stay on good terms outside of this."

To his surprise, Coby shook his head. "Friends," he said. "We're friends. Call it what it is."

Darian wrangled that over inside his head. They didn't know each other well enough to be friends yet, but... that didn't make it not true. *What even*?

"Friends," he agreed. "Friends who do this when they want."

"Good." Coby's mouth curved up. He stretched out one long leg and hooked it over Darian's, lazy but with intent. He'd be an octopus lay, all miles of arms and legs and Darian was *very* there for that. "Friends who do this whenever, as in more than once?"

"As long as one of them isn't a pushy bottom from the jump and gives the teacher a chance to actually fucking *teach*." Darian drew his wet finger down Coby's chin, his throat, and his chest, down and down and down. "That's rule three. I lead, you follow."

Coby bit his lip, briefly uncertain. "If I can. If I'm okay with what you want."

"That right there? That was the right answer." Darian lifted Coby's chin. Confidence sat better on his face than doubt, and that was all part of the lesson plan. "Whenever you can't follow, you say 'no' or 'stop' or 'I'll fucking twist your nuts off if you don't quit it.'"

Coby covered his face, laughing too hard to even think about developing a case of nerves now. "Oh my God. Okay. Fine."

"Good." Darian kissed him again, because some temptations *weren't* made to be resisted and Coby had the sweetest mouth now he was learning how to use it. "Lie still."

"What --"

"Shush." Darian lifted Coby's hands above his head, wrists together, and pressed down. "Keep them there, out of the playing field."

"Why?"

"Pushy question-asking bottom. Because I need room to work." Darian studied Coby's shirt, gave it a good sharp tug, and grinned fiercely when it ripped at the collar. Cheap cotton, easy to shred threads on once he'd gotten it started, and he parted that motherfucker like the Red Sea with his hands and his teeth, letting it come apart and fall at Coby's sides.

Now *that* was a stare of awe that he'd fucking *earned*. Coby lifted his hands carefully and put them at Darian's hips, a hard flex of his fingers the only clue -- besides his silence -- that he'd gotten too turned on to speak.

Excellent.

But that begged the question... *Where to start*? Coby had a hell of a lot of real estate to explore on him, and Darian hadn't been with someone so much taller and broader before. Made him feel like a wildcat stuck on a redwood branch -- and good God, a man could hope that'd happen in the next round or two, anyway. Darian bent his head to press his nose to the soft spot under Coby's jaw and breathed in deep, thoroughly satisfied when Coby gave a helpless grunt and jerked up.

Scent. That was what he wanted. What Coby would want too. "Breathe me in," he said, pushing himself back and down inch by inch, scenting everywhere he went. Muskier at the pits, but good musk overlaid with a hint of soap. Darian had to taste that, no choice about it, and flickered the tip of his tongue wherever he wanted to put his tongue -- first, second, didn't matter. Coby lay beneath him, but he couldn't stop moving his hips and it made the way he smelled even more lush. Darian could have gotten drunk off it, for fuck's sake.

But he'd better watch that and keep his head in the game. He'd gotten his dick wet plenty of times, but he'd never broken in a virgin before. Losing his own V-card had been so damn awkward he'd done his best to block it out of his memory and he wanted to give Coby a better experience.

Why? Be-fucking-cause, that was why.

Darian nosed and nuzzled his way down, but deliberately didn't make contact with anything between waist and thigh. He got plenty of scent, especially when he and Coby wrestled his jeans down and out of the way. Coby kicked them off, putting those miles of leg to good use. Darian took in as deep a breath as he could and held it, savored it.

At first. But when he spread Coby's legs open, his face good and in the crux of his thigh to get a deeper breath still, a glossy trail of Omega slickness slid down his skin and landed on Darian's tongue. He swallowed, and -- *fuck*. Either he'd been with some shitty lays before or he'd had a few fakers, because tasting *that* damn near made his brain explode. Bursts of color filled his vision like reverse fireworks.

Holy *shit*. Nope, no turning back now, Darian had to have a taste of everything. He raised himself on his elbows and put his mouth over the bulging head of Coby's cock to suck hard as he could.

Coby arched up with a cry that made Darian think he'd come, but he wrenched himself back at the last second and panted himself back down.

One word made it out through his ragged breathing: "More."

Toppy for someone who wanted to take it, but did Darian care? Hell no. He was busy being too breathless himself to object, and far too damn hard to protest. He'd believe Coby hadn't been with anyone before, it fit his nature, but there *was* such a thing as natural talent. If he could rev up the engines like this now, what would he be like with some practice?

Darian might not survive that, but it might be worth it.

And -- yes. More, all of the more. He shredded open Coby's jockeys the same way he had the man's shirt and got rid of *his* jeans while he was at it. Shorts could go as well, those wouldn't be needed, and for good fucking measure his shirt too. They'd lost their socks and shoes somewhere between the tequila and the pizza, getting comfortable, and there wasn't anything left between them now but sweat, Omega slick, and a matching case of *need-to-fuck-right-now-now-now*.

They were so close and Coby so wet that Darian really couldn't have stopped it. His cock slid down into Coby's cleft, not inside but kissing those hidden lips, rubbing at them and bumping the soft-swollen-open rim. Coby bowed up, arms and legs winding around Darian to clutch him tight. Exactly as Darian had wanted. He pulled back, and best believe that took some effort, and curled his fists against Coby's chest. Lightly, he scratched faint marks down Coby's chest. "You good?"

Coby let go to press a hand to his forehead. "Good. So good. Condom. Now."

"Hurry, hurry, hurry," Darian chided -- like he was any better off. He genuinely couldn't stop moving once he forgot to distract himself, and he'd slide right in if he wasn't careful. No one could have held back for long. Omega bodies were made that way on the regular, and when they were aroused they were like magnets with how they drew an Alpha in. "Fuck. Where did I --"

"God, tell me you have some. I don't."

"I'm an Alpha, I always carry at least one." Darian reached for his jeans, dug through the pockets until he found his wallet and *aha*, there it was, a foil square so new it still had a shine on the wrapper. He held it up between two fingers, considered, then decided it was Coby's turn to have a little fun. More fun. He dropped the foil packet on Coby's chest and sat back with everything on display, loving the way Coby's pupils dilated until there was barely a rim of gold left to see. "Well?"

Coby swallowed so hard Darian could tell his mouth had started watering, and pulses of slick washed out of him at about the right speed of a heartbeat. They'd have to hose down the damn floor after this but nope, still didn't care about anything else.

His hands shook as he tore the packet open -- inexperience showed there too but Darian wrestled his patience into the forefront and waited, letting him learn until he got the thing unrolled and, clumsily in a way that made it even better somehow, rolled it down the length of Darian's dick. "Monster dick yourself," he rasped when he let go. Then, he bit his lip again. "Don't laugh."

Like he could, but Darian shrugged anyway. "Why?"

"Oh God." Coby's face went redder still under the sex flush. He touched Darian with one tentative finger, jerking back when Darian jolted at his touch. "How -- how does it fit?"

Darian smoothed his hair back and kissed him one more time. *Mmm.* "Baby, your body knows the answer. You lie back and let it happen. Or get in the game and help make it happen. Two guesses which one I like better."

There went Coby's grin again, and Darian resigned himself to that being an addiction already. "Same one I think I like."

Good bravado. Darian would have applauded it and probably would later, but -- performance reviews: later. Getting inside Coby: now. "You ready?"

He was, and he wasn't. Scared out of his mind and desperate at the same time, but still brave. Coby nodded, put his arms around Darian's shoulder and let his legs fall apart wide enough to give Darian all the room he needed. "Ready."

Darian made himself move steadily. He positioned

himself right where he wanted to be, flush against that wet opening, and nudged. "Getting started feels weird, the first time. Hold on and breathe. I promise you it gets better."

Slowly as he could, careful as he never had been before, he eased his way inside. Coby grunted and squeezed his eyes and his fists tight shut, but that was natural, that was what it felt like to have someone inside for the first time. Darian went slow, letting Coby adjust, little push by little push until there was nowhere else to go.

Coby's fists dug into the meat of Darian's back, and those would be some pretty, pretty bruises later. He panted, almost sobbing, more so when Darian kissed him every-damn-where he could reach because he *had* to have his mouth on the man. To soothe him too, let him go from too full and tight to slippery-smooth and accommodating.

He unclenched as slowly as Darian had slid in, and in waves that coated them both. Darian bit down on one of Coby's nipples, surprised and pleased when that made Coby moan and squeeze around him. He slowed from panting to gasping, his gaze wild and dazed and high on adrenaline. Though his mouth moved, no words came out -- but that didn't matter. Darian could just about read the man's mind from the look on his face and the movements of his body: *I didn't know it would be like this. I didn't know I wanted it this much. Don't stop.*

Darian took Coby's hand, kissed every finger without thinking about it, and moved. Started slow, like before, each stroke a long drag in and out.

"Don't try to be gentle," Coby said one word at a time, between breaths. "It's not you."

"Want it to be good for you."

"Already is. I think -- better if it's harder." Coby brought his thighs up to cradle and clutch Darian's hips. "Fuck me like you mean it."

So help him. Darian did. Deeper, faster, harder. All the brainpower he had left melted out of his ears. The only thing he could concentrate on was how it felt to be inside this man. The way Coby reacted, so Goddamn responsive with wild clutches at him and nails scoring his skin. The heat of Coby's rapid breathing and the pounding of his heart.

When he started to make desperate noises and his cock throbbed where it was trapped between them, Darian had enough thinking brain left in him to recognize what that meant. He didn't stop fucking, couldn't have even if he'd wanted to, but he *could* take hold of Coby's cock and pump it in time with his pushes inside. "Come on," he muttered, over and over. "You can do it, you're doing so fucking good at this, come on, damn it, let yourself go and *come.*"

Coby's back left the floor, only his shoulder blades bracing him there, and bucked like a wild thing. Hot fluid flooded them front and back, and with one more deep, deep, deep shove, Darian let go too. Coby's startled gasp at what *that* felt like brought him over a second time, which was a whole new kind of treat, and he stayed right where he was until he'd finished.

Beneath him, Coby shuddered and shook as if battered by a strong southerly wind, but his lips were parted in pure blissed-out satiation until they softened into a disbelieving smile. "I didn't know," he said, out loud this time. "I didn't know."

Darian rolled his forehead against Coby's chest. "Mmf."

Slowly, Coby ran his fingers through Darian's hair. "Is it like that? Every time?"

Nope. It absolutely wasn't like that. Darian didn't say it and didn't know if Coby could see it written all over him as he propped himself on his elbows, slid out -- carefully, that condom was damned full -- and indulged in one more deep, wet kiss that was the only answer he'd give.

Coby didn't seem to mind. Nor did he realize, Darian thought, exactly how much trouble they were getting themselves into.

He should have been worried about that, himself. It'd be sane. It'd be savvy.

Yeah. He'd never been good at either of those.

Chapter Four

A wise man, who might or might not have been himself, had remarked to Darian that there was nothing better than going to bed with a hot piece of ass.

Yeah, he was one crude motherfucker, but he'd been right so far.

Darian woke up the way he usually did, taking one blink to figure out where the fuck he was and what he'd gotten up to, then all engines roaring. Looked like a nice morning out there. He glanced down. *Nice* morning wood too, and no wonder. His memory got a little fuzzy after finding a second condom in the bottom of his duffel, a second fuck, and the third and fourth round of tequila. He *thought* he remembered himself and Coby passing out right there on the floor in a tangle of arms and legs and all kinds of sticky things. Sometime during the night they'd rolled apart, leaving six inches of separation between himself and the big Omega.

Well. Technically no separation at all, given the morning wood thing and the space it took up. A little weird to wake up in the same place he'd been the night before -- Darian wasn't one for making a whole night out of one-night-stands -- but he could get used to it. He indulged in a good long up and down look at Coby. Mmm. Ass as fine as he remembered, and all those miles of torso and legs. As if he sensed Darian's gaze, Coby twitched once and took a startled breath. If he wasn't all the way awake yet, he was getting there fast.

And that gave Darian all kinds of ideas. No sense wasting a good hard-on, after all, not if you had something better to do with it than jerk off.

A little scoot nudged him close enough to snug his cock up good and firm against that sweet ass, and *now* Coby was awake if that deep grunt of shocked arousal was anything to go by. "Hey, baby," Darian said with his mouth at Coby's shoulder. He bit down barely enough for

Coby to feel it and liked the way it made him shiver. Snaking one arm around the man's middle, he slid his hand down to take hold of a hard-on as good as any Alpha's. "Turn around, gorgeous. Want to wake you up all the way with my mouth on your cock."

The rest of Coby went stiff. He held his breath -- Darian felt his chest stop rising and falling -- then shoved Darian's hand out of the way and went still again, pretending pretty badly to still be asleep after all.

You didn't get a much clearer *no fucking way* than that. Darian stared at him, too nonplussed to react. Well, damn.

There really wasn't anything better than going to bed with a hot piece of ass, but then there was the flip side: there was nothing worse than waking up with a cold shoulder turned your way.

Fuck. Darian folded his arms behind his head and stared at the ceiling. Some dickbrain had stuck a wad of gum up there, and a dozen graphite streaks around the pencil stuck in the middle told a whole story about how bored someone had been the last time it got noticed.

"You know, if somebody that I'd fucked blind and stupid last night was lying there pretending to be asleep when he knew damn well I was awake, I'd get annoyed," Darian remarked, calm as if he'd said *hmm, looks like rain later* instead. "If I'd tried to go down on him and discovered he'd turned into an Alphaphobe overnight, I'd be pissed."

There, *that* got a reaction. Coby jerked up, looking hard at him over his shoulder. "We don't have any more condoms, and I'm not an -- what you said."

"No? 'Cause I've got to tell you, that's not the usual reaction to what I was offering."

"It's not…" Coby fidgeted until he worked himself upright and slumped, hands between his knees and head low. "I don't feel like I thought I would. I mean, I did it, right? I got through it."

Whoa. Whoa. And also, what the *fuck*? Darian sat up too, indignation lighting his darker fires. "Okay, you better not have said what I think you said. 'Did it'? 'Got through it'? Like, what, I'm some mountain you had to climb or a bridge you had to jump off? Goddamn, man, thanks for the memories."

Darian pushed himself to his feet -- it was his turn to storm out anyway -- but Coby caught him by the ankle before he could make a getaway. "No! That's not what I meant."

The sincerity on him was almost painful to watch, and it made Darian slow his roll despite himself.

Not enough to damp down his temper, though. "Okay, fine. What did you mean? Try again. Use small words."

"Don't be like that. You know I don't think you're stupid. *Fuck*. I'm the stupid one." Coby's head lowered, but -- huh -- he didn't let go of Darian's ankle. His thumb rubbed at the bone there before he looked back up. "It wasn't what I thought -- no, let me start again. I'm not what I thought I would be, after. I wanted to be -- not me, and you were there, and -- God! Shouldn't it have been -- it should have made me different. Shouldn't it?"

Oh, for the love of *hell*. "You thought your first time fucking an Alpha would turn you into a Stepford Omega?" Darian asked incredulously. "You wanted that? And is that why you picked me? Convenience? Nearest one on hand to get the job done, and now that you did, you're over it?"

Coby's eyes narrowed. "If I said none of that was true, would you believe me?"

He would, yeah, and that pissed Darian off even more. Tugging his ankle free, he glowered at Coby. "All you had to do was ask, you fucker. I'd have told you. Sex doesn't make you all growed up. It just gets you laid."

"And that's what you wanted."

"I" -- Darian clamped *his* mouth shut because Goddamnit, he was starting to be unable to escape an awareness that that wasn't all he wanted and --"I could have told you sex is sex is sex and what it does to you, that's up to you. There's no Goddamn rules about fucking and no magic wands unless you really like the dick. And you want to talk about different? Shit, that was my first time with a virgin!"

Coby stared at him for a full count of five, jaw dropped. "What?"

Oh *hell*. He hadn't meant to say that. Now Coby would think it'd been a pity fuck or worse. Darian clamped his jaw shut and crossed his arms.

"I'm sorry, what?" Coby hauled himself to his feet, and good God, could that man loom when he wanted to. "Was that why you wanted it? You wanted to be the first one in there? Put your stamp on my ass?"

Yup. He'd thought "worse." Darian threw his hands up. "Oh fuck no, you're still the one not getting me and you know what? You're doing it on purpose, smacking me back."

"Oh my *God*, you are the most --"

"Yeah, and I knew you'd be that way!"

They were facing each other now, glare to glare, jabbing fingers, shoving each other knuckles first. "If you knew what would happen, why did you even bother?" Coby demanded.

Maybe it was the frustration, maybe it was the things Darian kept trying to stomp down finally breaking through, but he shouted, "Because you're worth it, you fucking moron!"

Coby's mouth opened and shut before his face went red with fury. "And you didn't even --"

A knock on the door cut him off halfway through what promised to be one hell of a fiery rant. Darian and he swung their heads around in tandem to find Oscar standing in the doorway -- shit, they'd left it unlocked, hadn't they?

Oscar jingled the change in his pocket, head cocked slightly. Oh yeah, he'd heard all of that. Darian didn't even need to ask. "Bad time?" he asked, too nonchalant to fool any of them. "I came to get my vape back and ask if you two wanted breakfast."

Coby's stomach roared, right on cue. So did Darian's.

Okay, fine. He wanted to tag all kind of Alpha bullshit on Darian? Fine. Darian'd give him something to really work with. Grabbing Coby by the wrist, he hauled the big man stumbling forward. "Let's go."

"Sure." Oscar shrugged. "Might want to put some clothes on first, though. And shower."

Coby went embarrassed pink as Darian clapped a hand over his face.

Oh yeah. This was going to be one hell of a day, and it'd barely even started. Who knew where it'd go from here?

* * *

Oscar, like Darian, wasn't a total asshole when he didn't want to be. By the time Darian and Coby had showered, separately and thank you very much, and made it out to the grassy quad, glaring at each other and anyone who happened to get in their way, Oscar had parked his ass under a tree with a cigarette in one hand and two giant bags of fast food kept safe from poachers between his boots. He gestured at those, then at the grass.

Coby shifted glances between the food, Darian, and Oscar, but the near-constant growling of his stomach won the fight there. He collapsed into a completely graceless heap of legs and grabbed one of the bags. Barely waiting to get the wrapper off a sausage biscuit, he shoved half of it into his mouth.

Darian shook his head at Oscar in warning, who shrugged. He took a long, long drag of delicious carcinogens and let it out in a streaming plume of smoke. "I ate on the way back, but there's burritos in there for you," he said to Darian. "Eat. You're not yourself when you're hungry."

Fucking bastard, he *knew* that was the Snickers tag line.

Darian curled his lip at Oscar, who smirked back at him, but now that it'd been mentioned he could smell those tortillas. They'd been stuffed with eggs and bacon and peppers hot enough to melt his face off and fuck it, he needed fuel too. He sat, deliberately graceful, and dug through his bag for his share.

For a few minutes, they chewed and swallowed ferociously, sinking their teeth into bread and meat like it was the chunks of flesh they'd wanted to bite out of each other. When Coby's stomach finally chilled the fuck out and he slowed down enough to tear bites from his fourth sandwich instead of damn near swallowing it whole, Oscar cleared his throat.

"I'd have won that bet," he said.

In tandem -- and what the fuck was up with that, seriously -- Darian and Coby showed him their middle fingers.

One good thing about Oscar, besides his willingness to shell out a small fortune on fast food, was how little of a damn he gave about that kind of thing. He snorted and kicked lightly at Darian with one boot heel.

But then, he got evil.

"Missed you last night," he said, lighting a second cigarette with the cherry of his first and stubbing that one out. "Thought you and I had plans."

Darian frowned. "The fuck are you talking about?"

"Fucking," Oscar said, still mild.

Oh shit. "Motherfucker, I will kick your ass,"

Darian warned. "Stop trying to stir the pot. You know damn well what's going on and unless I am sadly fucking mistaken I didn't ask for your help."

"Wait. You were going to hook up with him?" Coby looked half appalled, half dismayed.

"He was," Oscar said. "What? I offered, I assumed Darian accepted. I waited for you. Cleaned up and out and everything and there you left me, sitting all alone like an ugly boy on prom night. Makes a man feel un-damn-appreciated. I've gotten fucked by some good ones, but I had *ideas*, man. Eating you out, for a start." To Coby, he added, "You ever have someone eat your ass? He could give lessons, damn. Or get someone to finger-bang you while he sucks your cock? I have. A few times, but this one here, he's top tier."

"I will kill you," Darian said. "Kill you with my bare hands."

If Oscar heard him, he didn't let on. He had all his attention fixed on Coby. "I mean, you're an Omega. It's probably different for you. Who'd want a briefcase bomb like him? You need someone gentle. Sweet, maybe. Someone who'll treat you like you're precious." He gave Coby a lascivious once-over. "You want a taste of this, I'm still worked up, and you need a good claiming."

Coby's hands knotted into fists so tight the knuckles went white, and his glare could have set the whole campus on fire. That son of a bitch was goading him, wasn't he? Darian realized.

Seriously. *Kill him.*

"But then again, who knows. Maybe you like being the way you are, with all that sexual tension boiling underneath. You two were too busy fighting last night? Or, you know, screwing like rabbits? Like I said, I'd have won that bet. That whole dorm stank like sex."

Coby covered his face with both hands. "Oh my God," he said behind them, muffled. Darian winced with embarrassment on his behalf. Virgin that he'd been, he probably didn't realize others could smell what they'd been up to.

Oscar continued as if he'd never been interrupted, gazing thoughtfully at his cigarette ember. "I'd have won a bet that you'd fuck it up as soon as you could too. Stubborn bastards, both of you. After you've finished stuffing your faces on my dime, maybe try talking to each other instead of shouting. Works better."

"Nope. No. Not doing this."

Coby unfolded and stalked away. Even left his unfinished biscuit behind, but the back of his neck was as red as a sunset and he shudder-stumbled with a hitch of breath every few steps. No man who didn't have the most inconvenient boner of his life moved that way, and Coby confirmed as much with a quick glance over his shoulder before turning back.

"Damn." Oscar whistled. "How good *was* the sex?"

Darian calmly, slowly, reached out and put one hand around Oscar's throat.

Oscar knocked it easily away. "Like you would, dog. You're all bark and dick."

"I can change if I want," Darian growled. "What the fuck did you do that for? He was pissed off enough before. I'll be lucky if he hasn't moved all his shit out of the room before I get back."

"Will he?" Oscar took the last drag off his cigarette and let it fall where it could keep burning until it reached the filter and the dirt. "You want him. I can smell it. Judas fuck, man. Why'd I do that? So he'd figure out how much he wanted you too, even after whatever happened. Anyone could see that if they weren't being stupid on purpose. Sound familiar?" He knocked Darian upside the head, very much not gently. "Stop being stupid. That Omega's mad as hell at the thought of anyone even talking about having you."

Darian stared at him, struck dumb for the second time in one morning.

"I swear I can hear you thinking, *what do I do*?" Oscar snorted. "Go after him, dipshit. See what happens next." His grin went evil again. "Or are you chicken?"

Darian punched him in the ribs, hard enough to knock him sideways.

"Yeah," Oscar said from down in the dirt. "That's what I thought. And it was worth it."

* * *

So there were a few things he could do in response to that. There were always choices. Darian thought about getting right back on that train, drop-off to hell be damned, and hauling ass back where he'd come from where things were slightly more sane. Thought about going to the housing office and asking for another room ASAP. An Alpha changing his mind about rooming with an Omega? Nobody'd ask questions, not even Nutcracker Jaw. He spent the longest time wondering if he could pull off going back and pretending nothing had ever happened, not even the sex, and spending the rest of the session ignoring Coby until Coby did the same thing.

In the end, Darian did what he'd known he would all along, really. He went back to their shared rooms with all his sleeves rolled up, mind and body, ready to throw down however he needed to.

Not that he knew -- still -- what exactly he was fighting for. Just that he needed to fight for it.

The trick would be how Coby felt about it all. With his hand on the doorknob, Darian paused long enough to shake his head. Who even was he now, and what even was his life? *Fuck.*

He could taste Coby's scent right through the door. He was in there.

Darian squared his shoulders and turned the knob.

Coby sat on his bed, pretty much the way Darian

had figured he would -- but not with his back turned. He'd perched himself in profile, where he could keep an eye on the door, and rested his chin on his hand as he watched Darian walk in. "Hi."

Darian eyed him. Hard to tell what he was thinking, from the look on his face. Definitely wasn't playing to his strengths and it sure hadn't worked before, but he might want to tread carefully. He grimaced at the thought, then waved off Coby's worried glance. "Random thought. Not related."

Coby scoffed quietly. "Until now, I never believed all that about being able to smell lies."

Super. "Fine. Not unrelated. Still random. Mostly."

Coby cocked his head as if curious, then made an *okay, that tracks* face. Then it was straight back to neutral with almost concealed worry lingering in his eyes.

Darian shoved his hands in his pockets, but so help him, he couldn't hold it in. "All I want to do right now is kiss you. Push you down and fuck you harder than I did last night. Just so you know."

Coby's lips parted. He licked them and nodded once, very carefully. "But first."

Yeah. "First," Darian said, resigned.

"You need to understand, Darian. I fought like that with my family all the time. Not about sex! I mean."

"Jesus, I'd sure hope not." Darian sat on the edge of his bed, directly across from Coby, and rested his elbows on his knees. "You mean you fought about stupid shit instead of…" He winced again. "Talking about it."

"You know you make 'talk about it' sound like 'deliberately trying to catch gonorrhea,' right?"

Catching feelings, catching STDs, what was the diff… okay, there was plenty of difference. Darian spread his hands, palms up, and shrugged. "I'm trying."

"Yeah." Coby looked down, biting at his lip. "This is all so weird. Can you listen for a while?" His mouth crooked in a hint of a smile. "I mean, you might rupture something from not talking for a few minutes, but if you could give it a shot."

What Darian gave him was a rude gesture, but he settled back and indicated, *go ahead*.

Coby took his sweet time about it, drawing in a few deep breaths and moving his lips as if sorting through ways to put it and discarding them one after another, then finally gave a frustrated growl and went for it. He looked up at Darian, hawk eyes so fiercely locked on his that Darian damned near lost his breath -- not from being taken aback, but with a shock of pride in Coby's newly rediscovered backbone that rocked him from brain to dick and took a return trip all the way up. "Are you listening?"

Darian nodded.

"I didn't explain myself well this morning, and then you made it worse by pissing me off. Emotional STDs or not, if we're going to make this work, whatever it is, we can't throw words at each other like they're knives and expect no one's going to end up bleeding."

Darian blinked. "Damn. Shit, sorry, still trying."

Coby shook his head, but like he was doing his best not to laugh, before he went on. "I need to know something. Did you set all that up with Oscar on purpose?"

"I don't understand."

"Did you try to make me jealous, I mean." Coby held his arms open at his sides. "Did you know I would be?"

"No," Darian said. No hesitation. "You can smell that that's the truth."

"Yeah." Coby rubbed his knuckles against his chin. "I didn't consciously know myself until it happened. But -- I was. I am. Is that part of the whole Omega thing? You didn't stamp yourself on me, but *I* stamped you on me?

You learned a lot about the ways Omegas work. I didn't, and I still don't get most of it."

"There's... not a lot to get, aside from the obvious, and what happened last night. I don't know most of it myself. I mean, you could have done that."

There went those hawk eyes again. "If I had, would you mind?"

And there went Darian's breath too. He hesitated, knowing if he went too long that smell or not anything he said would sound like a lie, and hell, he had to go for it too. "No," he said. "I wouldn't. And I don't know that I didn't stamp myself on you either. I didn't plan on it. Fuck knows I didn't."

"But it happened," Coby said. "I didn't know it was going to be like that, Darian. Like the second I let myself think *I want him* I was -- gagging for it. I would have gone down on my knees if you'd pointed at the floor and said 'heel.'"

"Holy *shit*, don't say things like that if you don't want them to happen." Darian pressed a hand to his groin, because he wasn't lying about that either. "Fuck, Coby. You don't pull your punches sometimes, do you?"

Coby really laughed this time. "No promises, but what do I have to lose?"

Well, fair point. Darian gestured at him, asking him to go on.

"As long as you remember you asked for it." Coby shivered like a man on the very finest edge of coming. "I felt like I was going to die if I didn't get your cock inside me, and when you did -- I mean, part of me still doesn't believe it really happened, but, Darian, I can still feel you inside me, and all *I* want is for you to knock me down and blow my fucking back out."

"Oh my *God*."

"And so you know, you said 'don't say things like that if you don't want them to happen.' But I do."

"You are two words away from the deepest dicking of your young life, dude."

"Yeah. I know." Coby sobered. "But I need to know this too. I think it's an Omega thing neither of us knows much about it, but it keeps beating at my head and I have to at least ask. This thing -- is it going to last?"

"I don't know. I've never been there before. Didn't know I would now. I'm kind of an asshole. I could change my mind tomorrow. Or you could, yourself."

"Maybe," Coby mused to himself. "Maybe not. I guess we find out. That's the only thing we can do unless we find some other Omega to ask, and I know you'd rather be slow roasted on an open fire. I'm lucky you're talking this much with me."

"Not luck," Darian said, too abruptly but there was no taking it back after the fact. "It's just us, how we are."

"Is it all too fast?"

"No. Fuck, depending on how you look at it, it's been years in the making." Darian rubbed at his forehead, where the tension in his jaw was giving him the start of a fine-ass migraine. That, and the sexual tension that kept getting resolved and then unresolved, and if Coby called him on that… "It's just us. How we are."

Coby smiled. Small, but sweet, almost like the boy he'd been when they met. "Can you keep teaching me? Or when we come up against something neither of us gets, can we work it out together?"

Darian considered that, then jerked his head in agreement. Seemed fair.

And it satisfied Coby, who nodded. "Okay. Then can I do something?"

Curious, Darian leaned back to look at him. "Like what?"

"Like this," Coby said. He stood, slid easily across the small gap between their beds, and straddled Darian's lap -- and kissed him, long and deep and slow.

Mmm. Darian liked it. Except --"Goddamn it," he muttered into the kiss. "We're out of condoms."

"No, we're not." Coby bit the tip of Darian's nose and, when he pulled away, Darian got another peek at that shy little grin of his. "I bought a twelve pack."

"You are fucking amazing."

"You're amazing at fucking," Coby said. "So can we?"

"Twelve times, if we want." Darian's hands found their home at Coby's hips and pulled him in tight, grinding up slow and deep and long.

Yeah. He'd been right. This was them. How they were.

As for what the rest of that meant, they would find out.

Should be a hell of a lot of fun, actually. He was kind of -- no, strike that. He was fucking absolutely looking forward to seeing what came next. As he lifted them both, then gave Coby a good hard push back onto his bed and climbed on top of him, Darian didn't even give a damn about being careful what he wished for.

He'd probably wish later that he'd known better. But that would be then. This was them, and this was now.

And there was going to be fucking within the next few minutes so seriously. No complaints.

Chapter Five
Two weeks later

Oscar leaned back on his hands, squinting up at the sun. "Fancy seeing you again. I was starting to wonder if you'd ever come up for air or out of your Omega's ass."

Darian snorted without looking up from his study guide. Couldn't seem to get much studying done in the room, so he had to make do with the great outdoors. And the occasional bit of company that took way too much pleasure in razzing him.

"You know, getting laid on the regular's making you downright fucking mellow."

"Oh, bite me," Darian muttered, looking at his book.

"Yeah," Oscar said, lighting up. "You say that, but you know what?"

"What?"

"You're smiling when you do."

* * *

Maybe he was. So what? If any Alpha ever had a damn good reason...

Because it wasn't only sex on the regular. Oh hell no. Sex on the regular implied, he figured, falling into a routine. *Hey, it's time for bed, want to dick down first?* Not with Coby. Once that fuse had been lit, there was no telling when he'd pop off and Darian was 100% there for every last crack he got at that ass. Coby walked around twenty-four/seven smelling like he'd just gotten some and wanted more, and the looks he got now weren't weird -- they were straight up envious. Some confusion got added to the mix when Darian walked next to him, sure, but Darian didn't give much of a damn. He liked seeing Coby lift his head and walk tall and grin when he saw people mentally crash and burn wondering what the hell *that* was about.

And he liked being the one who knew for sure.

But what he liked best was never knowing when the powder keg was about to explode. Could be anytime, anywhere. They'd gone at it in bathroom stalls in the middle of the day and behind trees late at night where it would be so easy to get caught that the excitement made Coby lose his voice, trying to keep those sweet, sweet noises he made stifled behind his hand.

Then, there were nights like this. Ordinary? Maybe to someone on the outside, looking in. They'd called it early, stuffed full of some actually damn decent cafeteria sandwiches with no bullshit dished out on the side, and they'd topped it off with a pot of coffee Coby brewed -- and Coby knew the fuck his way around how to make coffee so strong it'd strip your stomach lining, make your mouth cry for mercy, and keep you awake as long as you wanted.

"Hit me again," Darian said, buried in the same textbook he'd been scowling at earlier. He held his empty mug out in Coby's general direction without looking. "I swear to fuck, whoever wrote this had some sick hard-on for confusing people. Or they were high. Or a bastard."

"Sounds about right." Coby slid his chair back and snagged Darian's mug. "Sugar? Cream?"

"Sugar, yes. Cream, no."

"You change it up a lot," Coby said with a shrug. He carried both his and Darian's to the tiny kitchenette, though honestly his arms were long enough he could have reached from where he was sitting, but watch Darian complain. Go on, watch. He leaned back in his chair and enjoyed the view of those long legs and that fine, fine ass.

Coby'd come pre-installed with a pretty good sense of when he was being watched, and it'd only gotten keener. He slowed his roll mid-fill and glanced back at Darian with a hint of a gleam in his eye.

Darian knew that gleam. He *liked* that gleam. He

arched an eyebrow and let Coby see what taking in the whole picture did for him.

Coby licked his lips as he put the mugs carelessly down. "Yeah?"

"What the fuck do you think?"

Another thing: Coby knew, now, how to separate the profanity from the profound, and he knew what Darian meant no matter how it sounded. The gleam in his eye brightened from intrigued to predatory and hot damn, they were off to the races. Three long steps took him from kitchenette to Darian's chair and straddling his lap, his hot mouth on Darian's before he'd even fully touched down. Quick learner, that Omega -- and that was another thing. The more he let his inner Omega out, the more he learned he liked, the more Coby shone. He appreciated what he could do now, and he was hungrier than an alley cat in winter for more, more, more.

There were things Darian had learned too. As Coby kissed him, mouth open and eager, he ran his hands lightly up and down Coby's sides. Made him shiver, always, and arch toward Darian. He tilted his head back to let Darian kiss down the side of his neck and slid his fingers through Darian's hair to scratch at the back of his neck. His feet dragged on the floor and Darian had to raise himself up, but: worth it.

They broke for air, eyeing each other up. This was the fun part. One among many, but one of the best, the *well? What've you got in mind?*

The gleam in Coby's eye turned downright wicked, and Darian only had one split second to appreciate it before Coby used all that athlete strength of his to lift, twist, and drop. Laughing in surprise and appreciation, Darian wrestled back before Coby could KO him and landed more or less on his feet. He grabbed Coby around the waist and twisted him back where they'd come from, but oh no, Coby didn't go easily. He slid one of those long legs between Darian's and overbalanced both of them, whirling them sideways until gravity took over and they collided with Darian's back to the wall and Coby looming over him.

Darian lifted himself on his toes to find Coby's mouth with his own, eyes closed but knowing by heart, by now, where and how to find the collars and hems and drawstrings he needed to work loose to get Coby as naked as he could as fast as he could -- except Coby stopped him this time.

Curious, Darian opened his eyes as Coby pinned him against the wall and buried his face in Darian's chest to kiss bites and bruises across his ribs. "Watch it with the teeth, Cujo," he said, giving him a light shove. "What am I, your chew toy now?"

"You love it."

"Fuck you."

"If you play your cards right." Coby pulled a move Darian had only seen strippers and Omegas ready to pop with lust pull off and slid down him as gracefully as he would down a greased pole. He stopped halfway to the floor and looked up at Darian with that gleam in his eye gone downright feral. "I was daydreaming about something today. I want to try it."

"Hell yes," Darian breathed. There were advantages to a man who liked thinking. "Show me."

Coby slid two fingers under Darian's belt buckle, and even trapped by denim and shorts, Darian's cock jerked upward all on its own. Still caught there, Coby lowered himself to his knees and pressed his face to Darian's groin. He breathed deeply, hungry on the inhale, starving for it on the exhale, and lifted up to lick below where jeans gave way to skin.

"I want to blow you," he said, already as gravelly as if he'd had Darian's cock down his throat. "For starters."

"You're going to kill me." Darian rolled his hips forward. "Keep going."

Coby laughed, ripples of movement that buzzed against Darian's stomach, but he did what he was told. Probably because he'd wanted to anyway, but there was a hell of a something to that. Darian speared his fingers through Coby's hair and gave him a push downward.

No matter why, Coby took directions so damned well. He kept his mouth where it was, wet tongue swirling and flicking, while his hands -- clever and nimble for their size -- jerked open belt, button, and fly. Boxers couldn't contain what the jeans had kept trapped, and he surged into the space Coby had made for him. God *damn*, that man got him so hard, and harder still when Coby pulled everything in the way down to knee level and got his mouth on Darian's cock.

He didn't play games about it. Lips tight and hard, a bare hint of teeth, and he bent forward to take Darian's cock deep as he could go -- and good God, that wasn't any small distance. Darian's balls hit his chin before he stopped, and when Coby looked up at him from under his lashes and swallowed --

"Shit," Darian said, arching up. "Shit, shit, shit, Coby, who the fuck taught you how to do that?"

Coby drew off wet and messy, a string of saliva connecting his reddening lips to Darian's dick. He wiped it off on his wrist and he didn't look away. "You did."

"I know, so what the fuck was I thinking?"

One more long, hot lick. "That you live for getting your dick sucked."

"Oh yeah. That. But damn." Darian wrestled him off. "This all you want? If it is, keep going."

Coby's grin went sharp. "That's not all I was thinking about."

Darian would have asked if Coby hadn't showed him. He thrust two fingers into his mouth and sucked as enthusiastically as he'd gone after Darian's cock, sliding them in and out with such enjoyment that Darian could have come from watching that -- if Coby had been done, but oh no, he wasn't. Face nuzzled in again, he licked one ball at a time into his mouth and slid his hand around Darian's backside. Those sopping fingers circled his hole, and Darian didn't open like an Omega but when he wanted it enough, he could damn well do his best impression.

Coby's fingers slid inside him and crooked up. He laughed, low and proud, when Darian groaned so deeply he made his own throat burn. "I didn't teach you *that*."

"Yes you did. You just didn't know." Coby tapped the side of his head with the hand not finger-banging Darian's brains out.

Still, not done. He set his mouth to the inside of Darian's thigh and shoved those fingers deep inside him, stroking and curling until *he* had to stop, panting and pressing a hand to his crotch. He wasn't the only one who lived for cocksucking, but he beat Darian hands down for knowing when to stop before the party ended.

Damn.

Darian swore and smacked at him, missing when Coby dodged. "I'm still not done." He slid out and reached for a suspiciously convenient bottle of hand sanitizer. Strong smelling, making both their noses wrinkle, but Darian had a glimmering of an idea where this was headed. Maybe. If he was wrong, he didn't give a damn.

Good thing too. Coby stood and took him by the arm, hauling him bodily toward one of the beds -- they'd stopped calling one his and the other Darian's. Why bother when they both got as much use out of both? He kept pulling until he fell and wrangled Darian down with him.

"There," he said, still rough and raspy. "Take the

pants off all the way. Mine and yours."

Fuck yes. Darian shucked his shirt while watching Coby do the same, and those pants came flying off no matter how awkwardly: didn't give a single damn about that, either. He was on his knees when they were both naked, pretty happy about it, but then had to take himself in hand and stroke -- carefully -- when Coby let his legs sprawl wide open and brought his knees up one at a time to put everything, every last bit, on display. Wet, swollen, the heat in his blood making a pulse throb where he was opening.

"*Fuck*," Darian breathed reverently.

"I haven't been thinking about just you," Coby said.

"No?"

"Nope. Watch this. Bet I can surprise you." Coby reached between his spread legs and rubbed himself with freshly clean fingers before sliding them inside. Before Darian's head stopped reeling, he moaned and arched up. He shuddered on a sharp keen, and if Darian hadn't seen it wasn't so, he would have sworn Coby'd come, and come hard.

"What the *hell*." Darian had to rub the smooth skin on Coby's inner thighs as he leaned in, too fascinated not to need a closer look. "What did you do?"

"Something I didn't know Omegas were able to." Gorgeously flushed, Coby gave himself one more hard rub before he slid his fingers out and took Darian's hand. "Your turn. Inside, a little higher than you'd go to hit -- you know."

It was way too damn endearing how he still got a little shy even at times like this. Studying? Who needed book learning? Darian had to be in there. He had an easier time of it with all the clear fluid leaking out of Coby, but he didn't know what he was hunting for either. Some kind of magic switch?

Coby undulated up. He guided Darian by the wrist. "Up," he said. "You'll know it when you feel it."

Darian wasn't sure of that until his fingertips glided over the weirdest damn thing ever, something between a rough bump and what he'd swear felt like a tiny cock that throbbed to the beat of Coby's heart. He rubbed it once, easy then hard, and almost swallowed his tongue when Coby jerked up fit to break his back and fucking *howled*. Fluid dripped from his dick, but he still hadn't come that way yet.

No. No way. Darian rubbed him inside again, hard and steady, drinking in the sight Coby made spitted on his fingers, coming in that unfamiliar way again and again, pulse after pulse. *There* was a whole new addiction, wasn't there? "What even?" he breathed. "Seriously, man. What?"

Coby drew in deep, air-starved gasps. "The best thing ever, that's what. I didn't know Omegas had these. Thought maybe I really was a freak, but I looked it up and we all have them. Not nearly as many know about them as they should, but me? I'm never going to stop playing with it as long as I live."

Darian couldn't argue with that -- a tiny internal dick that could make you come like a string of firecrackers without knocking you out for the count? Omegas really had these? All of them? *Judas fuck*, sex education sucked in Coby's part of the country. His too, apparently.

Wait, where had he been? Right -- he'd learned *his* important lesson for the day, but he wasn't about to let Coby take back over yet. Darian took his fingers out and sucked them clean for the fun of watching Coby shudder with an aftershock, then used his wet hand to set his dick against Coby's slick-slippery channel, stretched open from both of their playing around in there. Coby drew in a sharp breath and shuddered, legs falling farther open.

Excellent. But for the fun of it, Darian put his mouth to Coby's ear and growl-purred, "Maybe there's more than one way to skin a cat. Want to find out?"

"Oh God yes." Coby clutched at him, from arms to back, dragging Darian down. "And do it right now before I lose my --"

Didn't have to tell Darian twice, or even once. Darian slid home good and hard, jolting Coby up the sheets. He could *feel* it, that bit of Coby hidden deep inside, and he knew how to work a good spot with his dick, and neither one of them wanted to hold back. He went hard, jackhammering him without mercy even if they were both too revved up to last as long as they wanted. Coby wrapped arms and legs around him like an octopus and bit Darian's shoulder hard enough to draw blood when he came the usual way, a sticky mess between them, his howl muffled by the mouthful. Darian did the same, tasting salt and copper when he burst as deeply as he could get himself, flooding Coby with all he had to give.

His muscles gave way, lax as a puppet whose strings had been cut, and he collapsed on top of Coby. Coby too, going limp and wrung-out and sprawled on the bed.

But he had enough oomph left to take Darian by the neck and kiss him one more time.

Darian landed with his cheek pressed to Coby's left tit this time, struggling to catch his breath and listening to Coby's heart slow from pounding-fast to slow and smooth. "What the hell even," he said, astounded. "You win. You surprised me."

Coby shook both of them with his laugh, soft and satisfied as it was, and his arms were a languid, lazy weight around Darian's waist. "One to me," he said. "You still want that coffee now?"

Coffee? Shit. He'd forgotten. He did still want

some, but -- later. So much later.

He had the oddest feeling he'd forgotten something else too, but it disappeared from his mind just as fast.

* * *

The days passed in a series of snapshots, the kinds Darian wanted to keep stored safely in his head, saved in the same compartment where he kept that first time he'd met Coby. What, it was a good place to go when he needed it. He gathered more and kept on picking them up like lucky pennies on the sidewalk and seemed like every day there were more.

For one:

Heading out to classes in the same building and every time someone gave them a weird stare taking Coby's hand and holding it. Lifting his chin at Coby's startled glances whenever that happened. *Show them you're not afraid. I know you can do it.*

Coby's big, warm hand folding around his and Coby straightening his back, both of them walking tall.

Another:

Oscar twirled an unlit cigarette between two fingers. Sprawled back on one elbow, he grinned at them in the shit-eating fashion most guaranteed to make Darian want to punch him between the ribs, and somewhere along the way he'd acquired a completely douchebag sailor's cap that made him look like a wannabe leather daddy.

Darian rolled his eyes. "Go ahead before I have to hit you on general principle, asshole."

"Since you ask so sweet," Oscar drawled. "I know you, and I know you've got the kind of dick that'd make a grown Alpha weep."

Darian opened his mouth to answer, but Coby beat him to it. "Thanks for noticing."

Oscar's jaw dropped, and Darian couldn't help falling over, conveniently into Coby's sturdy bulk, laughing until he nearly pissed himself. He threw his arm around Coby while he was there and kissed the side of his mouth.

"Judas fuck, you two make me sick," Oscar said with frank admiration. "Okay, so you're both gifted? Proportional, I'd buy that. So who takes it and who gives it?"

This time, Darian waited for it, and Coby rose to the occasion. "I'll answer that if you can guess who the size queen is."

Goddamn. Darian couldn't have been prouder of him.

Another:

"No. You have my voucher, and you know it's valid." Coby slammed his tray down, glaring at that same old cafeteria dickhead who just didn't learn. "I'm not taking what you feel like giving. Not even when you grow a dick and learn how to use it. You don't scare me."

Had Darian thought before he couldn't be prouder? Coby kept on surprising him. Talk about unleashing the beast.

He liked it.

The fact that the meatballs in the spaghetti were a little off and Coby hurled them back up after the first two bites kinda took the shine off, but the way he grinned at Darian through the grossest mouth ever, that Darian would not be kissing until after some serious mouthwash, brought the satisfaction right back.

He liked that too.

And another:

Walking down the sidewalk, hands laced together, people getting used to it now even if they did still put off waves of WTF and catching sight of Nutcracker Jaw kissing a very pretty, *very* pregnant Omega against the side of the admin building. Noticing Nutcracker noticing him and Coby and giving them a nod of approval that wasn't nearly as subtle as he probably imagined. Plus an absolutely unsubtle caress of his Omega's belly when he turned back to the business at hand.

Watching them, the weirdest pang zapped across Darian's chest that he had to massage away. He thought he caught Coby rubbing his own stomach, absently, as they both stopped to enjoy the view, but he might have been mistaken about that.

Or the bottomless pit needed feeding after the meatballs that didn't stick.

And another:

Doing laundry. So much laundry. Splashing each other with the lakes left in the machines when they didn't spin, shouting and swearing at the shock of the cold water, then going back to their room to warm up in the shower together.

And another:

"Swear to God, you two really do make me sick," Oscar said. Not with admiration this time. More like envy.

Interesting.

And another:

Deciding to deconstruct the twin beds, boards in one corner and mattresses plus box springs pushed together to make one bigger bed in the middle of the floor.

"As often as we end up there anyway, it makes more sense," Coby had said, red-faced from exertion and grinning like an idiot. For which Darian had first kissed him because he was turning into a Goddamned sap that way, and then tackled him onto their DIY queen-size to test it out.

Those horrible springs still made a racket.

He didn't really care.

And one more:

Feeling, more and more, day by day, like this was

where he belonged. Darian didn't examine that one too closely. It couldn't happen for keeps, right? But he could let it float past, every now and then, and breathe it in when that happened. Then let it go where it wanted.

And so:

Darian didn't sleep much better at nights but that wasn't new; he drank more coffee than water, studied until his head hurt, and spent the rest of his time fucking that sweet Omega like he'd just hit puberty. If you wanted to play, you had to pay.

Fine by him. He had those flashes back to lull himself to sleep with, and he learned how to lie still enough that his tossing and turning didn't inspire Coby to kick him out of the bed.

Not a bad deal.

* * *

Until:

Someone pounded on their door around -- what the fuck, four thirty in the afternoon -- waking Darian up. As long as it wasn't before eight a.m. Darian wouldn't get too pissed off unless he was buried balls-deep in Coby or enjoying a snooze after enjoying said balls-deepness. He snarled under his breath as he untangled himself from Coby's too-many-miles of legs and arms and stomped to see who the fuck and what the fuck.

When he opened the door, no one stood on the other side, but a folded piece of paper fluttered to the floor. Darian glowered down the hall at what looked like an underclassman roped into doing the job moved at a rapid clip, knocking and jamming papers into door jambs.

"This couldn't wait?" he yelled, waving the paper. "You couldn't shove it under the door like a sane person?"

The underclassman flinched and started moving faster.

Coby chuckled sleepily behind him. "You're

getting a reputation."

Darian glanced over his shoulder to see Coby hadn't gotten out of bed, and wasn't really even awake yet, rubbing his eyes. He looked stupidly cute like that, far more so than any man had a right to. Even an Omega. "Good," he said as he unfolded the paper. He frowned at it, then cocked his head in low-key interest. "Huh. Fourth of July, fireworks display tonight. I'd forgotten what date it was. You?"

Coby made a sleepy noise and flipped the covers back over his head.

Darian switched his frown from the paper to Coby. Seemed like he never could wake up properly the last few days. Maybe he needed more rest than Darian had been giving him, but he wasn't the only one making that happen.

Still. He should work on that.

He needed to work on coffee first, though. So much coffee. Darian shambled to the kitchenette, still a little clumsy with leftover drowsiness, and flicked it on. The sweet, sweet smell of caffeinated happy juice flooded the room, as dark a roast as he could legally buy. He breathed deeply in appreciation and waved a cloud of the smell toward Coby.

That should have worked. Instead Coby groaned and shoved his head under his pillow. "Open the window, would you? That's too strong."

Darian's frown deepened into a concerned scowl. "You love coffee."

"Oh God, don't say that word." Coby pressed the pillow over his face. "I'll throw up."

What the... Okay, not making any sense, but -- leftover food poisoning? Darian shrugged and slid the window up. Coby'd set up a fan that could blow air in or out as they wanted, and he pointed it outward. There was enough coffee in the pot for one cup, anyway, and that shit would put hair on a hairless cat's chest, so it'd do. He stood at the window to drink it but kept his focus on Coby. "Have you eaten today?"

Coby muttered something under his pillow, not likely to be a compliment, and flipped him off.

Darian snorted. He hadn't lost all his spirit while he slept. Good.

After a minute, Coby tossed the pillow aside, but his eyes were red and puffy, and he looked halfway between comatose and dead. He scrubbed at his face. "Not hungry."

"The fuck?" Darian asked, nonplussed. "Since when?"

All Coby did was shrug.

So, he guessed they wouldn't be going to dinner. Darian chewed that over. Hungry or not, a man Coby's size burned through a hell of a lot of calories walking through an average day. Well, they'd laid in a few supplies to keep from spending their last cents on delivery food. Maybe something mild. He found the bread, decided against toasting it, and smeared the super-mild strawberry jam Coby liked on two pieces. Stuffing one piece in his mouth, he carried the second one to Coby and waved it under his nose. "Still not hungry."

Nope. Not just nope, hell to the fucking no. Coby took one whiff and lunged toward the opposite side of the bed. Darian couldn't see his head, but he did recognize the sound of gut-wrenching hurling when he heard it. "Jesus Christ." *That* sounded worse than food poisoning. Did he have the flu? "Get your ass out of bed, man. We're going to the health center."

"No." Coby looked up, his jaw set hard. He shook his head, softened his glare to something rueful, and made it all the way to sitting up. "I'll be fine. Go get something to eat somewhere else, though, would you? Bring me back something fizzy to drink."

Darian's stomach grumbled. He needed calories too, but... "You sure?"

"Fuck yes." Coby collapsed back into bed, but he smiled at Darian out of the side of his mouth not smashed into his pillow. "Call Oscar. He'll keep you company. I'll be more myself when you get back."

Darian wasn't any too sure about that, but for once in his life concern rode roughshod straight over the need to fight, and after a brief fit of foot-tapping indecision, he figured it might be best to do what *he'd* been told for once. "If you're not better when I get back, you're going to a doctor. I have better things to do than fret over your puking."

Coby laughed into his pillow. "Yeah, yeah, yeah, I care about you too. Go already."

Chapter Six

"Huh," Oscar said as he munched on the bagels and peanut butter they'd scavenged from the cafeteria, which wouldn't have opened its doors before dinner hour if they hadn't been scared shitless of Darian and whoever accompanied him by then. "Huh."

"That's helpful. Thank you."

Oscar chewed and swallowed, tossed the last bite of his bagel to a nosy crow, and leaned back. "*Huh.*" He eyed Darian, who hadn't bothered too much with his own bagel. "Hmm."

Darian shot him a sideways unimpressed look. "If you don't have anything to contribute besides noise, I'd rather go back to Coby and listen to the spewing for a while."

Oscar took out a cigarette and lit it, blowing the smoke away from Darian while he mused over whatever the fuck he might have been thinking. "Haul him to the doctor if you have to. You might have to toss him over your shoulder, and he'd skin his knees raw on the way there because he's taller than a giraffe, but you need to know what's going on."

Huh, Darian thought, then swore at himself because that shit was apparently catching. Still, he couldn't help catching a subtle emphasis on the *you* that made it singular, aimed solely at him. "What aren't you saying?"

Oscar gave him a sideways look right back, shook his head, and said nothing except, "Got any better ideas?"

Not exactly. Darian sat up on his heels, all the better to think, and racked his brain until one tiny spark went off. Maybe... Coby kept it buried these days, but he did have a taste for romance and that so wasn't Darian's strong suit. Maybe he needed a little wining and dining, or the kind of equivalent that wouldn't end up in a messy puddle.

It was as good an idea as any. Darian shredded his

bagel and tossed the pieces at a handful of curious squirrels, then stood. He liked it when he had a mission and a direction to point himself in. This one started with going back to the room. Which he would have done anyway, but he had a reason. Besides the usual.

As he walked away, he could hear Oscar lying back and laughing under his breath.

What the fuck even?

* * *

Darian took a few laps around campus, chewing over his idea until he was sure it'd be worth a shot, and the dinner hour was past by the time he got back to their room. Coby'd made it out of bed, had even showered and put on clean clothes, and Darian smelled the mint of mouthwash. He'd parked his ass back on the edge of the bed, looking as deeply self-focused and not-thrilled as he used to be, but he looked up when Darian opened the door and his grin was the new kind. "Hey."

"Hey to you too." Darian walked to him and nudged Coby's sneaker with the toe of his bed. "C'mon, out of bed. It's already sunset."

Coby raised an eyebrow. "And?"

"And we've got somewhere to be before it gets really dark."

"Not the doctor," Coby warned. "I'm serious, Darian."

Darian raised one hand. "Not the doctor. I like your knees with skin on."

Coby blinked at him.

"Never mind. Some shit Oscar said." Darian held out the hand he raised. "You trust me?"

"Okay, Aladdin," Coby snorted -- but he took the hand Darian offered, and let Darian lever him up and standing. "Where are we headed?"

Darian grinned at him. "You'll see. Follow me."

He turned to lead the way and might -- or might

not -- have imagined Coby murmuring behind him, "I always do."

* * *

"You brought me out here to play hacky sack?"

"Stop looking at the damn bag like it's a grenade." Darian caught the little grain-stuffed leather ball when Coby, eyebrow arched high in disbelief, tossed it back to him. "You have to have played before. It's a fucking college staple."

Coby caught Darian's return throw. The hack looked tiny in his palm, more like a ping-pong ball. "Yeah, if you grew up in the 90's. I think my dad played this with his buddies." He flipped it into the air, watched it spin, and caught it neatly as it fell. "Where'd you even get this?"

"Someone left it on a bench."

"Oh my God, you are such a dick!" Coby shoved him sideways, laughing. "You didn't really, did you?"

Darian nodded in satisfaction. That was more like it. Definitely worth a little petty larceny. "Hey, whoever left it there was long gone. I looked around. Even waved it in the air and asked if it belonged to anyone."

Which he had, no matter how crazy it'd looked, and it'd sent the few people around him running for cover.

Huh. Maybe he was getting a reputation.

Eh, there were worse things in the world. Darian caught the hack when Coby lobbed it to him, dropped it, and kicked it from foot to foot without breaking his stride. "See? Easy."

"Yeah, for someone who's small and nimble. I'd probably kick it through a window by accident."

"Windows can be fixed, and no you won't, it's not that heavy. Come on, at least try." Darian stopped kicking the hack long enough to turn Coby around to face him. He nudged Coby's ankles apart to about the right distance. "I kick, you kick back. First one to fumble loses."

Coby looked down at their feet, chewing at his lip, then shook his head. "No. Too much difference. In the height, I mean."

Darian swallowed a frustrated noise. He wouldn't even try?

As if he could read Darian's mind, Coby gave him a rueful shrug. "Sorry. Not feeling it tonight. But..." He reached out and took Darian's hand, lacing their fingers together. Such big hands. His swallowed Darian's as much as it had the hack. "We could keep walking and doing this."

When he put it that way... Darian tossed the hack over his shoulder. Someone else could enjoy it. He squeezed Coby's hand once, roughly. "Yeah, all right."

"Which in Darian-speak means 'thanks.'" Coby leaned into him, kissed his cheek, and pressed the sides of their heads briefly together. "I'm not sick, okay? Don't try to make me better. You're not a doctor and you're a terrible nurse."

Darian scoffed, but he gave Coby's hand a small tug to say what he wasn't sure how to. *I worry about you* and *I want to take care of you so let me, damn it* and *whatever, bitch* all rolled into one. He knew Coby understood that too. His chuckle said it all.

Slower than before, they ambled across the quad. Easy, peaceful. A quiet night for the Fourth, and for a college campus. A handful of kids with acoustic guitars clustered on the library steps, picking their way through learning new songs. Fireflies blinked on in the deepening dusk, flickers of light that danced across the maze of sidewalks and paths and under the trees they liked best for lazing beneath. Coby went slightly green every time they passed a trash can, but nothing worse, and when Darian pulled a plain granola bar he'd filched from the cafeteria out of his pocket and broke it in half to share, Coby ate his part without any gagging. Absently, probably not really tasting it, but getting some calories in him regardless. Darian nibbled at his share once or twice, and since Coby wasn't paying that much attention, put it in his hand and got him to eat the that portion as well.

Much better. Too pleased with himself to keep cool, he pulled Coby around in a looping circle more or less in time with the guitarists. Startled, Coby laughed out loud, bright and fucking gorgeous. "You're out of your mind."

For you, Darian thought, but kept to himself. "I know you can dance. I've seen it."

"Twerking to the radio doesn't count."

"Counted for me," Darian said, because that was another of those snapshot memories he kept safely stored away -- already kind of ragged at its edges from too much handling, but *damn*. He gave Coby a good once-over. "What song was that again, that got you so worked up? Asking for a friend."

Coby laughed more quietly this time, shaking his head, but he moved a couple steps closer to Darian, close enough for their body heat to warm each other as they walked. "I like crazy."

"Fortunate for me."

"That's one way to put it." Coby cocked his head. "Where are we going? I didn't think to ask."

More like he'd been too out of it to come up with questions, but he seemed to be waking up now. "Not far now." Darian tugged his hand, coaxing him to pick up the pace a notch or two. "Or really fucking far. I forget which."

"What?" Coby's face wrinkled in confusion, but he didn't stop walking. "Seriously. Where are we going?"

Darian glanced sideways at him and put a finger to his lips.

"You pick now to be the quiet type," Coby

grumbled. He knocked their shoulders together. "Okay, Mysterio. Lead the way. Show me what you've got."

Wouldn't he just. Darian had plans for that too -- but later.

He kind of wanted to see what Coby thought of this, first.

* * *

"The bridge?" Coby let go of Darian's hand. Eyes wide, he turned in a -- very careful -- slow circle. "You hate this bridge."

Darian shrugged. "Everyone, except you, who has a working brain hates this bridge. It's a death trap waiting to happen."

"Then why…"

In answer, Darian tugged the now-crumpled flyer out of his pocket and handed it over. He watched Coby read and process before saying, "No one else would even think about coming here, but -- look, see those lights down there? That's where they're getting ready to set off the fireworks. I figured this would be the best place for a private show."

Coby's smile dawned slowly, but it was one of his most beautiful ever, wide and delighted. "You brought me here because you knew I'd love it."

Darian made a face and grumbled, looking away because he knew he couldn't hide the twinkle in his eyes -- then looking back because he couldn't not look at Coby, especially when he was that happy. Coby ought to be happy all the time. Pissed him off when things upset Coby. He could deal with making it his mission to make that happen.

At least as long as the summer lasted, anyway. Darian's frown drifted back over his face. The Fourth already, and he hadn't even thought about how that meant their time together was nearly half over. Damn.

Coby let out a quiet exhale. Probably thinking the

same thing.

Well, that didn't gel with the mission Darian had assigned himself. He tugged Coby's hand again, leading him across the tracks and to the bridge railing. Way too close to the edge for his comfort, and when he looked down a swirling *whoosh* of vertigo made him feel like he was falling. He caught his breath, a sharp gasp, and grabbed the railing.

"Whoa. Darian, careful." Coby pulled at his shoulders, trying to walk him backward. "I don't know how strong that rail is."

But Darian could be really fucking stupid sometimes. He'd own that. And he fucking *hated* running headfirst into any kind of weakness. He shook off what he could of the vertigo, ignored the rest, and shrugged out of Coby's hands. "It's been here for a hundred years. It's strong enough." He took a deep breath, went to his knees, and crawled under the lowest rail, bringing himself up on the opposite side. *That* was how you faced your fears: head-fucking-on.

"Darian, don't --" Coby yelped.

Too late. Darian stood up. He clung white-knuckled to the wood, only the strength of his grip and his planted feet and some really old wood standing between himself and a nasty plunge that'd render him a formerly human pancake when he hit the bottom. *If* he fell.

Which he wouldn't. Coby wound his arms around Darian as far as they'd go and knotted them in his shirt. Strong as an ox, better than a harness. "Darian, oh my God, what the *hell*. Are you really crazy?"

"No. I knew you wouldn't let me go." Darian pressed his mouth to Coby's neck, then blinked in surprise at the frantic-fast hammering of his pulse. "Wait. Are you really scared?"

"What the fuck do you think, you idiot?" Coby

yanked at Darian, clearly meaning to haul him bodily back to the other side if he had to -- and frankly, Darian was too taken aback to stop him. The old wood held as Coby dragged him over the rails, the Omega holding his breath until he had Darian safe on less-perilous ground.

He let go to drag his hands through his hair and give Darian a wild, disbelieving stare. Darian opened his mouth, but lost whatever he'd meant to say when Coby kissed him as if it was the last chance he'd ever get, then threw both arms around him again. Nearly squeezed all the air and a few organs out of him with a grizzly-bear's bear hug. His heart hadn't slowed, not even a fraction.

"Jesus." Darian hugged him back, more carefully because Coby had started shaking and he wasn't too sure the Omega wouldn't shatter like an old vase if Darian squeezed him too hard. "I didn't mean to freak you out that bad. Swear."

"You did." Coby didn't let go. "Don't do that again, Darian."

"I won't. I promise." Even if he wanted to, and there had been an adrenaline rush there that made Darian understand the appeal of bungee jumping. But -- not if it did that to Coby. Not worth it. He peeled himself carefully out of Coby's hold enough to get some needed oxygen, and to put his hand to Coby's cheek. "You reading me? I promise."

Coby covered Darian's hand with his, shuddered, and let out a sigh.

He needed more than a promise. Darian took his arm and guided him down until he got the idea and sat on the ground safely behind the bridge railing. Darian sat behind him, tossing his legs over Coby's to help keep him anchored.

That got him a snort and a wry look over the shoulder. "I feel like you're about to ask me for a piggyback ride. Short-legged man."

"Long-legged giraffe," Darian retorted. He hitched forward and looped his arms around Coby's waist. "Deal with it -- and hey, there, look." Pointing, he traced a plume of smoke heading for the sky. As they both looked up, the first of the Fourth fireworks exploded in a ball of purple sparks overhead. "Say, can you see."

Coby's pulse finally started to slow to something not in heart attack range. He looked as enchanted as a kid, watching the purple sparks fall in slow motion, followed by bursts of gold and bright crimson and electric green, one after the other. "God. They're beautiful."

"I know." Darian tucked his chin over Coby's shoulder. "Roman candles?"

Coby stroked Darian's hands where they'd locked around his waist but didn't look away from the night sky and the exploding lights. "So far," he said, drawing loops and circles on Darian's palm with his thumb. "I love fireworks."

And I love -- Darian shook his head. *Do you feel the same way for me* --

He put his mouth to Coby's throat instead, wanting the salty taste of skin and Omega to replace the woodiness of bland granola and the sharp sourness of alarm. Once there, once Coby leaned his head aside to give him room, he had to burrow closer and splay his fingers wide across Coby's chest. Coby made a low humming noise and shifted his hips, and there was an idea, wasn't there? Darian hitched forward to bring them body to body and press himself against the too-inviting curve of Coby's ass.

"Oh my God," Coby laughed. "Are you never not horny?"

Darian pretended to consider that. "Hmm... nope." Least not when it came to Coby, and then he couldn't get enough. He rolled his cock against Coby's ass, and liked that so much he had to do it again. Liked it even better when Coby moaned a deep "oh God, yeah" and rolled back. He wasn't the only one who'd gone insatiable.

But it could get better. Darian slid backward, bringing Coby with him until their legs didn't dangle over the edge of the bridge, and turned him onto his back. Even with the fireworks going off faster and hotter, felt like slow and steady was the way to go. He draped himself purposefully over Coby, short legs be damned, and gave Coby one thigh to grind up against.

Plenty to grind with. Darian had to feel that, even if he already knew it by heart. He flicked open Coby's belt and slid his hand beneath it, taking Coby's cock in hand. Fucking hell, he was harder than ever before, straining up into Darian's palm. He kissed Darian rough and messy between startled gasps, already wet and leaking from cock and channel. Darian moved his fingers low and brought the lubrication high, making it easy, keeping it slow, but not showing him any mercy either. Coby clutched his shoulders in a different way, urging on his languid roll. He panted between kisses, small moans and groans and pleas that went straight to Darian's head.

Darian had to move faster. Had to. Had to grind down harder too, fully ready to come in his pants like he was a teenager again and to hell with pride. He could feel it coming already. Adrenaline, pride, whatever -- and love --

He stuttered to a halt, shocked still. *Fucking hell.* He'd thought something like that just a minute ago, but it hadn't sunk in then. It sure as balls did now.

Was he in love with the guy? Did -- did Coby love him too?

Coby hesitated beneath him. "What?"

Darian shook his head and went back for another kiss, as fierce as Coby this time. He yanked until he had Coby's jeans down past his hips, his own too, far enough for skin to meet skin, and shoved Coby's shirt up until he could press his mouth hard and hot to Coby's stomach. Didn't know why, only that he was hungry to all of a sudden. He caught a tiny fold of skin over Coby's abs between his teeth and bit down, wanting to feel the jerk he always gave and the keen he always made when Darian did that.

Which he didn't get. Coby went still as if he'd been carved from marble out of that quarry below them, then gave Darian a shove that nearly sent him over the railing and down after all. Before Darian could recover and ask what in the ever-loving fuck, Coby'd twisted onto his side so his head stuck over the edge -- and there went that lightly-digested granola bar, splatter-splash. Gross as hell and also, what. The. *Fuck*.

Darian's cock throbbed, indignant at being denied what it wanted -- blue balls were a bitch -- but he ignored them like he'd tried to ignore Coby's scent that first night in their quarters. He leaned over Coby, holding him steady as he gagged and choked on bile, then shuddered when there was nothing at all left to come up, but his guts kept trying to turn themselves into out.

"That's it," he said, hand on Coby's back. "I'm taking you to an urgent care, and you can argue if you want but I'm not arguing back."

"For once in your life," Coby muttered. He spat over the edge and let Darian turn him over in a mimicry of what they'd been doing though he'd gone limp as a rag doll except for the tension that held him rigid as a steel bar. He winced, probably sore as hell from that impressive round of hurling, and stared helplessly up at Darian, visible in bursts of the fireworks ahead. "Don't. Please don't."

"If I have to toss you over my shoulder like a fireman, I fucking will."

"Oh. That's what the skinned knees thing was about," Coby said, confusing Darian until Darian remembered mentioning that. "You're strong enough." He reached up to brush Darian's face with his fingertips, still looking so much like one of Peter Pan's lost boys that it made Darian's heart *ache*. "You always know what you want, and you never change your mind, not ever."

Darian stared right back at him. "You've got me scared shitless right now."

Coby's mouth twisted. "I'm sorry."

"Yeah, I'm sure." Darian took Coby's chin and lifted it, making sure of his undivided attention. "You remember that whole talking about things bit you were so set on? How about you tell me why you don't want to go to a doctor? If it's good enough, I'll listen. No promises that I won't haul you there if I have to, but I'll *listen*."

For a second Darian didn't think he'd answer. Then Coby shivered, visibly gathering his strength. He didn't reach up to caress Darian the way he usually would, instead lying still with his hands at his sides. It should have been a weird look on such a big man, but it only made him look almost smaller than Darian, instead. Almost fragile.

Nuh-uh. Darian lifted Coby's chin a fraction higher, pulling out a little of the Alpha dominance he didn't like to use with Coby -- but wasn't against playing now. "Tell me, right now. I'm not kidding. What's going on with you?"

"Darian," Coby said helplessly. He shook his head, but he did open his eyes. "Darian. You remember that night when I learned my new trick?"

Huh? "Not like I could forget," Darian said, trying to puzzle out the non sequitur. "You want to try that again?"

"No. Listen to me. You asked, I'm talking." Another deep breath, his hands shaking. "That got hot. Hotter than I'd thought it would."

"Not telling me anything I don't know." Darian

didn't get it. "What are you working up to?"

Frustration looked at least a little better on Coby than unhappiness, and he finally reached up to Darian, even if it was only to shake him. "*Darian.* You remember that night. I know it. You remember everything about it." He licked his lips. "But do you remember using a condom that night? I don't."

Come to think of it, they hadn't. Shit, that'd been irresponsible of him. Could have been some consequences there --

Oh.

Shit.

Wait.

Fuck!

The pieces came together like a car crash. It all made sense. The sleeping. For fuck's sake, the *puking.*

Coby hardened his jaw, daring Darian to react however he thought Darian was going to. "I know you're not stupid unless you want to be. Don't be a dumbass now. Please. Tell me you understand what I'm trying to say."

"What?" Darian rasped. "Coby. Coby, *hell.* Are you trying to say --"

"Yes."

Darian couldn't reply. He couldn't even blink. His brain had exploded like the fireworks building up to their grand finale.

Coby covered Darian's splayed fingers with his and pressed down, where even with all the not-eating, Darian could feel the faintest start of an outward curve. He said it, what Darian couldn't, and like Darian had taught him, he didn't apologize. Not for this.

"I'm pregnant."

Chapter Seven

Now that he'd said it out loud, Coby's spine straightened, and he didn't need Darian to hold his chin up for him -- but he covered Darian's hand lightly and rested his palm there. "I'm pregnant," he said again. "I took a test. More than one. I'm pregnant, and it's yours. It's your baby in here, Darian."

Nope. Did not compute. All Darian could do was stare down at Coby. Not breathing, not blinking, not believing what he'd heard even as his hand flexed over that so-unmistakable change in Coby's body.

He always used a condom. Always. Except -- *oh*. Also, *fuck*. Yeah, now he remembered what'd completely blasted past him at the time. They hadn't used a condom that night. Hadn't thought about it once.

His hand flexed again.

"I don't know if it was coming that many times, or if it was going to happen anyway," Coby said, steady as the earth. "But it's true."

Did not compute. Could not compute. Darian pulled roughly away and stood, careless of his closeness to the edge. He couldn't stop staring, and his palm burned and tingled where he'd laid it on Coby's stomach over -- over his --

Oh, *fuck*. Over his kid. A kid that neither one of them had planned on or imagined would happen.

Coby was pregnant, and Darian had done that to him without the sense to think twice.

He'd started backing up before he realized what he was doing, and then he couldn't seem to stop. Coby raised himself on one elbow, and somehow even worse than anything yet, he looked so fucking sad and so Goddamned stubborn that Darian's body wanted to jerk forward.

He didn't. Want and ability were two different things. He couldn't fucking move while Coby was looking at him like that.

"I knew you'd be like this," Coby said -- or at least that was what Darian thought he said. It was hard to tell with his ears ringing and buzzing from the shock. "I wanted one more good night. But I knew."

He lay back down, looking up at the stars and the very last sparks of the fireworks. Darian looked anywhere but at them, and his feet, damn them, carried him away at a stride, then a stalk, and then a jog.

Did not compute. Except for how it did.

It did.

* * *

His brain still hadn't stopped jolting around in his skull before he reached the quad, where the fireflies had gone but one bright ember flared and dimmed under a tree. The familiar, comforting smell of smoke filled Darian's nose, and he came to a stop so abrupt he left skid marks in the grass.

Oscar tilted his head at Darian, exhaling a thoughtful puff of smoke before holding the cigarette out in a silent offer.

Darian took it, and that was when his knees decided to give way. Went right out beneath him and planted him ass-first on the ground, head tucked hard against those useless knees, cigarette dangling dangerously close to his hair.

"If you burn yourself, I'm taking that back."

Darian passed it over blindly without drawing on it once. His lungs were telling him they weren't down with sprinting that far for that long anyway.

Oscar waited a minute before saying, "So. You figured it out."

"He told me," Darian said, muffled against his knees. "You were both right, damn it. I'm a dumbass."

"Only when you want to be." Oscar made a shrugging movement that jostled him against Darian.

Darian couldn't hear him inhale or exhale, and figured he was letting his cigarette burn down to the filter without smoking it either, just holding it steady, keeping him company. "Latex failure or fucked too stupid to think straight?"

Darian held up two fingers to indicate he'd guessed right the second time.

"The way you guys are around each other, the only mindboggling thing is that either of you are surprised." Darian could almost hear Oscar wince. Darian glanced up to see the cherry had burned low enough to scorch his fingers. He dropped the filter between his feet to grind it out, then leaned back against the tree. All the better to study Darian from, Darian guessed. "Anyone with a grain of sense could have seen it. He'd started to glow. You too. Something in your heads knew it, even if the rest of your brains didn't."

That was a hell of a soliloquy from Oscar. Darian raised his head, meaning to glare, but he couldn't find the oomph for it. "What do I do?"

"Be fucked if I know. That's what I was about to ask you. You've got options."

Darian couldn't think of any and frowned the question at Oscar.

Who snorted at him. "You don't do anything by halves, do you? Even when you get the shit shocked out of you, you've got to go full fainting goat."

"Full what the fuck, now?"

Oscar waved that away. "It's a goat, they faint when you startle them, not the point. Options. There's adoption."

Darian put his chin in his hand.

"Abortion?"

There was the glare Darian had wanted to give Oscar, right along with a flare of *no fucking way* and *how the fuck dare you*.

"Thought not," Oscar murmured. "Only one other choice. I'm not going to say it. You already know what it is. But because you really can be a dumbass when you want to, I'm going to tell you one thing for free, my friend. You know what you want."

He stood up, looking down at Darian. "So stop being stupid and figure out a way to make it happen."

Darian sat still a moment longer, looked up, shook his head, and stood. He turned to walk away with his hands in his hip pockets.

"I know you just stole my smokes, jackass!" Oscar yelled after him.

Darian raised the pack in the air, using his middle finger to brace it. Seemed fitting.

Oscar got him, anyway. All that there was as good as a hug and a pat on the back. You had to learn the languages people spoke, all in their own ways.

Sometimes it wasn't as easy as it could be. So? All that meant was he had to try harder. That'd be another thing to think about.

* * *

Good places to think on a college campus: surprisingly limited. Gym closed, track gates barred, library doors shut. They couldn't close the steps off for business, though, and Darian tucked himself into a corner where no one would tread too closely and piss him off, lit up with the matchbook he'd stolen from Oscar too -- why have one without the other -- and set the wheels of his brain in motion.

Or at least he tried. They kept on spinning without getting anywhere. Total dead hamster on a perpetual motion machine, and that thought made Darian snort with imagining the baffled/disgusted/delighted look Coby would have given him at that.

Coby. Coby, Coby, Coby.

One cigarette burned down to ash, unsmoked, and

Darian lit another without really noticing. He held this one to his lips but let the slow trickle of smoke drift up his nose instead of drawing it into his lungs.

Coby.

Coby was pregnant. Okay. He could start there. Darian went over that night one more time, and he couldn't deny what he recalled. No condom in sight, much less wrapped around a dick, and as hard as they'd gone after learning Coby's new party trick it was a wonder *he* hadn't ended up pregnant himself from all the spunk in the air.

Coby would wrinkle his nose and shove Darian for saying something like that. Darian rubbed his arm meditatively, imagining he could feel it.

Pregnant. Carrying a baby. His baby. Darian's child. *God.* Every time he thought it, it became more real, but those empty wheels still kept spinning in his head. He dropped his head into one hand and rubbed hard.

He gave himself ten seconds to do that, because he'd never run from anything before, and he'd be damned if he let himself start tonight -- for longer than he had already -- and the only way he knew to face this was head-on.

So:

Fact one. Coby was pregnant. Two weeks along, by Darian's reckoning, and Omega pregnancies only lasted nine weeks. Everyone would see it for themselves in two more weeks, and just about sooner than you could spit, he'd give birth. Probably right after they'd graduated summer session. *Judas fuck.* Darian was sure down to the soles of his feet that Coby was going to keep the baby -- their baby. He'd have to walk across the commencement stage to get his certificate looking like he'd swallowed a watermelon sideways. He could either do it with his head held high or hung low in shame --

Hell no.

Fact two: Darian would be damned all over again before he'd stand for that.

Which brought him to fact three: Oscar was right. He -- they -- only had a few choices. They weren't married, and holy hell that was a whole other crisis for another time. Didn't mean he couldn't sort himself out in the interim.

So: what did he feel? No lies. Darian rolled it over in his head and came to an inalienable truth that made him nod.

So: what did he want? No lies. More chewing on notions, and Darian knew the answer to that one too.

So: what was he going to do? That was a harder question. The hardest. He couldn't really know for sure, not until he knew what Coby wanted.

Only one way to do that. Carrying his phone in his back pocket had become such an ingrained habit that Darian mostly forgot it was there, but he had Coby's contact plugged in there from nearly the start. He slid it out, thumbed it on, and had his pointer a fraction of an inch from speed dial a literal split second before it blared out a ring that damn near made him jump five feet in the air.

"Fucking hell!" he barked into the speaker before he thought twice and slapped himself on the face. A quick look back confirmed what he'd figured, who'd called him. "Coby. Where are you?"

"You're one to ask, but I'm back in the room," Coby said. "I'm halfway packed."

Simple words, but they hit like a punch to Darian's guts. "You're what, now?"

"Should I stay?" Coby demanded, and oh damn, he was hopping mad now. "No, don't answer that. For once in your life, Darian, shut the fuck up and let someone else talk. You either listen to me or I hang up right now. Understand?"

Darian *almost* swore back at him, but some merciful force out there snapped his jaw shut and kept it there.

"I'm keeping it," Coby said. "And I don't give a damn if you don't want that."

Darian swallowed hard, loud enough for Coby to hear.

Coby growled. "You drive me crazy, Darian. You know that? You've got one hell of a nerve walking away, and I'd never figured you for any kind of coward, ever, but I knew you would be like this, and you know what? I know all the arguments you're going to make too. The way our families are going to flip out, how we'd live, what we'd live on, how we barely really know each other -- that is all *bullshit*, okay?"

Darian couldn't have spoken now if he'd wanted to.

Not that he thought Coby cared. He'd built up too much of a head of steam to stop and he blazed full speed ahead. "It's bullshit, Darian," he said. "Our careers? We're both going to fight to be teachers of what we want for the rest of our lives. Our families? Hell, Darian, yours is probably going to deal out high fives all around. Mine? Imagine what that's going to go down like. 'Hey, Dad, guess what? I came to get a degree you thought I had no business going after, and while I was here I got knocked up by a short, high-velocity Alpha who spends his life looking for things to punch.' Can't wait. It's going to be fantastic. And I don't care. I learned that from you too."

Darian closed his eyes, just breathing. He could hear the conviction in every single word, the truth blasting through Coby's voice.

"How would we get by?" Coby went abruptly quieter, steam gone, and sad. "We could make it work if we tried. I know that. We're smart. We could find a cheap place and stick to a budget. We could stay together. It isn't too fast to want that with each other. It's been five years coming and you feel that the same as I do. I've seen it in you."

He wasn't wrong. Not even a little.

Darian lit up a third smoke to let it burn away and listened. His heart had started aching again. He'd hurt Coby that way, and it made it hard to get enough air in. *Fuck.*

"We didn't plan on this," Coby said, quieter, so resigned that sorrow tangled up in with every word, and the growing heat of returning anger too. "We didn't plan on any of this, but I *want* it. Especially if I can't have you too. This is what I want, and what I'm doing. If I have to do it on my own, I will. But if you don't want that, come back here before I finish packing and stop me." He let out a shuddering sound. "It's up to you, but whatever you decide, that's it. No more second chances in Second Chance. So. Your move."

He hung up, leaving Darian holding the phone to his ear without a chance to say a single word.

Not that he could blame Coby. If their positions had been reversed, he'd have been there already, shouting all of that and meaning it.

Meaning it.

So, there it was. Darian did know what he wanted, and so maybe it scared the ever-loving shit out of him.

Yeah, well. That was what courage meant. What fighting was all about, anyway. He knew the right thing to do, and what his heart wanted. Had wanted for a while now, maybe since the beginning, if he was going to be honest with himself.

Okay. Darian stood, walked down the library steps, and took the left he needed. Headed for the residence halls, and as fast as he could. If he didn't get there in time, he'd go after Coby anyway, but better to get the jump.

He left Oscar's cigarettes behind. Didn't need them anymore and didn't want them.

Secondhand smoke wouldn't be good for the baby.

* * *

Coby could go fast when he wanted to. By the time Darian got back to their room and shoved the unlocked door open, he'd almost finished packing. His side of the room, nearly bare except for the tangle of sheets still on his half of the now-separated twin bed, each one shoved back into its original corner. When he looked up, his eyes were as red and swollen as before, and he'd taken off his shirt in a defiant show of the change in his body that Darian had somehow missed so far.

A dumbass when he wanted to be, no doubt about that. There were a hundred and one different ways to be a moron, and Darian had walked across a couple dozen lines so far.

No more.

Not saying anything, because he didn't need to answer the question Coby wasn't asking out loud anyway -- yet -- Darian stalked across the room, caught him by the nape, went up on his toes and hauled Coby down at the same time, and put his whole answer to the question, entire and true, into the way he kissed that man. Hard and fast, then slow and smooth, then sweet as he could, then hard again, with teeth and bruises to be left behind.

Coby went still at the first press of Darian's mouth to his, but he spoke Darian's language too. Aside from one soft, soft, soft "Oh," against Darian's lips, he didn't say anything out loud either. His arms went slowly around Darian's waist, then clung as ferociously as Darian was kissing him.

When Darian lowered himself to flat feet, his lips were as kiss-swollen as Coby's but he kept a hard hold on Coby's nape. "You're not going to do this alone," he said in a growl. "I'm not letting you. I don't back down. You want this? Guess what: I didn't think I did, I didn't know it'd changed, but it has, and I do. I want you."

Coby stared at him, searching his face.

He needed more? Darian could give him that. He laid his hand on Coby's stomach, possessive. "Mine. Yours. And we'll fucking well make it work. The hell with anyone who says different. As long as you can believe me when I say I'm sorry for bolting like a chickenshit, all right?"

Coby laughed. Kinda watery, but a real laugh, and when he grabbed Darian in another hug he lifted him clean off the floor. Darian went right along with it, letting himself be whirled around in a circle. He didn't care. He was where he belonged, and he didn't have to fight anymore.

He would fight, of course. So would Coby. They liked a good scrap. It was just that he knew, now, they'd always be able to make up after those fights too.

And speaking of which...

Darian's hand still rested on Coby's stomach, but he let it drift downward to stroke Coby's groin. Not hard, but Darian could work with that. Slow, lazy rubs started him on his way, making him draw in a sharp breath.

Coby spoke his language. His red eyes went darker, hawk-gold the way they should be, and his voice was a couple octaves deeper. "You still want me."

"Don't you ever doubt it again. I'm going to spend the rest of my life with you, inside you." He teased Coby's stiffening cock with one fingertip. "But tonight... I want *you*. In me."

Coby blinked at him, stunned still.

Darian had figured he would, but it didn't stop him wanting what he wanted. He grinned up at Coby, and it felt almost as good to finally let that go as it did to hold Coby in the palm of his hand. "What? It's not like you can knock *me* up."

There was that laugh again, the one Darian liked best. Coby studied his face again, and he must have believed what he saw there because he didn't wait a moment longer before spinning Darian around one more time and tipping them over, landing with Darian on his back in that tangle of sheets on his bed. Then, kissing him, as deep and dirty as Darian had kissed him before.

Darian surged up into the press of Coby's arms, the sturdiness of his strange, fantastic Omega, crushing him into the mattress, and he fucking loved it.

"I don't know how," Coby said against his ear. "But you do. And you'll show me."

"Bet."

And Darian did. He did like it both ways, and before he'd had Coby, during the times he hadn't had anyone else, he'd learned how to make himself feel as good as an Alpha could on his lonesome. He showed Coby, step by step, how to lubricate his fingers with his Omega wetness -- it smelled different, now that Darian was paying attention, sweeter -- and thicker too, which worked a treat. Showed Coby how to open him the harder way, and how it was worth it. Moved beneath him in waves and undulations and wrapped his legs hard around Coby's waist when Coby, shaking with nerves and lust, slid inch by inch inside him. God *damn*. Nature had made this boy a natural bottom, but nurture and being quick to learn had turned him into a fucking brilliant top.

Coby stopped when he couldn't go any farther, touching Darian's cheek. "You're making noises like you never did before. Am I hurting you?"

"I like it." Darian bared his teeth in a challenging grin. "I like to feel it." He hesitated, licking his lips, but -- hell, there would never be another moment. He arched his neck to kiss Coby again, and said, "And I love you. So you know."

Coby breathed out, long and rough, and pressed his forehead to Darian's. "It took you long enough. I love you too, you dumbass. I have since the day I met you, and you loved me that day too. I know you. I know it's true."

"Don't gloat about it."

"I will too." Coby tried a roll of his hips, one that made Darian arch and groan. "As much as I want to. Because you're mine, Darian, and you always will be."

He wasn't wrong. When Darian came, he was surer of it than ever, and when Coby came with a moan that shook the bed, flooding them both, he was surest of all.

They were like this, really, and no, it wouldn't be easy at all. But it was worth it.

Every warrior needed someone at his back.

Darian'd found his.

Epilogue
Several weeks later

"If you're FaceTiming me in the middle of the night for any other reason than what I think, I'm gonna take the next train from my nice new city of employment back to Second Chance and kick your ass in person. I just got here yesterday but I swear I'll do it." Oscar flipped Darian the bird and tossed a blanket over the head of the Omega asleep on the other side of his bed. "Well?"

Darian cocked an eyebrow at the phone and held it back far enough for Oscar to see the crook of his finger. "Walk with me."

"Jesus Christ. Coby's a bad influence on you."

"That's your opinion, and by the way, it's wrong. Also, watch your fucking language, would you?"

"This had *better* be the only call that'll save you from getting beat up."

"Wait and see for yourself." Darian started down the short hallway from the den of the tiny apartment he and Coby shared, heading for the bedroom. He kept one eye on Oscar, who'd helped them move in and knew the apartment's layout and noted with satisfaction his friend's growing wakefulness and interest. But because he had to his own self be true as well as bursting his own buttons right now, he asked, "So who's the HPOA in your bed?"

"The what now?" Oscar wrinkled his forehead. "The hoppa? The fuck is a hoppa?"

Darian made a rude noise. "H-P-O-A. Stands for Hot Piece of Ass, dumbshit. You never heard that? That's ten years old or more."

"None of your business," Oscar retorted. He sat up in bed, as if he could get a better look no matter how Darian held the phone. "Hurry up, would you?"

"All things in their own time," Darian murmured, quiet on purpose. There were sleeping bodies just behind the bedroom door he pushed open, and he'd already had his eardrums damn near ruptured a few times already that night.

Also, his hands would never be the same -- Coby might have cracked a bone or two squeezing them during all the excitement -- but honestly, Darian couldn't have cared less.

The door opened on a dimly lit bedroom almost entirely filled with a genuine queen-sized bed, extra-long to accommodate the length of Coby's legs when he wanted to stretch out. Good fresh sheets, clean duvet, pillows piled everywhere. Coby himself in the middle, not fully but almost drowsed off, the belly that'd frankly frightened Darian in the last two weeks gone down like a deflated balloon.

But that wasn't the best part. Darian pulled back a corner of the duvet to give Oscar a look at the red and wrinkled, squashed little face on the equally red, raisin-crinkled body otherwise swaddled up tight as a burrito and snugged into Coby's side. Coby sighed quietly, stirring at the movement.

"Shh," Darian said, touching Coby's lips with one bruised finger. "It's over, and you're good. Rest."

"Holy. Fucking. Shit," Oscar whispered. "This is the call."

"Yeah." Darian reached the bed and leaned over to brush wayward strands of hair out of Coby's drowsy face. "You want to know a weird thing about Omegas his height and weight? They don't calculate the drugs right at first, and nothing kicked in until it was all over. He's going to be flying high for days."

Oscar winced out loud, considered that, then whistled. "The universe has a way of returning to balance. Wait." The man had some keen-ass eyes, and he was craning his neck. "Wait. Wait, wait. The way he's holding that one arm. Is he holding the other the same way? You son of a bitch, he is, isn't he? Pull that blanket back."

"What did I say about watching your language, you comeslut?"

Coby stirred and laughed, sleepy and slurred. He mumbled something interpretable enough as, "As much cussing as they heard before, they already know all the words." He tugged at the other side of the blanket until it came back to display a second little face and body snugged into the crook of his far arm. He drew a fingertip over that one's fatter cheeks. "What d'you think about that?"

"I think if you knew, you kept that secret close to the chest." Oscar looked fascinated, and, interestingly, pretty damn envious. "You really don't do anything by halves, do you?"

Darian shrugged. "Technically. They're identical, so it was one fertilized blob that split in two."

"Tell me about it," Coby mumbled. He turned his head toward Darian, and Darian knew what that meant. He bent to kiss him lightly on the corner of his mouth, then the top of each of his son's heads. "Still blows my brain right out."

Coby flipped him off, and that was it, he went out like a light.

"Labor bad. Drugs good," Darian said. He settled in a rocking chair across from the bed, where he could keep an eye on his family and the other on the phone. "You know you're the godfather. Or if you didn't, you do now."

Oscar said absolutely nothing. Curious, Darian turned back to the screen to find Oscar looking unsure whether he wanted to bawl like one of the babies or swear an indigo-blue streak. Perfect.

"What? I'm not letting you out of it."

"Yeah, no." Oscar swiped at his face. "I hate you.

Now I've gotta buy them shit, and two of each."

"Yup," Darian agreed happily. "Or duplicates of what we got, because that second one surprised us just as much."

"As big as he got, it makes sense now. No one saw it on a scan? Were they all blind?"

"Nah. Deux --"

"Don't you fucking dare actually name the poor kid that. Judas."

"-- Twoey liked hiding behind Numero Uno," Darian went on, ignoring Oscar serenely. "Not that anyone got much of a chance to look. Coby skipped every Goddamn checkup unless I threatened to hogtie him and haul him in or marched him there myself. Not the most cooperative patient to start with. Then every time they got that wand thing out to do a scan he said it tickled, and he wiggled around too much on the table for anyone to get a real read." He cocked his head thoughtfully. "'Course, I think I'm going to have about as much trouble keeping Coby *out* of a pediatrician's office now every time one of them gets a sniffle."

"If he doesn't, I will. Over the phone, but whatever."

"Or you could come back to Second Chance," Darian suggested, deliberately careless, purposefully casual.

"Don't tempt me, you fucker."

Darian shrugged. Oscar had been recruited by a special arts school before they even finished the summer session and gone straight from commencement stage to the train station. Hadn't taken twenty-four hours before he and Oscar had known he hated the place.

As for himself and Coby? They'd stayed put in Second Chance where they belonged. In the last couple of weeks they'd kicked it into high gear, knowing every day was part of a countdown, but they'd made good use of their time. Found a cracker box-sized apartment to share. Touched base with a few universities who let doctoral students get a jump on their degrees by working from home. Did the paperwork for some assistance programs. Accepted a pair of suspiciously convenient offers of TA jobs at the university. Darian suspected that part of it was thanks to Nutcracker Jaw who seemed to like them both for whatever reason.

Come to think of it, with all he and Coby had doubled between them already, twins shouldn't have been a surprise to anyone.

"Come back to Second Chance," Darian said. "It's a good place."

Oscar made a dubious face. "I might. I'm not promising anything. But I might."

Which meant he would, and pretty soon. Darian grinned to himself, satisfied. Content. Pleased down to his bone.

A Snickers bar, a grin, a kiss, a lucky chance of supposedly unlucky housing, and a whole life unfolding after that. Good enough for him.

Good enough to be all he'd ever wanted, even if he'd never known it until it happened.

Some kind of a lucky son of a bitch, wasn't he?

Come for You (Second Chance Omegas 3)
Willa Okati

Gabriel, a dreamer and a librarian, is so shy and introverted that he's still a virgin Omega at twenty-five -- but he can't help wishing fairy-tale Prince Charmings were real and that one would find him. One does, a rough-hewn but outgoing, captivating quarryman Alpha called Wynn. For them, it's love at first sight. Gabriel doesn't care if they're an odd couple, no matter what others and his Beta co-librarian Cameron thinks about it.

But the happy ending is harder to come by. When Gabriel's almost full term with their first child, there's an accidental explosion at the quarry that leaves Wynn trapped behind a wall of rubble. Waiting for news – any news – and hoping against hope, all Gabriel has to comfort himself with is the memory of his fairytale of a love story. He's so lost in dreaming he doesn't realize he's in labor and needs to get to a doctor.

Who will rescue who?

Chapter One

Love at first sight was only for stories, or so Wynn had always been told. Fairy-tale princes that carried you away beneath their hills, who danced the night away with you, and left you changed.

So *he'd* always been told.

Everyone who'd ever told him that had been wrong.

The second he laid eyes on the cute little librarian with the glasses and the sweetest smile he'd ever seen, Wynn knew: everyone else was so, so wrong, and he was going to prove that.

* * *

Past

Tick. Tick. Tick.

The clock perched on their windowsill wasn't old enough to be vintage or antique, and wasn't new enough to be anything but old, but Gabriel liked it anyway. He'd painted the metal frame brass, then scuffed it with sandpaper until it took on a patina of age.

"Like it's been through a war or something," Wynn had said, turning the thing over in his strong, work-scarred hands to marvel at it. "What made you think of doing that?"

Gabriel took the clock away, his hands so much smaller and fairer than Wynn's that he let them linger there, so long that Wynn took one of them in his and kissed the back of his knuckles. "Because time matters," he tried to explain, lifting his hand to Wynn's hair to ruffle the short, still-wayward sandy strands. "Because I wanted it to be beautiful."

No one besides Gabriel ever got to see Wynn's best smile, the one that made him warmer than the sun, and that sent a slow-rolling wave of pleasure tingling down to his toes. "You're beautiful."

"Stop it, I'm not."

"Shh." Wynn pressed his lips to Gabriel's hot cheek and laid his hand on Gabriel's belly. "You're beautiful if I say you are, and I do. So there."

When he said it, Gabriel believed him. He raised himself to wind his arms around Wynn's neck and pulled him down into a kiss. One kiss, and then another, and then --

* * *

Present

Tick. Tick. Tick.

"Hey. Where'd you go?" Tucked up big and hard and solid behind him, his chest pressed to Gabriel's back, Wynn nosed against Gabriel's ear. "Come back."

Gabriel blinked out of the daydream he'd drifted into. It happened more and more often these days, but he'd been told that was natural for Omegas this close to giving birth. He looked down to where Wynn's big hand splayed wide over his belly, and even it wasn't big enough to cup more than the top. They'd been twined together for an hour, maybe more, taking their time and letting the fire build.

He glanced at the clock -- they had half an hour before the alarm rang, not enough but enough to make use of -- and covered Wynn's hand, turning his head as far as he could toward Wynn's mouth. "I'm here."

Wynn's quiet laugh made his mouth tickle, but he swept that away with a nip to the side of Gabriel's mouth and the downward slide of his hand. He wrapped it loosely around Gabriel's cock and gave him a slow, lazy stroke and smiled against his neck when Gabriel moaned and arched up, wanting more. "Better be."

"I am. I am." Gabriel reached backward, skating his fingers over Wynn's hip. It was all he could reach. Eight and a half weeks -- maybe eight and a half, maybe nine and a half weeks, they weren't sure and first babies were usually late -- kept them almost at arm's length. As Wynn stroked him, too slow and too lightly for anything but a tease, he tried to arch his neck backward to kiss his husband and only caught a brush of his skin. "*Wynn*."

Wynn's breath warmed his neck in small puffs. "What do you need?"

"I need -- *oh*." Gabriel's fingers spasmed as Wynn rolled his hips, light pushes against but not inside him, not nearly enough, not as much as he needed. His body clenched around nothing, and it wasn't enough. "Wynn. Oh God, Wynn, please?"

"Mmm-mm. Tell me what you want."

"I need to see you. I need more." Gabriel wasn't ever going to be able to say things like that out loud without his face burning, but Wynn gave him the strength to try. "Please, think of a way."

Wynn laughed as he trailed his fingers down the inside of Gabriel's slick-wet thigh. The small bedroom that already smelled like sex and sweat, and saline humidity should have been too thick an atmosphere to breathe in, but the air next to his skin was clean and sweet. "Oh, babe, you should know better than to ask things like that. Keep doing it." He bit the curve of Gabriel's ear, sending a thrill down his spine, then tickled him in the next second to surprise Gabriel into laughing too. "I've got you."

He threw one leg over Gabriel and before Gabriel could ask, came down with a thump on his other side. There was barely enough room between Gabriel's belly and the wall they'd pushed their bed against, but Wynn had a good eye for judging distance, and he didn't jar or bump a thing. Face to face with him, he grinned at Gabriel. "Better?"

"For a start," Gabriel breathed. Wynn had to arch his back into a C to get close enough, but he could and he did, and the heat of his mouth pressed to Gabriel's was worth the effort. His tongue flicked inside and curled against Gabriel's, drawing a moan out of him and a hitch forward with the need to get closer still.

"Oh God," Gabriel breathed between their lips. He fumbled for Wynn's hand and brought it down to his cock. "Wynn. *Wynn.*"

"Better," Wynn murmured, with a right to sound as satisfied as he did, and kissed Gabriel again but only let Gabriel nudge his wrist instead of taking him in hand. He moved his mouth down the line of Gabriel's jaw, soft and rounded as Omega bones often were, not hard or planed like his own, but he must have liked it. He nibbled lightly over the valentine's point of Gabriel's chin and nosed beneath it to kiss a path down his neck. "And this?"

All Gabriel could do was take hold of Wynn's head and try to slide his fingers through hair too short for that. The nails just scratched over his scalp, but it made Wynn groan and buck toward him. He moved his hand to Wynn's back then, drawing harder lines there, curling them upward.

"Better," Wynn murmured between the quiet panting of Gabriel's breath. He took hold of Gabriel's leg and lifted it to drape over his hip, then slid his hand between Gabriel's legs and two fingers inside him in one smooth, fluid sweep. He bit over Gabriel's collarbone when Gabriel gave a startled gasp and clenched down around him. "Oh God, you feel so good."

"More, Wynn, please, more." If only he could *reach* more than Wynn's back! He gave Wynn a taste of his own teeth, biting his cheekbone just shy of breaking the skin. "*Wynn.*"

"Shh, shh, baby, I've got you." Wynn crooked his fingers up, rubbing him from the inside, while his cock rubbed sticky trails on Gabriel's thigh. "Oh God, you're so hot inside. You open up like…" He shook his head and withdrew just long enough to stroke Gabriel's stomach with something like reverence and something like lust.

"Look at you, gorgeous, so full of our baby you're ready to pop. So *tight*. I didn't think you'd be that hard, I thought you'd be soft, the way you look."

"Not yet." Gabriel touched Wynn's mouth. If he kept talking like that Gabriel would come, and he didn't want to, not yet. They had time for a little more, even if the clock on the bookshelf kept ticking the seconds away. He slotted his mouth against Wynn's to keep him quiet and lifted his hips, finding he could get a little closer after all, breathing into his mouth. "Not yet, not just yet. *More*."

"Hungry little Omega," Wynn murmured, but he wanted it as much as Gabriel did. Always had. "Hold on."

Gabriel curled his fingers into Wynn's shoulder and arm as Wynn found a rhythm, somehow, two fingers and then three, spreading open in a fan shape, closing to slide higher and deeper. Nudging him and driving him, pushing him so close to that edge -- but it still wasn't enough. He whined and thrust back, trying to get him deeper and his mind throbbed in time with his cock, wild for it this morning.

The sharp, tight squeeze in his middle startled a moan out of him, a cramp that started at the small of his back and shot around to the front, drawing his belly up high and tight and hard. It didn't hurt but the *intensity* of it -- he let go of Wynn and folded over, hugging himself one-armed.

Wynn noticed, and went still as the marble he helped hew out of the quarry, risking his life for this -- for them -- every day, no matter how Gabriel begged him not to, because what choice did they have? What else would they live on? "Gabriel?"

Gabriel shook his head, his jaw clenched too tightly to answer. *Pressure*.

When he didn't answer, Wynn pressed his palm to Gabriel's bulging belly, feeling it quiver as the muscles drew tighter still. "Gabe? Is that --"

"No," Gabriel said when it ebbed, when he'd caught his breath enough to speak. "Strong, but. No. Just something that happens sometimes. The body gets itself ready. You just haven't been here for it before."

Wynn looked doubtful, uncertain, as young as he was, barely past twenty, even if years in the quarry had already left scuffs and scars on his skin. "You're sure?"

"I'm sure, and I don't want you to stop." Gabriel put his hand on Wynn's cheek, rubbing the firm bone there with one thumb. "Don't be scared. I just need you." His channel clenched, the last of the cramp melting away and leaving him so, so wet. "I need you in me."

Wynn pressed his face into Gabriel's palm. "I love you," he said, as breathless as Gabriel now, and so, *so* hard; Gabriel could feel it even if he couldn't see it when he reached down to stroke what he could reach. Sweat dripped into his eyes, making what he saw blurrier than usual without the glasses he needed when he looked up at his husband, his sweet husband, his Wynn. The man no one -- no one -- thought he should date, much less marry, much less start a family with, a rough-cut, dirt-poor miner without a high school degree or anyone to keep him in check, not a good match for a bashful virgin librarian who'd never even dated before, but Gabriel didn't *care*, hadn't then and didn't now.

All he wanted was Wynn, and all Wynn wanted -- he'd said so -- from that first day was him.

All of that must have showed on Gabriel's face; Wynn shut his eyes and pressed their foreheads together, though he was still smiling that roguish, Peter Pan smile that'd made Gabriel's heart skip two beats in a row when he saw it the day they met. "I love you, God, I love you so much. My Omega, my Gabriel."

"I love you more." Gabriel slotted his mouth to Wynn's, but he couldn't hold it there long, his neck aching with the stretch and his body moving restlessly. "My Wynn."

Wynn couldn't lie still either, rubbing circles against his belly, never too hard, but enough to make Gabriel's muscles clench in a hot rush. "Can't believe it," he muttered, pressing his mouth everywhere his mouth could go with their bodies aligned like this. "You're so beautiful this way, so hot, you make me want you so bad. What do you want?"

Gabriel's lips parted on a breath that was half rushed air, half sob. "I want it all."

Tick, tick, tick went the clock, but the sun wasn't up yet. They had some time.

Wynn stilled at last, his mouth on the lowest curve of Gabriel's stomach. Gabriel couldn't see him looking up in that wicked way he had, but he could feel the heat in it. "Tell me, baby. Tell me what you need."

"I want... Wynn, I want..." Gabriel swallowed, because even as shy as he was he wanted to give Wynn what *Wynn* wanted, just like he'd wanted Wynn's baby in his belly. "I want you to make me come," he said in a rush. "I want you inside me, and I want to come on your cock."

Wynn let out a delighted laugh that rattled the bed and their bones. "All you ever had to do was ask." He slid an arm under Gabriel and started to lift, shaking his head when Gabriel started to protest that he was too heavy for this. "You're not too heavy for me. Let me see you."

He didn't stop until he was on his back with Gabriel settled on his lap, his cock snugged up so, so close to slipping inside the opening he'd fingered loose and wet, wetter with every brush of skin on skin. Gabriel tipped his head back and put up his hands, knowing Wynn would catch them and give him something to brace against.

Almost. One hand. The other came back to his belly to stroke at it, and the pulse of pure *want* it sent through Gabriel made his muscles shake. And -- it made him brave. With the hand he had free, he reached under the heavy hang of his stomach to find Wynn's cock and guide it toward him, inside him -- almost.

When he looked down, Wynn stared at him as if he'd been hit by lightning, eyes wide and lips parted.

Gabriel had to touch his face, his cheek, even if all he could reach was the roughness of his stubble. "Like this," he said.

He raised himself on his knees, shaky though they were, and moved the way he'd learned how, and slid down, down, down, not stopping until they were skin to skin again and Wynn was as deep inside him as he could go. He clutched Wynn's hand as Wynn arched back and rolled his hips up, a push that should have hurt but only made his head spin and sparks light in front of his eyes.

But that wasn't all. He drew himself up, nearly letting Wynn go, then sank down. His inner muscles clenched and squeezed, not wanting to loosen, then going hot and eager to take him back again. Fresh sweat rolled down his back and chest, and they were so *wet* between them that the dirty, sticky, slippery noises made his cock jerk in an effort to come that he barely held back.

He stole a glance at the clock. The alarm would go off soon, and they would have to part for the day -- Wynn to the quarry, the dangerous quarry, and Gabriel to the work he could still do from home when he was this pregnant -- if he could only do more, if he could keep Wynn out of that awful place --

Tick. Tick. Tick.

They still had a little more time right now. Just a little. But enough.

Wynn's hands fell to Gabriel's hips, where his fingers would leave bruises. "Gabriel, oh God, Gabriel," he said between ragged breaths as he swelled harder, thicker, stretching Gabriel open further still. "I could watch that forever, me going in and out of you." He had to work for it now, Gabriel's body wanting to trap him inside and keep him there, but he was stronger and he was gentle with it, and there was enough slick to keep it smooth except when they wanted it to be rough. He built up speed, going faster until Gabriel could only hold on and ride him, rise and fall. He drew his hand up his belly, hard like Wynn had admired it, up his chest and to the changes there, a little softer, a little fuller. When he squeezed one nipple, a milky drop trickled out that he caught on his fingertip and slipped between his teeth.

"Fuck!" Wynn threw his head back, the tendons straining in his neck.

It tasted sweet, but not as sweet as that. Gabriel wanted more. He let go of his nipple and brought his hand up to his neck to caress it and rumple his hair, then rolled his hips so that Wynn could feel what this did to him. His belly clenched again, not as strongly and yet almost painful, but the heat building in his groin was far stronger, and he could feel himself rushing toward the end.

He let go of himself and fumbled for Wynn's hands, graceless again and not caring. Down, down, down, he rocked his hips, taking as much as he could and demanding more -- and Wynn gave it to him, red all over from effort and *so* hard --

Wynn's hand pressed against his spine when he came, or he might have arched far enough to break his bones when he came, milky like the sweet drops trickling from his nipples, just as hot, falling on him. He squeezed Wynn's hands and held tight, inside and out, still riding him, working him until he groaned and shuddered to a freeze, a stop, and then a long, long, long exhale as he let go. His seed flooded Gabriel until it overflowed and rolled back down to mingle with the mess Gabriel had made, a sticky pool between them.

He fell, letting Wynn catch him even as Wynn slipped out of him, not yet soft but satisfied, his head coming to rest over Wynn's pounding heart. Wynn carded his hair in uncoordinated pulls and cradled his belly, not feeling one last squeeze rippling faintly through Gabriel's muscles before fading and lifted his head to kiss him so deeply that they might have melted into each other, becoming one person instead of two.

Gabriel's eyes were closed, and he thought Wynn's were too, when Wynn breathed into his mouth, "I love you."

"Always," Gabriel said. "Always yours." He licked his lips, tasting milk and Wynn. "Just promise me."

Wynn wound his arm around Gabriel, easing him down, the pounding of his heart and the salty slickness of his skin soothing. "Anything you want, Gabriel. Anything."

Tick. Tick. Tick. The clock would go off any second.

"Promise you'll come home to me," Gabriel said, rubbing his thumb over the beat of Wynn's heart. "No matter what happens, promise you'll come home."

"Sweetheart." Wynn's light touch coaxed Gabriel's eyes open, meeting them. "You think anything could ever stop me, you're wrong."

"Promise anyway."

Wynn shook his head, but he took Gabriel's hand and kissed the knuckles again, and Gabriel could hear him mean it when he said, "I promise."

I promise.
Tick. Tick. Tick.
The alarm rang…

Chapter Two

Present

Just like always when something went wrong at the quarry, Gabriel felt the explosion before he heard it. A shock wave blasted through his and Wynn's little house half a second before the dull *roar-boom* that followed, both making him flinch and clap a hand to his chest. He turned toward the door even though he knew he wouldn't see anything -- instinct to protect, perhaps? Born or unborn, their baby had working ears and he hadn't liked the commotion either; the baby turned agitated circles inside him as quickly as he could with almost no room left in there to twist or flip.

"Shh, shh, shh." He couldn't cradle the baby against his shoulder the way he suddenly wanted to, needing the warmth and weight in his arms -- he'd heard it was like that, for most Omegas, when they were alarmed -- but he could rub soothing circles on his stomach, and that helped. Some.

It didn't help *him*.

Gabriel caught his lip between his teeth, not quite able to look away from the door. Second Chance had grown outward and upward in the past years, but it still wasn't any kind of industrial hub where noises like that might be commonplace. If Wynn was there, he'd have made a guessing game out of it: an explosion in the college chemistry lab? *Some poor bastard's going to show up for his date with no eyebrows and only half his hair*, he'd say, tickling Gabriel to make him laugh and relax.

Or the train had cracked its tracks again, but -- no, that wouldn't be an explosion.

Or a car wreck.

Something had happened at the quarry, and Wynn always, always told Gabriel when they were blasting the rock. So he wouldn't worry. And he called him afterward, so Gabriel knew he was safe.

Gabriel's phone, tucked in his pocket, didn't make a sound.

A thick, sour swallow knotted in Gabriel's throat. He touched his phone, knowing he should call, but somehow he couldn't seem to make himself move. He barely noticed a cramp that shot around his middle, except to dismiss it as another one of those things that'd alarmed Wynn. They happened.

He needed to call.

He went for the door instead and made himself open it. Their cottage faced the quarry, and that hadn't been on purpose, but they'd made a joke out of it, how Wynn would have a straight shot to work when he was in a hurry. They could load him up like a pebble in a slingshot and fire away and he'd always make it there on time.

Dark, ashy plumes of smoke rolled slowly, inexorably up from where the quarry dug into the earth.

Gabriel's knees wouldn't hold him up. He lowered himself to their front steps. *Wynn. Wynn, what happened?*

He might have been there for fifteen minutes, or maybe an hour or two. The baby went still, sleeping or bored or worried and straining his ears or just asleep; Gabriel hoped for asleep, but he kept a hand on himself just in case. He didn't hear any more explosions, but there were sirens and flashing lights, and the plumes of smoke never stopped rolling. He couldn't look away from them.

The first new thing he saw was movement in the corner of his eye. He glanced sideways, quick-there-and-back, because whoever this was, they drove a faded red sedan. Wynn had sold his battered gray-green work truck a few weeks back when they'd had no other choice. The one he'd kept running for years with duct tape and sheer stubbornness. It'd been his father's, and Wynn hadn't had anything else besides a wolf's bloodline that'd belonged to him.

"I'll give that to our son one day," he'd said the last time he tinkered around in there, pushing his ball cap back and leaving a long smudge of grease on one cheek that didn't mar his grin at Gabriel. *"He might not thank me for it, but tradition's tradition."*

Every time he talked -- thought -- about being a father, Wynn lit up from the inside. No one else ever saw him that way. Only Gabriel.

Gabriel ignored the driver of the sedan as they heaved themself out of it and trudged toward him, a grizzled old man saturated with the stink of smoke and burning rock, hands raw with sluggishly bleeding scrapes. What was the man's name? It wasn't coming to him. Gabriel was a librarian and had owl bloodlines; he studied and kept quiet, kept to himself, he wasn't a town councilman, and he only knew the man's face because he worked at the -- at the quarry, where --

"What happened?" he asked, turning away. "Where's Wynn?"

"Ah, hell." The old man stopped a safe distance away from a claimed Omega and let out a rough breath. "You're his husband, weren't you? Wynn's."

Present tense. Past tense. Both in the same sentence. *Titus.* That was the old man's name, though he didn't remember when he'd learned it. One of the foremen.

Gabriel took a breath of his own. "I am. What happened?" He didn't miss the wary look he could *feel* old Titus gave his midsection. "Don't do that. Please. I don't matter right now. Something bad happened out there. What was it?"

"I dunno," Titus muttered. "Hell, I told them we ought to get the NP out here with me."

"No. Everyone with training will be busy at the --" Gabriel stopped himself. "At the quarry. Titus, please."

Titus dragged a hand backward through his hair. *"Hell.* They don't know exactly what did happen, they're still figuring that out, but odds are a charge went off when it wasn't supposed to."

Gabriel's eyes slid closed. He'd been right.

"A few walls came down, couple corridors got blocked off, there's some flooding," Titus went on, gruffer and faster. "There's some casualties. People who weren't where they were supposed to be. Most everyone's accounted for, but not everyone." He shook his head. "The ones that are missing, they were down a tunnel that got blocked off with rubble. And..."

And Wynn was one of them. Titus didn't have to say it out loud for Gabriel to know that his husband was among the missing. He pressed a hand to his middle, though the baby hadn't moved.

And -- no. Just -- no.

Wynn wouldn't do that to him.

"You need to prepare for the worst," Titus said, rougher but closer, still keeping a wary weather eye on Gabriel. Either he'd never had children of his own, or he was a throwback to when Alphas were kept pacing in a waiting room until everything was all over but for passing out the cigars and tossing back a few glasses of whiskey. Not like Wynn, who wanted to be there for everything.

"Depending how gnarly it gets I might throw up a couple of times, but you try and keep me away," he said, tucking Gabriel under one wiry-lean arm and resting their heads together. "I'll be there. You count on that."

Gabriel had laughed himself half sick over that. Gnarly? That was one way to put it.

"He was coming home to me," he said, sounding faraway even to himself. He might be in shock, he thought dimly. Or maybe not. But -- still. "No. He's coming home."

"Are you hearing me?" Titus asked. He'd come around in front of Gabriel, all the better to study him for -- what? Signs that Gabriel was going to pop like an overripe plum right there, he guessed.

It irritated him into pushing himself back to his feet, away from the uneasy helping hand Titus tried to offer. "Thank you. I'm fine."

"The hell you are," Titus muttered. "I need to be back over there myself, all right? Just Wynn made me promise, if anything ever went balls up, I'd come tell you what was going on. Didn't want you to hear secondhand. He's dead, boy. Probably dead. If he's not dead yet and they don't get that tunnel open soon enough, it'll come to the same thing. I'm sorry, son. I'm damn sorry."

"I see." Gabriel put a hand on the doorframe. A splinter, small but sharp, slid into his palm, but it didn't seem to hurt, not like the cramp in his back that made him hiss and that he had to rub away. It was nothing; it happened. Standing too stiffly with a spine that wasn't used to carrying so much more weight in the front would do that. "Thank you."

Titus gave him the oddest look. "Look, son --"

"No. It's all right." Gabriel closed his eyes and breathed, one-two-three-four-five, then opened them. Titus almost made him laugh, ridiculous as that would have been, with how that'd alarmed the grizzled old man. "I'm not in labor. I don't need help. Thank you for coming to tell me, but you can go now."

Titus's wariness turned baffled. "Figured you'd want to go to town, anyway. Be near the hospital just in case. I can give you a ride."

"No!" Gabriel held up a hand and took a step back. It was strange, and he couldn't explain it, but all he could feel now was calm, and an unshakeable certainty of what he was going to do. "Thank you, but no. Wynn said he'd come home after his shift. I'll wait here for him."

"For fuck's sake, son." Titus really looked worried now, probably for his sanity. "You need checking out."

Perhaps he wasn't wrong. It wouldn't hurt.

And yet.

"I'll be fine," Gabriel said, still so calm. "Wynn promised he'd come back."

Titus exploded. "Hellfire and shitballs, son! You didn't see what it was like down there. I've never been to hell but that was damn close, all right? If he's alive, and that's a big if, he's staying under all that."

"No. He won't."

"You're not hearing me!"

"I hear you fine!" Gabriel never shouted, never, but the crack-boom of his voice at full volume now startled them both. He took a breath and held out his splinter-ridden hand to warn Titus off as he backed through the door, safely into his home. "None of that matters. Wynn said he would come back, and no matter what anyone says about him, he's never lied to me. I don't need to go anywhere. I'll wait here. Thank you again."

He took hold of the doorknob, and gently eased the door shut.

He'd always wondered what would happen, *if.* Now he knew.

Absently, he sucked the splinter out of his palm. He lowered his hand, bleeding a drop or two, to his middle, and let himself drift off the way it was so easy to do these days. He turned his gaze inward, looking not at the world around him or hearing Titus's fast, angry, hammering knocks, but at the past, the memories that lived as brightly as the day was dreary, all inside his head...

Back when he'd had a different name. When he'd been Vincent, not Gabriel. Before Wynn changed that, and so much more...

* * *

Past

Troublemakers.

Vincent saw them in the far side of his peripheral vision as they barged into the library, all big voices and jeering and ragged-edged flannel and heavy leather boots. It wasn't even two in the afternoon, but cigarette smoke and beer stink rolled in front of them in a wave. They strode through the front foyer like they were in a museum, peering around in frank, undisguised curiosity.

He and Cameron, the other librarian on duty -- a Beta who seemed like a kind man, so far as Vincent knew him -- exchanged speaking glances.

Definitely troublemakers.

Cameron gestured at himself and the circulation desk, saying he'd put himself in a position to keep an eye on them no matter where they went. Vincent nodded and went for the cart full of books to be reshelved. He could roam, and if anything looked dicey he'd give Cameron the signal.

He grunted with the effort as he got the cart, one wheel's axle slightly bent, started forward. It'd been story hour that morning, and Vincent loved children but oh, they could make a mess. Not one he minded cleaning up. It was worth it to see the looks on those sweet faces when they got lost in the story he was reading them, to look at them and wonder: *what will you be when you grow up?*

Hopefully not like these men: the definition of high risk, walking.

There weren't many of them in Second Chance. Less so than in any of the bigger cities surrounding their tucked-away valley, but no matter where you went, there were always a few. When he'd first moved here for the library job, Vincent had gotten his ears filled with plenty of stories and warnings about the handful of roughnecks who called this place home. Quarry workers and railroad men for the most part, a few bikers; some who'd grown up on the wrong side of the tracks or the ones who didn't give a drop for anyone but themselves and whatever entertained them at the moment. Vincent understood why, in a way. They lived dangerous lives and they worked hard; it only made sense they'd want to play hard too.

But Omegas were *always* taught to be wary of men like that.

Vincent kept a careful watch on the group as he slid books back into their places. The library wasn't that big, and someone who didn't understand how books work had constructed it as a rotunda so that all the shelves had been custom made to fit the curving walls. He wasn't afraid of the roughnecks, not exactly, but he'd always been shy. Painfully so. After he'd lost his family, he'd needed to find somewhere easier to breathe than inside a foster home. Libraries had been that for him wherever he could find one, quiet and peaceful and safe.

The men had lowered their voices -- a little -- but they were still treating the library like any other store or bar, trading jokes and jeers and jabs. Striding in as if they owned the place.

One of them, the youngest of the bunch, stayed more or less in the middle of the group. He might have been around Vincent's age, give or take a year, sandy brown hair a mess, red plaid flannel unbuttoned at the neck, and crackling with as much mischief in him as Peter Pan on a spree. Not so tall as some, but broad-shouldered with hands the size of spades. He looked like he could take down a brick wall without blinking. As Vincent watched he gave one of the older men a playful shove and peeled off to one side, ambling down a line of shelves by himself without a care in the world.

He didn't seem to be a threat. Vincent didn't need to keep his focus on the man and the group he'd come in with.

But he couldn't help himself. He kept his head down, yes, nudging his glasses up his nose whenever they slipped a little too low, and glanced up at the youngest miner every three books or so. Even away from the group he was still noisy, whistling off-key to himself as he poked through displays and opened books only to flip through a few pages, frown, and drop them back in place.

Not roughly. Carefully. Those big hands were surprisingly deft, and there was something about the look on his face, the key to his whistling... It took Vincent a minute of puzzling to recognize and understand what it was.

Happiness. Pure and simple happiness.

Vincent's heart tugged sideways in his chest. What must it be like, to live so carefree? He liked his own life well enough, calm and ordered and quiet, but he wanted to *know*, just then, how life could be when lived with that kind of uncomplicated joy.

He looked down to see his hands were shaking, made an impatient noise at them and at himself -- he liked books, loved reading, but he lived in the real world -- and went back to shelving one after another until the repetition lulled him into a serene, dreamlike fugue. He stopped paying attention to the roughneck miners, most of whom had either left or plunked down in front of their bank of computers and let himself focus only on the rough-and-soft book bindings, the rustle of pages, and the smells of paper and ink.

When he reached the end of the kids' books, Vincent gave the cart another good shove to get it around the corner to the nonfiction shelves. He pushed it forward without looking, too hard, and the axle chose that moment to finally give way. The wheel cracked, falling sideways and taking the weight of the cartload on a suddenly lower corner, Vincent too startled to stop it in time before almost all the books still on there skidded off its side. Only a quick shove of cart against shelf stopped them from falling.

"Whoa! Hey. You need some help?"

Vincent stilled, but he knew before he looked up who he'd see, and he was right. The sandy-haired miner had paused on the other side of the shelf -- or had he been there already? -- keeping it between them but leaning over it, propped on his wrists, his head tilted like a curious child's. He had a kind, friendly face, a sideways grin and the sparkle in his eyes was the kind that would never dim. *He* didn't smell like beer or smoke, but like cinnamon gum and strong black coffee.

Heat flooded Vincent's face, along with a deeply, deeply embarrassing rush of warmth in his lower belly. He didn't put off much Omega scent -- suppressants, no matter how unnecessary they were in his case -- but every now and then hints of sweetness still made themselves known.

Shyness made him duck his head; embarrassment made him brusque. "No. Thank you."

"You sure?" The miner craned his neck to look over the shelves and whistled again, a single note. "Wow, you broke that pretty damn good."

"Language!"

The miner laughed. "Okay, pretty darn good, if that's better. I could fix it for you. If you have a tool kit, it wouldn't take a minute. Here, look, let me show you."

He loped around the shelf as careless as could be and dropped to one knee beside the cart, poking curiously at its broken wheel. Vincent backed away one step, meaning to take two, but hesitated. He didn't know how to fix a cart, though he could find out within six seconds on Google, but he didn't know if he'd be able to do it properly, and there was something... something he couldn't put his finger on... that made him think this rough, troublemaking miner could.

Only that wasn't right. Somehow, there wasn't any trouble in *him*, as hard as Vincent looked for it. Just some rough edges and a good-natured disregard for what anyone thought about them.

"Wynn," he said with a glance up and another easy grin. "In case you were wondering."

Vincent blinked and adjusted his glasses. "I'm sorry, what?"

The miner raised one shoulder, as comfortable on one knee as if he'd be on an overstuffed couch. "If you're going to study me like a butterfly in a glass case, Mr. Owl, you should at least know who you're looking at. I'm Wynn."

"Oh." Vincent hesitated. He'd never liked his name; it'd never seemed to fit him, but it was the only one he had. He did have it on his library badge, clipped to his collar, but it seemed rude not to answer -- and he didn't want to be. "I'm. Vincent. Win, you said?"

The sparkle in the Alpha's eye didn't dim at all. "W-y-n-n. Sounds like a 60's country-western singer, doesn't it?"

Vincent's laugh surprised him so much that he clapped a hand to his mouth, but Wynn -- his grin only widened as he pushed himself to his feet. He casually reached over to push a wayward curl of no-color brown hair behind Vincent's ear. "I was right," he said. "I knew you'd be pretty when you smiled."

Oh. Vincent's burst of amusement died, and he took that second step back after all. He pushed his glasses back in place, very aware that he was as plain as an Omega could be, bookish and bespectacled and *so* socially awkward, never understanding how to dress himself any better than in sweaters and jeans. "Don't make fun of me."

"Who's making fun?" Wynn crinkled his nose in amusement when that curl popped free and fell over Vincent's forehead again. He nudged it behind Vincent's ear this time and his touch, so unexpected, made Vincent draw in a quick breath. Wynn's fingertips, rough but gentle, made his belly clench in the strangest way. "I'm not, by the way. You are pretty when you smile. I get the feeling you don't much. Maybe I could help change that."

Vincent -- had no idea what to say to that. It'd dawned on him that he was being flirted with, and that didn't happen. A virgin Omega at his age, even a loner owl, was almost never heard of, yet there he was. He'd barely dated, and he'd never even been kissed, too bashful for both, and somehow he felt sure Wynn could see that written all over his face.

Wynn, meanwhile, had tucked his hands easily in his pockets but hadn't stopped grinning at Vincent. That sparkle in his eye really never did go dim, did it? "So I'm Wynn, and you're Vincent. There you go. Meant to be."

Vincent hesitated before confessing, "I don't get it."

"No? Wynn and Vin, Vin and Wynn." Wynn winked at him. "Meant to be. Together, in case you missed the point I was trying to make."

Vincent's cooling cheeks flooded with heat again. "But --"

"But?" Wynn cocked an eyebrow.

"But," Vincent said in baffled helplessness. A friendly, kindly Alpha, handsome as the devil no matter how young, could have anyone, so... "Why?"

"I already said. You're beautiful." Easy as anything, Wynn took up Vincent's hand and ran his thumb across the knuckles. The feel of his hand made Vincent shiver the same way he would when he saw the first snowflakes of winter, his most favorite of all. "You are, you know. Vin." He laughed at Vincent's wince, but it wasn't cruel, not at all. "You're not feeling the rhyme? That's fine. What's your middle name?"

Vincent blinked, confused. "Gabriel."

"I should have known. A man with the face of an angel; it fits." Wynn stroked Vincent's face with just the pad of his thumb, so light, so sweet, so everything a man like him wasn't supposed to be but *was*. "I'll call you Gabriel instead, angel."

Such a line. Even a virgin like Vincent knew one when he heard it. He should have laughed, himself, told Wynn to go try it with someone who knew how to play his kind of games, but Gabriel -- because that was the day Vincent *became* Gabriel -- took the gift he'd been offered. He'd never thought of going by his middle name. Wouldn't have done it on his own. But on Wynn's lips, it sounded like it fit him just right and should have always been that way.

It felt so right that it frightened him, and he took a third, skittish step back, bringing a book up to hold against his chest. "I have work to do."

"You're a librarian, and this is a library. I figured." Wynn cocked his head to the other side. "When you get off, come to dinner with me."

Vincent -- Gabriel -- was shaking his head before Wynn even finished. He couldn't. He wouldn't have any idea what to do, and he couldn't bear the thought of Wynn looking at him in disappointment. How? Why did it matter so much, so fast?

"So that's a no," Wynn murmured. He studied Gabriel thoughtfully, then broke out into another smile. "That's okay."

"It is?"

"Sure." He touched Gabriel's face one more time, lifting his chin so gently. "I'll come back, and I'll ask again. However long it takes, I'll come back for you."

Chapter Three

Present

The pounding at his and Wynn's door had stopped; Gabriel didn't know when. He'd gotten too lost in his head to notice, and he still couldn't quite pull himself out of it even as he realized he'd started walking to the corner of the one-room shack that held their bed. The covers were still in a mess, tousled and tangled and sticky in places.

They needed to be changed and made to lie smooth. Gabriel reached for the edge of the blanket, meaning to do that, but somehow suddenly he was sitting on the edge of the bed instead, his palm resting in the divot Wynn's head had made on a squashy pillow he loved. He could smell them so strongly here, blackberries and cinnamon thick in the back of his throat.

Wynn. Wynn was trapped. There'd been an accident at the quarry, and Wynn was --

Gabriel pulled the pillow up to his chest and wrapped his arms around it, as much as he could with his belly in the way. The baby was still quiet, barely stirring inside him, only a tiny flutter every now and then. His back twinged, but he was used to that; Omega pregnancies went so fast that their spines were still compensating right up to the very end, and --

Wynn was --

No. It didn't make sense, and Gabriel's mind flatly rejected it. This was the year of our Lord two thousand and twenty-odd. They had high-speed Internet, they had electric cars, they had vaccines, and they had clean skies above them. Things like this didn't still happen. They couldn't.

He really should make the bed.

Instead, he slipped his hand beneath his own pillow. Old habit to stash valuable things where he knew they'd be safe while he slept, but aside from making sure he had a fireproof case for the thing Wynn had never commented on it. He thumbed it awake and tapped on his phone app. Five missed calls; he hadn't even heard them. Five messages. More texts. Cameron, Titus, some names he didn't recognize.

He should call them back.

He didn't.

Gently, gently, Gabriel clicked his phone off and slid it in his pocket. He folded himself over the pillow and pressed his face to it, breathing deep. If he did return any of the calls, what would he even say? His mouth felt numb besides; it couldn't shape words even if he'd wanted to. And he would scream, he knew it, if someone tried to be kind to him -- worse than that if they were just nosy, wanting the tea spilled in their dish before anyone else could get a taste.

It might have been different if any of the callers were family, but they weren't. He didn't have any family besides Wynn -- and neither did Wynn have any family besides him. Him, and their son, as soon as he was born. Another week, or a week and a half. He thought.

Absently, he pressed a hand to his side to ease a deep-tugging twinge until it faded. Wynn couldn't be dead. He hadn't met his son yet, the one he wanted more than almost anything.

And Wynn didn't give up on anything he wanted. Not ever.

* * *

Past

Gabriel hadn't expected it, not really, but Wynn had meant what he said. He kept coming back. Sometimes to flip through a book and wink at him, nothing more. Sometimes to leave a small gift, never signed, but who else could it be from? Coffee the way he liked it, an old coin with quarry dust ground into it, a bracelet woven from owl feathers, a rose just on the cusp of blooming. Once, a flash drive with one MP3 file on it, someone playing a soft, sweet melody on an acoustic guitar. Gabriel had never heard the song before, but he heard Wynn humming under the plucking strings and knew he was the one playing. That he -- might have -- written it for him. *Him.*

Cameron frowned over every little thing, but he never failed to pass them on. He also never failed to look exactly like he wanted to say more than a few things about them, all pointed, but he kept his mouth shut.

Still, nothing lasted forever, and even Cameron had a breaking point. His came the night after the morning where, when Wynn had asked Gabriel out again, and Gabriel had -- heart in his throat, pounding so so so hard -- said *yes.*

* * *

Some people thought libraries were strange, creepy places once they'd closed for the day and went empty. Abandoned stores too. Empty parking lots, old playgrounds and houses where no one lived. Liminal spaces like that.

Gabriel hadn't ever thought so. His idea of heaven had been a room with nothing but books, as many as he could ever read in one lifetime, and all the soothing quiet he could drink in.

Only things were... had become... not the same.

In the utter quiet of the library, Gabriel's ears pricked at the sound of the bathroom door opening. Standing in front of the mirror, he stilled for half a second before he recognized Cameron's reflection in the mirror and went back to tugging at his hair, trying to make it lie down smoothly or least not fly away in every direction. "Did you need something?"

He wouldn't have said he and Cameron were friends, exactly; they got along, and they worked well together, but they'd never connected on any other level.

He was the only Beta that Gabriel had ever known; maybe it was like that with them, caught in a liminal space of their own between Alpha and Omega, not knowing whether to carve out their own space or try to fit in one box or the other.

Or maybe they were all different, like every other person in the world. Cameron took charge more easily than Gabriel, but so did mice. He had a big heart, enough to share with those who weren't even really friends. He closed the bathroom door and leaned against it, frowning at Gabriel.

Ah. Gabriel thought he knew what this was about. He shook his head at the Cameron in the mirror: *don't, okay?*

Cameron didn't look away from him, frowning. "Are you sure you know what you're doing?"

Two weeks ago, Gabriel would have said *no.* But that was before Wynn had coaxed him into *yes.* "You already know the answer to that. You've asked before."

"I've asked around about him, you know," Cameron said after a pause. "I've heard some things."

Gabriel licked his fingertip and tried to nudge his hairline into place. He'd brought the outfit he was wearing to the library in its own special bag; he still didn't know what he was doing, but he'd tried. Black shirt, one that fit him, and black jeans that he'd been promised did the same. Boots, new but sturdy, surprisingly easy to stand in. His heart still started to beat too fast every time he met his own gaze, rattling against his ribs in a nervous gallop. "I don't want to hear gossip."

"Is it gossip if it's true?"

"You know it is."

"But do you know?" Cameron asked, still frowning. "I asked because I want to be sure you're safe, and this guy doesn't have a good reputation."

Gabriel held up one hand, telling him to stop.

Cameron didn't. "Word is he ran away from home when he was just a kid, went out on his own and went wild. Sleeps with anything that'll hold still for it and drinks like he's just come out of the desert."

"He doesn't. I would have smelled any of that on him."

"Maybe, or maybe all you're catching is the way he wants you." Cameron let out a breath. "I'm not stupid, Vincent -- Gabriel. You got hearts in your eyes the first time he looked at you; you didn't see it, but I did. Love at first sight isn't a real thing. Maybe in books, but --"

"No one said I was in love with him."

"Did they have to?" Cameron raised one shoulder. "Say you don't. You're going to get there if you let yourself think this is some kind of fairy tale. He's not Prince Charming."

Gabriel's hands dropped to the rim of the sink and held tight, his knuckles fading to white. "You think I should cancel."

"I think you should be careful. We both saw the crowd he hangs out with. You really think you could fold that into your life? You think he could stick to the wall with you for long without getting bored and wandering off?"

Gabriel's head shot up, as offended as he was startled, and he turned on Cameron. "Is that what you think of me?"

"It's the truth, Vincent," Cameron said, gently, but not the way "rough" Wynn would have been gentle. "We're not best friends or anything, you and me, but you're a good man. I don't want to see you get your heart broken."

Gabriel stared at him for a long moment, starting to shake his head so slowly he didn't realize what he was doing until it made his neck hurt. "Stop. Stop right there. I do know what I'm doing, and you don't know half of what you think you do." When Cameron tried to interrupt, he drew a sharp slash through the air. "People say things when they think you're not listening and this whole thing is the talk of the town. I *know* what they're saying. Wynn's rough. He grew up the hard way. He's poor -- but are we rich, Cameron? He's blue collar, but we're barely better than that, we're pale gray. And I don't care about any of that."

"Vincent --" Cameron started, frustrated and not hiding it. He dropped back hard enough against the bathroom door that it slid halfway open before he dug his heels in to stop its movement. "Come on. Vincent."

"No!" Gabriel slashed the air again. "That's not my name now."

"I swear to God, man -- you're already changing yourself to fit him. How do you not see that?"

"Because I want to change!" Gabriel burst out, voice echoing against the tiled walls. "I want to. I'm tired of living in the shadows. He lives in the light, and I don't give a -- a damn -- about things that don't matter. I want the light that's in his life."

"You *are* falling for him." Cameron shook his head in disdain and disbelief. "Are you out of your mind?"

Gabriel thrust his hands through his hair. "Am I -- I tried not to, at first when I was scared, but I need him, Cameron. Enough to --" He drew in a steadying breath and raised his palms to show Cameron how he didn't understand everything either, but he couldn't stop himself needing it. "Enough to try, even if it's fast. He's not your Prince Charming. That doesn't mean he isn't one. That he might be mine."

"He's keeping secrets," Cameron countered. "I don't know what, but he is. It's written all over him."

Stung, Gabriel flung back, "You're one to talk about keeping things under wraps, *Beta*."

Cameron went still and stiff. "Low," he said. "Too

low."

"And what you're doing here isn't? Wynn's sweet, Cameron. He's sweet. He's gentle. He looked at me when he met me, Cameron, and he *saw* me. How could I not fall for him?"

The door behind Cameron came open the rest of the way, leaving him to stumble or fall as he chose. The person who'd opened it wasn't looking at him, but at Gabriel instead. Only at Gabriel, dressed in black with his glasses in place, his hair neat and his boots shiny, his hand risen to flutter uncertainly at his throat.

Wynn. And the way Wynn looked at him -- like he'd never seen anything more beautiful, anything that'd surprised him more or better -- Gabriel could see it for himself, then, when he met those sparkling lost boy's eyes.

Hearts. Hopes. Amazement, delight, pride.

The future, if Gabriel was brave enough to reach for it.

He stepped forward, past Cameron, and took Wynn's hand in his, lifting it to his cheek as he said, so quietly, "Let's go."

* * *

Present

The pillow that Gabriel cradled against his chest smelled like Wynn.

All they'd had, then, had been each other. But what had that mattered? What else could they have wanted?

* * *

Past

The only *fancy* Second Chance had to offer a dinner date was the kind of fancy the people who lived in those old Victorians could afford, but Gabriel hadn't wanted that. He didn't like rarified atmospheres. Places where he'd spend more time worrying about how to pronounce what was on the menu or identify it when it reached his plate, or what kind of wine should or shouldn't go with what he'd chosen. He'd worried that Wynn might try to pull out all the stops, but no. As if he knew all that without having to be told, he'd gone left instead of right on the Main Street and driven them to the kind of small, comfortable place that Gabriel liked. Greek food, well cooked and with not a drop of pretension in sight; comfortable booths, lighting low enough to soften the room, and milky shots of ouzo to finish their meal with.

Wynn ran one fingertip around the rim of his shot glass and grinned at Gabriel as Gabriel tilted his glass back to get the last drops. "I thought you'd like it."

"More than I'd imagined I would." He gave his half-full plate a regretful glance, but he couldn't have held another bite if he'd tried. He'd never had half the things he'd sampled that night, and he wouldn't have thought he'd like them, but he *did*. Anxiety had been the only thing holding him back -- that and pausing every bite or so to glance up at Wynn -- and more often than not, finding Wynn's gaze just as much on him. His cheeks warmed and a small, pleasant ripple ran through him. "How do you do that?"

"Do what?"

Know me better than I know myself, when we should barely know each other at all, was what Gabriel wanted to say.

All Gabriel could *do* was raise one shoulder, but Wynn's grin crooked sideways and Gabriel knew he understood. "I'll bring you back sometime," he promised. He slid easily out of the booth -- sitting across from him like a gentleman, not squeezed in beside him though Gabriel wouldn't have minded -- and offered him a hand up. Gabriel didn't need one, but he took the offer anyway, only realizing when Wynn's hand closed around his, dry and warm, that it was the first time they'd done this.

He caught his breath uncertainly, but he didn't take

a step back. He didn't want to.

A flicker of heat brushed through Wynn's eyes. He squeezed Gabriel's hand gently, then let go to take his coat down from the hook on the wall near their booth, holding it out for Gabriel to slip his arms through. Gabriel blinked at him stupidly before he got it -- no one had ever done that for him, ever -- but he let Wynn ease the warm wool coat onto his shoulders and tucked his hands in his pockets while Wynn shrugged on his own battered jacket, just so he could imagine he was keeping the warmth of Wynn's touch safe and sound.

He could feel the people around them giving them curious looks. Some only curious, some disapproving, as if to ask what he thought he was doing, as if to say *one of these things is not like the other*. Gabriel didn't often get angry, but his temper prickled now. They didn't know him, and they didn't know Wynn. How dare they? He slid his glasses up his nose and stared back at one nosy parker until they hurriedly looked away.

Beside him, Wynn chuckled, and oh, he'd taken Gabriel gently by the wrist to slide his right hand out of his pocket and enfold it in his own again. "You're fierce when you want to be, aren't you?"

No, he thought. *Brave*, because Wynn made him that way. He flexed his fingers, then threaded them through Wynn's and smiled up at him, ridiculously pleased at how that made Wynn's lips part in appreciation. "That song you gave me. Did you write that yourself?"

Wynn looked surprised, then delighted. "You listened to it?"

Several times. Gabriel nodded.

Wynn must have been pleased by what he saw in Gabriel's face. His fingers closed around Gabriel's and his thumb rubbed at the back of Gabriel's knuckles. "I didn't write it down, I never do that, but I made it up and I borrowed a buddy's guitar so I could play it for you. You liked it?"

Gabriel nodded again. "I loved it."

Wynn grinned at him, bright as starlight, and before Gabriel realized what he had in mind, he'd lifted their joined hands to his mouth and brushed his lips across the soft skin at Gabriel's wrist.

Gabriel gaped at him, which made Wynn's smile widen. "Had to. You're too sweet to not taste." He lowered their joined hands and gave Gabriel a friendly nudge. "Come on, angel. I'll walk you home."

* * *

Nowhere in Second Chance was too far from anything else to walk instead of drive, if one had a mind to, and Gabriel wasn't surprised when even though he'd taken them to the restaurant in his truck, Wynn strolled past it on their way out.

He was glad, actually. Letting him drive safely would have meant letting go of Wynn's hand, and Gabriel didn't want to do that.

"You don't own a guitar of your own? But you're a skilled player."

"I borrow what I can when I can, and that's good enough. I remember everything I come up with anyway. I've got a good memory. Hey." Wynn gave Gabriel a small sideways grin and held his hand a little tighter. "You have cold fingers."

Gabriel wasn't any more used to being teased by someone who meant it affectionately than to any of the rest of it, but... he liked it. "Not right now they aren't," he said. He lifted their joined hands and, though he was shorter and it was a stretch, slid them into Wynn's pocket. "And that's even better."

Wynn whistled, but with a chuckle threaded through the noise. "Did I say fierce? I'm not sure that's the right word. Don't get me wrong, it's one of them, but there's something else that fits better. Let me think of it."

Gabriel shrugged; it wasn't as if he had room to cast aspersions on having trouble finding the right words when he needed them and he was content -- no, satisfied as a cat licking cream off its whiskers -- to amble idly down the sidewalks of Second Chance, meandering, taking their time, pointed toward -- his apartment.

He caught his breath deep in his throat. His apartment. Wynn. Was this how -- dates *did* end this way. Sometimes. A kiss -- a real kiss -- at the door -- lips against lips, tasting each other's breath -- a whisper -- *come upstairs with me.*

Wynn turned his head to give Gabriel a curious glance. "Something wrong?"

"I don't know. No." Gabriel pressed his free hand, which *was* cold, to his hot cheek. He could feel his heart pounding too fast. He wanted -- he wasn't sure -- he -- "I'm fine."

Wynn made a noise that said Gabriel wasn't fooling him, but that he could wait to figure it out, and kept walking. He did take their hands out of his pocket but didn't let go. He kept them tucked against the warmth of his hip instead and shortened his longer stride every time he pulled far enough ahead to tug instead of guide.

"Fierce," Wynn said as they turned onto Gabriel's street. He lived at the far end, and he hadn't told Wynn which building, but it didn't bother him that Wynn seemed to know. "Fierce, and..."

"It'll come to you."

Wynn tipped his head back to aim his grin at the starry sky above. "I know it. You're from an owl bloodline, right? Just one kind, or lots of different sorts? I'm a mix. Mostly wolf."

Gabriel could see that. Wynn would make a good hunter, and he had a nose for things. But... "I don't know anything for sure except owl," he said. "I was too young to ask my parents, and there wasn't anyone to ask afterward."

Wynn frowned. "After?"

Oh. He didn't know this, then. Gabriel took a deep breath, because this never got easier to talk about, but he didn't want to brush it off. "When I was nine, they tried driving home in a storm. Slippery roads, bad visibility." Or so the one police report he'd tracked down had said. "They didn't make it."

"Jesus." Wynn's hand tightened around his, a rough squeeze. He walked a few steps in silence, then said, "They must have been good parents."

As Gabriel remembered, they had, but -- "Why do you say that?"

"Because they made you." Wynn knocked elbows with him, teasing again before he sobered. "I didn't know. I'm sorry."

Gabriel shook his head, looking down. "It was a long time ago."

"Doesn't mean it can't still hurt."

The kindness in that made Gabriel's eyes sting. He bent his neck to wipe them quickly against his shoulder, then cleared his throat. "What about you?"

"They weren't good. Mostly, they were drunk." Wynn's jaw worked. "One of them left before I was born and didn't come back. One of them took off when I was around that age. I set out on my own."

"I'm sorry."

Wynn shrugged. "I like knowing I'm what *I* made of me, not someone else. Independent. *That's* the word I wanted. You know how to stand on your own feet too."

Did he? Gabriel hadn't ever thought of it that way… but it was true, wasn't it?

Wynn walked a few more steps. "I'll always come to you, you know. Whenever you want me, as long as you want me to, I'll come to you."

Would you come for *me*? Gabriel's mind put in, a startling intrusive thought. *Would... would I come for* you? *If you... if you kissed me, not on the hand, and you didn't stop, and...*

Would it scare you off if I asked that?

Would it scare me off?

This should be too fast. Weeks were nothing when it came to forming a bond with someone. And yet. And yet, when they reached his doorstep, dimly lit by one soft light glowing at the top of the steps, he didn't want to stop and think.

All he wanted was Wynn, and he wanted Wynn -- kind, sweet Wynn -- so *much.*

Only Gabriel didn't know how to show him that. He turned without letting go of Wynn's hand and looked up at him to find Wynn looking down at his face. At his mouth, tracing the firmness of his own lower lip with the tip of his tongue, leaving it shiny and slightly pinker than before.

"So," Wynn said, quietly, quietly. He lifted his free hand to cup Gabriel's cheek as lightly as a feather. "What you said to your friend, before. You're falling for me?"

Gabriel couldn't look away. "No," he said.

Wynn blinked. "No?"

He looked so surprised that Gabriel laughed, and -- *brave.* He lifted himself on the tips of his toes and pressed his lips to Wynn's. "No," he said, tasting the anise on Wynn's breath, spicy and heady. "I'm not falling. I've already fallen."

The smile that he could feel curving against his mouth -- he would have marveled at it if Wynn's hand hadn't slid away from his cheek and to the back of his head, not gentle at all now, pulling him close and tight instead. His fingers slid through Gabriel's hair when he pressed the tip of his tongue to Gabriel's lips, teasing them open.

Gabriel had never done this before either, but

something in him knew how to answer that. He parted his lips and let Wynn inside, and let Wynn teach him the rest of what he needed to know: how tongues could slip and slide together, how they could stroke hard and then slow, retreat and return.

He heard someone breathing fast, then faster. Two someones. *Oh.*

His arms were too empty; they needed to hold on. He wound them around Wynn's waist and locked his wrists at the small of Wynn's back. He groaned, breaking the kiss, but that wasn't a bad thing because he came right back, pushing the noise into Gabriel's mouth. Not just that. His arms went around Gabriel's too, his mouth moving over Gabriel's, taking Gabriel's lower lip between his teeth.

Gabriel gasped. He needed *closer*, and the deep flutter-pulse of *want* would have embarrassed him with anyone else, but not now. He shuffled his feet until the tips of his toes touched Wynn's and their hips were all but touching. The smell of arousal made the air sweet between them.

"Don't stop," he mumbled into Wynn's kiss. His hands wouldn't lie still, stroking their way up Wynn's back. "I…"

"Mmm." Wynn moved, nestling closer still. "No. Not stopping."

He slid one long leg between Gabriel's, their hips almost touching. He shifted from Gabriel's mouth to the rest of his face, drawing hot kisses and small bites down across his cheeks, his neck, behind his ear, the hollow of his throat. Gabriel could feel his hips shifting and could smell Alpha musk mixing with his own Omega sweetness. He gasped and found a home for his hands in Wynn's hair, holding tight.

One step forward, because he wanted it, needed it, and their hips fit together. Wynn grunted as his cock bumped Gabriel's, and he made a soft sound when Gabriel pressed tighter, desperate for still more.

He'd said it, thought it, so many times, but he'd never been like this with anyone. He couldn't stop kissing Wynn, copying what he could, and his body taking over with the rest. Pressing tight, then drawing back, his tongue darting in Wynn's mouth now, then parting to pant. A hot coil went tight in his lower belly, and he could feel slick wetness dripping suddenly out of him.

He didn't care, he didn't *care*. He worked a hand between them, and though it shook with uncertain nerves, he pressed his palm to Wynn's cock, the way it tented his jeans almost obscenely.

A rough noise tore its way out of Wynn, and he pushed Gabriel away, but before Gabriel could ask *what* and *why* and *didn't you like that* Wynn was guiding him backward, quick and fast, until Gabriel had the wall by the stairs to hold him up. Not just that. He lifted Gabriel as if Gabriel weighed nothing, until his feet left the ground and he had to wrap them around Wynn to keep from falling.

Not falling. Fallen. Being lifted.

Gabriel couldn't kiss back, his lips wouldn't do anything but part over his ragged breathing, but Wynn's mouth was everywhere, and his hips rolled deep against Gabriel's as if he couldn't help himself.

"Sweet," he muttered, making it a chant between kisses. "So sweet." He bit Gabriel's lip and pulled, a sting that he soothed with his mouth and the sweep of his tongue, a kiss that Gabriel *had* to follow and chase, deeper than before, deeper, deepest -- "Angel. My angel."

The coil of heat burst in Gabriel's belly, and between his legs, locked so tight around Wynn as he came, the shock of it making him gasp and drop his head backward until Wynn reeled him back in, mouth to mouth, swallowing the noises he made. He reached between them and rubbed his palm against Gabriel's cock and the mess he made.

"Angel," he breathed, and Gabriel shuddered hard with an aftershock. "If you knew how you looked right now…"

Gabriel covered his face, embarrassed. To have come that fast -- "I'm sorry."

"Don't you dare. That was a gift." Wynn nuzzled the corner of his mouth, gentling his question. "You've never done that before, have you?"

Eyes closed, Gabriel shook his head.

"Then it really was a gift," Wynn murmured. To Gabriel's surprise, and a flash of disappointment, he let go, lowering him to his feet. He took Gabriel's hand and kissed it again, a flicker of tongue to clean a drop of slick away. "Now that's the way to say good night."

Wait. He wasn't --

Gabriel stared up at him, trying to figure it out. He could feel how hard Wynn was against him, almost throbbing, and he could see the wildness in his face. "But you didn't…" he said, pleased when Wynn thrust forward into Gabriel's touch with a groan. "Come upstairs with me?"

Wynn shivered hard but shook his head. "Not this time." He cupped Gabriel's cheek. "Not because I don't want to, angel, because I want that more than I want air."

"Then do it." Gabriel tried to pull him. His blood felt like it was sizzling, and he wanted Wynn inside him, so desperately that he ached, and he knew he could get hard again in minutes. "I want you."

"Oh God, when you say it like that…" Wynn pressed his forehead to Gabriel's. "No. And it's taking everything I've got to say that."

"I don't understand. Why?"

"Because, angel." Wynn kissed the soft skin of Gabriel's left eyelid, his own lashes brushing Gabriel's forehead. This rough, rough man, so tender, made Gabriel want him past all reason. He could feel himself pulsing inside, but Wynn wasn't finished yet. "See, I'm too romantic for my own good. I'll own that. But you're special enough that I want that first time to be special too. I didn't know it'd be your very, very first time, or I wouldn't have let it get this far. I'd have given you more than a rut on the doorstep. I'm sorry."

"Don't." Gabriel pulled away and caught Wynn's chin, and there was yet another first. "Don't you say that. It was perfect. Do anything you want, and I'll want it too."

Wynn's grin dawned slowly, maybe ruefully, but he stroked Gabriel's hair back and traced Gabriel's jawline, soft as it might be next to his. "Then what I want is to wait. Dream about it for a few days. Don't worry, angel. I'll be back. As long as you want me, I'll always come back to you."

Gabriel leaned up and forward, kissing Wynn one more time. "Good. Because I won't stop wanting that."

Wynn's smile widened and eclipsed any other others he'd shown Gabriel before. "Good."

That was when Gabriel knew: he wasn't just falling, he hadn't just fallen. He loved this man, and with all his heart. It was fast. It hadn't been fast enough. And it would be for the rest of his life.

He thought -- no, he knew, even if he liked to wait and he could be so, so determined -- that Wynn knew it too.

But they had time. They had enough time to go however fast or slow they wanted.

Chapter Four

Present

Gabriel blinked out of his trance to find he'd made his way to the reading nook Wynn had insisted on making for him, snugged up across the room where the light was best and a squashy, comfortable love seat fit just right in that space. A bookshelf sat where it could be reached without too much of a stretch. Not many books on it, not yet, but there was one in particular that caught Gabriel's eye.

He leaned across the arm of the love seat, wincing as the movement made him cramp again, hard enough that he had to wait and breathe through it.

But he didn't let that stop him from stretching until he had the book in his hand, a small photo album marred with scorch marks and still smelling of smoke. That was all right. The inside wasn't damaged.

Gabriel let the book fall open on the few inches of lap he had left. He'd handled it so often, looking for one particular page, that it always came up first.

A marriage certificate, dated three months after that first date.

He laughed quietly to himself, stroking his belly as he did. The baby was asleep, he thought, soothed by the quiet. *Three months.* Wynn would have waited longer, but Gabriel had gotten *his* way that time. Any longer, and he'd have been closer to bursting than he was now.

Though… he did understand, now, why Wynn had hesitated.

"He's hiding something," Cameron insisted.

Gabriel traced the neat, prim loops of his own signature. Almost old-fashioned. Then Wynn's name, written in a clumsy hand closer to print than cursive. One letter was the wrong way around, and one awkwardly corrected halfway through. He'd drawn a heart at the end, because of course he had.

Gabriel loved it.

He touched his fingers to his lips and pressed them against the page. What it'd taken to get that far...

Not all memories were good memories or didn't start that way. It hadn't all been smooth sailing. They'd had their bumps in the road.

Even that had been worth it, in the end.

Gabriel closed the book, resting it against his leg, wrapped his arms around himself, and let himself slip back into memory.

* * *

Past

Days went by, then weeks, and the parts of Gabriel's life that had already expanded to include Wynn enfolded him, blending them together so they weren't just Gabriel and Wynn, but GabrielandWynn. Oh, people still gave them odd looks, and some muttered behind their hands, clicked their tongues and shook their heads about how someone should do something before it was too late.

In a way, they weren't wrong. This thing between him and Wynn *was* too soon, too fast, and they *were* too young for something so serious. They came from two different worlds, colliding where odds were they never would have crossed paths, let alone locked onto each other's trajectory.

Gabriel didn't care. He meant to make sure Wynn never did, either.

Sometimes he caught Wynn staring at him as if he wanted to pinch himself -- *is this real?* -- but Gabriel was learning how to tease him and give as good as he got, and how to kiss him so sweetly they both forgot what they'd been doing before.

Wynn still hadn't taken him to bed, even though Gabriel wasn't shy about asking. Scared, yes. But not shy. He wanted Wynn over him, inside him, filling him in every way... every way. He bit his lip when he thought about having Wynn's baby. Stroked the soft, pliable skin on his belly, as virgin-taut as it'd been since he matured into himself, but with potential that he *wanted* -- oh, he wanted.

Maybe soon. Maybe.

Gabriel thought about that a lot, and as if he could tell, storm clouds darkened Cameron's forehead when he caught Gabriel drifting off into daydreams about it. Oh, he didn't say a word, but he clamped his jaws together hard every time, and he kept his eye on them whenever they were in his line of sight.

"He doesn't like me," Wynn said one day in the library, the two of them sitting at each end of a couch long since relegated to the small staff room after a disastrous story hour involving finger paint that had *not*, in fact, been washable. A few boot prints and soot smudges couldn't possibly do it any more harm.

"Who? Cameron?"

"Hmm." Wynn nudged at him with one foot, their ankles and calves already tangled comfortably together. He took up more room than Gabriel, but Gabriel didn't mind. He could stroke his thumb across Wynn's sharp anklebone and make him laugh when it tickled. "Is he jealous?"

"What? Of you?" Gabriel almost laughed, then realized Wynn was serious. "No! God, no. He never even looked at me once, before or since. He's not interested."

"He's protective, though." Wynn turned halfway around to cock his head thoughtfully at Cameron. "I'm not saying I don't get it, but it feels more personal than that."

He's hiding something, Cameron's voice prickled in Gabriel's mental ear. "Don't know why," he lied. Or -- no, it wasn't a lie. He didn't know why Cameron said that, or what he'd meant, or what Wynn could be hiding, or would. Too many question marks, and not an answer to be found.

"Water, water everywhere, and not a drop to drink," Gabriel said, almost as absently as Wynn, watching Cameron walk past with a very deliberate not-glance at them. "And... darn. I don't remember how the rest of that goes. Do you?"

"Say what, now?"

"It's a poem by... by..." Gabriel snapped his fingers, searching for the name on the tip of his tongue. Wynn *had* been distracted, watching Cameron, but turned back to laugh at him. "Hush, you. Is it my fault you keep my mind on other things?"

Wynn waggled his eyebrows and reached down to lift Gabriel's leg across his lap. He stroked the smooth skin behind Gabriel's knee, a touch that made him draw in a shivery breath. "No more than it's your fault you keep me drifting, angel."

"Oh, that's not fair." Gabriel made no move at all to move his leg, instead extending it so he could hook his heel around Wynn's side, enjoying so very much the way Wynn's pupils dilated. They'd better be careful, though. Cameron put up with a great deal but locking themselves in the public restroom for a quickie might be the straw that broke him.

Besides, Wynn would want to wait.

Gabriel sighed and ruffled up his hair. *Wait -- aha!* "Coleridge," he said with a final finger snap of triumph. "I remember now. Samuel Taylor Coleridge, *The Rime of the Ancient Mariner.*"

"What, now?"

"It's a poem, silly." Gabriel leaned forward to caress Wynn's cheek because he could, and because he wanted to, and because he loved the way Wynn's eyelashes fluttered shut when he did. "Did you ever read it?"

"Mmm. Not that I know of."

Wynn seemed more interested in having his face petted, and Gabriel wouldn't have objected -- but it'd been years since he'd read any Coleridge and he wanted to know if he had the quote right. He pecked Wynn lightly on the lips. "Would you go get a book for me? The title just says *Coleridge*. It should be in the poetry section."

Wynn wrinkled his nose. "Seriously?"

"Anyone who loves music as much as you do has to love poetry too. Or if you don't, you just don't know it yet."

Wynn snorted. "You're ridiculous sometimes. C'mere."

He reached for Gabriel, but Gabriel scoot-danced back out of his reach, teasing him. "Poem first, then playtime. There aren't *that* many books in the poetry section. Go get it and come back, and..." He leaned just forward enough to slide his fingertips halfway up Wynn's denim-covered thigh. "I'll thank you properly."

He would have expected that to get Wynn out of his seat, willingly if not jumping to it, but Wynn drew his lower lip between his teeth and frowned. "What does the book look like?"

"I don't remember. Just ordinary?" Gabriel caught Wynn before he got his phone out of his pocket, as he so clearly planned on, laughing at him. "Come on, I'm comfortable too, but if you ask Siri to recite for us instead of going to get the actual book, that's not the way to a librarian's heart."

Wynn rolled his eyes, but he finally stood -- tousling Gabriel's hair past all recognition of a style as he passed, but he went. Hands in his pockets, striding amiably past Cameron and nodding to him when he turned, and --

And --

Gabriel sat up straighter. He could *see* the poetry

section from where he sat, and he knew the library's layout by heart besides. It'd be to Wynn's left, but Wynn went right. Hard right, into general mechanics and DIY guides. His frown was drawn so strongly that even if Gabriel hadn't known every expression the man could make, he would have felt that much concentration from buildings away.

He glanced up to see that Cameron had noticed too, and that he didn't get it either. At first. Then, Cameron's eyes closed and he sighed.

Gabriel still didn't understand. Not until he watched Wynn come out of the one row, scan another, and start down it, poking at books first with confusion, then frustration, and finally hard-jaw-set, tight-lipped frustration that didn't hide the fear in his eyes. Eyes that, when they picked up books to scan over the words on their spines, hadn't a drop of comprehension in them.

Oh. Oh God. The pit fell out of Gabriel's stomach. *He's hiding something.* This was it, wasn't it?

He was on his feet without thinking about it, passing Cameron and his startled attempt to stop him, and at Wynn's side almost before he knew it; he thought Wynn might have been just as surprised as him that he was suddenly there, taking a book about container gardening out of Wynn's abruptly nerveless hand.

The fear in Wynn's eyes -- "Gabriel…"

It was cruel, but he had to know for sure, not just guess. Gabriel licked his lips as he held the book up. "Wynn, sweetheart. What does that say?"

Wynn's eyelids slid shut, and he didn't breathe once while Gabriel took in three quick, shallow ones. "I don't know," he said, and then, vicious like Gabriel had never heard him, "*Fuck.*"

"Wynn --"

"Don't. Just don't." Wynn jerked the book away from Gabriel, dropped it with a bang, and gave him one wild, hunted look that *burned* before -- he turned his back, and he was stalking away.

Gabriel stared after him, stunned into silence and stillness, but -- *no*, no, he'd misunderstood. That wasn't what Gabriel had meant to happen at all --

"Hey," Cameron said behind him. "Gabriel, don't go and do something --"

He probably had something else to say, but Gabriel couldn't hear him over the roaring in his ears and the rattle-bang of the library door slamming open and closed.

Once upon a time, the Gabriel he'd been who was shy and scared of his own shadow, who didn't know what it was like to be kissed by a man like he was more important than anything in the world, *that* Gabriel might have stayed right there, frozen to the spot.

This Gabriel had learned a few things, and when he moved this time, it was fast and determined. A jog, then a run, through the library doors and out to the sidewalk, a whip-fast scan around, and then a dead sprint to Wynn's truck before Wynn could get in and drive away. He already had the keys in his hand, but he startled back when Gabriel slammed into the driver's side door to block it.

"Don't, yourself," Gabriel said, panting a little but not giving a damn. "Don't you do that to me."

Wynn wouldn't look at him. "You know, now," he said after too long a pause. "I didn't want you to know. That I." He had to stop and roll his neck to loosen it enough to keep speaking. "You know that I can't read. I never could."

Gabriel had a yawning pit where his stomach should be. "You --"

"Books mean so much to you, and you're so smart, Gabriel, you're so *smart*. I wondered if I shouldn't -- if I wasn't the kind -- but you're so -- I wanted to be someone good enough for -- I had to try --" Struggle and shame made Wynn's shoulders bow forward; he braced himself on the truck bed and shook his head. "I didn't lie to you. I didn't do that, at least. *Shit*. I'm sorry."

He tried to reach past Gabriel, but *no*, a hundred times *no*. Gabriel was shorter and smaller in every way, but he planted his feet hard and refused to be moved. He didn't understand, and *that* would not stand.

"Do you think I care?" he demanded, raising his voice for the first time since he'd met Wynn. "Do you think that matters to me? Do you think I love you even a little bit less, now?"

Wynn stared at him, not a wolf now but a deer caught in the headlights on a country road. "What?"

"Sweetheart." Gabriel took Wynn's hand and pressed it over his own heart. "Wynn. I care that you can't read, but only because I can see how much that hurts *you*. All right? Because I care about you. You worked your way in where no one else ever wanted to go, and not being able to find a book by a poet who lived and died a couple hundred years ago --"

Wynn still hadn't blinked. Just stared at Gabriel, still as if *he* was the owl, then wet his lips. "You love me?"

Oh. Gabriel's fingers flew to his mouth, but he let them fall away just as fast. "I do." He lifted his chin sharp and proud. "I love you more than anyone or anything. Even books. I don't know why you didn't learn before but if you want to learn now, I'll teach you. If you don't, I don't want to change you, but no matter what you say or do, Wynn, I. Love. You."

He couldn't tell what Wynn was thinking, with the way Wynn stared at him, and it made his heart pound all the harder --

But not as hard as it did when Wynn's arms went around him, holding him so hard his ribs creaked. Gabriel couldn't have cared less; fine shivers racked Wynn from head to toe, and all he wanted to do was hold him just as hard. He raised his face to meet Wynn when Wynn bent his head to kiss and be kissed, as hard and desperately as he'd latched on with his arms, the kind of kiss that made him moan and burn deep inside. Sweetness filled the air between them, rising in a thick cloud, and he was hard before he knew it.

"You mean it." Wynn thrust his fingers over and over through Gabriel's hair, kissing him between each word. "You love me the way I love you. *You*." He caught Gabriel's hair and bent his neck backward to kiss him harder, deeper, messier; took him by the hip and squeezed, bringing him close enough that if they weren't in broad daylight Gabriel would have ground against him until one or both of them came.

He might have, anyway, if Wynn hadn't stopped just before he'd have started to climb that hill. Still wild, still frantic, but focused again. Like he'd faced his worst fear and it hadn't killed him after all, which Gabriel supposed was true. "I love you. I love you so much. You know that now too."

Gabriel touched his lips, kiss-swollen but curved into a grin, and nodded.

Wynn kissed him one more time, quick and rough and with all his heart poured into that one touch, then pulled away. "Will you be home tonight? Or here?"

Gabriel caught his breath. "That depends. Which would you rather?"

"No. Tell me first."

Not understanding but willing to see where this went, Gabriel said, "I'm off work at five, and then I was going home. I hoped you'd go with me or come to me."

"I'll always come for you." Wynn took Gabriel's hand and raised it to his lips. He bit at one knuckle, then soothed the sting with a quick sweep of his tongue. "Be there tonight. I'll be back."

Wait, what? "You're leaving? Where are you

going?"

"You'll see." The sparkle of mischief that suited Wynn so well was back, along with a burning hunger when he looked at Gabriel, drinking him deep. "Be there and wait for me."

Gabriel could only nod, agreement and promise. "All right." He stepped back, letting Wynn in his truck now that he knew Wynn would be back. "Go do what you need to. I'll wait for you."

"Good." Wynn cranked his truck engine and grinned out the window at him. "Maybe in the meantime try to talk Cameron down before he comes after me with an ax, would you?"

Gabriel was still laughing as Wynn drove away, but that was all right. So was Wynn.

* * *

Present

Gabriel had a radio app on his phone. He'd forgotten about that for some reason, and he had the phone in his hand for probably the same reason. Dimly, he realized he might be in shock and that it wouldn't be surprising, but he couldn't pay attention to that. A local anchor was on air, and the few words Gabriel could pick out were *quarry* and *tragic* and *survivors.*

He shook his head hard, so hard it made his neck hurt with a sharp, burning ache, and made himself concentrate.

"... we still don't have a complete report regarding what happened or why. Witness account are mixed, ranging from an unknown fault in structural integrity to an accidental spark around explosives."

Gabriel shut his eyes tightly, listening. No one was allowed to smoke anywhere in the quarry, but plenty of the workers were two or three pack a day men, and sometimes they got caught. Wynn didn't smoke. It wasn't his fault.

Wynn might still be trapped down there. Was he?

Gabriel's phone rang, vibrating in his palm and making him flinch violently. He jerked it up from where it'd fallen at his side to look at the name on the caller ID, then scowled.

Cameron.

Gabriel clicked on "ignore and silence." He didn't need the interruption -- and he and Cameron might still have worked together until he couldn't manage going into the library anymore and had to work from home -- but they'd barely spoken before his pregnancy started to show, and never exchanged a word that wasn't absolutely necessary since then.

He didn't want to talk to Cameron *now*. He needed to listen.

That startled jump must have traveled down his spine, giving him another cramp in his gut. Gabriel massaged it absently until it eased, pressing his ear to the phone to hear better. They were reading the lists of the survivors. The injured. The dead.

Wynn wasn't on any of them, until the last one read: the missing. It wasn't a long list. Just the men presumed to be trapped behind a pile of rubble, where they'd be running out of air, and --

No. No. No. He wouldn't let it happen.

God, God, please, God. Wynn, I need you, and you said you'd always come back to me. You promised.

As the reporter finished and some God-awful country and western song twanged too loudly in his ear, Gabriel let the phone fall back at his side. He covered his face with the crook of one arm and let the darkness carry him back to a better place, a better time.

* * *

Past

Wynn hadn't come back as quickly as Gabriel expected -- not through the rest of his shift, hadn't pulled up beside him on his walk home, hadn't been there waiting for him, and no one slid a key into the lock on his door before the sun went down.

Curled up on his couch, keeping a weather eye out for any sign of the man, Gabriel vacillated between worry and growing frustration, then back to worry again.

Wynn loved him. He'd said so. Who said that and then ran away, even Wynn? Especially Wynn? He hadn't changed his mind. He wouldn't do that.

Drowsiness, then sleep overtook Gabriel at some point.

The first *rat-a-tat-tat* at his window didn't wake him, but the pounding on the floor beneath him did. Gabriel came awake with a sharp breath, looking around dazedly. "Wynn?"

No answer except for another rattling at his window. His fifth-floor window. *What on earth?* Gabriel stumbled, sleep-clumsy, to the window. Tiny pockmarks showed on the glass by the next pebble that struck the glass.

He pressed his lips together in a line. Whoever thought that was funny was about to have another think coming to them. Shoes, a jacket, his keys, and Gabriel pounded down the stairs with a piece of his mind all ready to deliver. Today was *not* the day, and he was *not* the one.

But when he got to the bottom and opened the door to the outside, no one was there. Not on the steps, not around the side beneath his window, though a small pile of pebbles *was*.

And under those, a folded sheet of printer paper with his name on the outside.

It might be a trick. A nasty message from someone with too much time on their hands and too many opinions on who he chose to love. Hesitant, Gabriel knelt to push the pebbles aside and slide the paper out, unfolding it and adjusting his glasses to read it better. Though he didn't need to. The writer had used a large font, bold and black against the stark white of the page, and while they didn't have a shred of punctuation in there the words were clear:

Hi Gabriel I know how you feel about Siri but I had to do it this way and you can't hear it but I'm laughing now because I know exactly what kind of face you're making

Gabriel snorted. "Wynn, what are you up to?"

I always thought I was stupid but you don't and I still can't believe it that someone like you would say I love you and mean it

"I do," Gabriel said. "I always will, you silly man."

And I love you more just so you know that but I'm almost out of room for one page so come to the library if you want to know where I went Siri put a question mark there okay?

Okay, Win. What else would you like to say?

The printing stopped there, so Gabriel started. He already had everything he needed, and he could walk to the library inside five minutes, after all. Faster, when he wanted to, and though he was out of breath again by the time he got there he considered the run to be worth it.

At this hour -- after midnight? Good Lord -- the library should have been closed. And yet there were soft lights glimmering inside. Someone was there.

Gabriel's pulse fluttered in his throat as he slid his key into the lock and opened the door. He thought -- he hoped -- but he didn't want to get his hopes up.

But it could be Wynn, waiting for him. Wynn would probably know how to pick a lock or jimmy a window latch. He was clever like that, and good with his hands. Gabriel thought he should be upset about the idea, but if it *was* Wynn in there he knew he wouldn't be.

He opened the door. At his feet, glowing warm amber at the bottom of white paper bags filled with quarry sand, luminary candles lit a path forward. A winding path that led around the stacks and shelves, past all the places Wynn had lingered to talk to him -- before.

The pulse in his throat solidified into a lump, and Gabriel had to stop to center himself before he walked on. He slipped off his shoes first, though; the sharp click of business shoes on bare floors didn't seem as right as socks -- or better, bare feet.

Cameron would have kittens if he knew, and the thought had Gabriel smiling to himself as he walked on.

And then, next to the poetry section, Wynn sat cross-legged on the floor. He held up the Coleridge book Gabriel had asked him for earlier and grinned at him. "I asked Siri to show me what the name looked like, and I hunted for it like it was a pattern until I found it. I learned how to do that when I was a kid."

"Oh, Wynn."

"It's the right one, isn't it?" At Gabriel's nod, Wynn brightened. "I found it."

"Found you," Gabriel said, quietly, quietly. He started to go to his knees, but Wynn shook his head to tell him *stay there*. "Why? I want to be near you."

Wynn -- he was such a romantic under that rough-cut shell that wouldn't fool anyone who knew him even a little, and Gabriel loved it, loved it -- laid a hand over his own heart. "You already are, angel."

He rose, but not to his feet. To one knee. Lying the book aside, he shook his sleeve and let a small velvet pouch slide out, bouncing it in his palm. "I'm sorry it took me so long tonight. I had to call in a favor. And I'm sorry it took that long until now too. I couldn't before, you know? Even if I wanted to from the minute I laid eyes on you."

Gabriel couldn't speak. He pressed a hand to his throat, but he poured everything he was feeling into the way he looked at Wynn.

Wynn grinned back, almost shy himself, and let a ring thicker than Gabriel had imagined slide out of the pouch into his palm. He held it up but pressed it into

Gabriel's hand instead of slipping it onto his finger. "Read the inside," he said. "That's why it took so long."

What...? Gabriel held the ring up, thick and sturdy stainless steel without a single chip of a precious stone that he wouldn't have wanted anyway and peered at the flowing cursive etched inside.

Water, water, everywhere, and all that I could want to drink.

At the end of the words, joining the circle they made, was the most ragged, lopsided "W" he'd ever seen, and he knew Wynn had written -- drawn -- that himself.

"Oh God," he said, hand at his mouth. "Wynn."

"The guy who made it for me said it'd be tacky if I went that big, but." Wynn shrugged, trying for cool but so very betraying his pleasure. "I told him I knew who I was marrying. I mean. If you --"

"Wynn." Gabriel held out his hand, and he didn't care if it was shaking, because he thought his smile would split his cheeks. "You -- yes. Anywhere, anytime, anyplace. It would have been yes if you'd asked at first, even if it took a while to get the word out. It's yes now. So put that on me already before I do it myself."

Wynn's grin could have lit up the library better than a thousand luminaries. He pushed himself fluidly to his feet, taking Gabriel's face in his hands to hold him and kiss him, deep and sweet. Somewhere in the middle of it, he slipped the cool, heavy metal on Gabriel's finger.

When he let go, they were both out of breath, but the best of the sparkles was back in Wynn's eye. "Anywhere, anytime, anyplace. Did you mean that?"

"I did, and I do."

"Then." Wynn kissed his knuckles, and grinned at him over them, Peter Pan ready to take flight. "How about tonight?"

Gabriel had to laugh. "Tonight. Tonight would be good." He pressed a quick kiss to Wynn's lips. "If it wasn't past midnight and the courthouse wasn't closed until eight in the morning."

"I --" Wynn closed his eyes, groaned, and then he was laughing too, swaying Gabriel back and forth in the circle of his arms. "I didn't even think about that."

"Which I'll take as a compliment."

"You should. You keep me distracted, angel." Wynn pulled the hood of his sweatshirt up and let it fall at a rakish angle. "Some kind of prizewinner you just agreed to marry, huh?"

"Yes, I did."

Wynn snorted, but he didn't lose his fond smile. "So what now?" His thumb traced slow presses and circles at the small of Gabriel's back. He brushed the tip of his tongue against his lower lip, leaving it shiny, and oh, he was eating Gabriel alive with his eyes. "We could drive around until morning, I guess. Find something else to do. Go inside and nap on the couch."

They *could* do that… and Gabriel could call in a favor of his own and pick up the acoustic guitar he'd been making payments on… but…

He leaned thoughtfully back, knowing Wynn wouldn't let him fall, and let Wynn see what he had on his mind. He could see the moment Wynn understood, when amusement shifted sideways into consideration, and when *that* moved toward intent.

He laid his hand, the one Wynn had put the heavy steel ring on, on Wynn's chest and stepped in again, not kissing him but not leaving any distance between them. Wynn's eyes darkened, pupils going wide.

"Or," Gabriel said, looking up at him, letting Wynn fill his world. He could feel, pressed against him, that Wynn's body already had the idea. His mind only needed to catch up. He tapped his ring finger in a slow rhythm over Wynn's ribs. "Or."

Wynn covered his hand. "Or?"

"You gave me this, and I said 'I do.' You said it too. What's a wedding but that? As far as I care, Wynn, it's already a done deal and I'm never letting go of you."

Wynn shivered; tucked between them, his cock jerked toward Gabriel. He had barely any color left to his irises; they were all pupil, blown wide. "What're you asking me?"

"I'm asking you to take me home, because there are other ways to spend our time between now and morning, and I've already wasted too much of my life alone. I want to make up for lost time." Gabriel pressed his ringless hand to Wynn's cheek and kissed him long, deep, just as hungry, putting everything he felt into the press of his mouth to his -- his husband's. "I want you to take me home and... and make love to me. Really make love. Everything you want to do, I want that tonight."

Wynn groaned and pressed his forehead hard to Gabriel's. "You're sure."

It wasn't a question. Gabriel answered it anyway, his lips moving against Wynn's with each word. "Of you? More than anything else in my life."

"Gabriel, you --" Wynn stopped himself. "On one condition."

"Name it."

"You teach me how to read, after. I'll do my best to learn."

Gabriel kissed him quiet, making sure he understood that this kiss meant *yes* too.

Chapter Five

Gabriel's phone shrilled to life in his hand. He'd picked it up again at some point, but he almost threw it across the room now. Only -- if Wynn, when Wynn was able -- he'd need to call, and it was the only one Gabriel had.

Wynn. Was it --

No. The caller ID showed the same name as last time: *Cameron*.

Gabriel growled, a feral noise. If he hung up again, Cameron would just keep calling back, blast his hide. He picked now to give a damn?

He thumbed the phone on and snapped, "What?"

"I heard," Cameron said, no foreplay about it. "I'm so sorry, Vinc -- Gabriel."

Too little, too late. "There's nothing to be sorry about. He'll be home soon."

"Oh." Cameron sounded blank. "I -- the last report on the radio said he was still among the missing. Did you hear from him?"

"No. I just know."

A long pause, then Cameron sighed. Gabriel could see the Beta all too well in his mind's eye, pressing his forehead and rubbing the bridge of his nose. "Gabriel…"

"Gabriel, what?"

No answer. Cameron would be too frustrated for words. You learned a lot about how to interpret the meanings of various silences when you worked eight hours a day with someone and never exchanged a word. *That* was disbelief, disapproval, and worry that he had no right to lay on Gabriel when Gabriel hadn't asked for it and didn't want any of it.

"Gabriel, what?" he asked again, swinging his legs off the love seat and planting his feet on the floor. The change in blood pressure made his head swim, but the baby was still asleep. He caressed his belly to soothe him, just in case he was having bad dreams -- oh, there, he'd woken him. Tightness and pressure, like he'd felt before when he tried to stretch out but didn't have enough room left to flex his legs, made him hiss between his teeth. "Either say something or hang up. I don't want to miss it when he calls."

"Gabriel." Cameron took a breath. "My God, man, do you have any idea what you sound like right now? Like you're a thousand miles away, talking to me from the end of a tunnel."

I am. At the end of the tunnel, behind the rubble, with Wynn. "And?"

"And that's shock, okay? That's why I called you. Is anyone with you?" When Gabriel didn't answer, Cameron made an impatient noise. "I didn't think so. I'm coming over."

"No!" The idea made Gabriel shout, then flinch away from the phone with the force and volume of it. He tried to breathe deeply, to center himself, but he ached all over and that made it harder. "No. I don't need company. I just want to be by myself until Wynn comes back."

Cameron ignored him. "What if you go into labor and don't notice until it's too late? What if you *are* in labor?"

"Don't be ridiculous."

"You really aren't hearing yourself," Cameron said after a pause. "Last time I saw you, you looked like you'd swallowed a beach ball. There's a calendar in the office and a date circled on it, and we're past it, okay? Days past. Do you even remember that right now?"

Gabriel made an impatient noise and shifted, trying to find a more comfortable position. "First babies never come on time, and we weren't ever sure of when it happened. I could have another week to go, or even two. We fuck like rabbits, isn't that what you said? So who knows?"

Silence from Cameron, but Gabriel wasn't done yet. The words churned out like falling rocks. "You didn't even come to the courthouse. I asked. Wynn asked. You didn't even say yes or no, you just didn't turn up."

"I couldn't."

"Why? You never explained that. You never explained anything, not even why you gave a damn about Wynn and me in the first place! All I got was an empty seat at the courthouse and then nine and a half weeks of silence. When the library wanted me to quit, you kept your mouth shut *then*. You've got a nerve, calling me now. You never cared before. Tell me I'm wrong."

Cameron sounded like he was speaking through gritted teeth. "You *are* wrong. Believe it or not, I'm worried about you."

"You have no right to be. None." Gabriel couldn't sit still, not for a conversation like this one that was going on for *far too damn long*. He stood and paced toward the window, but he couldn't see much through the old glass. Had the smoke from the quarry site stopped? He shook his head hard, no matter how it made his neck twinge. Why was it so hard to focus? Was he in shock, really? Uneasiness made him sharper still, striking to cut deep. "Did you want me yourself? Was that why you hated Wynn?"

A sharply indrawn breath answered him first, and then anger to match his own. "Fuck you, Gabriel. Fuck. You. I don't want you like that and you know it, but you don't know me, okay? You don't know a thing about me."

"You never told me anything!"

"You never asked," Cameron countered. "*Fuck.* You are in shock. I can hear it, and you don't need to be alone. If you won't let me come over, then I'm calling an ambulance to come and get you."

"*No.*" Gabriel almost hung up then, but if he did Cameron would make the call and the consequences be damned; he needed to understand why he couldn't do that. "Every one of them who can be spared is at the quarry right now, they have to be. Don't you remember what it was like that night when the train went off its tracks? And there weren't even any real injuries then, not like this. I won't have any of them diverted for me when I'm *fine*. There are men down there they could make the difference between life and death for."

"Just not Wynn," Cameron said. "Because he's coming home soon."

"He *is*."

Silence. Gabriel rubbed his belly to ease the too-tight muscles; he'd been told it was natural, that part of coming close was ligaments stretching and bones widening. "I'm not going to say I'm sorry, because I'm not. I don't need help, and I don't want it. And if you call anyone, I won't ever forgive you for that. Wynn keeps his word. He always keeps his word, and he always comes for me."

"God help you, and Goddamn all the rest of it," Cameron said. "I won't call anyone *now*. But I'm going to check in again. And if I think you're in trouble, I *will* call someone."

"You won't need to." Gabriel ended the call. If Cameron called, he wouldn't answer. Simple as that.

In the abrupt quiet, he pressed his hands to his face, pressing the balls of his palms into his eyes, and drew in three, four, five rattling breaths. He'd broken out in a sweat at the end there, making his clothes -- they already fit too tightly, even the sweatshirts he'd borrowed from Wynn -- cling wetly to his skin.

It wasn't enough. He needed air, fresh air, even if it wouldn't smell so much like Wynn outside. Gabriel wasn't wearing shoes, but he toed off the warm socks

Wynn insisted he wear instead of going barefoot and walked outside with nothing between his soles and the winter-fallow grass prickling at the tender skin.

Better. He could see the quarry site again, and the smoke had stopped. Red and blue lights flashed, visible even at the distance, but that was okay, that was fine. They were all where they should be, helping.

He didn't want to sit on the steps, but -- there, the maple tree, the one Wynn loved. There was a cradle between two of the roots that still fit Gabriel just right, cradling his hips when he lowered himself awkwardly to sit between them. The sleep pants he wore were Wynn's too, and they slid easily down over his belly to let it breathe. *Better still*, a relief to have as much of himself as decently possible unconstrained.

Yet even with his body secure, Gabriel's mind wouldn't stay put. Shock, yes, he'd accepted that, but he couldn't seem to care too much.

Instead, he closed his eyes and drifted, drifted, drifted away.

* * *

Past

Gabriel wiped the steam away from his bathroom mirror. The face looking back at him -- same old face. No glasses, but he could still see himself. His eyes were wide, too wide, white showing all around. He turned his head, focusing on other things. Soft hair that curled a little around his nape and ears as it dried, before it was combed into place. A robe he'd always liked, plush enough not to stick to wet skin, light enough to move when he moved. Skin red underneath, flushed from the hot water he'd washed himself carefully with. He wanted to smell nice… taste nice… be as good as Wynn seemed to think. Wynn had gone first, to get the smudges and dust off his skin, and the look he'd given Gabriel as he passed him through the open door --

Gabriel tilted his neck back and trailed his fingers up to where his pulse hammered away, far too fast. He swallowed hard.

Warm arms surrounded him from behind, so strong with working man's muscles, a body just as strong pressing itself against Gabriel's back. Wynn tucked his chin against Gabriel's shoulder and stroked his chest. Gabriel couldn't remember from before, or he hadn't noticed, but *Wynn* didn't have so much as a robe on. "You're trembling."

"It doesn't make sense. I wanted this so much. I do want this," Gabriel said, helpless. He opened his eyes to find Wynn watching him in the mirror. "I'm scared. Why am I scared?"

Wynn nuzzled the side of his neck. "Never been here, never done this."

Gabriel scoffed but reached up to card through Wynn's hair. "I've come with you plenty of times."

"Never had anyone inside you, though." Wynn nibbled over the spot he'd nosed at. His hand slid lower, where Gabriel's body reacted, filling and rising toward him. "It's different."

"Never had any *one* inside me." Gabriel's cheeks reddened more than they had in the shower. "But. Things."

Wynn's eyebrows shot up. "Oh really? That's a story I want to hear sometime. But we don't have to do this. I can wait."

"I don't want to. And neither do you."

"I don't want to hurt you. Ever."

"You wouldn't ever. And you're hard as I am." Gabriel rolled his hips backward, something he'd learned from Wynn. Liquid trickled from the pocket between his legs, making his thighs slippery and releasing a wave of scent that made Wynn press his head hard to Gabriel's shoulder and his hand clutch reflexively at Gabriel's flat belly. "I want that in me."

Wynn held him tighter. He didn't deny anything, and when Gabriel pressed back, he pushed forward until they were rocking together. "There's one thing, first." He licked his lips even as he slid farther downward, teasing just above where Gabriel wanted his hand. Both of them were breathing in shallow pants, and a small cry escaped him when Wynn pressed his other palm to Gabriel's belly. "Do you need me to say it?"

"No." Gabriel understood. He reached backward, holding as much of Wynn as he could as closely to him as he could. "I know. I want that too."

"Children?" Wynn's hand slid downward again, far down, sliding through the slick between Gabriel's legs. He inhaled sharply. "Mine?"

"Right away," Gabriel said. He wanted to arch forward, or back; whatever would get Wynn's callused fingertips deeper inside him, but neither worked. "Neither of us has a family. Isn't that what marriage is? Making a family? A family can be two. It can be bigger than that. I want that, Wynn. I want you to get me --" He swallowed again and pushed the words out. "I want your baby growing inside me."

"It's not too fast?"

"Too *slow*." Gabriel couldn't take the teasing any longer. He wriggled around, though he missed the thickness of Wynn's fingers inside him right away and molded himself to Wynn's front. He put his mouth to the base of Wynn's throat. "Even if I'm scared, I want this. Take me to bed, or I'll take you."

Wynn laughed, startled and delighted. "I knew I loved you for a reason."

"Only one?"

"Not even. I'm going to pick you up now, just so you know." Wynn's mouth moved over his neck as he did just that, letting Gabriel wrap both legs around him.

He could carry him without straining, and he kept talking. "I'm going to carry you to that bed, and I'm going to show you everything I've wanted to do to you."

He lowered Gabriel to the bed, made with fresh sheets just that morning, and stood over him, drinking him in. "You don't know how gorgeous you are, still, do you?"

"I know you make me feel that way." Gabriel licked his lips and reached for the loose knot tying his robe closed. He picked it open and let the light fabric slide away from his body, displaying himself so that Wynn saw it all. Softness, smoothness, and the gleam on his inner thighs.

Wynn's mouth fell slightly open. "Oh my God."

He couldn't have been Wynn's first, but it felt like that. And -- he wanted more. Hardly shaking at all now, Gabriel raised his knees to plant his feet flat on the mattress. Showing him *every* last part of him, stoking the heat in his stare to a fire that almost burned his skin, that would devour him before he'd even been touched. With the last bit of shyness left to him, he slipped his hand between his legs and traced a pattern around his opening. "Wynn," he murmured, eyes fluttering closed. "Come here."

Wynn came, dropping to his knees at Gabriel's feet and crawling forward. "I meant it," he said, looming over Gabriel. He moved Gabriel's hand out of the way and replaced it with his own, sliding his fingers back inside. "God, you're so wet."

"For you."

"Mmm." Wynn slid back the way he'd come, but he worked his shoulders beneath Gabriel's knees as he went, until his feet rested on Wynn's back and Wynn was -- oh *God* -- between his legs. He didn't move his fingers -- at first -- not until he let them glide out and his tongue slid in, in their place, curling deep and teasing the pleasure center deep inside. He laughed, dark and low, when Gabriel cried out and arched his back. "Tighten your legs. Hold on tight."

Gabriel did, but they almost wouldn't do what he told them. Wynn knew his work here, oh, he did, and he took his sweet time. Drew one side and then the other into his mouth and sucked; slid his fingers deep in a slow, lazy rhythm -- added a third that made Gabriel moan with the burn and stretch, but it was so, so good -- and rubbed his cheek against Gabriel's cock, leaking almost as much. Deep inside, he could feel the pulsing need for more, more, more, rising toward its peak.

"Stop," he begged. "Stop, or I'll come."

"You can do that more than once," Wynn said, stroking him. He curled his fingers up, brushing the *something* inside him that made Gabriel shake and soak the bed with slick, but not come. Not yet. "Hold on for me. I want the first time with me inside you."

"Then you'd better -- *oh*, oh -- hurry." Gabriel tried to drag him back up, where he'd cover Gabriel's whole body.

No. Wynn had other ideas, and he didn't waste time *there*. Fingers still inside, still but for spreading, stretching, he blew a warm stream of air over Gabriel's cock. Gabriel knew what he wanted, but still sobbed when Wynn took *that* in his mouth next, cheeks going hollow and his tongue curling around. Down, almost to the root; up, to curl his tongue around.

But his hair fell forward, hiding him from Gabriel's eyes, and Gabriel wanted to *see*. He reached down, hands shaking hard as leaves in a hurricane wind, and pushed Wynn's hair out of the way.

Wynn looked up at him beneath half-lowered lids. His face gleamed with Gabriel's arousal, and his lips were red as cherries, wrapped around his cock. Thicker smears smudged his forehead, where Gabriel's cock had rubbed while Wynn ate him out, and --

Pulse. Pulse. Pulse.

Gabriel arched up, holding on by the skin of his teeth. His thighs shook too, and he drove his heels into Wynn's back.

Wynn let go with a small *pop* and grinned at him. He spider-walked his fingers up Gabriel's chest. "Not scared now, are you?"

"Oh -- *fuck* you," Gabriel gasped, not even caring when that made Wynn laugh. He *wanted*, too much. "I know I never say that. Come *here*, Wynn. I can't -- not much longer --"

Wynn bent his head to one side. "Or I could keep doing this until you do come," he murmured, cleaning Gabriel off his lips with languid strokes of his tongue. "And keep on doing it until you're hard again."

"I will kill you if you do."

Wynn buried his face against Gabriel's quivering thigh, his smile a tangible thing. "Can't have that. Don't want you a widower before you're even married."

"I am married," Gabriel said. He opened his arms for Wynn to undulate up into them. Wynn had narrow hips, but he still had to stretch wide, wider, to give him room. "It won't hurt," he said before Wynn could ask. "I want it."

Wynn hadn't taken his fingers out yet. He curled them upward. "Just thinking. You stretch around me like... Just thinking."

A delicious shiver ran through Gabriel, and he wound his arms around Wynn. "Please," he said, not ashamed to beg. "Please, Wynn, please."

Wynn took the deepest of deep breaths and pressed his mouth to Gabriel's. "God, I love you," he said, and slid his fingers out of Gabriel. Another breath, a hand moving between then, and something blunter, harder, longer, pressing against him -- and -- *in* --

It did hurt, at first, only at first, the stretch so much more than just his fingers, but Gabriel muffled the sound he made by biting Wynn's shoulder. Not that he fooled the man, who shushed and soothed him and held still, waiting for Gabriel to loosen around him, to let him in. It didn't happen quickly, Gabriel overcome by the feel of Wynn inside him every time he tried to let go.

"I've got you," Wynn murmured. He put his head to Gabriel's chest and his mouth to one nipple. He licked, getting it wet, and then took the stiff nub between his teeth. He nipped once, bit down, then *sucked* as if -- as if --

As if to show Gabriel what it would feel like to put their child to his breast. Not all Omegas could do that, but Gabriel wanted that. He groaned and pressed Wynn's face down harder, and almost unconsciously his legs relaxed. Slippery slickness eased the way for Wynn to move his hips. Slowly, getting Gabriel used to it, never letting go of one nipple before switching to the other. Slowly, then faster, panting into the skin he'd bitten and wetted with his saliva, ripples of air that made Gabriel strive upward when Wynn drove down.

He was so wet, they both were, and Wynn filled him to the edge of what he could take. He moved faster, grinding deep, holding Gabriel's thighs up and apart to give himself more room. For how long, Gabriel didn't know. Could have been minutes, could have been hours. He lost his sense of time. All that mattered was rising to the edge, pushing Wynn's shoulders to warn him and Wynn slowing until he nodded, then pressing back in and holding him. Wynn too, stopping more than once to pant and grind his teeth.

Until -- too soon, not soon enough -- Gabriel knew he couldn't hold back, not any longer. The pulse was too steady and hard, too deep, too insistent, and he could feel his body drawing up inside, demanding things. Open and eager and hungry. *Throb. Throb. Throb.* His muscles clenched at Wynn to keep him locked in place and he dug his nails into Wynn's sweat-soaked back to warn him. "I can't, I can't, Wynn, I'm going to --"

"Wait for me." Wynn could barely move with Gabriel so locked on, but he nudged him from the inside, seeming to swell. "Not scared now."

Gabriel panted, mouth on Wynn's neck. "Not scared now. Not ever again."

"And you -- you meant it. You want my child. Mine. God, Gabriel." Wynn ground his teeth, fighting a struggle that Gabriel could feel from the inside; could feel how close he was too. "I want it. I want this, I want you, I want it so much. I want to see this soft skin on you stretching out *so* big and full, I want to be there when our baby's born, I want to hold you and catch him when he slides out of you --"

Gabriel came with a scream that made his throat raw, breaking Wynn's skin with his teeth, clamping down in ripples that made him climax again before he'd even finished the first one, this one inside instead of out.

Wynn bit down just as hard, shuddered, and came. Gabriel could feel it, not just the jerk and pulse of his cock, but the seed itself, so hot and thick and soothing. He could feel his body taking it in, greedy, milking him dry.

He came a third time, his vision going white, clinging to Wynn.

The daze faded when Wynn slipped out of him, not fully soft but the rest of him wrung out and looked up to see Wynn staring down at him, dazed but happier than he'd ever, ever been. Probably had the same loopy, stunned smile on his own face, didn't he? He stroked Wynn's face with both hands, still rippling a little inside, and Wynn put his hand on Gabriel's belly. He couldn't feel anything Gabriel felt, but Gabriel still wanted to ask. "Do you think..."

"If that didn't, what would? Besides. You're my

lucky charm, angel." Wynn kissed him lazily, the half-hardness he sported slowly filling again, sliding through the mess he'd made that dripped out of Gabriel along with his own arousal. "Never hurts to make sure, though…"

"Never hurts." Gabriel would let him back in when he was ready, though he felt -- satisfied -- inside. He cocked his head. "Would you like to know one of the reasons I love you?"

"Just one?" Wynn teased back.

"One for now." Gabriel kissed the corner of Wynn's mouth and let his hand linger on Wynn's side after. "One of the reasons I love you is that you take me at my word."

Wynn frowned. "What else would I do?"

So many others would have a different answer for that, or never have fallen in the first place. And that made two more reasons, Gabriel thought, lifting to kiss Wynn with almost all he had left in him, and guiding him back inside with the rest.

* * *

Present

Maybe he was Wynn's lucky charm.

First time lucky. Or second, or third, that night. Or the next. Or the next, or after that crack-of-dawn wedding they'd rolled into smelling exactly like they'd spent the whole night together. Or… well, there was no telling, not really, but Gabriel always thought it had been that very first time. No son of Wynn's would ever want to wait.

Gabriel smiled to himself, remembering that. Wynn had been so *pleased* to get the news, and even more so to have it confirmed. He couldn't wait to meet his child.

Like father…

Out in the back yard of their small, small house, cradled by the roots of the maple tree and so comfortable even with those cramps that kept coming, Gabriel stroked himself slowly, so slowly, remembering that night over and over, until he drifted off to sleep.

* * *

Gabriel came awake with a sharp, startled breath. The sky above him, steely-dark-blue through the winter-naked branches of the maple tree, spun and danced and made him dizzy until he took a second breath, a third, a fourth, and a fifth. It didn't stop whirling until he closed his eyes and put both hands to his forehead, and even then the world seemed to rock back and forth slightly.

No. No, wait. That was him, clumsy and awkward, but rocking his hips in the cradle of the maple roots.

Why was he...

Still confused, Gabriel leaned back against the comforting coolness of the maple's trunk -- or it should have been cool. Where he'd fallen asleep leaning against it the bark was almost skin-hot, fever-hot, and damp from how much he'd sweated on it. He shivered now, even though he wasn't any cooler. He was on fire, it felt like, angry flames crackling just below oversensitive skin. The sweat that'd soaked through his borrowed sweats had dried, stuck to his skin, and soaked through all over again, leaving them both stiff and sticky at the same time. He wrinkled his nose and pulled at them, tugging the cloth free of his skin -- and oh, that felt good, that felt *so* good that he had to, had to get the rest of them off. *Now.*

The thought that he'd be naked if he did that fleeted through his mind and was just as quickly cast aside. Naked or not, he was in his own yard, with no neighbors in his line of sight, and if anyone wanted to get a look, what did he care? To be *comfortable* instead of --

He sighed in relief as he wriggled free and kicked off the last of the foul sweats, even if he winced at calling them that: they were Wynn's, and they smelled like him. After thinking about it a moment, he managed to stretch just far enough to pull them back and pile them in a loose heap at his side. They mostly smelled like *him*, but with Wynn's scent underneath.

Gabriel exhaled, easier now with the cool wind on his skin and one hand on the pile of clothing. Absently, he stroked his belly, and the first prickle of alarm rang a bell inside his head. The baby never stopped moving once he'd started, except for a nap here and there, but he'd been quiet for a long time now.

Too long?

He pressed his fingers into his side, moving them in a rhythm that usually provoked at least a wriggle away, or a good hard kickback into his palm. Nothing, and nothing again when he pressed down hard. He could *feel* the shape inside him, lower than usual -- his lungs weren't as squashed under his ribs as usual -- but nothing worked until he slapped himself as hard as he could. The sharp sting didn't matter; the faint shift and roll inside *did*. Gabriel dropped back against the tree trunk, boneless with relief. *Still alive.*

Titus and Cameron had both said *shock*. He'd thought they were only talking about him, not about --

A cramp rippled through his belly, surprising Gabriel into hunching abruptly forward, arms wound around himself. He drew short, shallow breaths, all he could get in, as his brain tried to puzzle through what was going on.

Or -- no. *No no no no no no no. No.*

But his brain knew. His body knew. His *heart* still wasn't having any of it, and Gabriel fought against all other certainties with tooth and nail and claw.

That wasn't a contraction. I am not in labor. I am not. I won't let myself be.

He reached out blindly for his phone, but it'd ended up just farther than he could reach. Gabriel grunted with the effort it took to gather his strength and used the tree trunk at his back to help push him to his feet. His head spun and his legs were jelly, but he stood still until he was sure he wouldn't fall.

Then, one step forward. He'd call -- Cameron, maybe. Or -- who? He'd figure that out.

But he wanted to call *Wynn*. Even if Wynn's phone couldn't get a signal, and all he could do was leave a message. Why hadn't he done that before? *Stupid, stupid...* His head had gone fuzzy again. Gabriel moved forward, reaching for the phone.

He made it two steps forward before a dull *pop* inside jerked him to a halt. Water flooded down his legs, smelling strongly of ancient salt seas, hot as blood and so much of it that it could only -- it could only be --

Gabriel's legs gave way and he hit his knees. Not rocking this time. Praying.

Not yet. Not yet, please not yet --

* * *

Past

Gabriel held the door to their bedroom open for Wynn to stagger through with a giant flat-packed box too awkward for one person to carry. "I can still lift things. Let me help."

"Not a chance," Wynn shot back, muffled behind the cardboard currently smashing his nose. He eased the box down and leaned his elbows on it to grin at Gabriel. "You're already lifting, anyway. Carrying. What's the difference?"

Gabriel fought not to grin back. "A considerable one."

Wynn winked at him. "Yeah, but I can put this down. You can't, or at least you'd better not for a few more weeks." He gazed at Gabriel, drinking him in like water in the desert, the way he had ever since they'd confirmed he was pregnant. Blushing, Gabriel put a hand to his belly, still small enough to cup with his palm and invisible under one of his old loose shirts, but noticeable to someone familiar with the terrain.

"You're beautiful like this," Wynn murmured. "I

never really bought all that about glowing, until there was you."

"Oh God, stop." Gabriel's cheeks were going to catch fire, but his heart thumped happily. "Don't stop."

"I won't if you won't. Where's the screwdriver?"

Gabriel was sure there was a dirty joke somewhere in there, but he only clicked his tongue as he found the screwdriver, along with a hammer, on top of their dresser amidst the keys and coins and breath mints and things that always accumulated on flat surfaces. More so now that this wasn't just his dresser, his bedroom, but *theirs*. The little shack Wynn had mostly built out of reclaimed wood, baling wire, and chewing gum, then lived in for years, sat empty at the very outskirts of town, waiting to be sold for the value of the land it sat on.

He passed Wynn the screwdriver, handle first, and since there was no way Wynn would let him help with any of the unpacking or constructing either, sat on the edge of their bed to keep him company. From there, he watched Wynn frown at the instruction sheet that'd come with the bassinet and visibly argue with himself.

It took longer than Gabriel expected, but in the end Wynn shook his head and held the sheet out for him to take. "Keep this safe just in case I can't figure something out."

That might not happen. Wynn had a fine mechanical mind, and he could intuit his way through almost anything that needed to be put together or taken apart, but the fact that he'd asked meant more to Gabriel than being allowed to get down there and dig in. So did the little, rueful smile Wynn crooked at him, and his *thanks* nod. "If you want to drill me, you can. Just go easy while I'm concentrating on this."

Gabriel rested his chin in his hand and watched. "C-A-T. That spells what?"

"Umm." Wynn eyeballed a factory-sealed packet of

multi-sized screws and bolts. "These are crap. I have some better ones; I'll use those. C-A-T... Cat."

"Good! Now, 'cats.' Spell that for me."

"C-A-T-S."

"Good!" Gabriel praised again. He'd led story hour for years, but he'd never expected those children to know how to read or need to be instructed on it, and for all his willingness he wasn't sure he knew how to *teach*. Still, they seemed to be muddling through. It helped to have such an eager student. "Now write the word in the air. It's okay if it looks backwards to me as long as it's the right way around for you."

Wynn pursed his lips together, then used the screwdriver to trace the shapes of letters in the air between them, but that man -- instead of spelling cats, his grin shifted to wicked as he wrote K-I-T-T-E-N and pointed at Gabriel's belly.

"Why, you --" Delighted, Gabriel crinkled up the instructions and pitched them at Wynn's head; laughing, Wynn batted them aside. "*Owlet*, just so you know. Or *cub*. You've been studying on your own, haven't you?"

"To see you light up like that? You bet I have."

Wynn looked so pleased with himself that if the floor hadn't become a danger zone of screws and DIY Gabriel would have gotten down there no matter what and kissed him. Instead, he offered what reward he could, even if it did make him blush a little even now and peeled the light sweater he wore off over his head to leave his chest and belly bare. He laid his hand on the small curve and stroked it gently.

When he glanced up to see what Wynn thought of it, he burst into laughter. "Close your mouth. You'll catch flies."

Slowly, Wynn shook his head. "Warn a man, then. You almost gave me a heart attack, angel."

"Stop it. I did not."

"Says you. I'm the one behind these eyes." Wynn twirled the screwdriver in his nimble fingers. "And just so you know? You keep rewarding me like that, I'll start studying twenty-four/seven. Except later. No way I can concentrate on that and this *and* you at the same time."

"I could put my shirt back on."

"Or you could leave it off. I insist." Wynn brushed his tongue over his lips. He glanced at the guitar Gabriel had given him for a wedding present, then shook his head, drawn back to Gabriel's belly. "I'll play later."

"Sing now," Gabriel suggested.

"The song in my head doesn't have words yet. It's a lullaby. Those are hard. Turn on the radio app instead. Something quiet. Babies are supposed to like, what, classical? It makes them smarter?"

"I don't think he has working ears yet," Gabriel said, but his phone was at hand as always and he already had a subscription to a station that played nothing but classical. His hands trembled a little. Wynn was making a lullaby for them, by ear and memory. *That man...* "I am not holding it against my stomach, though. Loud enough for all of us to hear and I'll deafen the poor thing whether he's got ears or not."

Wynn snorted quietly, but as the peaceful sound of strings and woodwinds filled the room, he settled back down to his work. Gabriel made a mental note of that, wondering if white noise might help Wynn concentrate on reading when they got back to those lessons.

Or perhaps might make him think too much, Gabriel wondered, when Wynn asked -- very much *not* looking at him -- "Do you think he'll be like me?"

"Probably," Gabriel said, not understanding. "You're his father. He could be tall like you or have the same color hair and eyes. He might take after your wolf side or my owl side, but I'd be fine with either."

Wynn grunted. "Not what I meant." He drummed

the screwdriver against his knee, and he still wasn't looking at Gabriel as his jaw hardened. "Do you think he'll be. Stupid. Like me."

Gabriel's jaw dropped this time. "What? You --"

No. Nope. That wouldn't do at all, and Gabriel would not let that stand. He slid off the bed and onto his knees, crawling toward his husband despite Wynn's yelp of protest, not stopping until he caught Wynn's chin in his hand and gave it a shake. "Don't you ever say that again. Not ever. Do you understand me?"

Wynn looked like he'd just been flash frozen. He stared at Gabriel, wide-eyed and startled.

Before he could speak, Gabriel pressed a finger to his lips. "Never. Again. You are *not* stupid, Wynn. It's not your fault your teachers were too lazy to recognize a learning challenge when they saw one. It is *not* your fault that your parents didn't notice. You were a *child* and you learned how to manage the world, even the parts of it that never made sense to you. You made your way, and you grew up into a man who had the balls to romance a librarian and who I am *proud* to be married to, do you hear me?"

"Loud and clear," Wynn said, looking and sounding stunned. "You mean that."

That he would be surprised every time -- Gabriel understood it, but it still made his heart hurt. Gabriel took Wynn's cheeks between both hands and kissed him fiercely. "You're darned right I do. No, *damned* right."

"Language, language. You'd better hope the baby doesn't have ears yet," Wynn said, a faint grin starting to dawn. He put one hand over Gabriel's and leaned into it like an ordinary hound might.

"Peter Pan." Gabriel rubbed his thumb against Wynn's. "We'll have you reading that by the time the baby's here, and you can read it to him. Ten dollars says we'll get there."

"Five more weeks, though. Not a lot of time."

Gabriel lifted his head. "Five weeks, *maybe*."

"Five weeks, definitely. I was there, and I can count if I can't read."

"Oh, get back to your work." Gabriel dropped a peck on Wynn's lips and clambered back up onto the bed.

Five weeks? Very probably. He'd already started to get clumsy, and in another week, no matter how loose he wore his shirts, people would be able to tell just from looking at him. He rubbed the soft, flexible skin on his stomach thoughtfully.

"What's it feel like?" Wynn asked, slowing down to watch Gabriel's hand move. "All those changes, I mean. It happens so fast for Omegas. I can almost see you growing."

Yes, and it got him hornier than a three-headed bull in rut when he wasn't otherwise distracted. *Not* that Gabriel would complain. He spent most of his days, and all of his nights, hungry for Wynn's body on him and in him.

"It's... odd," Gabriel said after considering his words. "It doesn't hurt, it's so gradual, but I'm different every day. Things are starting to get crowded. I can tell he's there, now." In another week, he'd know for sure if the occasional odd flutter inside really was their son starting to move around. Wynn could feel it for himself then too, and if he hadn't been able to keep his hands off Gabriel before that --

Well. As fascinated as Wynn was by it all, Gabriel was no less so.

Cameron, on the other hand, and the library's board of directors, were going to have other ideas. They wouldn't legally be able to stop him from working until he was too big for it to be safe, but they'd surely try, and with them barely able to afford all the things they needed already --

"Are you sure?" Gabriel asked, frowning at Wynn. He'd burned his hand a couple of weeks ago trying to fix a machine in the quarry that was running too hot. It'd mostly healed, but if he hadn't had such quick reflexes it could have been so much worse -- and that was the least awful thing that could happen down there. But -- he wouldn't want Wynn to change anything he didn't want to. "You're sure that you're sure about quitting your quarry job? I know I was the one who asked you to think about it in the first place, and I'll never be ashamed of marrying a miner, but..."

Wynn shook his head firmly. "I'm a hundred percent sure. I'm quitting. Money'll be tight, but we can make it work. Take out a loan. Sell the truck."

"Don't you dare."

"I will if I have to, while I'm looking for other work." Wynn had his stubborn well and truly on now. "It's too dangerous down there for a family man. Things don't always get caught and fixed when they should be, and sometimes family men get killed. That's the last thing I want to put you through, and I want to meet our son when he's born."

Gabriel couldn't help but smile this time. "You keep saying that, over and over."

"Because I mean it. I'm going to be there when he's born. Bet." Wynn sat back on his heels, letting himself look his fill again. "I'm going to be there for him, all his life, stuck to both of you like glue. Double bet. Triple bet, when he has siblings." He grinned. "You just wait and see."

Chapter Six

Present

It'd been a good plan, and it could have worked. It should have worked. Wynn would have quit his job, just as he'd promised, and he would have found something else. A stretch here and there, setting up payment plans where they had to, and they'd have made ends meet until Gabriel could go back to work.

Only then there'd been the night of the fire. It hadn't been their fault, nothing they'd done. A downstairs neighbor, new to the building, had decided he wanted to grill inside while completely baked, himself, and fallen asleep with the coals burning and the grill lid open. Too much lighter fluid spilled on the carpet, a few sparks jumping from coals to carpet, and minutes later Wynn had shaken Gabriel out of the soundest sleep he'd had in weeks.

* * *

Past

"Get up, angel. Get *up*. We have to get out of here *now*."

Gabriel didn't understand why at first, not until he smelled the smoke and reek of burning drywall and froze where he lay. "Wynn, we're on the fifth floor."

Wynn knew that, of course. He'd lifted himself up to shield Gabriel's body, and though it shamed him now, Gabriel had curled into a ball beneath Wynn. Or no, it wasn't a shame, it hadn't just been himself that needed keeping safe. He remembered staring up at Wynn as Wynn's jaw muscles clenched and his gaze swept to and fro, calculations flying back and forth in his head.

"We have just enough time to get downstairs," he said seconds later. "If we go now."

"Our things --"

"There's no time, angel. Trust me."

Gabriel did. There'd been fires at the quarry before, and Wynn would have calculated right. He hurled himself out of bed and barefooted onto the floor, wearing nothing but a loose pair of boxers, and raced for the door with Wynn taking point in front of him.

People did the strangest things at times like those. Gabriel had no memory of the action, but he'd grabbed the photo album with their marriage certificate. Flames had come closer than he'd known, scorching its cover, but they made it out only just in time. Gabriel had to jump a third of the last staircase down, landing heavily in Wynn's arms a bare moment before it collapsed, and somehow he'd held on to that album.

At least he hadn't been the only one. Standing on the cold street below, hands joined so tightly Gabriel left bruises and Wynn made his knuckles ache, they'd watched their home burn. Nothing left, nothing at all, not Wynn's guitar or any of Gabriel's other books, and not a bit of what they needed for the baby and had already spent more on than they could afford.

All gone, in an instant, except for that album and a blanket Wynn whipped around Gabriel's shoulders to cover and warm him. Gabriel wound part of it around Wynn too and kept hold of his hand as they watched the fire eat the rest alive.

And that had been -- that. Wynn's truck disappeared overnight, and the next morning, after Gabriel was released from the hospital just in case the shock had put him at risk of miscarriage -- it hadn't, Wynn's son was as stubborn as his father -- they'd walked themselves to his old shack, still hand in hand.

When they opened the door, Gabriel had cried. Not because it was as bare and cold as he'd been warned, but because it was *full*. Wynn gaped around himself, question marks and exclamation points somersaulting over his head over what he saw: a bed, a tiny kitchen set up with a dorm-sized fridge and a double hot plate, a working toilet and shower -- and baby things too. It hadn't taken long to find out why: the men at the quarry, rough as sandpaper, had heard the news overnight and gotten together, some of them missing their one chance at sleep for days, to scour their attics and banded together to buy at the thrift shops things they didn't have on hand. All secondhand but scoured clean and smelling of fresh air.

Wynn had gone back to the quarry, day after day. No choice, and his pride demanded it. It killed him a little inside, Gabriel could see that, but there was *no choice*. He'd worn Wynn's sweaters long enough to fool everyone as long as he could and bargained for extra shifts at the library. Even after he couldn't hide his pregnancy, he'd argued for permission to keep going at home, doing the paperwork. Doing all the odd jobs he could pick up, typing until his eyes burned and his back ached from hunching over a computer bought from a pawn shop.

But they'd had each other, and that couldn't burn down. Not ever. They'd find a way.

Wynn always did.

* * *

Present

Gabriel couldn't sit still. He wanted to stay where he was, keep his feet tucked beneath him even as slippery and sticky as he was with amniotic fluid, because he could *feel* himself opening with each spasm.

No. He would *not*, not before Wynn was back home with him.

He wanted to stay put, but he couldn't. His body was taking over, doing things without his permission, and it'd shoved him upright before he could properly fight it. He staggered forward, both hands on his belly, then turned back again before he got halfway across the yard. It did help, he thought. Made his hips looser for the stretching, and he could breathe easier even when he doubled over.

They were coming so *fast* now. Smears of blood dappled his thighs, but not more than there should be. *If* he was giving birth. Which he was *not*. He wouldn't allow it. Besides, first babies took forever. Everyone knew that. All the books said so, even the children's ones he'd checked out from the library for Wynn to puzzle his way through.

But it's already been going on for hours, a small corner of Gabriel's mind whispered, insidious as a draft through a cracked wall. *It started when Titus first told you, and that was early morning. It's nearly nightfall now.*

It can't be that much longer --

Gabriel gritted his teeth and forced himself forward. He would not walk. He would not make this any easier than it had to be, body's wishes be damned. But he needed somewhere he could watch from, and he shuddered away from the thought of lying down in their bed. That would be far too easy. Where could he... *The shed*. It'd been a garage before Wynn sold his truck, no other choice, but even back then the corners had been packed with this and that. Old quilts. Those would do for softening the concrete floor, but they wouldn't be comfortable.

When he cranked the shed door open, a gust of gasoline-stink and engine grease and Wynn's essence, soaked into the walls, made him sigh with relief. He'd forgotten Wynn's clothes back by the tree, but this was better. This was pure Wynn.

Quilts piled up in a messy, hurried tangle, he lowered himself onto his side and shivered. Colder in there, but -- good.

Somewhere in the tangle, his phone rang, and the radio played on, music broken by news that Gabriel couldn't concentrate on. He raised one leg to plant his foot on the floor, then made himself thrust it back down to press his thighs as tightly together as he could. For as long as he could. That wouldn't last. He was too full there, stretching open.

"Wynn," he muttered, curling in on himself with a groan he couldn't keep swallowed down. "Wynn, hurry. *Please.*"

His phone rang again.

He didn't reach for it. He'd rather dream. He'd *make* himself dream.

"I'm here."

Wynn's quiet laugh made his mouth tickle, but he swept that away with a nip to the side of Gabriel's mouth and the downward slide of his hand. He wrapped it loosely around Gabriel's cock and gave him a slow, lazy stroke and smiled against his neck when Gabriel moaned and arched up, wanting more. "Better be."

"I am. I am." Gabriel reached backward, skating his fingers over Wynn's hip. It was all he could reach. Eight and a half weeks -- maybe eight and a half, maybe nine and a half weeks, they weren't sure, and first babies were usually late -- kept them almost at arm's length. As Wynn stroked him, too slow and too lightly for anything but a tease, he tried to arch his neck backward to kiss his husband and only caught a brush of his skin. *"Wynn."*

Wynn's breath warmed his neck in small puffs. "What do you need?"

"You."

The dream popped like a soap bubble. He -- he couldn't *concentrate* the way he wanted --

Gabriel bit his lip to keep himself quiet. If he made too much noise, their neighbors weren't *near* but they might still hear him at a distance. They might come running and find him, and the thought made him shudder in revulsion. No. No others. No one looking at him, seeing him, not if they weren't Wynn.

Wynn would be losing his mind, if he were there.

Gabriel laughed, even if it sounded more like a sob to his ears. Wynn and he had almost argued about hospital versus home, back at the beginning. Wynn had won the hospital argument after the fire, but before that Gabriel had stood firm for home.

I guess I win, he thought, before all his thinking ran out and his body seemed to wrench itself almost in half.

He came back to himself panting, driven by the need to move. He couldn't lie on his side any longer -- couldn't stay in any one place for too long before it grated at his muscles and skin -- but nothing was much better than another. He still had to. His arms shook almost too hard to use, but he managed to push himself to his knees, then dropped to his elbows as well and pressed his cheek against the floor.

Cool concrete, at least for the moment. He leaned hard into the soothing chill and closed his eyes to claw at fragments and shreds of better times.

Memories. Memories were better. He didn't have to concentrate on those. He could just let them flow through him.

* * *

Past

"Wynn?"

Gabriel had heard his husband come home, crossing the fallow fields between the quarry and their shack, boots crunching on dry grass, but he hadn't come inside for long enough that curiosity and concern drove him outside to see why. He found Wynn as soon as he opened the door. His husband sat on the bottommost of the three concrete steps that Gabriel kept swept no matter what, and he didn't care if it made him a stereotype of an Omega; he liked things clean.

Wynn twitched, not quite glancing back at him, but with a hint of his old smile. "Angel."

"What's wrong? Don't try to tell me nothing. I won't believe you."

Wynn's shoulders quivered slightly as he shook his

head. "Can't put anything past you."

"Not for long, no," Gabriel agreed. He was clumsy enough at seven weeks to make even three stair steps a dicey proposition -- he couldn't see his feet past his belly anymore -- but Wynn had put up a rail sturdy enough for safe holding-onto. One step at a time, and he nudged Wynn's hip with his foot. "Sweetheart. Stop sprawling and give me some room. Go up one step? I want to sit between your knees."

"Pushy, pushy, aren't you, angel?" Wynn mussed his hair, but did as he'd been asked, and sighed with the relief Gabriel had known he'd feel once Gabriel was snug between his calves. He rubbed his knuckles against Gabriel's scalp, almost petting him. "That better?"

Yes, much. Gabriel rested his chin on Wynn's knee and stroked his ankle; it was as he'd thought. Alphas needed to know they were taking care of their Omegas, and any perceived failure brought them down faster than hailstones in a summer storm. Wynn's sunnier nature and his stubbornness kept him from frequent, mercurial mood swings, but... Gabriel did see how their current circumstances would wear at him. He'd kept his dangerous job, moved them into a shack that barely had electricity and running water, and they still couldn't pay their bills.

Are we too young? Did we make a mistake? Should we have waited?

They would be the same questions that tormented Wynn, but Gabriel shrugged them impatiently away from his mind. What difference would it make to ask them? He wouldn't have chosen differently in any case. It didn't matter to him what they had or didn't; he'd spent too many years too lonely to value *things* over love.

He knew Wynn felt the same. Only it had to be hard, sometimes. Gabriel nibbled at the inside of his cheek, wondering if now was the right time. Very likely, he decided, and pressed down on the tops of Wynn's boots to try and boost himself to his feet.

"Hey, hey, careful." Wynn steadied him when his shifting center of balance almost tipped him too far forward. "If you need something, I'll go get it."

"No, I'll do it. Stay there."

Wynn frowned at him, then watched him dubiously. "Whatever it is, it can't wait? I was enjoying that."

"Patience." Gabriel put his fingers to his lips, and then his fingertips to Wynn's temple. "Stay there. I won't be a minute." He knew exactly where he'd hidden what he wanted, and how hard it'd been to keep it a secret.

Though he hadn't counted on how hard it would be to dig the surprise he'd planned out from underneath their bed. In the end, he had to use their broom to fish it out, and wasn't that some kind of a racket? Wynn had to be wondering what on earth he was getting up to -- Gabriel could *feel* the waves of curiosity even through the door -- but he stayed put until Gabriel pushed the door back open.

"Here," he said, hefting what he'd brought out and laying it in Wynn's lap. "For you, and for me too."

Wynn froze. Well, he would; nothing on earth looked like a guitar case except a guitar case. He snapped his head up to stare at Gabriel, then back down to the case. He clicked open the catches and stared at the old guitar inside instead. Secondhand instead of the new one he'd bought for their wedding, scuffed and studded with decals from bands Gabriel had never heard of as good as welded to the wood, but a fine instrument all the same. When Gabriel plucked one string, the tone was honey-sweet and mellow.

His husband swallowed hard. "Where did you... How?"

He sat beside Wynn, laying his head on Wynn's

shoulder. "I bartered a week's worth of tutoring to a Beta for it. He needed help with his college entrance exams, and he remembered me from the library. He couldn't afford to pay a teacher, but he *did* have this to trade."

"That's why you looked more tired than usual last week." Wynn's throat worked hard. "You did that for me? Just so I'd have this? But..."

Gabriel eased himself down on the step beside Wynn, amused at how Wynn had to scoot the guitar sideways on his lap to clear room for Incoming Belly. Their son twisted and stretched, as if he thought it was funny too. Was it counterintuitive, to give his Alpha something instead of encouraging the opposite? Perhaps, but Gabriel knew his husband. He needed to feel good about something to keep the rest of his spirits up. He needed to make and build and create to feel fully alive, and with an instrument he could give Gabriel as much music as he wanted.

He leaned over to kiss Wynn's cheek. "Yes, and I would do it again. Someone's got to take over lullaby duty, and you know I can't sing."

It surprised him when Wynn caught him by the back of the neck and dragged him closer, crushing their mouths together hard and fast, then pressed his forehead to Gabriel's in silent thanks. Gabriel rolled his head against Wynn's: *you're welcome.*

He lifted Wynn's hand and put it on the guitar strings. "Go on, then," he said quietly. "I want to hear you."

Wynn beamed at him, and --

* * *

Present

And the memory popped again, *snap* and gone. Gabriel curled in on himself, a ball of arms and legs clutched tight around his middle, wrist between his teeth now to muffle the sounds he couldn't help making.

He couldn't do this, couldn't do this, couldn't *do* this.

Eyes closed, he reached out a shaking hand to dig through the tangled mess of quilts for his phone. It fell into his hand as if it'd been meant to, still humming away with the radio and lighting up to remind him that he had unread texts and un-listened-to voicemails waiting for his attention, if he didn't mind, please and thank you.

Gabriel had meant to ignore those, to swipe straight at the *emergency call* button on the Lock Screen, but his thumb missed, and he only raised the volume on the radio app instead, blasting some kind of Top Forty he didn't recognize or like.

But that was good. Keep it loud enough, and it would disguise any noises he made. Gabriel cranked the volume higher still and laid the phone by his head, waiting for the next news update.

It didn't come. One song ended and another started, and then another -- as far as Gabriel could tell, as closely as he could concentrate, which was hardly at all. When yet another song kicked on without more than a "You're listening to" to break up the music, his shoulders sagged.

No news wasn't always good news, and if there was nothing more to tell, then that meant --

He shuddered away from the thought, but --

If there was nothing else to tell, and he had almost more unread texts and voicemails than his phone's minimal memory could manage, then that meant Wynn --

Wynn was --

Wynn would have called, if he'd been found alive. His name would have come up on the screen, and it hadn't.

Gabriel turned his phone's volume up as high as it could go, pressed his face to the floor, and screamed into the concrete beneath him. Raw howls right from the middle of his broken heart, driven by the pressure and relentless progress of his laboring body, salted with hot, angry, anguished tears that burned his eyes and tasted salt-bitter when they ran over his lips.

Then, he stopped. Drew in a shaking breath and let it out through his nose. Wynn wouldn't be ashamed of him, but -- if he wasn't coming home, ever again, *oh God, Wynn, you promised, why did you have to come if you were only going to go --*

No. Gabriel made himself stop. He turned over, slowly though he had to, and leaned his back against the wall. He laid a hand on his belly, bit his lip hard enough to taste blood where he'd already bitten it raw, and waited till he had the air to speak. If he had to do this by himself -- and what other choice did he have, now -- he would do it in a way that would have made Wynn proud of him.

That he could be proud of, when he looked back. In Wynn's memory.

"You'll know him," he said out loud. He sounded as raw as the inside of his mouth, voice strained and cracking. He reached out with one foot and kicked the door open wide enough to let in some fresh, cold air, and that helped. "I'll tell you every story there is to tell, the parts of them that matter. I'll tell you how much he loved you even if he never met you. I'll tell you who he was and where he came from."

He had to stop, then, but as soon as he could Gabriel started talking again, letting the words pour out of him.

"You'll know your father," he told his son, on his way to being born so, so soon. "You'll know that fairy tales come true sometimes. Peter Pan and Prince Charming. And you'll grow up like me or like him, but you'll know, and you'll believe, and you'll never be alone. I won't let you. I'll be there, always. And Wynn…"

In spirit, if not in body, he'd be there too even if only in memories. Good, good memories, like --

* * *

Past

Wynn stood behind Gabriel by the maple tree to watch the sun set with him from under its shelter, the very last of the autumn leaves clinging and drifting down around them in a slow, fragrant sort of rain. He tucked his chin into Gabriel's shoulder, the rest of him so warm and so comforting, sturdy and solid at Gabriel's back. Gabriel leaned into him, safe and sound. He could hear Wynn's heart beating a steady rhythm, soothing away any hint of raw nerves. He'd been told he couldn't go back to the library until after his bearing leave was over, but he'd argued -- and won -- the right to work from home as much as he could.

He'd stood up for himself and he'd won, and he never would have done it without the man who had his back.

"What made you come into the library that day?" Gabriel asked, only now realizing he never had, and wondering why. "Were you killing time until the bar your friends wanted to go to opened, or were you looking for something?"

Wynn's chuckle jostled him gently, waking the sleeping beast inside. He laid his hand on Gabriel's belly to feel their son stretch out and kick ferociously at his palm. Gabriel concealed any hint of a wince; he wouldn't make Wynn regret taking what he wanted. It wasn't pleasant from the inside, no, but what did that matter? He couldn't stop marveling at how the baby was so *lively* in there. Even if he didn't end up looking like Wynn, even if he was Omega and not Alpha, he had his daddy's spirit already: full of fire, ready to take life by the scrotum and roar his way through the world, to tell it like Captain America -- *no, you move.*

"The guys were killing time," he said after a moment. "I thought I was too, until I found something I hadn't meant to look for."

"And that was?" Gabriel asked, teasing him the way Wynn had shown him he could.

Wynn touched his lips to the corner of Gabriel's mouth and rocked him, swaying them both gently to and fro, and even though it was only a joke he answered Gabriel seriously just the same: "I found you. Everything I ever wanted, even what I didn't know I wanted, when I found you."

Gabriel closed his eyes and sighed, content. If he never had another moment as perfect as this one, he'd have this memory forever and ever and always…

* * *

Present

Gabriel opened his eyes to the shed, barely lit by twilight. Strange, how he'd never noticed before that this door faced the quarry too. Seemed like everything led to and from the place, but that was just as well. Their son would need to know where he came from, so let that be his first sight.

He could hear the *tick, tick, tick* of their old clock in his head, just as he had this morning when making love to Wynn, counting down the seconds. But there was a little time left, if only a little.

"I'll tell you about the day we met," he told his son, still safe inside him for now. "I'll tell you everything."

And he did just that, pausing when he had no choice, then picking up the threads he'd dropped. Telling story after story until his voice was barely a ragged whisper, and all he could do was hum in a ragged monotone.

The pressure between his legs -- *God*!

Panting, Gabriel reached down. He couldn't go far at first, there was too much in his way, but he drew his knees up until he could make contact -- then jerked away with a bitten-off cry of pain; he hadn't known he would be so *sore* down there already, though he should have, shouldn't he? Even if he was too exhausted to think straight, there was a reason they called it labor, wasn't it?

He gritted his teeth, but let his air go in a startled gasp as he understood what he was feeling, what had happened to him and left him like this: swollen yet and wide open and soaked with the fluids his body kept making to ease the way and blunt the pain, the last gift an Omega's body could give them at the end. It was meant to help but that meant it was almost the *end*.

And it didn't help. Unless that was his holding back? Making it harder on himself? Even with all the effort he'd put in Gabriel could *feel* their son's readiness to be born.

He pressed his legs together and held them there. He couldn't make it not happen, if it was going to happen, but he wasn't ready yet. He just wasn't.

A little longer. Only a little longer, before it's real.

A distraction. He needed a distraction, and the blaring pop songs playing nonstop on the radio app raked his nerves into a tangled frenzy. Gabriel switched the noise off and swiped to the voice messages waiting for him instead. Just to check, to make sure.

None from Wynn. One from Titus, less than thirty seconds long, and Gabriel flinched away from that. But -- two from Cameron, the first of them almost five minutes long. Curiosity fought a brief struggle with displeasure, but curiosity won. He put the phone to his ear and let it play.

"I don't know what you're doing," Cameron said without a *hello* or a *how-are-you*. He must have been in the library when he called, likely tucked back in the break room but with the door open. Gabriel could pick up the faint sounds of talking in the background, hushed but there. "I don't know why you're not answering your phone, and you don't know how hard it is not to call the paramedics *right now*, other emergencies be damned."

Why hadn't he? Gabriel would have locked the shed to keep them out, but --

Cameron was still talking. "I told you before that you didn't know me, didn't know anything about me, so I'm going to tell you. I've lived in Second Chance all my life. I grew up walking these streets. I used to live in the same building you did before I --" He stopped. "Before I got married too. Around the same age you did."

Gabriel caught his breath. He *hadn't* known that. Cameron didn't wear any kind of ring to hint at that, and he'd never, not once, mentioned a husband.

"I got married. To an Omega. Which doesn't happen, you know it doesn't, because what would be the point? Or at least that's what everyone thought. They talked about us as much as they talked about you. Maybe more. Even more when my Omega got pregnant."

He'd -- what? Gabriel's head spun. Betas married other Betas, if they married at all, and they mostly didn't. Only once in the bluest of moons could one of them get pregnant, and that was the driving force behind their world.

What had happened to them, that Cameron never said a word about them before now?

Gabriel moaned, losing his focus. He couldn't pause the phone during the next contraction, though he felt as if he were splitting in two. He couldn't keep his thighs together either. He reached between them and spread his palm wide, pressing in, and that was stupid, even he knew that, but --

Cameron was still talking, faster now, as if he had to finish this now he'd started and couldn't stop himself any more than Gabriel could, telling him what Gabriel could have guessed if he hadn't instinctively shied away from it. "Betas aren't supposed to be able to do that. Even when it does happen, it's almost a medical impossibility. Mostly the babies don't live to be born, and ours..." He stopped to draw a breath. "Ours didn't. It died just three weeks in, and it took my husband with it. We were walking to the store, just walking, and it happened so fast. He stopped like he'd been shot, just stopped, and then he fell. He bled to death in minutes, in my arms."

Gabriel listened to him take a deep, harsh breath.

"You wanted to know why I stopped talking to you. Why I never do story hour. I *can't*. I couldn't. I know that makes me a coward, but I'm calling now. I'm telling you, because if you're not all right then I'm going to wring your neck myself. Call me back, Gabriel. I mean it."

Disconnect. Message ended, and though Gabriel's heart was already broken, he discovered there were still places where it could crack deeper. *You should have told me. I'd have understood.*

But I understand why you didn't too.

It still hurt. Too much. Gabriel couldn't bear it if he couldn't shake it off, just for now, and he needed to move again. The concrete wall scraped at his back, burning his skin with friction. Could he even move, though? Would he be able to?

He couldn't. He ached for the grass under his and the sky above him, but his legs wouldn't budge. They were locked in place, and he could feel himself stretching open, burning with a fire he couldn't put out even with all the slippery fluid still trickling away. He could feel the baby's head without putting his fingers inside now.

He had hair. So much hair. Gabriel couldn't see, but it was so fine he thought it must be blond, like Wynn's.

He turned his gaze toward the horizon, and -- and --

Oh God. Oh God, he was hallucinating, and this was -- cruelty, this was cruel. He'd lost his glasses somewhere so that everything was blurry anyway, but he must have pushed himself too far and he had to be hallucinating.

Wynn was dead. Buried forever behind rubble too heavy to shift before he ran out of air. *Dead* and gone.

Not loping across the field between the quarry and their home, stiffly and with a limp so pronounced that something in his leg had to be cracked or broken. Livid scrapes, red and raw enough for Gabriel to make out even at that distance, marred his skin along with deep purple bruises. He was missing -- oh Lord, he'd lost half his hair, frizzled away and burnt off. Gabriel could smell -- imagined he could smell -- the scorched stink of it.

Grass crunched under imaginary Wynn's feet. Or -- Gabriel leaned his head back, needing the support to keep from turning away. This was Second Chance, where things that weren't supposed to happen did, all the time. Maybe this wasn't a hallucination. Maybe this was the last trace of Wynn, come to say goodbye. Come to keep his promise after all, because if anyone on this earth was stubborn enough --

"I loved you," Gabriel said, voice wet and heavy, cradling the top of their son's head instead of his belly, watching Wynn come closer still. Imagining he saw Wynn see him, stop, and frown, then stare. "I loved you with all my heart and life and soul and I don't regret a second of it, do you hear me? Not one second."

His fingers were slippery, and they slid to the next message from Cameron. Not pressing PLAY, not yet.

"It was worth it," he told Wynn's ghost. "You were worth it, and however long I live there will never be anyone to replace you. No one ever could. I love you."

He had to stop, then, chin tucked to his chest. It was happening, the very last of it. Slowly, so slowly, but happening.

Wynn's ghost ran toward him and skidded to a

stop at the edge of the shed. "I love you too," it said, then in disbelief asked, "Gabriel, what the hell are you doing?"

Gabriel's thumb twitched, and Cameron's voice came out of the speaker.

"Gabriel, pick up! Goddamn it, pick up!" the Beta shouted. "Wynn is alive. Do you hear me? They found him. *Wynn is alive.*"

Chapter Seven

Gabriel jerked back, away from the ghost. His ears rang so loudly that he couldn't hear anything else, not even the roar and whoosh of the blood that he felt rush to his head. "You're not here."

Wynn's lips moved. Gabriel couldn't read them and couldn't hear them. He saw Wynn scan him, frantic -- why would *he* be frantic? -- and his jaw drop as he realized Gabriel was naked. The shock on his face when he looked down between Gabriel's streaked thighs.

Gabriel shook his head and clutched at his belly with a moan. "You -- can't be here," he ground out, still fighting. His son's head slipped forward an inch, and then back. "You can't be. You're dead."

His ears popped.

"I'm. Not. Dead," Wynn shouted. He crawled forward, even though it made him hiss when he put weight on his now-bad leg, and wedged himself between Gabriel's thighs. "And you're giving birth right now. *Gabriel.*" Reaching out, he pushed sweat-soaked hair away from Gabriel's face, then reached down to knock Gabriel's hand out of the way and replace it with his own. The shock on his face *would* have made Gabriel laugh if he hadn't been stunned silent.

That touch was real. He could feel his body straining toward it, in it. Warm and real and hard.

Wynn was --

Gabriel held his breath until the contraction passed but he grabbed at Wynn's wrist, clutching down hard enough to feel the bones grind together. That was real too. "You're alive," he croaked. "How? How are you alive?"

"Now isn't the time, Gabriel, my God, you're almost --" Wynn kissed him once, and that was *real*, he was *there*. "Why isn't anyone else here?"

Gabriel did laugh, though it was breathless. "I

waited. For you. As long as I could." He let go of Wynn's wrist and brushed his fingertips across Wynn's bruised cheeks. "How?"

Wynn let out a loud, rasping noise, then set his jaw. "I was trapped on the other side of some rubble. You would have heard. The rubble didn't fill the corridor I was in, just blocked it off. Some of the men were hurt. I helped them as best as I could, and I got the rest of the men to lift stones. We came from one direction. The rescue workers came from another. *Gabriel*. You waited. How? No. Don't answer that." He leaned forward and pressed his forehead to Gabriel's. "I know how. Anything you put your mind to, you can do. Even stop yourself from *this*. Stop it, okay? I've got you. It's okay now."

Gabriel wanted to, but oh, the irony burned, and he didn't have the strength left. "I don't think I can anymore."

"You can. I know you can." Wynn shook him with the hand not between Gabriel's thighs. "I'll take care of you."

Gabriel shook his head. He truly didn't have the strength. No food, nothing to drink since the morning, and a day's worth of sweat and strain and shock; he'd known his body would do it for him, but to do it himself - - "I can't. Wynn, I can't, he's too big, it's too much."

"Wrong. You can. Let go, Gabriel. You can, now. I'm here. I've got you. Both of you. *Do* this."

And it was as if his body needed that permission. Another spasm, stronger than any that'd wracked him before, seized Gabriel in its fist and didn't let go. He bent forward, spreading wide and wider still, Wynn bracing those broad shoulders between his knees to keep him like that. Gabriel could only be distantly grateful, because everything, every bit of himself, was right there between his legs and the *relief* of putting what strength he had left into this.

It took longer than he'd thought, or he'd lost all sense of time, because there was wave after wave, push after push, keening noises when he couldn't take the stretch and burn, but always, always, Wynn's hand on him, guiding him. He kept going, he had no choice, he pushed and strained until he thought he would tear in half --

Then, Wynn's startled shout, and an absolute *emptiness* where he had been so, so full before.

The ear-splitting, indignant yowl of a newborn.

He fell back against the wall, the last of his strength drained -- almost. He opened his eyes and looked up to see Wynn had gone ghost white but lit up from the inside out, juggling small, slippery limbs until he had them under control and pressed to his chest. "Gabriel, Gabriel, look what you just did. Look who you made."

Gabriel's body throbbed, muscles howling out their protest, and agony coming in waves between his legs, from inside him. They all would for a while yet, and he didn't care. He reached out, pleading silently for Wynn to come closer now that he could -- and between one blink of an eye and the next, he did. One arm around Gabriel's shaking shoulders, one arm holding their son, putting him to Gabriel's chest, keeping his hand on their son's back.

He put his head on Gabriel's shoulder and cried, and Gabriel let him. Pressed his lips to Wynn's hair, his temple, the top of his cheekbone. "What *we* did. And you were here."

Wynn had kept his promise.

He'd seen his son born.

He'd seen them become more than two. A family.

Everything else but this moment, past or present or future -- it could wait.

* * *

They sat stacked together, in the end. Wynn piled

as many of the quilts as he could find that weren't ruined into a cushioned nest at the shed door. Gabriel wasn't sure he'd ever put an engine together with more caution or consideration, but all he could do was laugh and tease him for it and Wynn didn't mind. Once he was as satisfied as he'd get, Wynn made sure Gabriel had their son securely in his arms, then picked them both up and eased them into the cradle of his lap where they could look out, up and at the stars.

He hummed to them, supporting and rocking both, his head pressed to Gabriel's. Gabriel didn't have to worry about the strength to hold himself or their son. Wynn would catch them if they slipped.

"You dug your way out?" he asked.

Wynn raised one shoulder. "What else would I have done? I needed you. You needed me. I wasn't going to miss this."

"You were hurt, though." Gabriel trailed his fingertips along Wynn's leg, wincing when he winced. "This isn't broken, is it?"

"No. Maybe cracked, but I'm used to it by now and there's nothing else wrong besides scrapes and bruises. Didn't even hit my head when the wall came down."

Gabriel shivered. "Used to a cracked leg? Wynn, my God."

"Shh." Wynn pulled him a little closer, careful as handling an egg, but the warmth of his body would have made a jostle worth it. "A *maybe* cracked leg bone, that's nothing. We had enough warning to hit the deck, and enough sense not to get back up until we were sure we could."

"It must have been dark, though. Cold."

"We had flashlights, and trust me, cold wasn't a problem after we got to work."

Gabriel could imagine it. He could smell the dried sweat on Wynn's skin, but he was hardly the least fragrant of them right then and he didn't mind anyway.

"Once we broke through and crawled out they wanted to line us all up to see the ambulance crew, but I'd just spent twelve hours hoisting rocks with my bare hands. I figured I could manage a walk." Wynn chuckled. "So I made a break for it when their backs were turned."

Gabriel laughed out loud. "You didn't."

"Damn right I did." Wynn reached across them to touch his son's hand; his index finger was almost too big for the little fist to curl around in its sleep, but it did, and Gabriel felt rather than heard the small sound he made. Shock, awe, delight. "I just wish I'd been faster. Five minutes later…" He touched his lips to Gabriel's temple. "I wish you hadn't fought like that. You could have hurt yourself."

"I wasn't thinking clearly. Almost all day, I wasn't." Gabriel could feel an apology gathering and cut it off before it started. "Don't. None of this was your fault."

"You never let me blame myself for anything." The warmth of Wynn's breath curled against Gabriel's shoulder. "I'm not going back there. I'll get compensation and PTO and we'll figure out what comes next in the meantime."

Good. Gabriel nuzzled at Wynn's shoulder. "Figuring out a name for him is what comes next. Or maybe calling people? Letting them know we're okay?"

"Are you kidding me? His name's Triumph."

"He's not a cigar-smoking comic insult dog puppet," Gabriel objected.

"Victory?"

"No." Gabriel hummed along with the melody Wynn had begun. "I think his name's Ford. You sold that truck when you wanted so much for it to be his one day. We can still give him that much."

He felt Wynn's throat work hard, and the hard

bump of their heads together; it was all the answer he got, but it was enough. Gabriel rested his head against Wynn's until his breathing steadied, and he said, still just the tiniest bit shaky, "Is that why you hid in the shed? Because that's where I kept it? Or was it a Nativity thing?"

"Maybe both." It might have been, on reflection. Gabriel brushed his thumb along Ford's lips, starting to work and pucker in his sleep. "He's hungry, I think. Help me? I don't know if I can do this, but I want to try."

"You can do anything you want, when you try, but I'll help you anyway." Chin pressed hard into Gabriel's shoulder as he concentrated, Wynn's work-roughened hand guided them into place. He hissed when Gabriel hissed, then let out a long breath at the same time and what had been hungry whimpers gave way to gulping swallows. "Look at that. You really can." He kissed Gabriel's cheekbone. "You're a walking jaw drop, angel. Just so you know."

"Look who's talking." Gabriel pressed against him. "And since my arms are full, you are going to be the one doing the talking."

Wynn snorted. "Sir, yes, sir. My phone broke when I hit the deck, but I found yours. There's just enough battery left for a couple of calls."

Gabriel waved at him; *go for it*, too fascinated by their son and content in Wynn's arms for anything else to matter. The only other thing he could look up at was the sky, and once he'd tilted his head back he had to keep it there, marveling at the clarity and beauty of the stars scattered across their indigo night, freckles of light surrounding the moon.

"Text Cameron back for me," he said absently. "He can yell at you instead of me."

"Titus's going to do enough yelling for everyone once I get hold of him."

"Do you mind?"

"Nope." Wynn cocked his head. "Cameron? You two are talking again? When did that happen? Never mind, tell me later. There are messages from him already. Last one's from a couple of minutes ago. He says he's sending an ambulance out here and he doesn't give one single damn if you like it or not."

"That sounds about right. How long do you think we have?"

"Not sure. Let me call Titus and get that out of the way in case it isn't very long." Wynn hesitated. "I know you're all right. I just want them to make sure. Okay?"

"As long as you let them make sure you are too. No arguments."

"You drive a hard bargain, angel. But okay. Titus first." Wynn readjusted his hold on Gabriel and their son so he could tap one-handed on Gabriel's phone, then lifted it almost to his ear.

Titus picked up halfway through the first ring. "Gabriel?"

"Guess again."

Titus exploded right on cue, hollering so loudly the phone jumped in Wynn's hand and the speaker distorted his voice while Wynn laughed into Gabriel's shoulder. *"You dickheaded asslicker, what in the ever-loving goddamn* hell *did you think you were doing running off like that? You'd better have had a damn good reason for not --"*

Apparently, Ford wasn't going to be one to tolerate anyone besides him making a racket. He let go of Gabriel to wail, ear-splitting and in need of immediate soothing, but by golly it cut Titus's rant off right down the middle.

"Well," the grizzled old man said after a stunned silence. *"Fuck."*

"Good enough reason for you?" Wynn asked. "That's what I thought."

He kept talking, but Gabriel drifted off. Not into

dreams, or memories. He'd run through his store of both, but that was all right. He could make more, now. New ones. Was making them now, in fact, adding pieces to their story.

* * *

After Wynn ended the call, he kept talking, content to just make white noise while Gabriel drifted into a light doze. He stroked his mate's face and imagined he could read the man's mind. He had so much more in there than anyone gave a "shy boy" credit for. In his heart too. Wynn had seen that from the start, but he hadn't realized just how deep that ran. Or how true he was, or how hard he believed in things, how much he cared, and how *strong* he was.

Look at what he'd been through today, what he'd done. Digging yourself out of a mine? Far as Wynn was concerned, it didn't come close. It'd been the bravest thing he'd ever seen, even more than when he'd decided to take a chance on Wynn.

And look what it'd gotten them, huh? They didn't have a horse and carriage or a palace -- yet -- but they had a starry night, a newborn son, and *he* had a husband who loved *him* that much, who would never, ever let him go.

"Prince Charming is real," Wynn whispered to the baby he helped Gabriel hold safe and sound. "I found him, didn't I? Fairy tales do happen sometimes. Sometimes you fall in love right away. Sometimes there really are happy ever afters, no matter what people try to tell you. Impossible things happen every day, especially when you believe they can. You wait, little one. You wait, and you'll see."

And so would he. Always, and evermore after too.

Take You There (Second Chance Omegas 4)
Willa Okati

Thoughtful, quiet, and just a wee bit on the dryly sarcastic side, Ethan teaches music at the university in Second Chance. With barely enough time to breathe between hysterical students and faculty shenanigans, he's not looking for Mr. Right -- just Mr. Right Now -- and only when the moment calls for it. The beautiful man who calls himself "Blue" in a quick, dirty alley encounter should have satisfied him. But now Ethan can't get Blue out of his mind, and can't seem to stop looking for him.

Carter -- "Blue" when he wants to stay anonymous -- wears his scars on the inside, but they're deep and still bleeding. He doesn't venture far outside his antique & pawn shop unless he's desperate for someone to touch and hold him and make him feel good for a little while. He promised himself he would never want more again. The smoldering musician who caught his eye, and what they did in the alley, should have been enough. That should have been the end of it.

It wasn't. It isn't. Their encounter left him pregnant, and he's been frozen since then, not knowing how to break free of his shell or what he should do. Until Ethan finds him -- and then, everything changes. Again.

Author's Note: Also featuring Oscar, everybody's favorite sarcastic best friend. We all need an Oscar in our lives.

Prologue

Was there a place like this in Second Chance?

Of course there was. Carter's lips curved wryly around the rim of the highball glass he held to his lips. There was always a place like this no matter where you went. It just depended on whether who you asked knew what you wanted. And if you wanted a bar that didn't serve chicken wings but did pour good beer and better tequila and top-shelf vodka, you wanted the bar called *Speakeasy*, just off Main Street. You could only get in through the back door and only if you knew where and how to knock, but once you did...

It wasn't a place where everyone knew your name, but for most people there, that wasn't even close to the point and sometimes --

Carter kept to himself when he could, lived silently and solitary, and he'd chosen that kind of life on purpose. It was better that way. Safer. He could watch his twelve and his six, and he could walk away from anything before it overwhelmed him. But sometimes --

Sometimes, he needed this.

Tucked quietly and carefully in one corner of the room, he kept the rim of a glass of tequila at his mouth, but only for show; he'd already sipped his way through two shots. Enough to work the tension out of his knotted muscles, but not so much that he'd do something he'd regret in the morning. Or if he did, to know it'd been worth it.

Carter's hand spasmed around his glass, remembering it all too keenly, and knew he'd keep remembering until --

He should have turned the radio at his antique-slash-junk shop workbench off as soon as the first broadcast about the quarry disaster came through, but it'd caught him before he could switch the app off and he'd been lost. Drowning in it. He'd spent the day ignoring a workbench full of things that needed repairing, fixated on the steady voice of the broadcaster droning on and on and on with the lists of missing, injured, dead. On and on and on. Heartbreak after heartbreak after heartbreak, and he'd felt them all. Even now he could feel the echoes in his chest, cracking with each one --

He *knew* better.

Carter rubbed the heel of his palm against his eyes. He'd always been like that, ever since he was a kid. *Too sensitive, even if he's probably going to be an Omega*, they'd said. *Strange, even for someone with -- you know -- his kind of bloodline, and everyone knows how they are.*

So.

He'd taken that to heart too. He'd learned how to turn himself off -- but too well. Even if he hadn't intended it, he'd gone too far in the other direction. Unless he was as careful as careful could be and didn't slip up as he had with the radio, it took him so long to warm up to people and let them in that it turned them off, made them look at him oddly and give him a wide berth.

What'd happened today at the quarry wasn't about him. Carter knew that.

But if he ever wanted to sleep again, he needed this.

Carter tilted his head back and gulped, letting the whole shot burn its way down his throat. He came up breathless, but -- better. Much better, even if it left him gasping and with his heart pounding. He lightly thumped the heel of his shoe on wooden floorboards worn smooth from years of others doing the same. The owner, who set the playlists every night, had a sense of occasion. No wailing jazz or mournful blues tonight. Just hard, driving beats that made a man want to shout, stomp his boots, pump his fists to the sky.

To dance, and --

To erase everything except feeling good for a little while. To fuck.

Fuck, no playing around, no sugarcoating it. A soundtrack like this demanded hard kisses and hands on harder bodies from anyone who was willing, who was able, and who was old enough to know better but still didn't give a damn.

But who?

Carter ran a finger around the rim of his glass as he searched the room and sorted through his options. The locals all knew him here. He had to do his hunting among the new-to-town men, but there were plenty. Firemen and rescue crews who'd done their jobs and been turned loose to celebrate, for one. Graduate students, a whole crop of them.

A few who weren't nearly so easy to pin down. Those were the ones he wanted. Carter wanted that, to chase after the distraction they provided.

Or to be chased, instead. That was new.

Carter could feel one of them watching him. Staring at him. He wasn't sure how long the man had been looking. He might have started while Carter emptied his glass and had his throat on display; that would have piqued any Alpha's interest. Slowly, slowly, he swept the room, searching.

Finding.

There. Someone he'd never seen before. An Alpha in a dark green shirt, well-worn jeans that hugged his ass, and scuffed leather boots. Long hair pulled up in a messy knot -- to hell with fashion for this guy, he clearly liked what he liked and he liked his man-bun -- and a feral grin. Lean as a lone wolf in early spring but lined with lean muscle and blessed with a sense of rhythm. He'd probably had just as many drinks as Carter, or more, but he could still keep up with the beat, swinging his hips and raising his hands to the roof.

When Carter met his hot, interested stare, the Alpha raised an eyebrow in both dare and invitation.

Yes. That. *Him.*

Carter licked the last drops of tequila off his lips, put his glass down, and slid out of his corner to glide across the room. The sheer number of men packed in there made for tough going, but the way that Alpha watched him was a good motivator to keep moving. Carter didn't stop until he'd reached the man, eyed him up and down to let him know they were on the same page, then turned away only to lean backward -- his own invitation.

He sighed in relief when the Alpha took him up on it. His chest nestled against Carter's back and the rest of him came along for the ride, cradling Carter's ass and guiding Carter's hips with his hands on them. He *could* keep the beat, and he could manage a good, deep, dirty grind at the same time. Already hard, Carter could feel the man's length pressed against him as he rocked and Carter rolled back, a hot buzz running through him that had nothing to do with tequila or a driving bass line.

Not that he didn't enjoy both. His head went calm and empty, and his body took over. When he leaned his head back in pleasure, deliberately exposing his throat again, the Alpha put his mouth there with his lips over the thumping pulse in Carter's throat. His beard, though short and neat, prickled and tickled and made Carter part his lips on a silent moan.

"What's your name?" the Alpha asked against his ear.

Carter stiffened, then shook it off before the man could notice. He didn't do real names, not with one-night stands. For this to work, to truly satisfy him, he needed the safety net of anonymity. "Blue," he lied. "Call me Blue."

The Alpha said something in reply, probably his

real name, but Carter deliberately chose not to listen. Besides, his senses were otherwise engaged. Another soft cry escaped him when the Alpha ran strong, agile fingers with callused tips through the length of Carter's hair. It'd come loose of the ties he kept it back with, but he liked his hair -- glossy, black, silky -- and he'd let it grow as long as he wanted, until it fell nearly to the center of his back. It seemed to fascinate the man. He reached backward to cup and cradle the Alpha's jaw, stroking beneath it.

Blunt teeth nipped at his neck -- not marking Carter but teasing him. Reminding him that an Alpha could use his teeth for fun and games as well as leave a stamp of ownership if he chose. Just give him an excuse.

Carter had teeth too, but he only shivered with pleasure and ground back harder as the Alpha held him tighter. Still in time with the music but adding his own rhythm. He tucked one hand into Carter's hip pocket, teasing a finger along the side of his hard-on, then slipped it around front to cup him.

Oh, they *were* on the same page. Carter moved into the touch, letting him know how hard he was too, how hungry, how he wanted what the Alpha was offering.

The Alpha leaned closer to his ear. Carter could feel the tickle of his lips moving, but the music was too loud, and he couldn't make out a word. Probably his name. Definitely a question. Maybe even something filthy. It all came down to the same thing: *want to get out of here*?

Yes, and the sooner the better. Carter peeled away from the man just far enough to take his hand and tilt his head toward *Speakeasy's* door.

Coming?

The Alpha grinned again, bright and fierce. *I will be.*

He switched their grip so he held Carter's hand instead of the other way around. He was the one who led the way forward, back the way Carter had come but right past his corner, opening the door to let a gust of cooler air in and showing them both out into the night. They moved quickly enough to raise Carter's heart rate and speed up his breathing with pure anticipation.

He wasn't wrong to let it race through him. The second the *Speakeasy* door closed behind them, the Alpha spun Carter around to press him against the cold brick wall of the alley and put his hot mouth to Carter's.

Warm, golden light from the one lamp next to the door, the kind of light Carter liked best, bathed them both in a soft glow. Carter moaned again, more freely and louder, and wrapped his arms around the Alpha's neck. The Alpha hummed in appreciation and slipped his tongue through Carter's obligingly parted lips. He knew what he was doing, shifting angles, hands roaming and roving, changing it up and keeping Carter guessing what he'd do next. He was a sensualist, wasn't he? He reveled in taste and touch and texture, on making sure his partner wanted what he wanted and would chase after it, and he could kiss like a fallen angel who'd flown straight back out of hell.

Like he'd known somehow what Carter needed like he needed this Alpha's cock inside him.

The Alpha didn't stop kissing him until Carter was limp in his arms, reliant on the wall and the pressure of the Alpha's body to keep him upright and finished with an almost-too-sharp bite of Carter's lower lip. It stung in a way Carter hadn't known he wanted until he got it. So good, almost too good, but stopping just short of the line.

Carter's eyes had slid closed somewhere in there, lashes heavy on his hot cheek. He bit back when the Alpha put a thumb to the lip he'd bitten, tugging it open.

"More," he breathed, though he could barely hear his own voice even out there in the quiet. His heartbeat was too loud, and the volume inside *Speakeasy* had left him with numb ears anyway. "I want some more."

He felt the Alpha's chuckle vibrate against his chest. He tickled under Carter's sides, startling a laugh out of him, and he felt the Alpha's mouth part in a puff of warm amusement. His breath smelled like every kind of alcohol, fruity dry wine and hops-rich beer and sharp tequila, but his hands and his body were steady where they touched Carter. His lips moved near Carter's ear again, but Carter still couldn't hear him, and he was too far gone to care. He couldn't have concentrated anyway when those strong hands with callused fingertips were busy caressing him, undoing a couple of buttons at his neck and then sliding back down to his groin to flick a couple of buttons open there too. *Yes. This.*

Just, just right.

The Alpha's lips moved again, and Carter made an educated guess as to what he wanted. He wriggled in the man's arms until he could turn around, the cool brick bliss when he pressed his forehead to it and canted his hips back in invitation. The Alpha paused with the jerk of an inward breath so abrupt and harsh Carter could feel it if he couldn't hear it, and then those hands were back to stroke his ass appreciatively.

His mouth moved against the top of Carter's spine as he reached backward. Carter would have protested the loss of his body heat if he hadn't come back right away and touched one sharp corner of an unopened condom packet to the side of Carter's hand. Skin-warm; he must have dug it out of a pocket, and he wanted Carter to know it was there.

Warning, promise, or question? Maybe all of those. It only mattered that he had one and was willing to use it. One argument they wouldn't have to have, and all the sooner they could get down to what they both wanted.

Carter glanced back over his shoulder, licked his kiss-swollen lips, and nodded. He rolled his hips just in case the Alpha had missed his point.

He hadn't. Deft fingers opened the rest of Carter's fly and tugged his jeans clear of his hips, down to his knees. Limited how far Carter could spread his legs, but he did his best and leaned forward on crossed arms to present himself. Already dripping, his inner thighs buttery-slick and his opening pulsing with the need to be filled.

Being an Omega had its drawbacks, but *this* wasn't one of them. Carter tilted his hips and arched his back, putting himself on display. He liked this, knowing what he had -- even if every other Omega had it too -- could knock the air clear out of an Alpha.

He felt rough, quick movements behind him; that would be the Alpha tugging his jeans down. *Good.* A slide, a nudge, and the slipperiness of a condom-covered cock was abruptly almost exactly where he wanted it. *Better.* A rock of the hips, the prelude to a good hard fuck. *Best.* The Alpha was still moving to the beat and bass thumping inside the bar, and it almost made Carter laugh. Instead, he groaned, light-headed with appreciation of the reminder. Anyone could have come out or headed into *Speakeasy* and gotten a free show at any time, but that only made it better, made the fizziness running through him spark brighter. Made Carter shiver, wanting and fidgeting, knowing he was about to *get*. He widened his stance. *Take me. Fuck me. God, please.*

But the Alpha wasn't done teasing. He stroked a pattern through the slick on Carter's thighs and brought it to Carter's lips, making him cry out in startled appreciation. He drew those fingers into his mouth to lick and suck them clean.

A sensualist, for sure. *More.*

"Fuck me," he growled, letting his animal nature and the wild heat of his bloodline thread through his voice just to see how crazy it made this wolfish Alpha. "Fuck me hard, and don't stop until we both come."

The Alpha said something, nipped at him where neck met shoulder, *almost* hard enough to break the skin -- then slid straight inside, deep and hard and smooth and --

Oh yes. Oh yes. Yes.

Carter moaned and moved back, trying to keep up. The Alpha knew what he was doing here too, hitting that sweet spot inside with every stroke and not wasting time. Every stroke, bottoming out, going fast and rough and keeping Carter's mind a peacefully buzzing blank -- pulling him back with lips and hands -- letting him sink into sensation, and then doing it all over again.

Reaching behind himself, Carter tried to cup the Alpha's jaw despite the angle, to urge him on.

Not that he needed to. He could feel the Alpha throbbing inside him with every deep push, and the faint tremors in his muscles. Good enough he had a hard time keeping control of himself, and didn't that go straight to Carter's head, where he needed it.

Carter arched into the man, begging for more.

He asked, and he received. The Alpha bit kisses at the back of his neck, fucked him deeper still, and kept his hands on Carter. Tight at his hips to guide him. Firm, over the pliable skin of Carter's stomach -- Alpha instinct, even with a condom -- but Carter shrugged it off. He could feel the slippery condom; he was safe. And even if he didn't mean to get pregnant again anytime soon, his body buzzed with excitement over the possibility that it *could* happen. Blame *that* on Omega instinct.

He covered the Alpha's hands and worked his fingers, kneading them, laughing when it made the hard length inside him pulse and swell. "Oh God. Oh yes. More, more." His breath panted hotly between his lips, sharp gasps and stifled keening that only made the Alpha go harder, fucking deep and hard and rough and fast enough to make Carter chase after him. "More. Please, more."

Carter thought he felt the Alpha's lips quirk into one of those bright, delighted grins -- and somehow, that was what did it for him.

Familiar warmth coiled inside his belly and tightened his muscles inside, squeezing the Alpha's cock. "Going to come," he panted, thrusting his ass back to take the Alpha as deep as he could go. "Going to come, going to, going --"

Not just him. The Alpha shuddered to a stop when Carter said that, body straining against it and then toward it. Never could feel the heat of spunk inside with a condom to catch it, but he imagined he could instead. It made him moan out a deep, bone-wrenching climax, bearing down as if he *was* pregnant and close to birth, *was* having this stranger's baby. The unfamiliar notion jolted through him like electricity, a shock to the system, and he grunted in just as much surprise as his cock jerked hard and he drenched them both with slick from a second, inner finish.

His legs wouldn't hold him up any longer, but the wall was there for that. He protested wordlessly when the Alpha slid out of him. Gentle now, he pulled Carter's jeans back up and refastened his buttons. Caressed his hip and pressed his lips to Carter's neck one more time as he did up his own jeans and drew the zipper shut.

Then he was gone, leaving Carter in quiet and peace just before it would have become too much if he'd stayed. Like he'd known, somehow, the same way he'd known what would drive Carter desperate and wild. A good lover. Maybe the best he'd ever had.

Whoever mated with him, down the road, they were one lucky bastard.

Carter turned to slump against the wall, deliberately not watching the Alpha walk away. Better to savor the memories. He looked up at the sky instead as he caught his breath, wishing he smoked so he could have a cigarette after *that* and kneaded his belly absently. God, he'd never come that hard in his life -- but he'd needed that so much. Now he could relax, and he'd even be able to sleep tonight.

He almost wished he *had* caught the man's name. That he might see the man again someday, when he needed this again.

If wishes were horses...

Chapter One

List: Ways To Be An Idiot.
Item the first: fall in love at first sight.
Item the first, part two: with a man you've never seen before.
Item the first, part three: and may never see again because you were too damn drunk to realize "Blue" was a spur of the moment pseudonym because absolutely no one you asked afterward would know anyone by that name.
Item the first, part four: while managing all of the above, make sure everyone else is too drunk or distracted to remember you were there, much less when you slipped out for a quickie or with whom.
Item the second: choosing to teach music. At the college level.
Item the third: forget the second item on the list because you can't do anything but fixate on item one.
Problematic.

"-- Dr. Gold? Are you listening?"

He blinked, snapping back from his memory of the street corner and into the present moment, focusing on the student in the front row of the lecture room. Where he was supposed to be teaching Music Theory 101 and, apparently, failing badly. *Damn.*

"Sorry. Didn't sleep much last night." Ethan lifted the tankard-sized coffee cup he'd toted in with him for another swig only to discover he'd drunk it dry without paying attention to that, either. "Could you repeat the question?"

Ethan's TA, a short, stocky, took-zero-bullshit Alpha named Oscar, who tended to take up a guard position on the corner of the lecture desk, cleared his throat. "The essay counts for ten percent of your final grade, which you'd know if you'd read the damn syllabus."

"Oscar," Ethan warned.

Oscar ignored Ethan with aplomb and addressed the student, who looked almost adorably confused. "The essay is ten percent, quizzes are fifteen percent, and seriously, all of you need to read the actual syllabus after you beat it for the day. Now scram."

"*Oscar.*"

Too late. The students were only too glad to take that as an early dismissal, and they were gathering their laptops and travel cups and the occasional pen in a clattering hurry that reminded Ethan of frightened bunnies bolting for their burrow. He rubbed his forehead as they rushed out in a few brief bursts of bolt and bottleneck. "Was I that bad today? Really?"

"You weren't that good," Oscar said. He slid off the desk. "However much coffee you had in there, it wasn't enough. Two or three more of those and you might be fit to lecture without sounding like a zombie. We heading back to the office?"

Ethan raised his eyes to the heavens but fell in step with his TA as he headed for the door. Oscar kept him on his toes, did a good job of it, and he wasn't wrong about the caffeination situation.

He really hadn't been sleeping well. Naps here and there, filled with dreams of the man in the alley, always waking up hard. So hard he ached. Head full of fantasies and memories: Blue's mouth open on a moan, Blue's head falling back against him when Ethan slid inside him, Blue's slim hips canting back to meet him, demanding more and more and still more, to be fucked deep and hard and giving as good as he got --

Lord help.

Ethan wasn't a teenager. He could control himself. He had, however, stopped even trying to rein in his mind after the first time he'd woken up humping the mattress like a two-dollar sex worker with a stopwatch in hand and so turned on he was barely conscious before crossing the actual finish line. It was either spend his entire salary on laundry or take the matter in -- as it were -- hand, do the best he could, and try to pummel his brain into coming up with a better solution.

And to find out the man's *name*. If someone was going to cast a spell like that on you, they should at least give you something to curse or bless. He'd done his own hunting, but with no luck for almost two months. Either no one recognized Blue by description or they did, and they weren't telling a newcomer-outsider like Ethan.

Speaking of which...

Oscar. He was too irreverent for most professors to want to work with, but insightful enough to appeal to Ethan. And if Oscar couldn't exactly control his tendency to use salty language in class, he wasn't nearly as bad there as he was with his friend Darian. Now *there* was a world-class cusser. Hand to God and so help him if Ethan wasn't going to record one of Oscar and Darian's conversations sometime just to count how many swear words they managed between them.

But Darian wasn't Oscar's only friend, of course. Oscar seemed to know everyone, every place, and every thing there was to know in Second Chance. It wasn't the first time that'd occurred to Ethan, but...

Oh. Well now.

Blame the sleeplessness and the energy it took both of them to wrangle five classes' worth of hyperfixated basket cases, but now was the first time Ethan tumbled Oscar's social pollination together with his own preoccupation and came up with a full-blown idea. If anyone would know --

He dug for his keys as they reached his small office and asked, as casually as he could, "Ever hear of a man called Blue?"

"That's a Johnny Cash song, isn't it?"

Ethan snorted. "You're thinking about *A Boy Named True*. I'm talking about a man called Blue. Or not." He unlocked the door and waved Oscar ahead of him. "Met him in a bar a while back."

He had Oscar's attention now. For such a rough and tumble sort of guy, he sure had a romantic's heart thumping away in his chest. He rubbed his chin in thought. "Describe him."

Ethan flipped on the overhead light with one elbow and then the coffeemaker by the door with other as he passed it. *More caffeine. Always more.* "Omega. On the small side, not like your friend Darian's husband."

"Pretty sure God broke the mold after he made that one. You ever meet another Omega that comes in NBA size, let me know."

"I'll make a note of it." Ethan rounded his desk and dropped the assorted papers, keys, and cell phone onto the pile of other junk that'd sprouted up like mushrooms after rain as soon as the semester began. He drummed his fingertips against the topmost book, thinking. *Fuckable* might be an accurate description of Blue, but it wouldn't be helpful.

"Small. Slim. Long hair, really long, down to the middle of his back if not longer. Either black or brown." He frowned. "Blue eyes. Or green. Or hazel."

He glanced over his shoulder to see Oscar raising a pointed eyebrow. "So *memorable* is what you're saying," he drawled.

Ethan had eyebrows and knew how to use them too and fired an identical arch look right back at Oscar. "Memorable is exactly what I'm saying. I'm also saying I didn't get a great look at him from behind and in the dark. You can't put 'sweet ass' or 'pretty little cock' on a *Have You Seen This Person* poster."

Oscar flicked off the coffeepot, which had begun to

smoke and smell like burned dregs. "You need to start paying attention to shit like that before you burn the damn college down. As for a poster? Me, I think you'd get plenty of interested eyeballs reading if you used that kind of wording, but whatever. Short and long of it is you got a little something and you want to go back for another taste. That about sum it up?"

Ethan lifted one shoulder slightly in acknowledgment. Why lie? Lies were almost never worth the fuss and bother. "Do you know anyone like that?"

"Hmm." Oscar picked up the scorched coffeepot and aimed himself at the door. "Gonna fill this with actual water and put actual grounds in there next. But yeah, I know him. He called himself Blue? That's interesting."

He slid out of the doorway as smoothly as Tom Cruise dancing in his underwear, leaving Ethan staring after him with his mouth slightly open. When he returned, a hint of a smirk firmly in place, Ethan couldn't even be mad. Too impressed.

"You are a rare son of a bitch, aren't you?"

"It's a dirty job, but someone's got to do it." Oscar's smirk widened, but he relented before Ethan would have needed to consider punching him. He started a pot of coffee going and hopped up to perch on the corner of the desk. "I don't know a lot about the guy. No one does."

"Then give me what you have."

"That's what *he* said," Oscar muttered. He kicked the desk idly with one heel, visibly thinking. "He owns a junk shop. Slash antique shop, slash pawn shop, slash repair shop. Buys, fixes, sells. I haven't needed anything done, but he's supposed to be good with his hands."

Hadn't he just been? Ethan remembered that perfectly every time he closed his eyes, and sometimes when he didn't, the sense memory of those lovely hands caressing him enough to set sparks running through his veins. "And?"

"And? That's about it." Oscar made a face. "From what I know, he keeps to himself, does his job, and doesn't say much. Not friendly. Not hostile, but most people think he's kind of weird for an Omega."

Ethan arched an eyebrow. "Like I'm a strange kind of Alpha?" One who got mistaken for an Omega -- often -- by people who mistook *quiet* for *meek* and *patient* for *passive*. "So other people think he's weird. What's your opinion?"

Oscar shrugged. "I usually think what most people think is at least a little wrong. I've got papers to grade. Drink the coffee before it burns back down to sludge again or go home and get some sleep because I'm taking your last class. Or, if you want to know anything else about the guy, his shop's two streets left of *Speakeasy*, far end of the block. Go find him for yourself. His name's Carter."

Oscar exited stage left before Ethan could say anything else. Not that he would have. His ears roared, his fingertips buzzed, and he might or might not ever be able to blink again.

He could move, though. Fast.

Carter. He had a name.

A shop. He had a location.

Now, finally, he had a place to start.

* * *

Outside, a glance at the sky warned Ethan that snow was on its way. Winter didn't play games in Second Chance, though he'd been told that what he considered a blizzard was barely a dusting by their standards. Still, he wasn't feeling the cold just then and like everything else in Second Chance, Carter's shop wasn't far. Ten minutes' walk, and he was there at *Old & New*.

He paused, just for a moment, to take its measure. From the outside the shop didn't look like much. One of a small row of shops nestled underneath a four story stack of apartments, probably built a hundred years ago and mostly unchanged since then except for paint and the advent of electricity. Carter might not have heard of that last one. The other stores boasted bright colors and eye-catching displays, but not this one. *His* had low-wattage lamps that didn't cut the dimness inside, and piles of clutter crowded into his window.

Or -- was it clutter, really?

Maybe not. A second, thoughtful glance told Ethan a different story. Nothing displayed there seemed to go together at first -- blown-glass ornaments, a stuffed mourning dove, a tin miner's lantern -- and was that an antique viola? It was, and so old it made Ethan's fingers itch to touch it. Nestled next to it he saw a single delicate cup that'd been shattered once upon a time and mended with moon-pale gold. The dim light didn't hinder your view but enhanced it -- made treasure out of what other people might have discarded as trash.

This was an artist's shop. He might mend and fix and make, but he did it all with the kind of subtle skill that took a life's worth of devotion to master.

That was a man worth falling for.

Ethan pushed open the door and let himself in to the tune of a silvery, soothing door chime instead of a jarring clanging one.

The inside matched the outside. Somewhat. A little more clutter, and a lot more... what was the right word? *Ah. Yes. Foreboding.* As if Carter hadn't been able to resist showing off just a little on the outside, but inside his cave of wonders, he kept the emphasis on *cave*. Almost too dark to see anything by until you got up close and personal enough for a good hard look.

Then, you saw the wonders.

Ethan moved carefully though the haphazard walkways, marveling at everything and touching whatever wasn't behind glass. Was there anything the man couldn't fix? Shaker chairs. Meissen china. A whole collection of ship's clocks and pocket watches and delicate rings. Wax cylinder records with a restored Victrola underneath. Slightly creepy taxidermy. Hundred-year-old Singer sewing machines, gleaming like new. Racks of vintage clothing.

As far as Ethan could see, the only thing missing from the shop was a proprietor.

Ethan turned to the left and the right, searching, but no, there was no one else walking the aisles or stationed behind the counter and a cash register as old as anything else in the shop. *Odd*. It didn't track. No one who cared as much about things like these would abandon them. They couldn't. It would cut them to the bone.

Which meant...

Ethan had a good ear. He'd trained it for years. When he closed his eyes and cocked his head and concentrated, he heard it: a quiet inhale from the far corner, behind a stack of railway trunks.

There.

A turn of his head, and there he was: *Carter*. Ethan had caught him trying to stand up slowly, maybe planning to sneak out or into the back of the shop, but too slowly for an Alpha on the hunt, who'd caught his scent.

"There you are," Ethan murmured, drinking him in with greedy gulps. "Found you."

"You," Carter breathed. Only that, and no more. Barricaded behind the stack of trunks that came clear up to his sternum, he stayed put like a soldier in a bunker, pressed a hand to his throat and stared back at Ethan. His eyes *were* blue, a bright silver-blue, huge and unblinking. Ethan remembered those eyes going wide, and the lids falling shut with a flutter of sooty lashes against his pale cheek when he moaned in pleasure.

Those hadn't changed.

Almost everything else had.

He'd cut his hair. All that beautiful hair gone, trimmed down to a Roman soldier's crop with a short fringe falling over his forehead. Might have been running his hands through it, for it to stand up in the mess of tangles and spikes that it did. Fingers still slim and delicate, but slightly swollen. A little fuller around the cheeks too? Yes. Not weight gain; the rest of him looked on the edge of too thin -- or at least the parts of him Ethan could see. He'd wrapped himself up in at least three layers, coat and turtleneck sweater and who knew what else underneath there, all the visible pieces in varying shades of black that turned his skin from ivory to porcelain. Dark circles ringed those beautiful eyes, and concern started Ethan moving forward, toward him.

"Don't." Carter flinched back and brought his hand up to say *stop*.

Ethan came to a halt, just about leaving a skid mark under his heels. He frowned. "What are you -- are you scared of me? Do you think I'm here to hurt you?"

Carter's hand fluttered and dropped to rest against his throat. His pulse hammered so hard Ethan could see the vein fluttering beneath the thin skin. "What are you doing here?"

Not scared. No. More like terrified, and of him. Ethan's stomach dropped through the soles of his feet. How was he supposed to handle this? Like dynamite or glass no thicker than a breath?

Or -- *ah* -- like a student who'd lost their voice before a recital. Carefully, lest they throw themself off the nearest convenient high ledge out of sheer animal nerves.

Deliberately casual, Ethan tucked his hands in his pockets, and no matter how much he wanted to move toward Carter, stayed put. He shrugged. "Looking for you. Finding you."

"Why?"

Carter's face had become a mask, too still in an attempt to cover his alarm to read anything else there, so Ethan kept a careful eye on his body language. He noted the way Carter clung to the edge of those trunks, fingertips curled under, and frowned on the inside. "Because I promised you I would. You don't remember?" He'd been tipsy, but not hammered or Ethan wouldn't have touched him in the first place.

"The music. I couldn't hear anything."

Damn and damn again. It had been loud in there. *Damn.* Things were starting to make sense. "You didn't even get my name, did you?"

"Not the -- no." Carter swallowed hard. He still hadn't blinked. "How did you get mine?"

"Asked around until someone told me. I'm smarter than I look."

Carter made a quiet noise of disbelief that made Ethan grin despite himself. "You teach at the college. You're not a stupid man."

Oh? He knew that? So Ethan hadn't been the only one trying to find out a thing or two, just the only one who'd acted on it. *Interesting.* Ethan wasn't sure he liked it, but he meant to find out the reason.

"Why?" Carter asked.

"Hmm?" Ethan eased slowly, slowly closer, sizing Carter up while pretending to be more fascinated with a display of trinkets and more of the mended teacups. He wasn't sure he liked the changes in the man. Those were some dark, dark circles under those unblinking eyes. The man must have had some kind of lizard in his animal bloodline to manage that without going blind on the daily. "Why, what?"

"Why were you looking for me? You walked away."

"Because I can tell when someone's over-stimulated

and needs a breather. Also thinking you knew who I was and that you wouldn't mind seeing me again," Ethan pointed out gently. One step closer, and then one more, keeping his interest surface-focused on the shop's stock until he could flick his glance upward and catch Carter off guard. "Was I wrong?"

Carter's tongue touched his full lower lip. "I…"

That was a *no*, then. Ethan nodded noncommittally. "You have trouble sleeping?"

"I -- what?"

"Like you said, I teach. I know what it looks like when someone isn't getting enough rest. I drink enough coffee that I barely sleep myself, but I don't think you've had an hour or two at a time for a while. Am I wrong? Not that it makes you any less beautiful, mind."

"*Don't.*"

"Don't what? Call you beautiful?" Ethan cocked his head to one side. "You are. Tired or not, you are."

"I'm not --" Carter's fingers flexed on the trunk edges as Ethan essayed a few more steps toward him, near enough to breathe in the scent of myrrh he'd had etched into his memory since that night in the alley. He flexed his hands again, too hard. He'd break off a corner or one of those delicate bones if he wasn't careful. "My bloodline isn't one that needs much sleep. I'm fine."

"You're a liar, is what you are," Ethan said frankly. "And you're hiding from me. Why?"

"Don't."

"Too late. I promise I'm not here to hurt you. I'm just keeping the first promise I made, looking for you, and from what I can see there's no one looking out *for* you except yourself. If you'll let me, I can help. I want to."

Ethan turned the corner, around the stack of trunks, even as Carter stumbled back with another *don't!* -- but -- too late. He came around that corner, and he saw what he saw. Though it'd been hidden all too well by the trunks, it wasn't now. Carter had lost weight everywhere but at the swollen middle.

Pregnant. Not just pregnant, but ripe as a plum and ready to burst.

Ethan drew up short, almost too startled to think but not for long. Eight weeks since he'd last seen Carter. Eight weeks of silence and absence, and no one knowing a damn thing about the man that they'd been willing to tell him. They might have known. As good as Carter was at hiding, they might not have picked up on a thing.

But Ethan did. And even if he hadn't, the way Carter's hands flew protectively toward that huge belly told their own story.

He'd used a condom. He knew he had. He always did. He knew that just as he'd known Carter wasn't too drunk for informed consent to get fucked good and hard.

Only condoms weren't always effective. He knew that too. *Eight weeks.*

Though his cheeks had gone from pale to blazing red, Carter lifted his head at last and his terror melted into a fine, fierce fury. He held his chin up, daring Ethan to say something.

Damn right he was, if in his own way, and while he was acknowledging truths then Carter wasn't the only one whose temper had started to heat. Ethan inclined his head at Carter's belly. "That's mine, isn't it?" he asked, quiet as a growling North wind. "Isn't it?"

"No," Carter retorted. He cradled himself defensively. "You put it in there, but it isn't yours. It's *mine.*"

"But I fathered it," Ethan said. "Tell me otherwise, and I'll know you're lying. Again."

Carter opened his mouth, teeth bared, and there was no telling what he might have said if the chimes over the door hadn't pealed out again. He melted down behind the stack of trunks again -- looked like instinct to

Ethan -- hiding himself away as pre-storm sunlight poured in alongside a rough-and-tumble Alpha with a boyish Peter Pan grin.

"We're not done with this," Ethan warned Carter in a rumble of an undertone. "Stay there."

He turned his back, keeping himself between Carter and the customer. Ethan had put in his share of retail work before getting his degrees, and it wasn't hard to summon up a good customer service smile at the new Alpha. "Can I help you?"

"Hope so." The Alpha limped slightly but gamely toward and turned his smile on Ethan. "You're new. Where's Carter?"

"I'm minding the store for him."

"Are you? Good. I've been telling him he needs some help. He told you about the layaway thing, right?" The man's beam brightened to headlights-on-high. "I'm here with my final installment."

"He mentioned you were on a payment plan," Ethan lied. Even if this guy was trying to pull a fast one, which seemed doubtful, he could swallow the cost. "Refresh my memory on what you wanted?"

"The pocket watch. It should be behind the counter. He said he'd put it in a box with my name on it so no one else could get it. I'm Wynn."

"W-Y-N-N?" Ethan asked, bending at the knees. Wynn's package wasn't hard to find, a small and plain but neat cardboard box with the name written across the top in the neatest print he'd seen outside a computer. Seemed too big and heavy for just a watch, but what did he know about the way Carter packaged his goods? He took the money that Wynn passed over, ten dollars counted out in wrinkled ones, and passed him the box.

Wynn frowned at the weight too as he opened the box with work-hardened fingers. He took out the watch first and held it up to admire, and so Ethan could see.

"For my husband. So he'll know however long it takes, I'll come home to him. All he has to do is wait."

There was something in the sweet simplicity of the statement that made Ethan's heart twinge with jealousy. Whoever his husband was, that was one lucky Omega.

Or doubly lucky. Carter had put a book in the bottom, an old one with a frayed-soft blue cover. Wynn turned it over with the kind of polite but uncomprehending interest that Ethan saw all too often even at the college level. Not that he'd shame this good man for it, or even mention it.

"A bonus gift for paying on time," Ethan improvised. "Enjoy and say hi to your husband for me."

Wynn grinned again, brilliantly beautiful. *Damn.* Ethan would bet cash money that Omega husband of his had fallen for that smile at first sight. If not for Carter, and if he'd been the type to go for Alphas, it would have tempted him.

"I will," Wynn was saying, tucking watch and book away, and the parcel under his arm. "I'll have Gabriel help me with -- I mean, it's probably for Gabriel anyway. Gabriel loves to read out loud to me, and to our son. He's three months old today. I can't believe how fast time goes. Anyway, you say hi to Carter for me, and thanks!"

Ethan waited for the shop door to close behind Wynn before asking, very quietly, "He can't read, can he?"

As slowly as he'd gone down fast, Carter stood. "He can read a little, and he's learning. His husband's a librarian; he's teaching him. It's a book of poems by Robert W. Service. A miner, like he was, back in the gold rush days. Who got out, like he did. He's doing odd jobs now. I don't do payment plans but I made an exception."

It was, by far, the most Ethan had heard Carter say at once, but he pretended not to notice. Had other things on his mind, anyway. He glanced outside the shop --

those skies were darkening, sure enough. Not quite so dark that he needed to be on his way home to beat the snow there, but suitably dark for his purpose. "Stay there." He headed for the door, taking the same winding path that Wynn had.

He couldn't see Carter stiffen behind him, but he could damn near feel it. "What are you doing?"

Ethan didn't see an OPEN sign anywhere or he would have flipped it over, but he did draw a hand-painted shade down over the glass and shot the deadbolt home. "Closing you down for the day. I told you we weren't done, and I meant it."

When he looked back, Carter's lips had parted again and there was a visible struggle on his face between alarm, defiance, and resignation.

Even though he only planned to take one thing for an answer -- he was owed that much -- Ethan waited for him to say it.

Finally, Carter let out a breath, though he kept a hand on his stomach. "Upstairs," he said. "We can talk there."

Good enough to be going on with. Ethan inclined his head. "Lead the way. I'll follow you."

He'd promised, after all, and he kept his promises.

Chapter Two

Ethan let Carter take the lead. He didn't look back to see if Ethan was following, though Ethan had no doubt the pretty, pregnant Omega was hyperaware of every move he made. His ears pricked like a cat's and his breath stayed light, shallow, quieter than their footsteps.

It would have made Ethan want to be gentle, and he would have if this wasn't so important. He could go easy, though, and he did, keeping a couple of paces behind Carter. Letting him have his space.

"Up here." Carter opened a door behind the register that let them into a small workroom, even more cluttered than the shop, but with a definite sense of *I know where everything is* to the scattered tools and mysterious repair jobs in progress. A second door, on the far end, already stood partially open with a view of a stairwell leading up. "One flight."

"Right behind you."

Ethan kept a careful eye on Carter as Carter put his foot on the first step. He took it awfully slowly, as if he still hadn't adjusted to the changes in his center of gravity. They happened so quickly that most Omegas never did get their balance; he'd seen it before. Carter's weight tilted him forward, and he overcorrected backward. Dangerous enough on solid ground, but on steps --

On steps, they could slip too damn easily. Carter leaned a touch too far and missed a step that he couldn't see under himself. Startled, he let go of the railing, then missed his frantic grab in reaching for it.

"Whoa!" Ethan darted forward just in time to catch him with a hand to his back and the length of his body in place just in case Carter fell the rest of the way. His full weight rested against Ethan for a moment, as warm as Ethan remembered and --

Electrifying. His touch, a shock that shot down his

spine and back up again. *That* hadn't changed. Ethan drew in a sharp breath, tasting myrrh on the back of his tongue, and exhaled the aftertaste of bitter aloes. He barely noticed that. Carter's body molded itself against his, sweet and pliant for just a second, head dropping back toward him in a graceful arch. Ethan wanted to kiss him. Burned to put his mouth on the curve of that beautiful neck and scrape his teeth across the pale skin.

Until, that was, Carter stiffened and glanced over his shoulder.

Ethan cursed himself. Not the time, not the place. "Careful," he said instead of giving into his impulses, and eased Carter away, holding him steady until his feet were firmly on the step and his hand on the railing. "Steady now?"

Carter didn't answer him. He touched the tip of his tongue to his lower lip and searched Ethan with too-wide eyes.

Not good. The last thing Ethan wanted was for Carter to be afraid of him. He stayed where he was but let go except for one hand at the small of his back. "I won't let you fall, but I promise you I don't have any funny business in mind. I'm not planning to jump you. Not in any sense of the word."

Carter's free hand lifted from his belly to curl upward over his sternum. "I don't understand."

He really didn't. Ethan could see it on his face. *God in Heaven.* What kind of life had Carter lived, that he thought every Alpha out there was only interested tapping his ass or *being* an ass?

"I said I wanted to talk, and that's all I want." Nodding once at the weight Carter carried in front of him, Ethan said frankly, "I think I'm owed that much."

Carter still didn't blink, but he caught that pretty lower lip between his teeth and worried briefly at it. "All right," he said after three heartbeats had passed. "All right."

"Good." Ethan gave him a light nudge. "Go ahead of me. I won't let you fall."

Carter's look changed from embarrassed to -- odd -- but he didn't explain. Just shook his head and started back up the stairs.

He let Ethan's hand rest on his back all the way to his door.

There, Ethan stood back and let Carter dig a set of keys out of his pocket. His hand shook as he fumbled for the right key and nearly dropped the whole bunch not once but twice. He shot Ethan a wary look both times, but Ethan was ready for it. He kept his calm face on and his hand steady, only waiting.

Carter unlocked the door on his third try and bumped it open with his hip. "It's messy," he warned. "Be careful not to trip."

Ethan raised one shoulder. "Can't be messier than my office."

Carter frowned. "Don't say I didn't warn you." He tapped a switch set into the wall with his elbow, producing a soft glow no brighter than his shop lights, and shuffle-slid inside.

He didn't invite Ethan in, but he left the door open. Ethan could follow him there if he chose, and he did choose.

He let Carter go ahead of him now there weren't any steps to navigate, wanting to get his own bearings. Nice architecture, one large room that took up the whole floor like a studio apartment on growth hormone, with painted or folding screens separating each area from another. No overhead lights, just lanterns mounted on the walls and a few fragrant beeswax candles in holders. There was a sense of solitude to the place that said, clear as a bell, that only one loner lived there. Silence that echoed off the walls, broken only by quiet breathing.

Beyond that? Carter hadn't exaggerated. Ethan had seen worse messes before. Just not often. Chaos incarnate had run through the apartment, whipped up a quick hurricane on his way through, and ridden a tornado back out.

It wasn't filthy. No old pizza boxes or dirty underwear or beer bongs. No naked students trying to hide under the bed. Clean laundry wrinkling contentedly away in piles on chairs and couch. Dry goods still in plastic shopping bags. An absolute cat's-cradle of things dropped on the floor wherever there was room. Most of them baby-related, three quarters of those still in boxes or piled in heaps. Ethan tracked them, frowning thoughtfully. Looked like Carter dropped things where they fell when he ran out of energy to finish whatever needed doing.

He really didn't have anyone to help him. Did anyone else even know?

Possibly not. Carter was good at hiding what he wanted hidden, and that Alpha named Wynn hadn't said a word about Carter being in a delicate condition. If there was anyone guaranteed to ask how he was doing and ask if he had any scans to show off, it'd be that guy.

He turned around to find Carter watching him wryly from a safe distance. "I warned you. Are you happy now?"

No, but each piece of the puzzle Ethan could put together was a step toward seeing the whole picture. He considered for a moment, then said, "Yes."

Carter blinked at him in a strange way. Not quite like other humans would blink. Was there something non-mammalian in his bloodline? Perhaps, but more than anything he reminded Ethan of a fallen angel. Was his family line crows, maybe? Magpies? He frowned at Ethan with one arm still around his belly and the other at his side, fingers flexing around a handful of his coat as if he wasn't sure what to do with them.

Ethan waited to see what he'd say.

"You don't look like I remember," Carter said abruptly. "I thought... No, never mind."

He didn't look away. With an inner shrug, Ethan let Carter study him as much as he wanted. He wasn't much for the eyes to feast on, himself, though it'd long stopped bothering him. He *was* an unusual Alpha, smaller and slimmer than most with longer hair and a beard he kept trimmed into shape instead of shaving bare or allowing it to run wild.

Carter let out a breath, shook his head, and bent awkwardly to strike a match from a box on a table and touch it to the wick of a thick white candle. Flickering light caressed his face.

"Why all the candles?" Ethan asked, curious enough to be distracted.

"Anything brighter hurts my eyes." Carter made a brief face. "And I like them."

"I like soft light too. I have to use brighter lamps at the office, but this is better. Relaxing." Ethan glanced around, picked a likely-looking chair set catty-corner to a mismatched recliner, and moved an armful of machine bits he couldn't start to identify off it. He dropped down to a seat and gestured at the recliner. "Sit down."

Carter did. Awkwardly, still not able to balance himself. No matter how much Ethan wanted to help him, he didn't. A man needed to have some pride, after all, Alpha or Omega or Beta.

Perched on the edge, he kept an eye on Ethan as he cradled himself, hands moving in soft, soothing sweeps across the heaving movements Ethan could just make out even under all those layers. It hit Ethan like a length of rebar right between the eyes, but he'd challenge anyone not to take a second to appreciate that kind of sight. The soft light bathed Carter in warmth, smoothing out the sharper angles of his bones and hiding the dark circles under his eyes.

Ethan said nothing and waited.

Carter ducked his head. The long slow sweep of Carter's sooty lashes reminded him of how they'd felt fanning across the back of his hand. The movements under his sweater had stilled, but Carter carried on caressing himself absently, as if it comforted him. He glanced up from beneath those lashes, wary again. "You said we needed to talk."

"And I meant it." Ethan leaned forward, letting his loosely cupped hands fall between his knees. "I can start, or you can. Up to you."

Carter took a deep breath, then nodded. "What do you want to know?"

"Start with everything you're not telling me."

"I don't know where to begin."

"Begin at the beginning." Ethan projected patience. Easy did it with this one, easy and slow. "Go on to the end, and then stop. The beginning being that night, and the stop being now. Take all the time you need."

"You really are a strange sort of Alpha," Carter murmured.

Ethan raised his shoulder in reply. "It's been said."

"Mmm."

Carter passed one hand across his face. He leaned back, still awkward, but more practiced, and rested his head against the back of the chair while still watching Ethan. He didn't say anything, and after a moment his cheeks went a darker shade of rose.

Ethan cocked his head, waiting.

"Sometimes I get..." Carter said, visibly frustrated. "I'm not good at words. Out of practice."

Another piece of the puzzle clicked into place. Carter might be distant, but for a reason. He was shy, wasn't he? Bashful as a deer, though *that* had to be nurture, not animal nature. Shy, and completely unused to company. No wonder, if he'd spent most of his time around customers who didn't bother getting to know him or Alphas just out for one night's worth of a good time.

"That's all right. I'm not going anywhere."

"Not in any sense of the word." Carter cupped the apex of his belly, thumb drawing circles there. "I didn't do it on purpose. If that's what you're thinking. I didn't go out planning to get pregnant."

Ethan believed him. He inclined his head and gestured for Carter to go on.

He did, more easily now that he'd gotten started. "I went my own way on purpose that night. Wasn't planning on seeing you again, even before…" His fingers flexed. "I figured it out early. Didn't want to believe it at first, but. Couldn't pretend it wasn't happening. I wasn't sure if I wanted to…"

Wanted to keep it, or not? Ethan stiffened as something protective and possessive snarled inside his mind. He held his tongue until it quieted. Abortions weren't illegal. They happened. Especially in situations like this.

That part of him growled again. *His* child, it insisted.

"You decided against that," he said instead.

"More like I waited too long. Couldn't make up my mind, and then…" Carter's thumb moved in smaller circles, and something that might have been second cousin to a flicker of a smile crossed his lips. "And then."

And then, probably not wanting to, he'd still fallen in love. Maybe for the first time.

Ethan sighed quietly and shifted to rest his cheek on one palm, watching Carter drift into memories of his own. The picture he made, tucked up in his chair with his arms around the treasure he'd found, hugging it to himself. He might not have planned on it or wanted it, but now that he had it he'd defend it with his life.

Oh. The light dawned. "I know what you are," Ethan said. "Your bloodline. You're a dragon."

Carter brought his head up sharply and blinked again, but not with his eyelids. White slid sideways across his sclera and over his pupils. Dragon, for sure. They were so rare Ethan had never met one before, but how had he missed it? The gathered treasures, the dark den, the stillness. "I never told anyone that. How did you --"

"I paid attention. I guessed."

"I don't understand you." Carter pressed two fingers to his forehead. "What are you? I can't tell. I'm not good at that."

"Wolf," Ethan said. "Gray wolf, out from Alaska. I never fit in there. I do better here. What happened next?"

Carter's lips quirked briefly. "What you saw. What you see. No one knows about this. Never told anyone about it either."

"Not even a doctor?"

"No. I couldn't…" Carter tapped one foot against the floor. "I don't like doctors."

Brooding Omegas didn't, though Ethan had never understood why. Maybe a genetic throwback to when they were more animal than man and would den up whenever they were expecting, waiting their time.

"Nothing happened to make me want one, anyway," Carter went on. He turned his face toward the window, then stood with an effort and walked toward it, to a lantern mounted against the glass. A deft twist brought the kerosene lamp to life, casting light and shadows over him. "Time went by. Then you found me."

That was that, Ethan supposed. Missing so many details, things that he needed to hear, but as complete as he'd get. For now. "And we came up here."

"We did." Carter turned his head abruptly, pinning

Ethan in place. There was something like fire in his eyes, a dark flame that took Ethan off guard. "You didn't let me fall down the stairs. Caught me. I could feel you. The way you shuddered. You're a gentleman" -- he made that sound like accusation and confusion at the same time -- "and you're so shocked by all this I can taste it, but you still want me. Don't you?"

Ethan stilled. Couldn't have moved if he'd wanted, watching Carter watch him through dragon's eyes. Neither could he help the way his heart slammed against his ribs, or how his cock stirred at the blunt question.

"I can feel that too," Carter pressed, intent on him now, searching him. "I can see it. I can smell it. I don't understand. I lied to you, or as good as. Didn't tell you when I knew you needed to know. But you want me."

No sense trying to hide it, not if Carter could be that acute. Ethan stopped trying to conceal anything, and let his feelings show on his face. "Yes. I do."

"Why?"

"Because I do."

Carter made a noise of pure frustration. "But *why*?"

"If you have to ask…" Ethan stopped himself. He stood, slowly but with purpose, and moved toward Carter. Hands out, not a threat, but still a hunter and not hiding that either. "Because you're beautiful. Because you're carrying my child. I didn't do it on purpose either, and I didn't come up here with schemes on my mind. Believe that. But you -- standing there in that light -- God, Carter. You make me want to take you like I did in that alley once upon a time."

Carter's lips parted and he stared before covering his face with both hands. Whatever response he'd expected, it hadn't been that, and it shouldn't have been as appealing as it was, but oh it was. Already half-hard, Ethan wanted to stop and adjust himself but -- no. Why should he? He hadn't lied.

And he could smell desire too.

Ethan was close enough now to scent him. Underneath the myrrh and aloe, he caught a hint of Omega sweetness. Richer, changed as he was, denser and deeper, but still the scent of arousal, the first drops of eagerness slicking him between his legs.

Carter's fingers curled, hiding himself. That wouldn't do. Ethan needed to see his pretty face. He took Carter's wrist and guided it away, replacing it with three knuckles nestled beneath his chin.

Carter's lips parted. "What are you..."

"If you have to ask," Ethan murmured. He brought the pad of his thumb up to press against Carter's soft, full lower lip, coaxing his mouth just a little more open. He could feel Carter's breath slipping across his skin, warm and shallow, as he stroked the man's satiny cheek, then down to a featherlight brush across his hips that made Carter hitch toward him. "You are so beautiful. Do you not know that?"

Carter shook his head but leaned into Ethan's touch. His throat worked. "I don't know why I... Or why you... Why it's like this."

He closed his eyes fully and pressed his forehead to Carter's wrist. "Neither do I. But it is."

"Ethan," Carter whispered, reaching for him then drawing back, reaching and retreating. "*Ethan.*"

Ethan couldn't help it. No one could have helped it. He lifted Carter's chin, lowered his head, and brought their mouths together.

He'd meant for it to be quick. Sweet. Chaste. And it might have started that way.

It didn't stay that way. One taste of his lips, and Ethan was drowning. He tasted so sweet, like jam and tea with honey, softening the myrrh into something like chai, and he yielded even more sweetly, leaning into Ethan. He pressed one hand to Ethan's chest, but not to push him away. His fingers flexed, then knotted in a handful of Ethan's shirt and clung tight; he lifted his face into the kiss and parted his lips again when Ethan brushed them with the tip of his tongue in silent question.

"Beautiful, beautiful boy," Ethan murmured between shifts and changes, teasing at Carter's lips and tongue. Even as short as it was, Carter's hair slipped like strands of silk between his fingers and his neck flexed like a willow, going where Ethan encouraged him to go.

Carter shook his head. "I'm not."

"You are." Even with all that belly in the way, when he turned to the side Ethan could feel Carter going slowly hard against him. He wanted to make this man come, to make him feel good, happy, as precious as any of his treasures. Moving his mouth to Carter's neck, he trailed soft kisses down its side. "Beautiful, beautiful boy."

"I'm…" Carter broke on a moan and brought his other arm around Ethan's neck. He clung tight and tilted his head back to give him more space, a silent plea for him not to stop. "I need…"

Ethan could feel the fine shivering in Carter's muscles and the desperation he only just held back. How skin-hungry and touch-starved this man was, and how much he needed to be cherished. Was that why he wanted it so much himself? Or was that just Carter?

It's both.

"If you need, then take." He bit lightly at Carter's shoulder. "I'll give."

"Shouldn't."

"Should," Ethan countered. "Can."

He took Carter's neck in both hands, thumbs beneath the pockets at the back of his jaw and tilted his head the other way. He was fully hard now, his hips starting to rock ever so hesitantly forward, the scent of Carter's sweetness thickening the air between them.

When he caught Ethan's scent -- or felt how hard he was -- or both -- he made a sound like a strangled sob and bucked into him.

Oh -- God. So good.

If Ethan hadn't learned how to be patient and careful, he'd have pushed that beautiful dragon onto the floor and taken him right then. It took all he had not to give in and reach down to unfasten his jeans then and there.

But that might be what Carter wanted. Or needed. And didn't know how to ask for it, like this.

Ethan nipped at the point of Carter's chin and nosed underneath, his mind working all the while. His hand too, tugging absently at the soft, finely textured collar of his sweater. A turtleneck, but the weave was loose and the fabric stretched easily; he could nudge it down easily enough, and then he just had to bend his head and taste the dip between Carter's collarbones. Not asking permission, but just to see, and when his tongue brushed over Carter's skin, Carter keened under his breath and dug short nails into Ethan's nape.

He needed to -- he had to touch. Ethan cupped his palm against Carter's belly, amazed at how hard it was. Shouldn't it have been soft? It looked soft, but it was solid and so, so heavy, so ripe. Full, with *his* child. The thought took his breath away. He drew his hand up, tracing the broad curve to where it stopped beneath Carter's breastbone, and back down against, marveling at it. He could feel a stirring from inside that made him hot with pride and possessiveness.

Mine, he thought as Carter speared both hands through his hair in turn and tipped back, mouth open. His hard-on, almost obscene in the way it distorted the line of his fly, fit perfectly in Ethan's hand when Ethan took and cradled it in his palm. *Both mine.* He stroked the length, thumb at the head, and pressed the rest of his fingers to the soaking wetness seeping through Carter's jeans.

"God. Oh God." Carter was panting now, pale skin flushed warm with need and want. "Shouldn't. Shouldn't."

"You should." Ethan pulled Carter closer. Pressed, with his fingertips, pushing just a little inside him. "You should let me have you."

Carter jerked back, eyes wide and shocked, and then pulled his body sharply away. Ethan caught him at the last second, one hand curved lightly around Carter's cheek, the other firm at his wrist.

"Let me go." Carter turned his wrist but didn't pull at him. He trembled, head to toe, and leaned toward Ethan before catching himself and leaning back. "You don't understand."

"No. Not yet." Ethan kept hold of his wrist. "But I will."

"You can't."

"I can. I'm starting to." Ethan drew his fingertips across Carter's cheek and took a leap into the dark with the dragon who didn't fly and almost never burned, asking, "Who was it that put out your fire?"

Carter stared, then clapped both hands to his mouth and shoved Ethan away. "Don't ask me that! Oh God."

They both stopped there, panting. Ethan knew, could see for himself, that even now Carter still wanted him as much as he *was* wanted, but -- as torn as any man Ethan had ever seen, he took another step back. "I can't. I'm sorry. I can't, I just…"

Ethan closed his eyes and counted to ten. It killed him and made his inner wolf howl, but he let it go. For now. He wouldn't force any man, much less the one carrying his child. They mattered too much, even if he barely knew them.

"All right," he said. "I hear you. It's all right."

"It's not, though." Carter wrapped his arms around himself. He wouldn't look at Ethan, but kept his gaze trained out the window instead. He looked so unhappy that Ethan ached to take him in his arms and hold him for an entirely different reason. "I can tell."

Ethan turned his head to look outside too. He ached, too hard to have been denied, and he needed the space to get himself under control. His inner wolf howled again in frustration, but it could howl on. He'd be damned before he took the unwilling or the unsure. Wouldn't have taken Carter in the first place if he'd known -- but that had been a different time, different place, a different man, driven past the walls he'd built around himself out of sheer desperation to touch and be touched. Without that, those walls were built strong. Hard to break through.

"You're angry," Carter said.

"I'm not." Randy, yes, and fighting himself, but not angry. "If you can sense everything else you say, you know what truth tastes like."

"I don't understand," Carter said again, though not to Ethan. He laid his palm on the glass. "It's not snowing yet, but it's cold."

True, though not as cold as it would be. As the sun went down, the temperature dropped and it'd keep on dropping. The clouds hanging heavy in the sky hadn't shed their blizzard yet, but they would. Soon.

Carter tapped at the glass. "What are you going to do now?"

"I don't know." Carter wrapped his arms around himself again, visibly thinking, visibly struggling, then glancing at Ethan through the very corner of his periphery. "We aren't done with this yet. Are we?"

Silently, Ethan shook his head.

"You said it before, that you weren't going

anywhere. I think I believed you, but --" Carter bit at his lip, bringing Ethan's attention away from his body and back to his face, to the dark circles that'd only gotten darker. He pressed his fingers to them. "But I *can't* think. I --"

Sympathy took the place of frustrated lust. "You're exhausted," Ethan said, gentling again. He had to remember: easy did it, with this one. "Go to bed. Sleep. I'll stay here and keep watch from the couch."

Carter struggled again, briefly, then nodded. "I owe you that much."

"It isn't about owing." Ethan waited for him to turn away, then took him lightly by the wrist. Easy did it, but attention had to come where attention was due, and he caught it, and held it fast. "But if you want me in the night for anything, Carter -- anything -- then you know where to find me. I told you before, beautiful dragon. I'm not going anywhere."

Chapter Three

Ethan meant what he said, every word of it, and he knew Carter knew that too.

He still fled. Past a set of screens and, from the sound of the footsteps, nearly to the back of his apartment. Ethan tucked his hands in his pockets and kept his back to the bracing cold of the window, his head tilted, listening until he heard the steps come to a halt, a pause, and then the weary rustling of sheets. A bed creaking under more weight than it was used to, and then silence.

He still meant it. Carter could sleep a while. When he woke up, Ethan would be there, lying in wait, sleeping with one ear open.

Speaking of, though. The couch wasn't bad, as couches went; old, like everything else; lovingly restored, like everything else. But -- fragile. Ethan grimaced when he'd shifted the clutter off, tried to lie down, and heard something go *crack* inside. Fine, then. The floor would do. Rummaging through a few of the laundry stacks netted him enough sheets and blankets to make a decent nest, with one of the couch pillows under his head.

Though honestly, he could have made a bed out of sticks and nettles for all Ethan noticed once he lay down. He tucked one arm beneath pillow and head and let the other fall idly on his chest as he looked up at the ceiling.

Painted.

Ethan chuffed quietly. *Might have known*. Hand-painted, by someone who knew what they were doing. Beautifully so. Swirls of dark and light with sparkling mica, impressionist whirls of color. Carter wouldn't have been able to help himself.

He liked it.

Ethan trailed his fingers near his waist, half tempted to take himself in hand, but -- no. He wasn't a horny teenager who couldn't keep his hands off. Just a man who didn't want to, and even if he cracked a molar or two grinding his teeth there *was* a difference.

He could be patient. He would.

If Ethan had to court Carter like an old-fashioned gentleman, he would do it. He'd win the dragon over, piece by piece. They didn't know each other well; true. They were ships that'd passed in the night; also true.

Didn't change the fact that that man was his. The child was his. Now that he'd found them again, Ethan wasn't letting either go again. He'd find a way to make them see it.

As he drifted off to sleep, he let himself wonder what would happen next --

And then, it did.

* * *

When he opened his eyes, Ethan couldn't tell if he'd fallen asleep or not. It was dark outside, truly dark with most of the streetlights dimmed and the moonlight hidden behind clouds. He smelled the icy coolness of snow, starting to fall at last, and could hear the way it muted out sound like nothing else.

But that wasn't what he cared about. Not just now.

The blankets he'd put down shifted, tugging under the weight of light footsteps, and a shadow fell over him. He looked up at the silhouette of the man standing above him as that man looked down. He wore nothing but a long robe that smelled and moved like real silk, the ends of a belt that didn't have a hope of reaching far enough to tie around him as he was fluttering loose.

Carter. More beautiful than before, even now.

Ethan's thoughts were fuzzy, but he knew he needed to be more careful than ever before. He murmured Carter's name under his breath and reached up slowly, curling his fingers and pulling them back down as if he'd caught the moon in a net and was coaxing it out of the sky.

Carter shivered, full-bodied. "Don't ask me what changed my mind," he said as he lowered himself to his knees, one on either side of Ethan's. Not quite straddling him, but close enough for Ethan to feel his burning body heat. He stared at Ethan, wary and shy and so many other emotions that Ethan didn't have names for all of them, tangled up in him and written over his face.

Patience. Within reason.

Ethan glided a hand up, laying it lightly on the heat of Carter's lower thigh, and waited for him to find his words.

"You asked me who put out my fire," Carter said abruptly. "I can't answer that. I won't answer that. But I..." Lip caught between his teeth, he drew his palm down Ethan's chest. "I, and you, and..."

"You don't have to say it out loud." Ethan covered his hand and guided it slowly lower, not touching his groin but coming so close it almost made no difference. "This says enough."

Carter shuddered, but now Ethan could feel how hard he was -- whether still, or again. And how conflicted too. He broke Ethan's heart, and made Ethan want to rebuild it with his bare hands. "I need this," he said, so quietly Ethan almost didn't hear him. "But I don't understand how you can -- with me, now, like I am."

"Like how, dragon?"

"Like *this*." Carter rolled his shoulders and shed the robe like autumn leaves, silk falling away with a nearly liquid whisper of fabric over flesh. With nothing but his skin underneath, he turned his face away but leaned back on his heels and arched his spine. He stroked his front as if he wanted to offend with the startling change in his shape, so different from the man he'd been in the alley but couldn't be rough with something he loved even if he didn't understand that either. "Look at me. You can't want me like you did."

"I don't." Ethan put two fingers to Carter's mouth, then lifted himself to a sitting position so that he cradled Carter in his lap. Lifted his chin so he could see those beautiful eyes, and brush his mouth against those soft, bite-swollen lips. "I want you more."

Carter stilled, and for a heartbeat Ethan thought he meant to pull away again.

He didn't.

He moaned and melted against Ethan instead, arms twined about his neck, and parted his lips to be kissed as if no time at all had passed between the alley and now. He opened so sweetly that Ethan had to taste his mouth, draw his tongue across Carter's and startle a gasp out of him. First a gasp and then a moan, softer and more desperate.

"I see you," Ethan said, bending his head to bite at the side of Carter's neck. "All of you, and I didn't lie. You are so beautiful."

Carter whimpered and hitched forward on Ethan's lap, straining to get closer. His hands came to rest at either side of Ethan's neck where his fingers dug into Ethan's shoulders, trying to cling harder and tighter than he could. Ethan could feel the strain in his muscles every time he shifted. Carter's arms were as long as any man's should be, but with all that belly in the way, he knew the man couldn't reach and hold the way he needed to.

But they could do something about that.

Ethan took Carter's hands and eased them down, guiding them to the clothes *he* wore. "Even the field," he said, his mouth against Carter's, making each word a kiss. He coaxed Carter's fingers to his collar and hem, groaning when hesitant fingertips brushed against his skin. "So you can see too."

Carter hesitated. "It's snowing. Light, but snowing. You'll get cold."

"I won't. You'll warm me up." Ethan trailed slow

caresses down his body, front and back, knowing if he stopped moving, he'd give Carter a chance to start thinking too much. "And I'll keep you warm too."

He felt Carter's neck work as he swallowed, but he let a shuddering breath escape him and he bent his short-cropped head. He slipped one button after another free of their holes in the shirt Ethan had worn to teach in -- seemed like a hundred years ago, now, the morning as far away as a fairy tale. When he'd opened them all, he swallowed again and bent his head further still to put his mouth over Ethan's heart.

Carter had been wild and reckless in the alley, but that'd been different. Here and now, the courage that took -- it should be rewarded.

Ethan could do something about that too. He guided Carter down to his button fly and nudged the first of those open, helping Carter find the next. Grunted deep in his throat with relief at the ease of pressure when the parting buttons couldn't hold him any longer and his hard-on escaped out the opening, spilling into Carter's palm.

"You're so..." Carter stopped, short of breath already. His hips rocked, though Ethan didn't think he knew he was doing it, searching for friction like that. Sweet-smelling, slippery stickiness rolled in fat drops down from between his legs to patter against Ethan's thighs. "I didn't see you before, but I felt you. I knew you were big. Not this big."

"Too big?"

"No. God no," Carter said. He brought his mouth up with a flare of the hunger a dragon *should* show, took Ethan's mouth, and wrapped his hand around Ethan's shaft almost too hard and not hard enough. "Bigger than me."

And Ethan could tell he liked it. He rolled his hips forward and eased Carter as close as he could get by clutching his taut ass cheeks and tugging a half inch at a time. When he pressed down, meaning to leave fingerprints there, Carter's cock jerked so that Ethan could feel it against his thigh, and let out a moan that was more than half a sob and just as much a hungry keen.

"More," he breathed, his eyes falling shut. "More. Please. I need it, but --" He stopped, cupping his belly in frustration that he clearly didn't know how to circumvent, asking without asking: *but how*?

"Like this," Ethan answered out loud. He eased Carter off his lap, though he hated to lose even a second's worth of the weight on his legs, and back to his knees so they faced each other.

"What are you --"

"Shh." Ethan got his own knees beneath him, shifting the angle just right to allow him to bend his head and take Carter's mouth. He slid his tongue between Carter's lips and licked at him, nibbling until the Omega moaned and melted into him, letting Ethan take all his weight. "Like this. Just like this."

Carter knotted his fingers and pressed fists to Ethan's ribs. "Please, more."

Ethan wondered if he'd said that in the alley, and he just hadn't heard. He remembered, then, how Carter had responded to being directed. It took him out of his head, Ethan realized. Kept him falling. *That* was what he needed, and that made all the difference. He could work with that -- and he wanted to, with a hunger that rose up growling in anticipation in his mind.

"More," he agreed, thumbing Carter's lower lip open. "If you do what I say."

Carter's sharp teeth grazed his thumb, and his lips closed around Ethan's to suck. He rested his full weight against Ethan, pliable except where he was hard, and let go of Ethan to incline his head. "Yes. Oh, yes."

That deserved rewarding too. "Then lie down."

Ethan helped him, easy but firm, down on his back. As Carter watched him with wide, unblinking eyes, his mouth a little open, he coaxed the Omega's legs apart. Knees first, bringing them up to brace around him. Feet flat on the floor, to push against it. Thighs last, trembling as he eased them apart slowly but as wide as they would go, not stopping until he had room enough for his shoulders to fit between them.

"What are you doing?" Carter breathed, even as he reached to push his fingers into Ethan's hair and take hold. "What are you…"

Ethan was the one to keep quiet now; he wanted to use his tongue for other things and with Carter like this, the full moon of his belly out of the way, he could reach as well as he liked. Dropping to his belly, flat against the floor and only supporting himself on his forearms, he nosed inward and touched the tip of his tongue to Carter's straining erection. Smaller than his, slimmer, but dark with arousal and as wet as his inner thighs. Slick beads trickled steadily out of him, falling like rain on Ethan's nose and chin. Ethan let them cover his face, wet him down, so that he could do this: press his mouth to Carter's channel and breathe against him.

Carter moaned and lifted his hips, silently begging Ethan for more.

Soon. Ethan wanted to see before he tasted, and he pressed Carter's hips down to keep him still while he drank it in. Different here too. Softer, skin smoother, swollen like the rest of him. Shut tight, as he'd heard Omegas were when they were carrying, but when Ethan traced a fingertip down the seam he slid inside without even trying, gliding on the slickness leaking out of him. Inside, heat and yielding flesh, tight but giving way for him.

Sweet, so sweet. But it could be sweeter still.

Ethan lifted Carter's knees one at a time, hooking

them over his shoulders and nudging Carter's bare feet behind his back and then, only then, sliding his tongue inside the man.

Carter arched backward, his cry louder and wilder. He let go of Ethan's hair after one hard pull and knotted his fists in the blankets. His cock jerked, leaving its own trail across Ethan's cheek, and rested there, the pulse that kept him hard throbbing gently and moving without any guidance. He didn't taste like myrrh anymore, but something closer to cinnamon and chai, hot spice and soothing sweetness. Sensitive, perhaps a little sore already from the pressure he'd have weighing down in him, but he clenched at Ethan and didn't let go.

Ethan drank him down, adding another finger to the first -- and then another, when he took those and clenched around him. He hooked his knuckles around the opening and tugged down to open him wider in the midst of all those delicious shudders and put his mouth there. Sucked at him one side at a time, heavy on his tongue but rolling easily, not stopping until Carter was on the edge and writhing with it, hands on his belly and the rest of him quivering with the need to come.

In one way, he could. Ethan slipped deeper until he found the inner nub that all Omegas could be glad they were Omegas for, and pressed hard.

No matter the heaviness of his belly, Carter's back cleared the floor as he made a noise Ethan had never heard before, high as a wild hunting bird's shriek and low as a man who'd had the air punched out of him. His channel squeezed Ethan's fingers so tightly his knuckles ground together as Carter bore down and made a deep, chest-deep grunt. But what was a little pain in his body when the man who caused it was driving him out of his mind?

Was this, Ethan wondered wildly, what Carter would feel like inside in labor? Would he make those noises when he was stretched even wider than this, straining with all his might to drive that burden out of him?

God. Ethan wanted more.

He didn't stop until Carter came back down. Cock still hard, pulse hammering where it twitched and drooled thin strings on Ethan's cheek, panting so hard he couldn't be getting much air.

Gentle. Gentle, before we pick up the pace again.

Ethan reached up without looking and let himself feel, really feel, the hard rise and curve of that ripe belly. It quivered under his touch, going hard and rising higher, then came down, firm in his palm. Carter keened until he muffled the sound, most likely with a fist to his lips, but he let Ethan do it. Let Ethan stroke and caress him, and even laughed when movement inside surprised Ethan into lifting his hand in brief alarm.

A taste of mischief, coming back to life. Ethan liked it.

So much that he burrowed into Carter just one more time, licking him clean as he could with all the arousal that buttered his face and Carter's thighs. Carter moaned and shifted as if it hurt this time, and the flesh there had gone puffy, sore-looking.

"Too much?" Ethan asked, lips lighter on him now. "Answer me."

Above him, Carter had lifted his hands to cup his chest. "No," he said, sounding far-away. "I… I like it. I like to feel it."

"Good." Ethan stroked him, light and teasing, pressing firmly with his knuckles, then lifted up to look at Carter. Let him see the gleaming wetness there and grinned in a way he knew looked feral as he felt.

Carter couldn't reach all the way but stretched out an arm to try. "What you just did. You…"

"Me," Ethan agreed. "Me and you."

"Oh," Carter breathed. The way he stared down at Ethan -- and how his eyes had gone dark instead of blue, dark all the way across, dragon's eyes -- "Ethan. *More.*"

Almost -- too good, that was. Ethan pressed a hand to his groin to keep himself from coming until the coiling tightness eased and he could move again. Up, on his knees, pulling Carter's hips into his lap. He took himself in hand and slid himself up the tender line between Carter's legs with enough pressure to be felt.

Carter clutched at his thighs, stretching them wider. He bit at his wrist but couldn't keep quiet. "Ethan -- Ethan -- don't torture me. Not you. Please."

"Shh. I won't." Ethan rubbed a little deeper, relishing the way Carter writhed against him, and bit a line of kisses down his hip and over his smooth inner thigh. "Soon. Do you want me to use a condom?"

Carter laughed -- really laughed, if wildly -- and tossed his head in a frantic *no*. "You can't knock me up twice, for God's sake."

That made Ethan laugh too. He rubbed at Carter's chest to show his appreciation and noticed he was swollen there too. A pinch at each nipple that made Carter cry out and drew a fat bead of creamy white out of each. He really wasn't far from the end. Another week, or less.

Another week, and Ethan would have missed this. Or he might never have known.

Mine, his wolf growled.

Air in. Air out. "Say it," he told Carter. "Tell me what you want."

Carter's eyes drifted open. He covered Ethan's hands and twisted hard at his nipples, though he didn't notice the wetness. Drew his fingers down his belly, not seeming aware of that either, but lifting his hips in bold invitation. "I want you to *fuck* me."

That was what he'd needed to hear. Ethan pushed

forward, one long, deep stroke, and didn't stop until he couldn't go any farther.

Carter bit his wrist, let go, threw it over his head, and a scream burst out of him, a dragon's full-throated shriek. He clutched at Ethan inside and out, grinding, making him work hard to drive in and out, but it was work worth doing and it felt -- so -- Goddamn -- good --

Ethan tucked his chin against his chest, focusing everything he had left on making this last though no matter what it wouldn't be as long as he wanted, both of them too worked up and on the edge of coming.

But he wanted Carter to climax first. Wanted to feel that again, this time around his cock, a drug he'd gotten addicted to weeks ago. Carter's cock, rigid and dark and straining, felt like steel when he took it in hand and worked it without mercy. He savored every wild noise Carter made without even trying to keep quiet now, each arch of his neck and clench deep inside, straining toward climax.

Did he need -- yes. This.

Ethan went deep again, stopped there, and drew the sharp edge of his thumbnail *hard* over the slit at Carter's tip.

The noise Carter made then -- God! The arch of his back, the rattling shudders that racked him, the rise and clench and fall of his belly, and the gush of liquid that almost pushed Ethan out of him -- Ethan couldn't wait, couldn't make it better for him. The tight coil in his groin burned hot and -- let go -- and he came with a wolf's howl to the pale moon he worshiped with his body.

He hadn't let Carter fall on the steps and didn't let him fall now. He tilted back, bringing Carter with him to rest on his lap again, kissing him rough and messy in time with his racing heartbeat. Kissing him until they both shuddered to a halt, moving their mouths clumsily across each other's faces.

"I've got you," Ethan said against Carter's temple. "I've got you."

Ethan half expected to be thrust away -- his brain wasn't working well yet, but he knew this, what they'd done, would be too much for anyone else -- but instead of pushing him away, Carter pressed his forehead to Ethan's chest and gripped him tight.

"I know." Carter scored lines down Ethan's back with his nails, stinging hot as fire. "You did want me. That much."

"And more," Ethan promised again. "And still do, whenever you'll have me."

"Is it still snowing?"

A glance out the window showed only light, fluffy flakes, lazy in their drift downward. "Not much, and not hard." He touched his lips to Carter's temple. "Do you want me to go?"

"No." Carter's nails dug deeper. "I -- no."

"Then I won't."

"That easily?"

"It shouldn't be?"

"You know it should, but..." Carter shivered and pressed his head closer still. He still didn't understand; Ethan could tell, but... he was trying now. He leaned into Ethan, starting to say something else, but then shifted abruptly and made an uncomfortable noise. His belly moved of its own volition, going tight. Hissing between his teeth, he rocked against Ethan.

Ethan stroked him the way he'd seen Carter stroke himself until the tension ebbed away. "That happened before. Does it hurt?"

"Little. Not much. It's a..." Carter's blush made Ethan's chest hot. "The body, it..."

Was getting ready for what would happen, Ethan figured. He really had made it just in time.

He started to open his mouth. He wanted to ask

more, to get answers to questions about everything he'd missed, but -- later. Carter was going laconic again, starting to think and having to force words out, and that wouldn't do.

Better to just feel, for now. And rest, while he could.

"Close your eyes," he said, easing Carter back down and following beside him without letting go. He lay the Omega on his side and curled up like a comma next to him, twining their legs together. The sweat had begun to cool, so he cast about until he found a good heavy quilt and drew it up to cover them. "I'll stay with you until you're asleep. And after."

Carter yawned, but he was a stubborn one. "Not tired."

"Yes, you are." Ethan touched the thin, still-dark skin beneath Carter's eyes to make his lids fall shut. "Close your eyes. I'll be here."

Carter murmured something Ethan couldn't make out, relaxing by inches in his arms -- then, clearly enough to understand: "It's different, why is it so different..."

Different wasn't a bad thing, no matter what anyone might think, but there would be time to mull that over for himself and to tell Carter about it in the morning, when they were both... hmm...

Ethan didn't notice when Carter drifted away, already asleep himself, but he kept his promise. He stayed.

And, as it turned out, it was a good thing he did.

Chapter Four

Ethan stirred.

The sun hadn't come up yet -- had it? No. He couldn't ever sleep after dawn, but usually he couldn't be dragged out of dreams before then by anything short of an explosion. *Then what...*

He couldn't put his finger on what'd woken him until the man who'd been lying at his side shifted, sliding slowly out of bed. Carter, trying to be quiet and stealthy, and to be fair, he was good at both, but not good enough to not disturb an Alpha in protective mode. Ethan reached for him and, mostly out of blind luck, caught his hand.

Carter stopped. "I might have known," he murmured. He laced his fingers briefly through Ethan's, then pressed his hand gently back down on their makeshift mattress. "I told you I don't sleep a lot and I can't sleep now but you don't need to be awake yet. Go back to sleep."

Ethan grimaced and muttered his disagreement, fully intending to get up and keep Carter company, but that sneaky dragon had moved on to lightly stroking his hair. "Not fair."

"Whoever said life was fair? Not me." Carter drew his fingertips along Ethan's nape. "Shh, now. Go back to sleep."

Ethan was already halfway there, soothed into bonelessness from the touch and quiet voice. "Do ASMR," he mumbled.

Carter made a quiet, possibly-amused noise. "I don't know what means. Sleep now."

Ethan had different intentions. He meant to get up. Instead, he slid back under the quiet darkness, and his plans dissolved back into sweet dreams.

He'll be a good parent, when it happens, was his last thought before he drowsed off.

* * *

Ethan opened his eyes.

Hours had passed; he could tell before the room blurred back into focus. Pale light filtered through the drawn blinds, not even as strong as the candlelight or lanterns from last night, but enough to announce a new day. Odd that he'd slept through *that*. He sat up, blinking and frowning at the windows, trying to figure it out.

"It's snowing." The quiet voice came from beyond a tall screen painted with water lilies. "Snow makes dawn as dark as dusk."

Ethan squinted at the screen. Strange how he felt so fuddled, like he'd just woken from a coma instead of a nap on a barely-cushioned floor. "Huh?"

Something very like a breath of laughter floated through the air. "You sound stoned."

"I feel stoned," Ethan admitted. He sniffed, hoping there was a kitchenette behind that screen and that that was coffee he smelled brewing -- possibly toast being toasted too. His stomach rumbled as he rubbed the back of his neck. "How hard was I sleeping?"

"Hard. You didn't move once after I got up and it's been hours."

Hours? Ethan sat up too straight too quickly and swore as his back kinked in protest. "The university --"

"Is closed. I checked. No one's expecting you there today."

Good, but how hard was it snowing? Second Chance knew snow. It didn't roll up its sidewalks for less than a... *well, shit.* "Blizzard?"

"Not quite, but not far off." He could almost hear Carter's diffident shrug. "Go and see for yourself."

Ethan dragged himself out of the nest they'd made over the protest of his joints -- he was getting too old for floor-fucking shenanigans, no matter how much they'd both enjoyed themselves -- and padded barefoot to the window. He whistled at what he saw when he peeked between two slats of the blinds. The snow wasn't too high yet, but those clouds weren't the kind that planned to stop now that they'd gotten started. They could go all day and they were going to prove it.

At least no one would be looking for him. Except Oscar, who for all his salty language had a not-so-deeply buried streak of mother hen. Ethan found his phone and checked it, mildly surprised he didn't already have a text or three. *Huh.*

"I should have woken you when it started coming down like that, but you were sleeping so hard I didn't..." Carter's voice trailed off. "You can still go now if you want."

"I don't want."

Silence answered him, in which it was easy to visualize Carter's surprise, struggle, then uncertain acceptance. After that, clinks and clanks, pouring liquid and scraping butter knives, sounded from what Ethan was almost sure was a kitchen and made his stomach rumble. "Is that breakfast?"

"For you. I'm not hungry. I --"

What should have happened next, in the normal course of things, would have been Carter putting his head around the screen to tell him breakfast was ready. Instead, his ears pricked at the jolting clatter of a knife falling into a sink basin and the almost but not quite stifled sound of a deep hiss followed by a moan.

Damn it, had he cut himself? Burned himself? Ethan bolted from the window and past the screen before he even realized he'd started moving. He fully expected either blood or red-scorched flesh to greet him, both of which he knew -- more or less -- how to deal with.

What he saw instead didn't make sense at first. Carter stood bent double, forearms and forehead pressed to the edge of the sink. Fists flexed and tightened, and though his face was hidden tendons stood out on his neck. He drew in deep, shuddering breaths, harsh through his nose, and held the rest of himself taut as bent iron.

The hell... Ethan came to a sharp stop, baffled. For a moment. Until his gaze trailed down to the belly hanging beneath Carter and he saw how it'd changed, drawn upward and tighter -- and then how it relaxed as Carter did, the rest of the man sagging in relief.

He hadn't noticed Ethan was there yet, too lost in his body and head, which told Ethan everything else he needed to know. A gun-shy, fire-wary dragon should have been, had been, acute enough to notice a pin dropping, much less an Alpha galloping into their space. As far as Ethan knew, only recitals and hard labor distracted people that much.

His heart jumped into his throat and panic thumped through his brain, but Ethan swallowed those both down. He crossed his arms loosely, well and truly wide awake now, but keeping it cool and relaxed as Carter finally looked up and flinched to see him standing there. He caught his lip between his teeth, very obviously trying to figure out if he could get away with any kind of denial, then looked away without a word.

"How long's it been going on?" Ethan asked when it became clear that Carter wasn't going to volunteer anything. "Since before you woke up that first time?"

A reluctant half-shrug was the only answer he got.

"So that's a yes. How long ago was that?" Damn it, he should have looked at a clock. "At least three or four hours?"

Carter made a frustrated movement. "Coffee and toast on the table. Have it if you want it."

"Don't try to distract me. How long?"

Carter shot him a diamond-hard glare, then exhaled and rubbed his belly. "Five hours."

Ethan bit the inside of his cheek, hard, to stop himself raising his voice. "You didn't wake me. You didn't call anyone either, did you?"

"I don't need anyone."

"You don't need anyone." If Ethan had bitten any harder, he'd have tasted blood. "You didn't ever plan to call anyone, you mean. Is that a dragon thing, or a you thing?"

Carter didn't answer. He'd started drifting away, focus shifting toward the middle distance, then drew in a sharp breath. He bent again, but the sink was out of his reach as a brace. Anyone less quick than a wolf might not have caught him before he took a tumble all the way to the floor, but Ethan did. He was strong enough to both hold Carter up and not make a fuss when the Omega squeezed his forearms so hard he was sure to leave bruises behind.

Ethan gritted his teeth and let Carter mangle him as much as he needed to. Helped keep him from losing *his* cool -- twenty-four hours ago, something like this hadn't been anywhere near his conscious horizon, for Pete's sake -- and that was what they needed. And fair was fair, after all, after what he'd put Carter through. Otherwise? *That's what we call enough of that.*

He waited until Carter relaxed again, abruptly as a puppet with its strings cut, and sagged against him. He could feel the shudder and quake of muscles not used to that kind of strain jerking against him and hear the soft panting keens Carter couldn't completely stifle. "Did I do this to you?"

Carter laughed, really laughed, breathless though it might have been.

When Ethan understood why, he wanted to smack his own forehead. "Did I start *this* happening last night, I meant." He laid his hand on Carter's belly, wincing internally and running some numbers. "Should have been another week to go. This is early."

"I know." Carter shivered, but somehow Ethan didn't think that one had anything to do with what his body was caught up in -- but he didn't give Ethan a chance to ask, either. "You probably did start it. But I did too."

"Too late to stop it?"

"Mmm." Carter rested his head on Ethan's shoulder. "I think."

"That's what I figured." Putting his arms around Carter's back to hold him still and keep him safe, and just in case he bolted, Ethan put his lips to Carter's ear and said, "Ambulance. Now. No arguments."

"*No*. I -- can -- take care of -- myself."

"I'm going to go ahead and call 'bullshit' on that one, beautiful boy. Ambulance. Now."

Carter bit his shoulder in sharp annoyance and glowered up at him, sideways, eyelashes spiky with sweat. "I said no. Don't want help. Don't need it. I can. Myself. I -- *ohh*."

Ethan had been ready for that. He dug his heels in and let Carter bow and bend and grip him as hard as he needed, though watching this made *him* grimace in sympathy. No wonder they called it labor. You couldn't work harder swinging a pickax to break rocks in full summer heat.

Do it himself? Maybe dragons could. Ethan didn't know enough about them. But he did know a little about the fragility of Omega bodies when they hadn't been cared for properly. What could happen to them.

Not a chance. Not on his watch.

As soon as Carter's body relaxed on a sob of relief, Ethan took the man's pointed chin between his fingers and growled, "Do it yourself, you said? You want to *bet*?"

* * *

When he shoved the door of the shop open -- there

was likely another exit, but Ethan hadn't wanted to waste time getting Carter to tell him about it -- it almost wouldn't budge against the weight of snow holding it in place. He snarled and put his shoulder into it and got the door open just enough to let him out, shoved it closed without locking it, and started running.

Hallelujah for growing up in Alaska. Ethan didn't think that all too often, but he surely did now. He knew how to run across snow, the ancestral memory of going on four legs showing him how to move just as fast and fluidly on only two. He'd never slipped or fallen before, not even on ice, and he damned well wasn't going to start now.

When he told Oscar about this later, Oscar would kick his ass. And laugh so hard he fell on his own ass. But that would be later.

This was now:

"If you won't go anywhere, I'm going to bring someone to you." Ethan gripped Carter's slim biceps as Carter gripped his forearms, hating to cause him any more hurt, but needing to keep him focused. "If I have to tackle an ER doctor and drag them here by the scruff of their neck, I will. You might know how to do this, but I don't."

Carter laughed, arms tight around Ethan's neck. Ethan didn't think he was really aware of doing either, but he kept that to himself. One battle at a time.

"I mean it," he insisted. "If there's anyone you'd trust more than someone else, tell me now or I'm going to the hospital and leading an ambulance back here."

Carter shuddered against him -- not a contraction, but the betrayal of fear he'd kept well-hidden before. "There's a nurse practitioner," he said at last, grudgingly. "He lives on Main Street, on the rich end. Big brownstone on the corner."

"Where he lives, not where he works?"

Carter didn't answer, caught up again in fighting with his own body. Ethan held him until he -- they -- could breathe again, then led him to the couch and eased him down. He almost gave in when Carter didn't want to let go of him, but only almost. Instead he uncurled Carter's fists and pressed him gently as he could down.

"Stay here. I'll be back. I promise you."

He meant to keep that promise too. Snow be damned, even if he'd almost never seen it come down like this back in Alaska. He pressed forward, running when he could and stalking when he couldn't, kicking snow out of the way when he had no other option, but making progress against a world that would much rather he stay put.

Fuck that.

Ethan was red, hot, and sweating despite the cold by the time he got to the "rich" end of Main Street, where the brownstones sparkled with mica chips and the air was rarified as well-aged wine. Frankly, he didn't give a damn. The brownstone on the corner looked like all the others, but he saw a discreet shingle with a red cross on it mounted next to the front window. He plowed and plundered for it, up steps that someone had swept and salted, and pounded on the door with all his strength.

It flew open between one knock and the next -- the NP must have had a sixth sense, or seen him coming and been ready just in case. An Omega, slim as most of them were but sturdy as steel yet gentle-handed where he arrested Ethan's flight. "Who needs me? Are they with you?"

Almost winded, Ethan shook his head. "No. Back at his place." For heaven's sake, he was talking like Carter now. He gulped air and tried again. "It's over the antique shop. He wouldn't let me call emergency services, but I finally got him to tell me where you are."

"What's wrong with him? No, never mind. I know that look when I see it." The NP clicked his tongue. "I had no idea he was expecting. He hasn't had any prenatal care? No, he wouldn't have. I've bought a couple of things from him and he doesn't seem the type."

"Dragon."

"Ahh." The NP nodded as if it all made perfect sense now. "How far along? How close together?"

"What?"

The NP sighed and shook his head. "Double the newbies, double the fun," he said with a pat to Ethan's shoulder to soften the words. "All right. I need to get some things together. Can you wait five minutes -- no, I can see standing still that long would give you angina. Go back to him. I'll follow."

"The snow --" Ethan started to protest.

"Snow doesn't bother a fennec fox." The NP flashed a sharp, white grin at Carter. "Canadian. You're Alaskan? I thought so. All right. Back as fast as you can, and if anything happens that worries you between now and when I get there -- I do mean anything -- call 911 no matter what he says. Yes? Good. Go on. I'll be right behind you."

"Not in that, you won't," a second voice growled behind the NP, making them both jump and look sharply back at the owner of that voice, a burly Alpha with shoulders like barrels and the stubbornest chin on the planet. He shot Ethan a dark look. "Call an ambulance."

The NP jabbed a finger at the man's chest. His husband? Had to be. "We've been over this, Nathaniel. Too many times." He stopped himself long enough to give Ethan a *hurry-it-up* wave. "Go! I'm coming as quick as I can."

Ethan went. Last thing he wanted was to get involved in a marital squabble. First thing he needed was to get back to Carter. He *kept* his promises.

He just hoped that squabble didn't take too long. That could be bad.

* * *

It took far longer than Ethan would have liked to fight his way back to Carter's studio, but he made it.

Pounding up the steps, he found Carter's door cracked open -- well, that was better than being locked, which he'd half imagined Carter would try as soon as he left.

Whatever. He'd take what he could get. Ethan jogged into the apartment, shedding snow as he went. "Carter? Where are you?"

Not on the couch where he'd been left, but Ethan had good ears. He followed the sound of quick, panting breaths around screen after screen until he reached the back of the studio. He found Carter there, lying naked and on his side in the middle of his bed, the sheets soaked beneath him. He shivered, goose bumps visible on every inch of his skin.

Carter glanced up at him, then squeezed his eyes shut. Silent, he curled onto his side and gripped the sheets instead of reaching for Ethan.

Stubborn little -- well, that wouldn't do.

Ethan shed his jeans, sweater, shoes, and socks, sopping-wet as they were with melted snow -- decided at the last second he'd rather not flash the NP when he got there and left his boxers on -- then grabbed the warmest-looking quilt within sight and clambered onto the bed.

"You're soaking and you're freezing," he said firmly when Carter tried to protest. "I don't know much about dragons, but I know you need heat. Shut up and let me help you."

Carter glared at him and started to say something, but the words didn't make it out. Ethan gathered him up and held him tight until he yielded and grabbed back, hanging on with all his strength.

And, when he could speak again, what he said was: "Go. Away."

Ethan rolled his eyes in frustration. "Not on your life."

Carter punched him in the chest, surprisingly strong even now. "I said *go. Away.*"

"Not happening, and why are you trying to make me?" Ethan tightened his hold. "It's like dealing with a bag of angry snakes."

"Or a dragon," Carter panted. He moaned and ground his head against Ethan's chest. "I hate you. For doing this. To me."

"Can't say I blame you," Ethan retorted. He didn't know if this was helping or not, but if he kept Carter talking it would distract him at least a little. "I'd hate me too, but I did do it, and so did you, and here we are, and I still want to know why you're trying to drive me off."

Another punch to his ribs, harder the second time. "Because this is *mine!*" Carter shouted -- almost a dragon's proper roar. He sagged into Ethan's hold, and Ethan felt the heat of sudden, angry tears rolling down his bare chest.

"Hey. Hey," he tried to soothe Carter. "It's all right. I've got you."

Carter hadn't heard him. "It's mine. Mine," he insisted. His body rippled -- the strangest-looking sort of movement, almost snakelike -- and he let out a shaky breath. "I don't want anyone staring at me or saying things under their breath. I don't want them to spoil it."

"They won't. I won't let them." He tucked Carter's head to his chest and rocked him. "Where the hell is that NP?"

Carter only shook his head, the rest of him undulating gently. Ethan very deliberately did not flinch. If it helped, he'd roll with it. He tested to see if rubbing Carter's back lightly helped. Carter moaned, in relief this time, and melted into him. Ethan felt him lick his lips and the warmth of his sigh. "I told you I don't need him."

"Forgive me for saying so, but how do you know? It's not like you've done this before either."

Carter raised his head as quickly as a snake and fixed Ethan with a stare just as diamond-bright and hard, his teeth bared. "You're wrong. I have."

"What?"

No time for answering, not for almost a minute, but Ethan wasn't going to let that comment just pass by. He jostled Carter as gently as he could and still get his attention. "What did you just say?"

Carter scoffed. "I know you didn't think I was a virgin."

Fair point, but even so.

Ethan pushed his jealous-Alpha side down and stomped it flat to keep it there. He needed to, for more than one reason. Carter had started talking, as if some kind of cork inside him had come loose and he couldn't stop the words now they'd started. "I had a fiancé. A long time ago. I didn't love him and he didn't love me but it was better than being alone. We didn't bond. He didn't want to and I didn't fight him, but it was better."

Ah. Ethan's heart sank. He'd heard stories that started like this before, and they never ended well. "You don't have to go on."

Carter did anyway. "I got pregnant. I wanted to. I wanted a baby. He didn't. He left me, and I… I didn't… I didn't sleep or eat, and I woke up one night with it already half born. Or miscarried. I don't know which. But it was wrong. *Wrong*." He keened, the remembered grief tearing Ethan's heart in half too. "It didn't even have a head, it didn't have a chance, and I lost him too, and there was no one, no one, when he'd promised me --"

As soon as he could, Ethan was tracking down an Alpha in dire need of an ass-kicking. Probably take Oscar and his friend Darian along, Oscar for the backup and Darian because he'd enjoy it.

In the meantime, he had a heartbroken Omega who had damn good reason not to trust anyone to take care of, panting hotly and maybe half an hour away from giving birth. Though Ethan didn't know what to say, now that

Carter had fallen silent, he didn't think speaking would be of much use anyway.

He still did it when Carter undulated hard and then slid out of his grip, slipping sideways and sliding one leg off the bed. "Hey! Whoa, whoa, whoa. I don't think you should be doing that."

"Stop me."

Before Ethan could try, Carter slid as neatly off the side of the bed as a beached walrus and landed on his knees. Ethan hurried to follow him. "What are you doing?"

"I don't know. I just -- I need to --"

Carter pressed his forehead to Ethan's thigh, nearly startling him into jumping back. Surely it had been on purpose, but his mouth rested damned close to dead center and so help him, his perverse body responded to the hot breath curling across it. He jerked forward instead with a grunt, coming up hard and thick, unmistakable, and so inappropriate it made his face burn with embarrassment.

Cheeks flaming or not, he stroked Carter's sweaty hair back. "Don't pay that any mind."

Carter wasn't listening. He'd fixated on Ethan's erection with the kind of laser focus that would make a man go soft if he hadn't been this hard. More so when his fingers crept forward on Ethan's other leg, tentatively toward his crotch. "Can I?"

"Can you -- is this a dragon thing?"

"Please." Carter brought his palm up to cup Ethan. "Please let me."

Did all Omegas lose their minds right around now, or was Carter a special case?

Carter hitched closer. "Say no and stop me."

Ethan should have said *no, nope, get back in bed right now and by the way, I feel this is one of those things the NP would have wanted me to call someone about.*

But he didn't.

His hand fell to the back of Carter's neck instead, guiding him or not denying him, watching in amazement as Carter opened his mouth to suck him through his boxers. No playing around, hard and deep as he could go with fabric in the way, soaking it with saliva and breathing hot and fast. Ethan groaned and dropped his head backward, his lips parted, and rocked into the press of that eager mouth.

"What," he breathed, "The. Fuck."

Carter's shoulders quivered with amusement, but the next undulation of that belly didn't seem to faze him nearly as much. Ethan shook his head, baffled, but if it helped… and *God*, Carter had a sweet mouth. Helping where Carter's hands shook too much for fine work, they pulled his waistband down far enough to let Carter have a real taste. He took the head into his mouth and nursed, moaning steady and low, his hips working in a gentle rhythm.

"Oh, *God*." Ethan threaded his fingers through Carter's hair and cradled him, still confused but too caught up to stop now.

More than. He'd teach Carter to trust him, if he could. But he wasn't letting this man go again.

He didn't know how long it went on, only that he came far sooner than he wanted to, and still couldn't believe he'd done it but didn't care. He tipped up Carter's pretty, pointed chin, but since that left him too far away to kiss, pressed two fingers first to his lips and then to Carter's.

Carter smiled at him, a smile of surpassing beauty. He pulled himself up from all fours to kneeling again, a knee on either side of Ethan's, and pressed their mouths together in a real kiss.

Ethan fell in as if into deep, deep water, drowning in it. Sleek tongues curling and stroking, tilting for the best angle, his hands at the sides of Carter's neck, Carter's fingers digging into his back. Labor between them, shared somehow, until Carter stopped abruptly and began to shudder as if he were shaking apart. He rippled in sharp curves and jerks, as if he wasn't doing it on purpose and couldn't stop.

"What?" Ethan's lips were nearly too kiss-numbed to speak, but he kept hold of Carter's face to search it. "What's wrong?"

Carter didn't answer in any predictable way but took Ethan's hand and brought it downward just as Ethan realized where he'd seen that kind of movement before: reptiles laying their eggs. He almost expected to find a hard shell between Carter's legs, but no, he'd seen it moving inside and that wouldn't happen with an egg. It wasn't that at all, and it was so *fast* he almost couldn't follow, but then, there it was. There *he* was. *Their* child, sliding into the world as easily as labor had been hard.

The Omega laughed, breathless and shocked, and Ethan couldn't help joining him.

"Oh my God," Ethan heard himself say over and over as he tried to gather up the now-shrieking, slippery armful. "Oh my God, oh my God, oh my God."

"I did it," Carter chanted, a counterpoint to Ethan's babbling, trying to help him. He held the messy thing tight to his chest, kissing its wrinkled forehead and murmuring, "I did it I did it I did it look at him just look at him he's perfect, he's alive --"

Ethan kissed him, hard as he could, because he was right and because he wanted to. And *that* was when the door flew open, footsteps clattered toward them, and the NP charged in only to screech to a halt when he saw them. He pressed a hand to his face. "You know, I might have expected that," he murmured. "It's been that kind of a day."

Hadn't it just, though?

Chapter Five

"Well! Everything looks as good as could be expected." The NP, whose name Ethan still hadn't quite had the mental capacity to retain, patted Carter lightly on the knee and more firmly on Ethan's shoulder. "Healthy parents, healthy baby. Who could ask for more?"

Ethan could think of a few things, but he couldn't seem to focus on those any more than the NP's name. Every time he tried, he drifted back to Carter and the baby -- his son. Once Carter had gotten the little one in his arms, he hadn't let go and Ethan itched for a real, proper look at his son.

Who did the baby boy look like? Or was it too early to tell? He'd never seen one newborn that didn't look more or less exactly like another, but somehow Ethan thought this one might be different. There would be something he could point to.

But it wasn't that, not really. He wanted to meet his son as a father should. He had some promises to make.

Later. Perhaps not in front of Nameless NP.

The NP lifted himself gracefully off the bed and nodded down at Carter, taking no notice of how Carter, who'd gone shy again, curled slightly in on himself and wouldn't meet the man's eyes. "You did well," he said. "You can be proud of yourself for that. Ethan, isn't it? Dr. Gold? If you don't mind, I'd like an escort back to the street."

Ethan frowned. Call him paranoid, but whenever someone was that casual about pulling you aside, they weren't going to talk about happy things. He sneaked a sideways check-in on Carter, relieved to see the subtext had flown over his head. Too busy rocking his armful, brushing the baby's face with hesitant awe, totally wrapped up in him and otherwise too stunned for anything else in the world to register.

The NP cleared his throat; when Ethan looked up,

he had his bag in hand and his coat on. "Shall we?"

"Right." Ethan shook his head to clear it. "Carter?"

"I'm fine," Carter murmured.

The NP laid his hand on Ethan's forearm -- big on the physical contact, that one, which probably *was* comforting to his patients -- and left it there, as clear and gentle an impatient hint as he'd ever seen.

"I'll be right back, Carter. I promise."

Carter hummed something and didn't look up. Ethan ran a frustrated hand through his hair, sighed, and turned the NP toward the studio apartment's door. "It's this way."

He hoped. Hadn't exactly been paying attention to the path through the screens the first time he pelted through there, and he hadn't had architecture on his mind afterward. Still, a scholar's mind remembered, and he navigated the NP out to the stairs without making himself look like a fool. With a little luck.

If the NP noticed anything odd, he ignored that as serenely as he had Carter's abrupt reticence and kept up a steady stream of soothing patter. "He really will be fine, you know. You'd be surprised how many home deliveries happen, you honestly would, and most of them without assistance. We're made that way. Gestate fast, heal fast, but do try and avoid another pregnancy for a while."

Ethan's face went hot.

The NP laughed. "Don't be bashful, now. I saw the way you two looked at each other."

Had he? Ethan turned his head toward the NP, curious. "I forget your --"

"My name is Julian. Don't worry about that either; it happens all the time too. As long as you remember the brownstone on the corner, we'll be fine."

Ethan couldn't help admiring NP Julian's aplomb and had to wonder if anything ever got under that smooth, competent skin of his.

"Very little," Julian replied. Somehow, though he couldn't say why, Ethan's radar pinged that as a lie. "I'm good at compartmentalizing."

"And reading minds?"

Julian chuckled. "It's a useful skill when your clients aren't terribly verbal when you meet them. Ah, here we are, at the street, and I suppose you're dying to know why I wanted to talk with you before I walk out there."

Ethan raised both shoulders. "It'd be helpful."

"Yes." Julian looked up at him, clear and direct and thoughtful. "You are aware that your partner shows significant signs of PTSD. Correct?"

No, he hadn't known that, actually, but the pieces clicked firmly together and made sense. Ethan kicked himself for not comprehending as much before -- on the inside -- and nodded on the outside.

Julian returned the nod, decided and firm. "I won't ask what happened to cause it. That's not my business. What I need from you is your promise that you'll take good care of him, mind and body. He'll need help more than ever now -- parenting a newborn isn't an easy job -- and if he isn't already seeing a therapist, he needs to be convinced to find one *and* make regular visits. He may need coaxing. An Omega might get away without prenatal care, even if it isn't advisable, but if he wants to be a good parent without breaking down on the regular, he needs that kind of help. Can you give me your word that you'll do your best?"

"Yes." The word flew out without planning or thought, but it was still true. Ethan met the NP's assessing stare with everything that he felt deliberately on display. "I promise you I will."

"Good. Do that, call me if there's anything at all you're not sure of, and we'll be off to a fine start. Has it started snowing again? Tsk. Well, with a little luck the path you and I plowed down the sidewalk won't have gotten covered. Good thing too. I've got some other patients I'll have just enough time to get to on my way back."

Alone? Ethan frowned at that, but when he glanced out the window relief flooded him. Sort of. The big Alpha he'd seen before, at Julian's house, leaned against one of the lampposts with his hands in his pockets, waiting like a statue. "Looks like you'll have an escort."

Julian drew up short. "Ah."

And if that wasn't the shortest sentence the man had come out with so far... "If you don't want to go with him, I'll call law enforcement to clear him out. It'd be the least I could do."

"What? No, no, no." Julian waved him off, his brave face and stiff upper lip firmly in evidence and utterly betrayed by the way he took a deep breath as he squared his shoulders. "That's my husband."

"That doesn't change my point."

"As long as I've known him, Nathaniel's never raised a hand to a fly in summertime. We do have a conversation to finish, but that's all." Julian smiled at him -- he had a beautiful smile, though not as sweet as Carter's -- and patted his cheek. "Me, I'll be fine. You: remember what I said and go take care of your man. Deal?"

* * *

Deal, with no twisting of his arm required.

Ethan paused only long enough to make sure the door was locked before he jogged back up the stairs. He made it to Carter's landing in a trice and had the door open before he realized he'd run into an unexpected problem. He wasn't the only one waiting on that landing.

He eyed the new arrival, irritated and frustrated and not inclined to like them. Not that that was a stretch. The man looked like a Beta, one of the ones who'd gone sour and bitter over his otherness like some did. Sixtyish, narrow-faced, and pinch-lipped, radiating disapproval. Not nearly as pleasant to deal with as Julian, but Ethan handled worse at every faculty party and most conferences involving a parent and a student.

He put on his most authoritative, professorial demeanor like a cloak and looked sharply down his nose at the man. "Can I help you?"

"Hmmph!" the man snorted.

Good lord, did people actually do that in real life?

"What," the sour old twist demanded, fists knotted on his hips, "was all that racket about just now? Were you having a party? You woke everyone up."

"Given that you're the only person complaining right now, I sincerely doubt that," Ethan replied calmly. "Are you on the third floor? Fourth? Ah, the fifth. Just in case you're not aware, this is an old building constructed back when they made walls thick and floors solid. The only way you could have heard any racket coming from us is if you had your ear pressed to the door. Does that sound about right?"

The old man spluttered. "Well! Why, I never --"

"Somehow, that fails to surprise." Ethan crossed his arms. "If that's all, I suggest you be about your business."

He turned, but the old man caught him around the forearm with a hand as cold and bony as chicken claws. When Ethan turned back, he saw the Beta's eyes were fever-bright. "He tried to hide it, but I saw him thickening up and I know what I know, I've seen what I've seen. There was a bastard born here this morning, wasn't there?"

"You might want to watch your language," Ethan suggested through gritted teeth, reminding himself that young healthy men didn't punch wizened old ones, no matter how much they deserved it. "And go back to your apartment. And mind your own Goddamn business while you're at it."

The old man ignored him, too busy relishing every drop of this. He rubbed his hands together so gleefully Ethan pinpointed his bloodline in an instant: *vulture*, come to pick the bones of the dead bare. "I knew it. Knew it! Why, back in my day -- an unmarried parent in this building? The committee will hear about this. Good people live here, and we won't stand for any such nonsense. A bastard, a single parent -- for shame, for shame!"

Enough. Ethan's temper, frayed thin, snapped. "Single parent? Hardly. Who do you think I am, you old turkey neck? *I'm* the father. That's *my* son, and *my* Omega, and I'm where *I* belong while you very much do not and moreover are not welcome. Am I making myself clear?"

The old man gaped at him, shocked into silence until he stammered, "I never saw you before."

"Get a better pair of binoculars," Ethan shot back. "Expect to hear from the committee yourself and piss the fuck off before I really lose my cool."

The old man might have had something to say to that -- men like him almost always did -- but Ethan decided he didn't care, wondered whether the fluency in cursing had come from too much exposure to Oscar, and stepped into the apartment, almost-but-not-quite slamming the door behind him.

To be greeted by the sight of a worn, weary, pale-as-paper Carter standing near the first screen. One of those little cots with a carrying handle rested at his feet, and his eyes were fixed on Ethan.

Ethan sighed and leaned back against the door. "So I'm guessing you heard that."

"Every word," Carter replied. "That was Tommo. He's a --"

"Vulture? I noticed."

"He's horrible," Carter said. "Everyone in the building's terrified of him."

Including Carter, no doubt. "That might change. The thing about bullies is most of them are weak under all that bluster and they can't stand up to any kind of pushback. Poke them and they crumble like wet cardboard. I wasn't going to stand there and let him get hard over the thought of shredding you even if it was the first erection he's likely gotten in years." Ethan raised one shoulder. "If you want to give me twenty lashes for defending you, have at it. But I'm not sorry, and I'd do it again."

"I know," Carter said. He looked at Ethan a moment longer. A glimmer of a smile dawned on his lips, curved slightly at the corners, and was that a hint of mischief in there too? "I see that now."

"Do you?" Ethan grinned at him, feeling as light as champagne bubbles. Look at that, would you? Look at that man, smiling for me. "You want to know something?"

Carter cocked his head in question.

"You're beautiful."

"Stop." Carter touched his own cheek slightly, but he couldn't hide his startled pleasure, or anything else behind whatever walls he wanted to throw up. Not anymore. Ethan had learned how to see through all that. "I haven't even taken a shower yet."

True, but Ethan shook his head and let Carter see everything in his heart written across his face, just as he had with the NP. "Still beautiful."

Carter's blush warmed and deepened and he looked down, but that smile lingered. "Well," he murmured. "Since this is apparently your place too, you might as well come in and make yourself at home. Hadn't you?"

No persuasion needed, again. Ethan's smile

widened into a grin. "I might as well just."
* * *

Ethan followed Carter back inside, taking the carry-cot with him, surprised by its weight. Even subtracting the bulk of plastic frame and blankets, it was no wonder carrying that around had kept Carter from finding his center of balance. How did any Omega do that? He couldn't wrap his head around it, but he could marvel.

And be grateful.

And marvel a little more, while he was at it. Ethan craned his head, trying to get a look at the face in between its swaddling of blankets, and once he did, came to a stop then and there. Babies did all look mostly like other babies, plump cheeks and button noses and all, but -- were the shape of those eyes the same as Carter's? Was the point of that chin like his? One minute hand had worked its way free of the blankets, and Ethan couldn't help it. He set the cot on the floor, knelt next to it, and brushed the hand with his fingertip.

Small, so small, but he knew the shape of that hand. He used two of them just like it every day.

Caught up in awe, Ethan only came back to himself when he heard Carter chuckle. Though rusty with lack of use, it still sounded sweet, and when Ethan looked up, he saw Carter trying and failing to hide a smile behind his hand.

"He's beautiful," Carter said. "That's what's beautiful."

Still kneeling, Ethan grinned at him again. "Can't help notice you didn't specify which 'he' there."

He startled a real laugh out of Carter, if not an answer, which was actually answer enough for Ethan, content to sit there and wait to see what happened next. He felt pretty certain he'd like it.

Carter's expression slid sideways into thoughtfulness and shyness, fidgeting in the robe the NP had helped him into, nibbling at his lip. "I... really could use a shower," he said, then added in a rush, "Could you help?"

See? He'd been right. Ethan did like it.

* * *

Ethan had seen the bathroom before, but only in passing. As it were. He'd kept the lights off so he didn't wake Carter during previous visits, but the soft lights that Carter clicked on with a bashful glance over his shoulder didn't even make the baby stir in his cot. Light metal frames with bulbs made to look like lanterns flickering.

"Is that a dragon thing?" Ethan asked, touching one delicate light cage in admiration. He could see where it'd been broken once upon a time, then fixed. "I remember you told me before that light hurts your eyes when it's too bright."

Carter didn't answer for long enough that Ethan looked his way, curious. "Yes," he said at last. "And no. Sometimes. I remember liking the sun. It's just... been a long time. So long I'm not used to it anymore."

Ethan digested that, hearing the NP say *PTSD* in his mind's ear. "Maybe you'll enjoy it again someday."

Carter shrugged; *I might.* He reached for the tie to his gown, hesitated, visibly gathering his courage, and turned to Ethan with the end of that tie held out to him. "Do you still want to help?"

With everything. Yes. Whether or not Carter knew it, this dragon had captured him like his other treasures. Ethan secured the cot in a snug corner, stood, and took hold of the tie. He pulled gently, steadily, slithering it out of its loops until it came free and Carter's robe fell open.

But he didn't stop there, and Carter didn't stop him from stepping forward to ease the loose robe off his shoulders, letting it fall to the floor and leave him in nothing but his bare skin. Carter held a little too still as Ethan took him in, almost but not quite concealing his worry about what Ethan would think of him now.

He didn't need to. Carter looked like a man who'd just given birth, of course, but to *his* child. Anyone put off by that kind of thing didn't deserve to be a father in the first place. And it was true, what he'd always been told, that Omegas healed fast. Not like a snap of the fingers or a lightning strike, but fast enough to fascinate: flexible skin tightening where it'd stretched, legs steadier, ankles slimmer.

"Beautiful," Ethan murmured. He picked up Carter's hand and brushed his lips across the knuckles, deeply satisfied to hear him catch his breath.

He thought he might just make it a mission to draw that sound out of Carter more often.

But in the meantime -- *hmm.* Ethan reached past Carter to turn on the spigots in the tub but reached for the stopper instead of the shower attachment. "You must ache," he said when Carter frowned at him. "If it's safe, a bath will feel better than a shower. And you won't slip."

Carter studied him for another of those long beats before nodding -- and, with another of those flashes of bravery coming to the surface, took Ethan's hand. "If you come in with me. There's room for two."

Ethan dropped the plug into its socket and lifted Carter's chin. "Try and stop me, beautiful. Try and stop me."

Carter shivered, his lips parted around a sigh and curved around a whisper of a smile.

What more of an answer did anyone need?

* * *

It was interesting, Ethan thought, though he was aware that word didn't go nearly far enough. But *interesting* nonetheless. Part of him kept wondering when this would start to turn awkward and uncomfortable. He and Carter were, technically, almost as good as strangers. They wouldn't be the first barely acquainted pair to produce a baby. It wasn't this easy for almost anyone. It should be at least a little strange.

Yet it wasn't, and it didn't turn.

Ethan got Carter settled in the tub, the carry-cot situated where they would both be able to keep an eye on it, and shed his clothes quickly and efficiently -- then more slowly when he sensed Carter watching him keenly, seeming to like what *he* saw. He glanced up and sideways to wink at him, just for the fun of making him blush and feint a swat his way. "Stop that."

"Do you want me to get in the tub with my socks on, then?" Ethan teased. "I could, but I don't think either of us would be happy about it."

Carter wrinkled his nose but was laughing quietly. "No socks. Please."

"Your wish."

Ethan shed the last stitches without making a show out of it, no need to, and stepped into the tub of warm water. He eased himself down behind Carter, cradling the Omega's hips with his and bracketing his thighs the same way. Even smaller than most Alphas as he was, his legs were long enough that their bare feet brushed and bumped together. Gentle, he eased Carter backward until he got the idea and let himself lean into Ethan, his back to Ethan's chest and his head resting against Ethan's breastbone.

Carter sighed as the water lapped warm around their skin. "How did you know?"

"Know what?" Ethan nuzzled at the nape of Carter's neck. Such an elegant arch needed to be kissed, but he reined it in. There would be time, and he meant to make sure they had it. But he could enjoy the way his Omega smelled: salty, a little coppery, but far more like cinnamon with a bite than bitter myrrh. "Hmm?"

He arched his back, a luxurious stretch that ended on a noise almost like a purr. "That this was what I needed," Carter said, sounding almost drugged. "Are you magic?"

Ethan laughed. He found a sponge, soaped it, and started to draw it gently over Carter's lax body. "I'd ask what kind of question that was if it didn't come from a dragon."

"No, I mean it." Carter closed his eyes, letting Ethan wash him. "I... don't know anything about you. Not really." He bit his lip. "Tell me?"

Ethan could see it, every time Carter remembered where he was and what he was letting happen, and the courage it took to let it happen. That deserved rewarding. "Let's see... you already know I'm from Alaska."

"Because you never fit in there," Carter murmured. He laid his fingertips on the back of Ethan's hand, not stopping him, just going along for the ride. "I grew up hundreds of miles away. I never fit in there either, and after... *after*, I had to leave."

Ethan hummed his understanding. "I came here for the job, but not just for the job. It's a year-long artist-in-residence position and a good one -- there aren't as many professional-level opportunities for what I teach as you might think, but --"

"You teach at the college," Carter said, interrupting him. His eyelids drifted halfway open. "I remember that now. What do you teach?"

Ethan couldn't help it. He skated the calluses on his fingertips along Carter's smooth shoulder. "Music," he said into the crook of Carter's shoulder. "Anything with strings, I can make it sing for me. There was a job here, and I took it, but that's not why I stayed. There's something else about Second Chance. It seemed like a place where things could happen. I wanted to see if they would."

Carter turned his head sideways, pillowing his cheek on Ethan's chest. "I think you got your wish."

He didn't know the half of it -- or maybe he did. Ethan did feel Carter smile and felt the shy brush of the Omega's hand on his flank under the water as well.

"I'm staying, by the way," he said into Carter's hair. "Even when the job ends, I'm staying. Just so you know."

Carter's body undulated under the water as he sighed. He licked his lips, starting to say something, but noises from the carry-cot distracted them both. Propped up as it was, with a clear view of the baby, Ethan could see their son starting to stir fretfully and smack his lips.

"He's hungry," Carter said, but laid his hand over Ethan's rather than get up. When Ethan craned his neck for a better look at the man's face, he found worry instead of an action plan. "I wish I could..."

Could what? Ah. "You don't want to try?"

Carter's skin warmed more than the water had managed so far. "I do. There are things you can -- things I heard about, to practice beforehand -- but I could never get -- I --" He covered his face. "The NP left me some formula and bottles. I can use those."

He could, but... Ethan stroked Carter's arm as he nudged Carter's hands away from his face. His mind raced ahead, remembering what he'd seen the night before when Carter forgot to be self-conscious, and it wasn't much of a leap from there. No one could let their body do what needed doing when they were too caught up inside their own heads. Only stood to reason.

The baby wasn't fully awake, not crying yet. They had a little time, and Ethan had an urge to touch that he couldn't resist once he had a good reason not to hold back. He put his lips to Carter's tempting nape and savored his startled shiver, his sound of surprised pleasure.

"I'll never get tired of that," he murmured as he kissed down the line of Carter's neck. He missed the hair, but all that skin readily available was a delight in its own right, and Carter bent his head to let him go where he wanted. Under the water, he laid his hand on Carter's stomach and started to draw slow, lazy circles. "I want to tell you a story."

"You -- what?"

"Shh. A story. Listen to me."

Carter shifted uncertainly, then subsided when Ethan took his earlobe between his teeth and bit down gently. Under the water, he took hold of Ethan's thighs, lightly and with shaking hands. "A story about what?"

"When I was a boy, in Alaska, I thought I'd stay there forever. Most of the wolves did. And why not? It's God's country up there, wide open and mostly wild, with more space than you can imagine to run and hunt in. Cold and dark in the winter, but sunlight almost all day in summer."

"It sounds beautiful."

"It was. It is." Slowly, slowly, Ethan traced lazy patterns that led higher up Carter's torso. "When I got a little older, I didn't love it any less, but I started thinking about the future. About who I wanted to be. How different I was. Where I would fit, in the world. Who I wanted to fit with. I'm old to never have had a mate."

"Not that old."

"Older than most, but I didn't mind that. I wanted to be sure about *who* I wanted. I had it all planned out too. Careful. Methodical. I knew where I'd go looking, and when, and why, and the kind of person I thought would be the best fit." He could tell Carter didn't like this story -- yet. But he would. "Do you know one of the things I like best about plans?"

Carter made an uncertain noise.

"I like it when they don't go the way I expected," Ethan said, lips at the shell of Carter's ear.

"Oh," Carter said, breathless. He lifted one wet

hand and reached behind himself, moving blindly until he found Ethan's head and threaded his fingers through Ethan's hair. "You."

"You. And me. And you." Ethan rubbed the pads of his thumbs underneath Carter's nipples, deeply pleased to find them so sensitive that Carter arched his back and moaned. "I like being surprised. I met someone when I wasn't looking like I'd planned. I met you, and you had me right away, did you know that? Cinderella of *Speakeasy*, of the alley, and I've been looking for you with a glass slipper in hand ever since. Beautiful dragon, it was magic. You looked at me and I was yours. I've wanted to find you, to be with you, ever since. More than. You make me want to give you the world, Carter."

Ethan took Carter's hands and raised them to the Omega's own breasts, pressing down so he could feel them. He held Carter as Carter startled and stared down at the fat beads of milk that formed steadily and trickled down his chest. Held Carter tighter when the dragon started to shake.

"I... how did you know what to... Ethan?"

"Like that," Ethan said. "We don't know everything about each other yet, but I think we're both good at learning." He kissed Carter's shoulder one more time, purely because he wanted to. "Stay there, stay warm, and stay safe. I'll bring your son to you."

Carter waited for him to step out of the tub before he said, "Our son." He was looking at Ethan when Ethan looked back, and said it again. "Our son. If you're sure. If you're really sure. If you mean everything you just said. Did you? Do you?"

There was only one answer for that. Ethan lifted their son from his cot and held him so they both faced Carter as he made his reply. "I do. I promise."

Chapter Six

Ethan woke to the humming sound of voices outside, the grinding roar of a snowplow drowning them out and fading away, and the light brush of fingertips on his cheek -- and then an even lighter press of lips against his. He made a sleepy, pleased rumbling sound and reached up without opening his eyes to find the back of his bedmate's head. Carter's head fit in the cup of his palm as if they'd been made to go together.

Instead of startling back or flinching away he only stilled for half a breath before his lips curved against Ethan's in a smile instead of a kiss. "You're awake."

"Not yet." Smiles were wonderful, especially from Carter, but Ethan wanted more of those sweet, soft kisses. He teased the back of Carter's head with the tips of his short-cut nails, coaxing him closer.

Carter's shoulders rocked with quiet amusement, but he was an obedient one. He rose up on one arm and bent his head properly to Ethan's, letting him bring their mouths together and interlocking their bodies like puzzle pieces. He laid his hand over Ethan's heart, light as the brush of a feather, and curled against Ethan as if he'd drink up every bit of his body heat.

Though Carter was warmer than he had been. Less of a frozen doll and more of a living, breathing, flesh and blood man. He splayed his fingers wide over Ethan's chest and curled them closed, slid them up to his shoulder, and parted his lips when Ethan teased them with the tip of his tongue. He tasted sweet inside, a hint of last night's toothpaste and tantalizing cinnamon, and his breath was hot as sunlight through clear glass.

The dragon was waking up from his long sleep, wasn't he? Finding his fire again.

Ethan had to see. He blinked his eyes open, three slow sweeps, and had the pleasure of watching Carter come back to himself from inches away. He broke the kiss with another smile, shy but not ashamed, and when he caught his lip between his teeth it wasn't with embarrassment, but to taste their kiss-swollen pinkness.

"If you're not awake, am I dreaming?" Carter stroked his forefinger down Ethan's cheek. "The way you're looking at me. As if…"

Ethan caught his hand and pressed his lips to the center of Carter's palm. "As if, how?"

Carter's cheeks went pink. "As if you like what you see."

"But I do like it."

"Stop it. You can't." Carter put his hands to his face, then pressed it into the pillow. "Even now?"

Did he really not believe that? Did he not know?

Time someone showed him.

"Even more than before, now." Ethan gazed at him, drinking in every drop of him and not hiding a thing. "You have a face that angels would fall for, a voice like silk, the cleverest hands, and as for the rest of you…" He grinned, letting his wolf bloodline out to play in its wickedness, then gentled it with the slow skim of his palm down Carter's thigh. "I could say a thousand words about how beautiful you are, dragon. But I'd rather show you."

"What are you -- *oh*." Carter arched his back as Ethan slid downward, tracing a path along both his thighs. "What are you doing?"

"Showing you." Ethan touched his tongue to Carter's navel. "Stop me if you're sore. But if you're not, then." He traced a fine line besides the trail of fine hair arrowing downward. "*Then*."

Slowly, slowly, Carter's fingers slid through Ethan's hair. "Then," he said, sounding dazed, sounding breathless. "Then?"

"Then," Ethan murmured, and put his mouth to the crease of Carter's hips. "And then. And again."

He moved as gently as he could, as firmly as he dared, and as slowly as he thought either of them could stand. If Carter had told him to stop, he would have, but it might have killed him.

But Carter didn't say *stop*. Carter let his legs fall apart a shivering inch at a time, as if he couldn't help it, inviting Ethan to slip between them with each hitch and fall of his chest and curl of fingers in his hair.

Ethan slid a knee over Carter's and eased into the cradle of his legs. He tasted the salt in the crease of Carter's hip, where it met the soft skin of his inner thigh and kissed the marks his beard left behind. That was good, but not enough. He wanted more. Needed more. Craved it, like a drug.

He coaxed Carter's legs a little more apart but arrested himself when that made Carter wince. "Stop?" he asked.

"No. Please, don't stop, no." Carter shifted, sinuous again, shoulders rolling down and hips arching up. "I'm only a little sore. Just -- be gentle."

Gentle, Ethan could do. "Gentle as sunrise," he promised, shifting deeper and easing Carter's thighs over his shoulders. He rested his weight on his forearms and pressed his mouth to the dip just above Carter's groin, breathing him in. Half hard before Ethan really got to work, he thickened and lengthened until his cock rested on his belly, flushed dark and leaving tiny drops of clear fluid on the skin. Ethan licked those up without touching Carter's cock, chuckling when he made a frustrated noise and tried to nudge closer.

"Not yet," he murmured, smoothing Carter's hips back down. "Patience."

He pressed his nose to Carter's soft skin, breathing deep. He smelled like life -- like everything ripe -- like all Omegas did, sweet and tempting -- like the traces of bittersweet and myrrh he'd almost left behind. Ethan nuzzled his way down, tasting him in light, delicate flicks of his tongue, and stopped where Carter could feel curls of warm breath against his center. He blew once, a thin stream of heated air.

Carter cried out, sharp and surprised, his hips jerking hard and his cock slapping his belly, drooling thin strings down to pool on his skin. Ethan swept those up with a finger and slid it into his mouth, tasting him. *Mmm. Sweet.*

"Please," Carter said above him. His thigh muscles quivered with the effort to lie still. "Don't tease, Ethan. Please."

Because he'd asked so sweetly, Ethan nudged Carter's center ever so lightly with his nose, then drew back -- reluctantly -- to shush and soothe him. "Easy, easy. Too soon. But for now..."

"For now?" Carter asked, sounding puzzled, before Ethan tongued Carter's cock into his mouth and suckled at it. Carter cried out sharply, then stifled the sound with the back of his wrist over his mouth. "What -- what are you --"

Ethan drew off to rub his cheek against the length of Carter's shaft, a good size for an Omega, but one of the prettiest he'd ever seen. "If you can't tell, I'm doing this wrong."

"You -- I --" Carter arched his back, hips coming clear of the bed, then pressed himself down when any fool could have seen he wanted to thrust *up*.

Ethan could help with that too, with his hands at Carter's hips to guide him. Showing him how to rise and fall, how not to go too deep, but how to go deep enough to feel Ethan's throat squeeze when he swallowed, how to ride through it when he fluttered his tongue. This was going to be another addiction, he could tell: teasing Carter into falling apart. He spread his hand on Carter's stomach, fingers spread wide, to feel the flex and tighten of his muscle. The scent of sweat, slippery and salty, and their panting made the air around them humid and saturated with sex. And the sounds -- those were the best of all -- startled mewls, guttural moans, rapid panting breaths, and scraps of what might have been his name amidst all the wild pleading noises. They urged Ethan on too, though he'd gone into this looking out for Carter's pleasure, not his own. But those *noises* -- Ethan found a rhythm with his own hips, rolling them down and rutting against the mattress, slow and sinuous, stopping when the coiling heat inside came too close to tipping him over the edge.

Not yet. Not just yet. He took Carter in hand to stroke his shaft while he lavished his mouth over the rest and hummed a brief snatch of a song he remembered from that night outside *Speakeasy.*

"Oh God, oh God, oh God." Above him, he sensed Carter lifting on his elbows, looking down, then collapsing back on his elbows with a groan. He brought his knees up to cradle, then to grip Ethan's shoulders, and tugged at his hair. "Ethan, I… I'm…"

He was; Ethan could feel it. The cock in his mouth stiffened, pulse beat hard against his soft palate, leaking musky sweetness on his tongue. Ethan stroked him, but not as gently as before, grinding into the mattress for relief while wanting it to be Carter's wet, welcoming body he sank into.

"*Please,*" Carter begged. "Please, Ethan, I don't know what, please, please just…"

Ethan let go with his mouth, but not his hand, and slid back up Carter's body to kiss him. Carter startled at the taste of himself on his own lips but pressed his mouth desperately to Ethan's and clung tight. His hips stuttered and found their own rhythm when Ethan stroked him again, and he brought his thigh up for Ethan to grind against.

Warm, hot, soft, smooth, rough, and so, so -- *there*, they were there, Carter tightening into a drawn-up knot, jerking in his hand, wet heat trickling down his fingers. Ethan caught Carter's lip between his teeth and bit it himself as he rolled himself forward and through it, coming just as hard, just as messily, and neither of them stopping before they were drained dry.

God. That'd been... Something Ethan wanted to do again. As much as he could. And more.

In the meantime, he had an armful of pliant, fucked-out Omega to gather up. Ethan stretched out alongside Carter, rolling the man toward him and putting an arm around his ribs to keep him safely there until the aftershocks faded.

Carter stared at him, more confused than before. "*Am* I dreaming?"

"No." Ethan thumbed at his chin, pulling his bitten lip a little down. "Not unless I'm dreaming the same dream with you."

Carter smiled quickly, rusty from lack of practice, but almost boyish and -- beautiful. "Maybe we are still asleep. Maybe it is a dream. *I've* done, to... but no one's ever..."

He trailed off, embarrassed, but not before Ethan had gotten the point. He lifted himself on his elbow. "No one ever did that for you before?"

Carter hid his face in the pillow, but his blush was its own answer.

Ethan wished he could say he was surprised, but from what he'd learned about the men Carter had taken to bed before, he truly wasn't. Well. That would change.

"Get used to it," he whispered against Carter's ear. "Because I liked it just as much as you did."

When he pulled Carter toward him, Carter came, curling into his body. He touched two fingertips to Ethan's bicep, stroking him as if puzzled. "I keep trying to wrap my head around you, and I can't."

Because you never did that before either, Ethan thought. What he said instead was, "Give it some time."

"Time?"

"All the time you want. As long as you want me, I'll be there."

Carter lifted his head, studying Ethan with the kind of intensity it was hard not to look away from, but Ethan had meant what he said. He held Carter's gaze until the faintest of smiles crossed Carter's lips, and then he had no choice but to kiss them. Show the man he meant it as well as tell him.

Their mouths had barely touched, though, when an earsplitting air horn blasted outside the window, making them both jump and laugh, then wince at the immediate and indignant shriek following from the portable bassinet. Ethan didn't think it was his imagination that the little one's loud wail had the edge of a hunting hawk to it. It'd be a roar, somewhere down the road. He could already tell their son was more dragon than wolf, but the wolf shored up the dragon's odd edges and made them both sturdier.

Ethan couldn't wait to watch him grow up.

"I'll get him," he and Carter said at the same time, then burst into laughter together.

Carter shook his head and dropped one more light, sweet kiss to Ethan's lips. "No, let me. The more I move, the quicker I'll heal, and we've been in bed for hours. It's almost noon."

"No kidding?" Ethan reluctantly let Carter slide out of his arms and sat up, quilt almost but not quite falling away from his bare hips. He squinted at the window, surprised at how bright the light that filtered through the blinds was. "I can't remember the last time I slept this late."

"Then you must have been due."

"Hmm," Ethan said, not paying attention to himself but distracted by watching Carter make his way to the cot and kneel to pick the baby up. He *was* moving better than yesterday, wasn't he? Still a little stiff and sore, but his gait was smoother and he didn't wince.

Amazing how Omega bodies worked. Not hard to understand why some mated pairs had baby after baby like assembly lines, and not that it wasn't tempting, but -- there would be time, plenty of time, and Ethan wanted to enjoy Carter on his own merits right now.

"Bring him back here? I'll change the sheets while you're up. There would be enough room." Ethan liked the idea of lying face-to-face on their sides with the baby between them, fighting sleep and trading drowsy caresses.

But Carter was already easing down into the padded chair in the corner of the room, as careful with the baby as he would be with a glass egg. "Shh, shh, shh," he murmured, until he had them both situated and the howling silenced. "He's a hungry one." Dark lashes fanned across his cheek before he glanced up at Ethan from beneath him. "Gets that from his father."

A starburst of warmth exploded behind Ethan's breastbone, making him grin like a fool and not mind in the least when Carter laughed at the look on his face. What? It must have been priceless.

"Will you do something for me?" Carter asked. The chair only rocked a little, but he'd set a slow, easy rhythm. "Go downstairs and get something from the shop? I won't open today, maybe not for a few days, but -- that's all right. I just want something I remembered."

"Easy enough. What do you need?" Ethan slid out of bed, found his pants, and tugged them on. He found his sweater in the opposite corner and wriggled into it as well. He could feel Carter watching him and threw in a little hip twist to make him laugh again -- which he did.

"What am I looking for?"

Carter was watching him fondly, chin tucked on one hand. "I wonder if I just imagined you," he murmured, then waved that off. "One of the lanterns in my workshop. I'd finished repairing it before you came in, but it had to set and dry. It's tin, painted blue, with stars and moons cut into the barrel. Only big enough for a tea light candle to go inside."

"A nightlight." Ethan crossed to the chair and reached down to rub one knuckle across the back of his son's hand. "You made it for him?"

"I fixed it for him," Carter corrected. "I want to be sure it's working before it gets dark again, and there's only five hours of sunlight left. Would you mind?"

Ethan shook his head; not at all. "Back in five. Or less."

"Maybe more," he heard Carter call after him, wry and rueful. "I'm the only one who can find what he's looking for in there."

"Good thing for me I'm a quick learner. I'll figure it out."

The stairs were becoming as familiar to Ethan as the ones he used every day at the college, and he was light enough in heart to take them two at a time, hopping the last three to land at the bottom and lope into the workshop. Carter hadn't been joking about the clutter; Ethan remembered that from before -- had it really been less than forty-eight hours ago? -- but it still wasn't the most chaotic office he'd ever seen.

As he sorted through the projects in progress, he heard the faint sound of a phone ringing upstairs. No, his phone, ringing. It'd been silent for so long that the familiar ringtone made him look sharply in that direction. A rapid-fire stream of text noises followed, making him snort quietly. Cell towers must have been down and the signal just come back. Lord only knew what he'd find when he opened those. *Are you alive* and *if you are alive I'm going to kill you*, that kind of thing.

For the moment, Ethan ignored it in favor of hunting for what Carter had wanted. Easier once the phone cut off mid-ring, but harder since he kept getting distracted by the fineness of Carter's handiwork. The man needed more recognition for his work, and yesterday if not sooner.

Ethan had balanced a teacup in his palm, brought up close to one eye to try and see the almost invisible cracks Carter had mended, when he heard footsteps coming down the stairs. Fast, and that was enough to concern him, but not just fast. Hard, as if they weren't being descended so much as stalked. Ethan only had enough time to look up at the partially opened door before Carter pushed it open with a rough shove and fixed Ethan with a stare so cold and fiery it could have melted glass and frozen blood.

He had Ethan's boots in one hand and his phone in the other and threw that at Ethan without warning. Startled, Ethan fumbled the teacup to try and catch his phone; he couldn't manage both, and the teacup dropped to shatter all over again on the icy floor.

Carter didn't flinch, or even seem to notice. His face was set in hard, cold lines, and he stared at Ethan as if he hated him.

Surprise, confusion, and frustration at going back to square one made Ethan sharper than he would have liked. "What the hell, Carter?"

He thought, at first, that Carter wasn't going to answer him, not until the frozen mask on his face cracked. "Someone named Oscar just called."

"And?" Ethan spread his hands, still baffled. "He works with me, he's my TA. Did he grill you or something?"

That would have been bad. What Carter said next

was worse.

"He wanted me to tell you that Ry mailed you the ring, asking you to get it resized."

Oh… *hell*. Ethan shut his eyes tight. Killing wasn't good enough for Oscar. He'd string the man up by his balls. "It's not what it sounds like."

Which was the worst thing anyone could ever say to an angry lover aside from *it's not you, it's me*, and he figured he deserved Carter's derisive bark. If that'd been all, but it wasn't. "You're married. Aren't you?"

"What? No, I --"

Carter didn't give him a chance to finish before he threw Ethan's boots at him one at a time.

Ethan didn't bother trying to catch those, only dodging out of reflex. "I'm not married. It was an engagement ring."

Hell!

"Wait. That's not what I meant." Ethan stepped barefoot over the broken teacup, reaching for Carter. If he could bring them back to skin on skin, Carter might be able to sense the truth in him. "Listen to me."

Carter dodged. "Not married but engaged. How is that better? You belong to someone else, but you still fucked me." Ethan could tell he was being crude on purpose, drivingly cruel. "You fucked me, you pretended you'd been looking for me, and you let me -- I trusted you enough to be there when -- go to hell, Ethan." He took two steps back. "Liar."

Ethan's temper flared to life. He stopped trying to reach Carter. "*Listen* to me. Ry isn't my fiancé. He was once. Not now. Not for a long time."

"That's still not better."

"No. It isn't," Ethan agreed. "But if you want to talk about lies by omission, take a look at yourself. If I hadn't found you, you never would have let me know I had a son. You would have kept that to yourself for the rest of your life, and maybe I'd have taught him one day and wondered why he looked so familiar, and why his father never showed up for conferences. You would have told him I didn't care, and damn you for that. You want to tell me to go to hell? I'll save you a seat."

Carter flinched, but he set his jaw and dragon fire burned in him, a dark and smoldering flame that scorched everything it touched. "Get out."

"Carter --"

"*No.*" Two more steps, and Carter was out of the workshop now. "Get. Out. I wouldn't have told him, and we'd have been better off. I was a fool twice. I won't be a third time. I don't want you here anymore, Ethan. Neither of us needs you. Go. *Now.*"

He meant that. Every word of it. Ethan stared at him, furious and frustrated and almost able to hear that door slamming shut between them. He could feel, as sure as it beat out of time in his chest, that Carter had just sheared his heart in two.

Caught between fury and howling his anguish at the moon before it'd risen, Ethan did the only thing he could.

Picked up his boots, shoved his feet into them, and turned his back. Stalked away, without looking back once.

Fuck!

Chapter Seven

Ethan stalked through the snow, kicking up drifts where they'd been unwise enough to blow across the sidewalk, murder in his eye and a snarl on his lips that made any human who thought about crossing in front of him think twice. Then get out of his way. Fast. There were more than he'd expected, but that was human nature; get penned up for any reason, no matter how short a time, and the first thing men thought of was breaking free.

He bared his teeth at a few of them, and it almost made him feel better.

Firing off a text to Oscar, pithy but to the very sharpened point, almost helped too.

He started to shut his phone down, but hesitated. What if Carter called him? No, he wouldn't. He didn't even have Ethan's number. All they'd shared over the past couple of days, and he hadn't even thought to ask. Of course, Ethan hadn't planned on leaving him long enough for that to matter, but he had to scoff at himself there. The professor had gotten good and schooled there, hadn't he?

The phone went into his back pocket, silenced but not shut down.

Ethan would have liked to say he was surprised his path led him straight back to *Speakeasy* but he wasn't, not really. He glanced up at the alley when he walked in, snorted, and kept walking, shoving *Speakeasy's* door open with a crash and a glower that dared anyone to make something of it.

No one did. Smart men.

Oh, he got a few curious glances and a few muted whistles, but apart from that the day drinkers minded their own business. All of them, and a bigger crowd than Ethan had expected. More excited than he'd have imagined too. Someone had fired up a grill -- he hadn't known they served food -- that made the air smell of charcoal and browning meat as well as hops and yeast and cigarettes. His stomach rumbled, but Ethan ignored it.

Elbowing his way through the congestion at the bar and waiting for a beer to be uncapped and slid down his way, he caught a few words about *quarry* and *union* and *safety regulations*, with a *fuck the foreman!* thrown in here and there for good measure. That was right; hadn't he heard something about a disaster there not long before he'd met Carter? Was it the day he'd met Carter?

Might have been. Either way, good for them. Ethan lifted his beer grimly and clinked with someone he didn't know, then took bottle, thundercloud mood and himself off to a far corner.

Leaning on the wall, he drank in small sips and pretended to watch the room. Lots of couples, he couldn't help noticing. All kinds. Work buddies or miners with their mates. An old, old Alpha kissing his just-as-grizzled Omega on his cheek, then raising his glass with a whoop *and* a holler. The guy who'd bought a watch from Carter -- Wynn, the one who was learning to read -- and *his* mate, a young Omega with the sweetest face Ethan had ever seen and a baby with his daddy's curls and smile that he carried strapped to his chest. Two old bachelors toasting each other and bellowing a song filthy enough to scorch a sailor's ears.

Ethan shook his head, but almost laughed. Human nature was a hell of a drug, wasn't it? Got you hooked, made you fly, brought you crashing down, left you figuring out what to do next every day. His stomach rumbled, but he ignored it and took a deeper pull on his beer.

He had thinking to do.

Given that he needed all his concentration focused inward, he was even less surprised than before when he looked up at some jostling to see Oscar wedging his way out of the crowd and into his corner, a full bottle in each hand: left hand beer, right hand water. Ethan narrowed his eyes at the man, who ignored that to fetch up on the wall beside him and pop the beer for himself. He held the water casually out to Ethan, who growled about it but took it, and pointed it at him with his mouth open to ask a question.

Oscar beat him to it. "How'd I find you?" he asked the air. "That little computer you carry around with you has GPS, and I've worked with enough professors -- I *am* one, almost -- and I know how we are about losing shit. Then needing to find it. So. You pissed enough to really fire me?"

"Don't test me," Ethan said shortly. He finished his beer and shoved the empty at Oscar. "I might be."

"As long as you're not pissed enough to try and geld me with a rusty fork like you were saying, I'll live." Oscar shrugged. "Probably. Might have to go on a Ramen diet or sponge off Darian and Coby for a while if I do lose my job, but it'd be worth it. What's it worth to you, not to lose that little dragon that's been hiding in his cave for oh, right around nine weeks and change now?"

Ethan snapped his head around to give Oscar a disbelieving look.

The man didn't even flinch. "You heard me. What, you think this is my first rodeo? You think it was a picnic watching Darian and Coby run around in circles with their heads up their asses trying to figure their shit out?"

Ethan blinked. "I hope you don't mean that literally."

"Likely not, but I don't kink shame. You mind?" Oscar dug a crumpled pack of cigarettes and a lighter out of his coat pocket, using one deftly on the other. "Good, didn't think so." He took a deep drag and let out a plume of smoke. "God, that's better."

The only thing Ethan could do was shake his head

slowly. "You knew all along and you didn't say anything?"

"I did know, and hell no, I minded my own business. I just got done helping Darian and Coby with their bullshit. Once is one time for the one time but sticking my neck in someone else's romance woes kicks off a pattern. I told you when I told you to put us *all* out of our misery, but the third dumbass with hearts in his eyes and rocks in his head who comes to me for advice to the lovelorn isn't getting anything but a boot to his backside and a --"

Oscar was going too fast for Ethan's boggling brain to keep him. He held up a hand to cut the man off. "But -- how did you know?"

"*Pfft*. You forgot you went to *Speakeasy* in my company the second you set eyes on Carter. You pull a disappearing act with that pretty little thing and come back with sex hair half an hour later. Then, Carter starts plumping out. Doesn't take a genius." Oscar took a few contemplative pulls on his smoke, then sighed. "Look, man. First times are for fucking up. That's just facts."

A frown wrinkled Ethan's forehead. "I don't follow."

"Yeah, most people don't. That's the problem. Beginner's luck is a thing, but it's called luck for a reason: it's lucky, and it's rare enough to stand out. The rest of us, the rest of the time? It's all trial and failure and trial again until we figure out what the hell we're doing." Oscar gestured with his cigarette while he spoke, a pillar of ash building on its tip. "The first time you have sex? Odds are it's going to be bad. Sucks to suck at sucking, but I remember my first and I'm pretty damn lucky I didn't get gelded way back then, let me tell you. Shit."

Ethan watched him, awed. No wonder Darien liked getting Oscar wound up.

"Anyway." Oscar exhaled. "Every time you

mentioned that ex-fiancé of yours you had a face on like you'd just bitten into a lemon, and every time someone brought up dating or even just getting your dick wet --"

"Good God, Oscar."

"-- it was a face like someone had just fisted you with two cut lemons and an orange, but him? He got to you. You were looking for him, and that meant you cared. So I took pity and gave you a clue. You found him, and he was pregnant. Right so far?"

Ethan inclined his head. "With my child."

"I didn't think it'd belong to Elvis or Bigfoot." Oscar lit a second cigarette with the ember of his first, though he let it burn down instead of breathing it in as he gestured. "I've seen that kind of shell-shocked look before. On Darian, for one. So I'm guessing he went pop during the snow, and you were there. Damn. Postnatal hormones are a bastard. Maybe I should have waited to tell him about the ring."

"Wait." A startled flare of fury spiked behind Ethan's eyes. "Wait a damned minute. You told Carter about that ring on purpose. Did my ex even send it back at all?"

"Yeah, it's in your desk. And also, yep." Oscar popped the "p" in satisfaction. "Why? Because, dumbass --"

"Dr. Dumbass to you, or 'boss.'"

Oscar laughed. He had an interesting face, what the French would call ugly-handsome, but amusement gave it a whole new dimension. Nothing comparable to Carter, but -- Ethan pushed back the distraction.

"Why?" he asked. "Why did you tell him? Not just for shits and giggles, and by the way, your language is wearing off on me."

"A little cussing does a body good. And I told him because I wanted -- you needed, both of you -- to see what would happen next. If it was something worth fighting for, you'd figure out how to fight. If not, you'd be better off going your separate ways. Basically the same principle as teaching a kid to swim by tossing them in the deep end."

"Unless they drown," Ethan pointed out dryly. He took Oscar's beer from him and drained it half dry. "And if I don't want to drown? Or want him to drown? If I want him and our son? How do I fight? How do I fix this?"

Oscar mulled that over. "I'd start by talking to him."

"Not that easy. He kicked me out."

"Might have," Oscar allowed. "But he also came to find you."

Ethan stilled. "Say that again?"

"He came to find you. Either that or he really wants a drink, but since he's carrying a baby in a sling I'm guessing not. Also people don't usually look like they want to literally murder a beer in cold blood." Oscar pointed at the door with the tip of his cigarette. "No one ever looks up, you realize that? Look up."

Ethan did. Moses must have swept through on the tail edge of the storm, because a path had opened between himself and Carter as if through the Red Sea. Or perhaps quarrymen were better than most at sensing when to get out of the way of an oncoming conflagration. Carter stood by the door, coat on, baby wrapped in multiple blankets and strapped to his chest, a heavy leather carryall resting at his feet. He was pale as milk with cold and white as marble to the teeth with fury, dark-eyed with wrath, and looked like nothing so much as an avenging angel. All he lacked was a sword.

The spike of hunger that shot through Ethan at the sight of him might as well have been fired from the barrel of a Gatling gun, it pierced him so straight and true. He tried to catch his breath, but it wasn't there to be caught, and when Carter's glare landed on him the Omega's lips parted slightly.

Oscar chuffed quietly and stole the beer back to empty it down his throat. "Yeah, that's what I thought. Well? You love that man. Go get him. I'm not letting another friend get within a hair's breadth of throwing away his shot."

It wasn't what Ethan had planned, but... hadn't he been learning that wasn't how life worked? Throw yourself in headfirst, and swim.

But -- one last word to Oscar first. "However many times you've watched *Hamilton*, it was one too many."

"Fuck you, he might be married but I have a crush on Mr. Miranda's brain. Go, already."

Ethan went.

Slowly at first, then faster. Anyone who'd thought about straying across the path thought twice and skipped back before he plowed them down, and he didn't have to stop once before he was nearly toe to toe with Carter. Carter, who lifted his chin sharply and proudly and met his stare without fear.

He could have done any number of things then, he knew. Shouted. Sworn. Shaken him. *Could* have, but couldn't have, either. The only thing he wanted to do, and did, was take that proud, stubborn dragon, shaking with nerves behind that defiant exterior, into his arms and kiss him hard enough to mark him for life. To keep kissing him until Carter gasped into his parted lips and brought his hands up to dig his fingers into Ethan's shoulders and mark him right back.

Ethan kept on kissing him until the whoops, cheers, catcalls, and shouts for a round on the house deafened him more than the music those short few weeks ago had. He pulled away, fascinated by how kiss-reddened Carter's still-parted lips were, and cupped the man's cheek but warned him with a look that he meant business.

Outside, he mouthed.

Carter licked those pretty lips and nodded.

Outside it was, then. Full circle, all over again.

* * *

Speakeasy had a good solid door, and the music wasn't so loud at this time of day. Some of the noise filtered out, but as Ethan's ears popped and cleared he could hear over them. Muted street sounds, cars and chatter and rock salt pinging off turning tires, were all dimmed by the snow into a quiet hum. Not that he cared. He'd fixed all his attention on Carter -- but didn't say anything. Not yet.

Carter searched his face. "You're not going to yell at me for bringing him out," he said, laying his hand on the baby's back. "I thought you would."

"I will. Later. Right now he's swaddled like a mummy, probably warmer than either of us. You're a good father."

Whatever Carter had been expecting, it wasn't that either. He blinked rapidly, once with that odd reptilian sideways shutter, and stared at Ethan as if he were the strange one. "I don't understand you and I don't know if I ever will."

"Wrong. You do, and that's what scares you." Ethan took one of Carter's hands, cold even through the leather gloves he wore. "For what it's worth, me too."

"You kept a secret from me." Carter licked his lips again. "But. A secret. Not a lie."

Ethan inclined his head once. "Only because I didn't know how to bring it up, and I didn't want to hurt you."

"But you did."

"Without meaning to but yes, I did. And I'm sorry for that. Here's the truth: I never loved Rob. I only thought I did, because I wanted to be in love. He never loved me either. He loved money, and I didn't have nearly as much of it as he decided he liked. I was glad to see him go, and that's why I let him keep the ring. I don't know why he sent it back now, and I don't care. I'll send it back to him or toss it in the quarry lake."

"But you --"

Ethan caught Carter's forearms gently, but firmly, not meaning to let him step back or run away a second time. "I never loved him. But I do love you. I'm in love with you, and I think I was from the first second I saw you. And..." He put his thumbs over the pulses in Carter's wrists, feeling them thud and rush. "I think you started to too. I'd do a lot of things differently, given a chance to go back and make other choices. And I'd have figured out where to find you much, much earlier. But those are the only things I'd change. I'll never regret being with you that night. Or having a son. Will you?"

Oscar's unexpected eloquence must have rubbed off as well as his swearing habit did. Ethan wouldn't complain. Not when Carter was looking at him that way, with all the heart and feelings he tried so hard to keep so guarded all nakedly displayed on his face. Ethan wanted to kiss him again, but -- not yet.

Carter had opened his mouth, and he wanted to hear this.

"I'm not good at words," Carter said, watching him steadily as a rock even though his hands trembled. "I'm not good at talking. Out of practice. But I want to. When I came here, I came here thinking I would never love again. Never wanting to. Tried my damnedest not to, but then you... Then *you*. And then him. And then here." He struggled and shook his head. "Tell me you understand."

Ethan stroked Carter's arms, then his cheek, a warm glow starting to fill him when Carter closed his eyes and leaned into his touch. "I do."

Carter shook his head, silent at first, then barely

whispering, "No. Or -- or you. But I don't know where to go from here."

"Yes, you do."

"Where?"

"Back home, for starters. Both of us. Back to that studio above your store. Where you feel safe." Ethan took a deep breath. "But you let me in too. And then, we start over. No more secrets. No lies. Nothing hidden."

Carter shivered but leaned harder into Ethan's hand. "I don't know if I can do that."

"You can. It won't be easy for either of us, but it's worth it to me. Is it to you?" Ethan brushed Carter's hair away from his forehead. "Do you want to do that? Try again?"

Carter put his hand to the back of Ethan's and turned his face, warm breath tickling his palm before he pressed his lips to the heart line running across it. He nodded, and that was all, but that --

That was enough.

Ethan touched his lips to Carter's forehead. "Then it's you and me. A second chance in Second Chance."

He felt Carter smile against his skin. "You promise that?"

"I do," Ethan said, knowing he meant more than just agreement. Ethan put his arm around Carter to lead him away. "I do. We'll try our best, you and me, and you'll see what we can do. Come on, dragon. Take me home."

Carter fell into step next to him, leaning into him, warming up. His lips quirked. Ethan thought they would make the walk in silence, until --

"On one condition: don't get me pregnant again," Carter murmured, glancing up at him with pure mischief in his eyes. "For a while."

Ethan tilted his head back and laughed to the skies.

Epilogue

Things happened, in Second Chance. Things you never thought would, or could, or even should, but they did. Oh, they did.

Carter wrapped the last of his teacups, one of the half-dozen he'd mended using real gold melted down from old jewelry no one wanted, and handed it to the Omega who'd bought the rest of them -- every last one he had in stock. He tried a smile at the slight, intense man, who gave him a fiercely pleased look in return.

"Let me know when you have more of these," he ordered, wrapping the handles of the string bag Carter had given him around one wrist while cradling a newborn in his other arm and keeping an eye on a little boy with as ferociously strong a presence standing next to him. "I'll buy them all. Standing order."

Carter nodded. He still wasn't the best with words, but as for the rest… well. There he was. Out in the sunlight, in the heart of a street fair he'd never attended before, closing his shop doors and hiding away from deep inside until the party was over. Selling things, to people whose eyes were caught by glittering metal and doeskin soft leather, wood polished to a deep glow, and everything else he'd cleaned and coaxed back to life.

The Omega he'd been talking to before his customer strode up, the town librarian Gabriel, cleared his throat to get Carter's attention. He had a smile sweeter than Ethan swore Carter's was, but Ethan had his biases and stuck by them.

Carter didn't mind.

"Do we have a deal?" Gabriel asked. "You'll teach me how to fix ordinary books, and I'll bring you in as the archivist when you have time?"

Carter nodded but confessed, "Not much time with a ten-month-old around."

"Lord, tell me about it." Gabriel stretched. His son

was almost a year old, a bouncy little sprite with a head full of dandelion-fluff curls and a gigantic smile, happily playing with toy soldiers at Gabriel's feet, content with the shade his parent provided -- and with a nearly full-term belly on him, that made for considerable shade. Gabriel stroked himself, unashamed, and grinned at Carter. "It's worth it to have everything you ever wanted, though, isn't it?"

Carter smiled at him without meaning to, as broadly as the little boy might, and it didn't fade. Gabriel knew him well enough by now to understand what he meant and how he meant it and smiled back as he waved goodbye.

Left to himself for a moment, Carter watched Gabriel gather up his things and walk away. He kept on watching the man make his slow way down the street toward his mate -- then across, to where *his* mate was coming down the street toward him. He'd surrounded himself with good company, ambling side by side with Oscar, Darian and Coby, their twins, and Joseph. His son, and Ethan's too. Ethan swore he looked like Carter; Carter swore the opposite; they were likely both half right. Sometimes he still couldn't believe it, really. That he'd made a person, him and Ethan, and how it'd all come together.

Not easily. They'd had their fights, but they'd had their reunions too. When Ethan's tenure as artist-in-residence ended, he'd gone straight into private teaching without a hitch in his step, and he'd nudged Carter relentlessly until he opened an online shopfront for his repair work. That'd caused some battles, and some fences that needed mending, and it was so strange how it brought them closer together every time. But it did. It did.

Gabriel had been right. It was worth it.

Carter laughed to himself when one of Darian and Coby's twins tried to climb Coby like a piece of jungle gym, and Coby turned him upside down to dangle him by his ankles and make him scream with laughter. Was Coby pregnant again too? It was hard to tell with an Omega as tall and muscled as Coby, but Carter thought it might be so. *Good luck to them*! Carter thought, meaning it, and laughing again as the second twin launched himself at Darian to demand the same treatment. Then a third time, harder, when Joseph took advantage of their distraction to steal the peppermint stick Oscar had shoved in his mouth instead of a cigarette clean away from him.

Sometimes, Carter's heart felt so full he wondered if it would burst. Sometimes, he wanted to go back to the shadows and the corners and hide there. Sometimes, he did.

But more and more often, he went out into the sun.

Ethan leaned over the stall counter when he reached it, catching Carter easily by the nape and pulling him into a light, sweet kiss. "Everything good here?"

Carter tilted his head to a side to say *yes* before kissing him back. He put his arm around Ethan and Joseph, holding them close. That alley outside *Speakeasy* seemed a thousand years ago and a hundred miles away, but -- he liked to remind himself of it.

He leaned against the counter, not too hard, and pressed his forehead against Ethan's in a silent *thank you*. Tonight, he thought. Tonight might be the night. They'd promised each other not to keep any more secrets, but Ethan might forgive him just this one secret just this once.

Or -- he might have the fun of telling him now.

Why not?

Carter ruffled his fingertips through the soft hair at Ethan's nape and took his other hand, guiding it over the counter to rest against his stomach. Still flat, but only for now, and he let the curve of his smile tell the story against Ethan's lips. Ethan's hand spasmed, springing open in surprise, then pressing in and kissing him more deeply, hungrily, not able to stop grinning for even a second.

It was good, and it was right, and it was everything, to stand gilded by the sun surrounded by a world of second chances.

Will Okati

Will Okati (formerly known as Willa) has lived through a few Interesting Times, but come out the other side a little grayer, a little wiser, and ready to get writing. Still as passionate about coffee, cats, and crafts as ever, but knowing that to your own self you must be true. Also still one of the quiet ones to watch out for, but life -- like storytelling -- is always a work in progress.

Will at Changeling: changelingpress.com/will-okati-a-213

Changeling Press E-Books

More Sci-Fi, Fantasy, Paranormal, and BDSM adventures available in e-book format for immediate download at ChangelingPress.com -- Werewolves, Vampires, Dragons, Shapeshifters and more -- Erotic Tales from the edge of your imagination.

What are E-Books?

E-books, or electronic books, are books designed to be read in digital format -- on your desktop or laptop computer, notebook, tablet, Smart Phone, or any electronic e-book reader.

Where can I get Changeling Press E-Books?

Changeling Press e-books are available at ChangelingPress.com, Amazon, Apple Books, Barnes & Noble, and Kobo/Walmart.

Changeling Press. LLC

ChangelingPress.com